CYNTHIA HARROD-EAGLES

Dynasty 16
The Devil's Horse

sphere

SPHERE

First published in Great Britain in 1993
by Little, Brown and Company
This edition published by Warner in 1994
Reprinted 1994 (twice), 1996, 2000
Reprinted by Time Warner Books in 2006
Reprinted by Sphere in 2008

5 7 9 10 8 6

A CIP catalogue record for this book
is available from the British Library.

ISBN 978-0-7515-0080-6

Printed and bound in Great Britain by
Clays Ltd, St Ives plc

Papers used by Sphere are from well-managed forests
and other responsible sources.

MIX
Paper from
responsible sources

FSC
www.fsc.org   FSC® C104740

Sphere
An imprint of
Little, Brown Book Group
100 Victoria Embankment
London EC4Y 0DY

An Hachette UK Company
www.hachette.co.uk

www.littlebrown.co.uk

Cynthia Harrod-Eagles is the author of the contemporary Bill Slider Mystery series as well as the Morland Dynasty novels. Her passions are music, wine, horses, architecture and the English countryside.

Visit the author's website at www.cynthiaharrodeagles.com

The Morland Dynasty series

THE FOUNDING
THE DARK ROSE
THE PRINCELING
THE OAK APPLE
THE BLACK PEARL
THE LONG SHADOW
THE CHEVALIER
THE MAIDEN
THE FLOOD TIDE
THE TANGLED THREAD
THE EMPEROR
THE VICTORY
THE REGENCY
THE CAMPAIGNERS
THE RECKONING
THE DEVIL'S HORSE
THE POISON TREE
THE ABYSS
THE HIDDEN SHORE
THE WINTER JOURNEY
THE OUTCAST
THE MIRAGE
THE CAUSE
THE HOMECOMING
THE QUESTION
THE DREAM KINGDOM
THE RESTLESS SEA
THE WHITE ROAD
THE BURNING ROSES
THE MEASURE OF DAYS
THE FOREIGN FIELD
THE FALLEN KINGS
THE DANCING YEARS
THE WINDING ROAD
THE PHOENIX

The War at Home series

GOODBYE, PICCADILLY

For Hannah, with my love.

THE MORLAND FAMILY

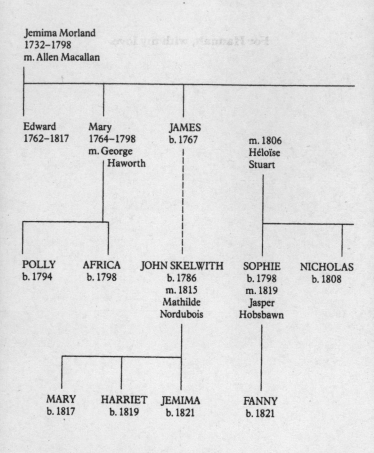

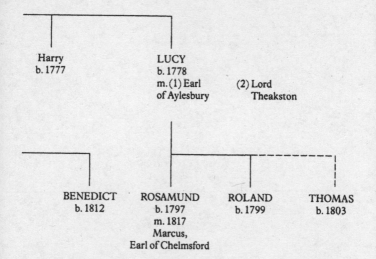

Harry
b. 1777

LUCY
b. 1778
m. (1) Earl
of Aylesbury

(2) Lord
Theakston

BENEDICT
b. 1812

ROSAMUND
b. 1797
m. 1817
Marcus,
Earl of Chelmsford

ROLAND
b. 1799

THOMAS
b. 1803

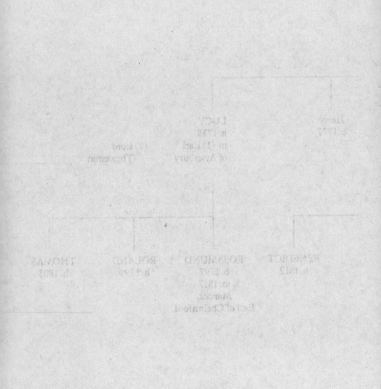

SELECT BIBLIOGRAPHY

Baines, Edward	*The Social Educational & Religious State of the Manufacturing Districts*
Battiscombe, Georgina	*Shaftesbury 1801–1885*
Briggs, Asa	*The Age of Improvement 1784–1874*
Clapham, J.H.	*An Economic History of Modern Britain 1820–1850*
Fay, C.R.	*Life and Labour in the Nineteenth Century*
Finlayson, Geoffrey	*England in the 1830s*
Hartcup, Adeline	*Love and Marriage in the Great Country Houses*
Heaton, Herbert	*The Yorkshire Woollen & Worsted Industries*
Hobley, L.F.	*Living and Working*
Holland, A.J.	*The Age of Industrial Expansion*
Hopkins, Eric	*A Social History of the English Working Classes 1815–1945*
Inglis, Brian	*Poverty and the Industrial Revolution*
Jackman, W.T.	*The Development of Transportation in Modern England*
Norman Smith, David	*The Railway and its Passengers*
Pollins, Harold	*Britain's Railways: An Industrial History*
Prothero, R.E.	*English Farming Past and Present*
Ransom, P.J.G.	*The Victorian Railway and How it Evolved*
Rimmer, W.G.	*British Factory Towns During the First Industrial Revolution*

Rolt, L.T.C.   *George & Robert Stephenson: The Railway Revolution*

Royle, Edward   *Modern Britain — A Social History 1750–1985*

Thomas, N.W.   *The Early Factory Legislation*
Ward, J.T.   *The Factory System (2 Vols)*
Woodham Smith, Cecil *Queen Victoria: Her Life and Times*
Woodward, Llewellyn   *The Age of Reform 1815–1870*
Ziegler, Philip   *King William IV*
Ziegler, Philip   *Melbourne*

BOOK ONE

Public Clamour

Stern Daughter of the Voice of God!
Oh Duty! if that name thou love,
Who art a light to guide, a rod
To check the erring, and reprove.

William Wordsworth: *Ode to Duty*

BOOK ONE

CHAPTER ONE

Flowed seemed to be the wrong verb for the River Irwell where it passed between the mills: it *toiled* between its grim banks, its waters black and stinking and laden with detritus, the unfiltered outpourings of privvies and tanneries, glue factories and soapworks. Between the river and the factory walls was a sad strip of earth where no grass grew, a footpath in keeping with its surroundings, as devoid of natural life as the black water or the blackened walls.

The man who stumbled along this footpath cared nothing for that. He was drunk, and meant to be drunker as soon as he had found a place to hide himself. He was a thin, undersized, shabby creature; pale under a layer of dirt that had ingrained itself so that his skin had the characteristic greyish patina of poverty. His clothes were hardly more than rags held together with dirt. His wooden shoes had worn a ring of ulcers on his feet which were far beyond healing now. He had a bad gash on his left palm which was wrapped around with a piece of rag. He had done it over a fortnight ago but it would not heal either, and where it had oozed day after day, now it had started to swell and send hot throbs of pain up his arm.

The man's name was Jack Flanagan, though it was a long time since anyone had used it. There was no-one to call him by it now. He'd had a wife and five children back in Ireland, a mother and a father and two brothers. They were all gone now. He was alone, and he was the last of them.

Hughie went first, his younger brother. Hughie said he was going to walk to Galway and get work on a ship going to

3

America. He said he'd come back one day with his pockets full of gold, and buy Ma a silk dress and a green umbrella. Ma had cried, knowing she'd never see him again. Hughie was the one she loved best out of them all.

She and Daddy died within a month of each other, the winter a year after Hughie went — died just of being old and tired and not being able to care about anything any more. The baby went that winter too like a sparrow dropping off a twig, such a very little baby. They'd called it Hughie, trying to make it up to Ma, and she'd pretended to be pleased. Mary cried when the baby died. She did it silently when she thought Jack was asleep, but he knew all the same. He could tell by the way her shoulders hunched.

She didn't cry when Cathie died next winter. Cathie was their eldest, eight years old, a good girl and a hard worker. She was a dairy maid at the farm down the hill at Clare-morris, and never complained though her hands were often cracked and raw from milking cows in the open fields in all weathers. She didn't complain that her chest hurt her, and only when she was too weak to get out of bed one morning did they know she was ill. The priest said it was pneumonia. He closed her eyes and gave her absolution, and then complained bitterly because they had no money to pay him, only a loaf of bread and a tiny bit of bacon, their last.

That was a hard winter, the hardest he remembered in the old country. There was never enough to eat, no matter what they did, or how hard they worked. The last of the potatoes went, and then there was nothing but the scrapings from the flour bin and whatever they could glean from the hedges.

Then one day Con, his elder brother, had come back with a chicken. It wasn't much of a chicken, all skin and bones, but Jack was worried anyway.

'I found it wandering loose in the lane,' Con kept saying; and then, 'For God's sake, Mary make some soup out of it and feed those children. I can't stand looking at their staring eyes day after day.'

They all had something off that wretched bird. Never did a chicken go so far amongst so many. But Jack had been right to be afraid: it had been stolen all right. Con had gone to a farm a long way off, and taken the oldest and scrawniest bird

4

hoping no-one would miss it; but two days later they came and took Con away and put him in prison, and then they hanged him.

That was when Jack decided they had better emigrate. He and Mary and the three children packed all they had into two bundles and walked all the way to Dundalk. There they sold the only thing they had of value — a gold chain given Mary by her grandmother — and bought passage to Liverpool. It was the autumn of 1818. The factories were on full-time working, and they'd all managed to get work, all five of them. They found a room to live in — shared with an old couple, but a blanket hung across the middle divided off their half and they were eating every day.

The work was hard, especially on the little ones, but at least they were indoors in the warm through the winter. But then in the spring came the slump, and one by one they were laid off. No work to be had anywhere, no wages — no food. Someone said there was more chance of something in Manchester, so they packed their bundles and walked there; but it was no better. They got a day here and a day there, not enough to keep them from starvation. First their youngest died, little Brigid, just five. She'd eaten something, they never found out what — some filth or other, maybe just a sod of earth — to keep the pangs of hunger away, but whatever it was, it poisoned her. She writhed in agony for hours, but they couldn't save her.

It was the worst time. To watch your children starving to death and not to be able to do anything to save them is enough to break any man. The children's bones stuck out as though they might break through their skin, and they huddled together in silence, too listless even to cry, only their eyes moving, looking up in automatic hope when Jack came in from his fruitless searches for work. In the end they didn't even look up. It was hard to know when they died, it made so little difference to them.

The next year things got better and there were jobs again — for Mary, but not for Jack. They didn't want men in the factories, only women and children, so Mary went to work, and he lay all day on the bundle of rags they called a bed in the dark, stinking cellar room they called a home and waited

5

for her to come back. There was nothing else to do. When she did get back every night, she was so tired after fourteen hours standing at the jenny that she was no use to him or herself.

He talked sometimes about maybe going back home — if they were going to be miserable, he said, they might as well be miserable in their own country — but she was too weary to care. She said that standing all day gave her pains in her back. One morning when she tried to get up to go to work she gave a terrible cry and fell back down. A savage pain in her belly, she said: she lay hunched up all day, crying and moaning and sweating with pain. By noon she had a fever too, and by evening she was delirious. In desperation Jack went up to the street and hammered on the door of the people who lived above them, begging them for help. The old woman came and looked at Mary and shook her head. She said she thought Mary must have ruptured something inside, something female. Nothing anyone could do, she said, and went away quickly. Mary lived two days. If only he'd had a gun, he'd have shot her, to put her out of her pain.

That was a year ago. Since then he didn't really remember much about his life. There was no regular work for him. He stole to keep himself alive, and when there was nothing to steal, he went hungry. He slept where he could, and there had been nights, many of them, when he had laid himself down on the bare earth in the shelter of a wall.

Now and then he got a day's work, and when he got any wages he spent them on drink. It seemed the only thing to do. He felt ill and light-headed most of the time, and he had sores that wouldn't heal. He thought he was probably dying, and he wasn't sorry. He had no reason to live, now all those he cared about had gone. When a man loses even his name, he thought, he has no business staying alive. God could take him as soon as he liked.

This would be a good night for it, he thought as he stumbled along beside the river. He had picked a man's pocket in Grape Alley — almost recklessly, for it was daylight and there were plenty of people around and he hadn't been careful. But with the perversity of things in general he had got away with it, and found himself safely in possession of a leather purse, which proved to contain some tobacco and a

6

strike-a-light in one compartment, and several coins in another.

It seemed like a gift from God to him: tobacco, and enough money to buy food and drink. One last taste of human pleasures before he went to meet his Maker. He bought a plate of faggots from a street-vendor and gorged himself almost to sickness, and spent the rest on drink. Now with a bottle of spirits and the tobacco in his pocket, warming his thoughts like young love, he was looking for a place to spend the night and consume them.

His luck held out. He found a building with a broken window on the ground floor — newly broken, by the look of it, so perhaps undiscovered by the owners. He managed — not without difficulty, for his swollen hand was almost useless — to get through and found himself in a storeroom piled to the ceiling with bales of cotton.

It couldn't be better; it was almost luxurious. He took a little time to rearrange the bales to make a space in the centre so that when he crawled inside and pulled the last bale after him, he could not be seen by any watchman who might discover the broken window and come to look around. Here he might stay for some time, several days perhaps, warm and snug and safe with his bottle and his old clay pipe, until either he died, or they pulled out the bales in the natural course of things and discovered him. He rather hoped the former would happen first. It was so nice here, he really didn't want ever to have to leave.

Jack Flanagan crawled into his nest and loosened one of the bales to make something soft to sit on, and with a sigh of comfort he pulled out the cork from the bottle and lifted it to his lips. You can come for me any time, he saluted the Angel of Death through the fumes; only it would be nice if you'd wait until I've finished the bottle and smoked a pipe or two. But if you can't wait, so be it. I'm in no case to argue any more.

Sophie and her friend Prudence Pendlebury came out from Jackson's Court into Water Lane with a sense of relief. Water Lane ran parallel with the river, a gloomy street flanked on both sides by mills, between whose fortress walls were

7

crammed narrow courts and alleys of grim dwellings. Sophie had once heard them spoken of as 'teeming with life', but as far as the human inhabitants were concerned, teeming was far too active a verb. The only things that teemed in a place like Jackson's Court were rats and bugs.

Sophie's carriage was waiting for them a little way along the road, and the two women turned towards it and began picking their way through the mud, lifting their skirts carefully and trying to avoid the human and animal excrement. Above them the smoke from the mill chimneys hung on the air like winter fog, through which the sun could be seen only as a yellow smudge as it moved across the sky. The mill hands who lived under the shadow of the chimneys never saw more of the sun than this, Sophie thought; in winter, when they began work before sunrise and finished after sunset, they saw nothing of it at all.

'Sophie, you're not listening to me at all,' Miss Pendlebury complained.

'I'm sorry, Prudence. What did you say?'

'I said that I don't believe the Keenans' sickness can be typhoid. That rash on the baby's stomach isn't typical. I think it's something they've eaten. There's simply no way of knowing what they put into the bread at that bakery in Moss Street.'

'I'm sure you're right,' Sophie said. It was another worry amongst the many that when the poor had money for food, what they were able to buy was as likely as not to be adulterated. Last year Frederick Accum had published a treatise on the subject, and Prudence had acquired a copy. It spoke of 'wheat flour' which was a mixture of inferior grain and ground beans whitened with alum; 'porter' blackened with any number of noxious substances and made bitter with ginger, copperas, quassia, even sulphuric acid . . .

Sophie dragged her mind back to the Keenans. 'You don't think we ought to ask Dr Hastings to call, just to be sure?'

'Oh no, not Dr Hastings,' Prudence said firmly. 'His time has too many demands on it as it is. It's so good of him to visit these people at all, I feel obliged only to refer the most serious cases to him.'

'Everything we've seen today is serious,' Sophie said sadly.

'Nevertheless, Dr Hastings is a rare resource, and we ought to spread him thinly.'

'Oh Pru! But I know just what you mean.' Sophie sighed. 'No matter how often I come here, I can't get used to it. They live such terrible lives, and there's so little we can do.'

'The Augean Stables,' Prudence said drily. 'In more senses than one.'

'It's the smells I hate the most. They seem to coat the inside of your throat so that you can't get rid of them.'

'But you do follow Dr Hastings' advice when you get home, don't you?'

'Yes, don't worry. I'm very careful. My clothes are all hung out to air, and I breathe aromatic steam for half an hour. It can only be my imagination that the smell lingers. Do you think I would risk Jasper's life, and little Fanny's?'

Prudence gave a grim little smile. 'If anything happened to you or to Fanny, I rather think Jasper would murder me. My life is in your hands as well.'

'Oh Prudence!' Sophie laughed. 'Jasper would never hurt a fly whatever the provocation.'

'Don't you think so? I wonder. When it's a matter of something he cares passionately about —'

They had reached the carriage and were about to climb in. A horseman who had been posting along the road towards them slowed to pass the carriage, and then stopped with an exclamation. His hand which had gone automatically to his hat fell away with the polite gesture uncompleted.

The women looked towards him. It was Mr Olmondroyd, owner of the mill beside which they were now standing: the high iron gates were just a few yards further on down the street. His hand dropped from his hat to the rein to check his horse: a magnificent animal, Sophie thought, but over-curbed. It fretted against the restraint, its neck so arched that its chin was almost touching its chest, foam spilling from its mouth over its breast and knees.

Sophie was a Morland by birth and didn't like to see a horse so uncomfortable, but a glance at its rider's face told her this was not the moment to speak. Mr Olmondroyd was scowling horribly.

'Well, ladies, so you didn't heed my warning!'

9

Prudence raised an eyebrow. 'I was unaware that you had issued one,' she said coolly.

'Nay, Miss Pendlebury, you can look hoity-toity from now till Easter,' Olmondroyd said, red-faced, 'but it doesn't change the fact that you've been interfering again where it doesn't concern you!'

'It concerns every Christian person who has —'

'I warned you last time not to go meddling amongst my workers,' he interrupted, working himself into a rage. 'You spoil them with your charity and your mollycoddling and make them fit for nothing. I won't have them stirred up and made discontented, and so I told you!'

'Mr Olmondroyd, you have no right to tell me anything,' Prudence said. Sophie admired the steadiness of her voice. The angrier Olmondroyd became, the cooler she grew. 'You have no authority over me. And as far as I am concerned, these poor creatures I have been visiting are not your workers, but simply Christian souls who are suffering —'

'Suffering? Suffering? I'll give you suffering!' Olmondroyd shouted, making his horse waltz on the spot, its ears flicking back and forth in alarm. 'If I was your pa I'd give you the leather as long as I could stand over you! Go and meddle with your ma's workers if you must poke in where you're not wanted! By God, I think she'd give you short shrift if you did, and never mind all this Christian nonsense! And as for you, Mrs Hobsbawn, you may tell your master I shall speak to him straight if he doesn't keep you in order — straight and true, I shall, and no mincing, the next time I come upon him, so now then!'

Sophie had been gently reared, without ever having been spoken to harshly in her life. The loud voice and angry words made her tremble. She wanted most of all to run away, but while Prudence stood her ground, her lips pressed tightly together and her eyes bright as a cat's, Sophie must stand with her.

'Mr Hobsbawn knows where I am and why,' she said, and was angry with herself that her voice sounded so faint and tremulous. 'He approves of what I do.'

'Aye, well, he would, wouldn't he,' Olmondroyd retorted cruelly, 'coming out of the gutter as he did! And with his

10

fancy ideas he'll be back there before you can say knife, but I'm damned if he'll take me with him, and so you may tell him! And now, *ladies*, perhaps you'll be so good as to move this carriage out of the way of my gates so that hard-working folks may get on with their honest business.'

The carriage was not obstructing the gates in the least, but Prudence laid a warning hand on Sophie's arm, and urged her gently into the coach. Olmondroyd plainly did not consider they warranted even the ordinary courtesies, so there was no knowing what he might not say next. She climbed up after Sophie and the carriage moved off.

'That uncouth man!' she exclaimed as they lurched over the ruts of Water Lane. 'He's the worst of all of them; but if he thinks he can stop us visiting the poor and sick — why Sophie! You aren't crying are you?'

'Oh, no, not really. It's all right, I'm just being foolish. I hate unpleasantness, that's all.'

'You aren't used to it,' Prudence said. 'Now if you'd been brought up by my mother . . .'

'Oh Pru!'

'Foolish, I'm teasing you! That's better — I just wanted to make you smile. You mustn't worry about Mr Olmondroyd. No-one shall stop me from doing what my conscience bids, and as long as you have Jasper's approval, you can care nothing for that rude man.'

'I don't care for myself,' Sophie said. 'But he has influence amongst the mill masters. I'm afraid he will stand in Jasper's way, and prevent our scheme from getting on.'

'He'll try,' said Prudence bluntly, 'but I think your husband is a man to be reckoned with, and there are other mill masters who will side with him against Olmondroyd.'

Sophie murmured agreement. Prudence wanted to comfort her, so she didn't add that the very idea of there being sides and having to be on one and against the other made her feel unhappy.

At the same time, Jasper Hobsbawn was talking to Jacob Audenshaw, another mill master, and father of five sons, four of whom had courted Sophie during that heady Season when Jasper couldn't pluck up his courage to speak for her. The

11

Audenshaws were friendly, unassuming people, and Jacob not only owned a large mill but a half share in Droylsden and Audenshaw's Bank. He was an important man for Jasper to have on his side.

But Audenshaw was shaking his head. 'I know, I know. You've said all these things to me before. It's just the same with the factory reform and the minimum hours: I agree with you in principle, but I just don't see that there's anything we can do about it in practice.'

'We can change things if we all act together,' Jasper said urgently. 'That's the whole point —'

'The whole point,' Audenshaw interrupted, 'is that we *won't* all act together. Olmondroyd, for instance, will never agree to reduce hours, and there are many who look to him for their lead. I'm sorry, but I can't afford to go out on a limb on this particular tree. If I cut hours or increased wages, I'd have to put my prices up, and then I'd lose my customers to the likes of Olmondroyd, who'd kept his prices down. I've five sons and three daughters to find for, Hobsbawn. I can't be throwing my business away; and I think when you've more than just the one, you'll feel the same.'

Jasper took a deep breath, and then let it out slowly. He had told Audenshaw, and the others, time and time again that experiment had proved that cutting hours *increased* both the amount and the quality of work done by the hands. They simply would not believe it. They said it was impossible, and that was that; and when he insisted otherwise they smiled politely and went away shaking their heads over him and pronouncing him unsound. The fact was that however badly the mill masters felt about the condition of their workers — and there were many, like Audenshaw, who were decent sorts and did worry — no-one was willing to risk being undercut by harder-hearted competitors.

He knew there was no point in pursuing that particular matter for the moment, and he was more immediately interested in his housing scheme. So he said as calmly as he could, 'Well, never mind the ten hours business, Audenshaw. What about this other plan of mine?'

Audenshaw laughed and shook his head. 'You're a funny one, Hobsbawn, and no mistake: always riding some hobby

12

horse or other! Now you want to build new houses for the mill hands, and you expect me to pay for it!'

'They must live somewhere.'

'Aye, aye, so they must. But they manage somehow as it is. It's not my business.' Seeing Jasper with the light of battle in his eye, he went on hastily, 'And in the name of reason, man, why d'you want to build in that particular place?'

'Because that's where the houses are needed most.'

'Right up against the walls of Olmondroyd's mills? It's a red rag to a bull. He'll never agree. Besides, there are houses there already —'

'Houses, you call them? Filthy, verminous, fever-haunted sties! No, worse than sties: I warrant you even Olmondroyd wouldn't keep pigs in conditions like that.'

'Maybe not, but you're picking yourself a hard row to hoe. There's a nice empty field down at the bottom end of Deansgate — now why don't you build your houses there instead? You wouldn't annoy anyone then.'

Jasper looked at him cannily. 'Would you come in on the scheme if we built there instead of in Water Lane?'

Audenshaw looked uncomfortable. 'Well, now, you know, this isn't a scheme I can put to my partner with any confidence, is it? Capital must have its return, Hobsbawn, you know that. And the rents you propose — well, a man would be foolish to invest in your scheme for an uncertain one per cent when he might have a certain five almost anywhere, just for the asking.'

'The return would not only be in money rents,' Jasper said. 'Well-housed mill hands will work better and harder. There's the greater part of the return on your capital! Its value would be beyond calculation —'

'Exactly so: beyond calculation! I can't put a scheme like that forward to our depositors, even if they are mill masters. And as for my own money,' he went on hastily, anticipating Jasper's next question, 'I can't afford to take risks. I've two daughters out, and one coming out next Season. Have you any idea of the expense involved in that?'

'Not yet,' Jasper smiled, giving up for the present. He knew that like water wearing away a stone, he must go on and on, but gently and imperceptibly. 'Fanny's not six months old yet. That pleasure is still to come.'

Audenshaw softened. He liked Hobsbawn, liked Sophie, and thought the whole story of their courtship and marriage very touching. He said, 'Well, look here, Hobsbawn, if you can get some of the others to agree, and if you can get the right side of Olmondroyd, you can come to me again, and I'll think about it. That's the best I can promise. But I still think you'd do better to look at an empty site. What about over on the other side of Swan Street? There's a nice, flat piece of land there.'

'Thank you. I'll think about it,' Jasper said neutrally, and prepared to take his leave.

Audenshaw called after him. 'If you'll take a word of advice—' Jasper paused enquiringly. 'Don't make an enemy of Isaiah Olmondroyd. He's a hard man, and he makes a bad enemy.'

Jasper nodded. 'Thank you for the warning. But he may find that I'm not the man to cross either. When I care about something, I don't give up easily.'

The man who had been Jack Flanagan ended his life more comfortably than he had ever lived it. Cradled in his warm nest of cotton, his head full of the fumes of raw spirit, his senses were pleasantly numbed so that he did not feel the stab of the infection creeping up his arm towards his heart. He puffed on his clay pipe and the stolen tobacco tasted better than anything he had ever smoked. Drowsiness came slipping over him. The Angel of Death, he thought, was hovering somewhere very near; he could almost see the big drooping wings in the shadows on the ceiling above the cotton-bale walls of his hiding-place. He thought he ought to say a prayer, but no words would come to him. He slid down wordless as an animal into his alcoholic stupor, made the more profound by his long famine and weakness.

The clay pipe slipped from his fingers to the floor, rolled over once, and spilled its glowing dottle of hot tobacco against the bottom of a cotton-bale. Almost at once a faint thread of smoke wavered upwards, and in a moment a little red-gold tongue of flame appeared and licked greedily at the edge of the bale. The man did not stir, sunk deep in a half-world between sleep and death; his own flame guttered low as the vigorous new flame he had lit jumped up the side of the cotton and then leapt merrily across to the next oily bale, eager for adventure and excitement.

Jasper Hobsbawn had his offices in Number Two Mill, the largest of the three buildings of Hobsbawn Mills. It was the only one which as yet worked through the night, for he had only just installed gas lighting in it. He meant to put lighting into the older Number One Mill within the next year. Number Three he wasn't sure about. It was a weaving shed, still one of the few power-loom sheds in the country; but the looms themselves were old and crude and not very satisfactory. He felt they needed new and better looms before it would be worth lighting the mill and working nights as well as days. He studied new designs for looms whenever he could get hold of them, and as soon as they had capital enough —

But one thing at a time. The first capital expenditure must go on rational housing for the hands. As Robert Owen said, the human machinery must be as carefully looked after as the wooden or metal. Jasper turned over the latest design for workers' houses sent to him by John Skelwith and studied it carefully. Later this month he and Sophie would be going to York to visit her parents, and he and Skelwith would be able to get down to some real planning. The drawing Skelwith had sent looked very nice, very nice indeed, but there was a great deal to be considered. The dimensions, for instance . . .

The sound of some distant disturbance brought him back to the present, and he fumbled for his watch, realising that it was dark outside, and he had sat later than he intended. He had told Sophie he would dine at the club, where he had meant to sound out another mill master or two, but he might have left it too late. It didn't matter. He could go home instead to cold beef and pickles. Cold cuts with Sophie's smiling face across the table were more to be relished than a hot steak pudding with strangers.

What *was* that disturbance? Shouts and running feet — and now the door burst violently open and Bates, the manager of Number Two, rushed in. Behind him was the watchman of

15

Number Three, Hodges. He had been a spinner until he had lost three fingers in an accident, and Jasper had given him the caretaker's job out of compassion. Both were looking agitated — Hodges, in fact, seemed quite wild.

'Good God, what's the matter?' Jasper said, jumping up.

'Fire, master! A terrible fire! Oh come quick!' Hodges cried in an agony of anxiety.

'Fire? Where?'

Hodges waved his hands helplessly, too overcome to find words. But Bates was a good man. He laid a steadying hand on Hodges' arm and spoke succinctly. 'It's Olmondroyd's, sir. Started in a store shed, and now it's spread to the mill building. It's burning fiercely. There's no wind, but everything's so dry it's going up like tinder.'

'What about Number Three?' Jasper asked tersely. It was the nearest to Olmondroyd's, divided from it only by a narrow lane down to the river.

'It hasn't caught yet, sir, but sparks are flying over all the time. We must get some people down there at once and organise a chain. I think we ought to shut down Number Two.'

'Shut down?' A whole night's production lost. Half of tomorrow, too, by the time they'd got steam up again.

'Sir, we need every hand in the mill if we're to fight this fire. If Number Three goes up, we'll never keep it out of Number Two. And remember, sir, that all the machinery in Number Three is wooden, and quite a lot in Number Two as well. We could lose everything.'

Jasper read the urgency in Bates's face, and nodded. He trusted this man: Bates would never recommend it if it were not necessary.

'All right, shut down. Get the overseers to organise their own sections; you are in overall command. Get a chain formed down to the river as quickly as you can. Hodges, we'll want every bucket and every broom and blanket — anything that will hold water and anything you can beat flames with. And send someone to warn Croggs in Number One to stand by.'

All three were in movement even as he spoke. There was no moment to be lost. As Jasper stepped outside into the yard he could smell the fire, even through the sulphurous reek of his own mill chimney — the fresh, charcoal smell of burning wood and the scorched reek of burning cotton. Looking up he could see a red glow outlining the tall oblong of the mill building. Above him the sky was blank, starless as always. The natural lights of night were obscured by clouds, but they were only clouds of smoke. Would to God that there were any chance of rain — but there was none, had been none for weeks. He heard a tearing crash somewhere over in the direction of the red glow, and began to run.

The puniness of man against the powers of nature had never been more obvious to Jasper as during that night when he and his mill hands fought to keep the fire from Number Three. As to saving Olmondroyd's, he saw from the beginning that there was no chance of it, even though the whole of Olmondroyd's workforce was out too. Indeed, they would not have kept it from Hobsbawn's, had it not been that the main burning building at last fell in on itself in a fountain of sparks, partly smothering its own flames.

There were others out fighting the fire besides the mill hands; not just those whose homes were threatened, but people from all around drawn by the sight of the flames to help. When fire was on the loose, every man and woman fell to without regard for personal interest, all one kin in the face of the terrible enemy.

They fought through the hours of darkness. There was no time or space for thought, only heart-tearing effort: sore hands, sore lungs, streaming eyes; faces scorched by the dragon breath of the monster, clothes singed by flying sparks, front hair melted away, voices hoarse from shouting against the roar of the flames.

And when dawn came at last, sulkily through the lingering clouds, they paused at last to survey both their success and their failure. Hobsbawn Mills were saved, but Jasper felt no elation as he stared at the charred and smoking ruins of Olmondroyd's factory. Beyond them he saw now that a large extent of the dwellings which had ben crowded up under the walls had also been consumed. The teeming, close-packed courts he had been so anxious to replace with rational

17

housing were gone, razed to the ground by the fierce flames. Largely built of wood, with walls of withy daubed over and repaired here and there with rags, they had burned up like straw.

Jasper was too weary to draw any conclusions from the sight, but there was someone else who was not. His shoulder was suddenly seized and he was dragged around to face Isaiah Olmondroyd, whose face was black with soot, his eyes red-rimmed, his eyebrows gone.

'By God, Hobsbawn, you've gone too far this time!' The big man's voice cracked with smoke and emotion. 'I'll see you damned for this! I'll have your blood! I'll ruin you!'

'What — what are you talking about?' Jasper croaked.

'You did this!' He shook Jasper as a dog shakes a rat, beside himself with rage. 'You burnt my mill down! But I'll have you for it, I swear to God! You won't get away with it! Arson's a hanging matter, and I'll see you swing if it's the last thing I do!'

'You're mad!' Jasper gasped, too close to that suffused, blackened face for comfort. 'You're out of your senses. I've been fighting all night to save your damned mill.'

Others were coming to his rescue now, seizing Olmond-royd's arms, prising his fingers loose, pulling the two men apart. Olmondroyd glared, his teeth looking oddly white against his drawn-back lips and sooty face. He obviously wanted to go on yelling, but his voice failed at last, and all that emerged was a formless croak which broke up into a paroxysm of coughing. Jasper took the chance to escape. When Olmondroyd calmed down, he would realise the enormity of what he had said and feel foolish. Meanwhile Jasper was desperate to get home, to bathe, to eat, and above all to sleep.

He stayed at home the next day, partly because he was so exhausted by his efforts, but mostly to allay Sophie's anxieties. Bates came up to the house in the afternoon to report that there was no damage to the spinning mills, and nothing worse to Number Three than a few broken windows and a great deal of soot on the walls and ceilings. Number Two had been started up again, and the hands were back at the machines after dinner, so a night and half a day had been lost.

'What's the damage to Olmondroyd's?' Jasper asked when his own business had been discussed.

Bates shook his head. 'It looks bad, sir. I don't think he'll be able to save anything from that mess.'

'Poor devil,' Jasper said. 'Fire's the thing we all fear most. I wonder what he'll do?'

Sophie asked Bates about the damage to the workers' dwellings.

'From what I've seen, ma'am, three courts are completely destroyed — that's the three nearest the mill, Grey's Court, Moss End, and Jackson's Court. Then there are three others which are more or less damaged, but still habitable, as far as they ever were.'

'What has happened to the people who lived in the three that were destroyed?' Sophie asked anxiously. 'I was there only yesterday. Some of them were sick, and all of them were poor.'

'Yes, ma'am, it's always the lowest sort who live in the old buildings like that,' said Bates kindly. He knew of his employers' strange preoccupation with the dregs of society. 'I don't know what will become of them. I dare say they'll crowd into the remaining buildings. That's how they get so crowded in the first place, of course — dividing the rooms, and then dividing again.'

Sophie turned to Jasper. 'We must do something. Now there will be nothing to stand in the way of our scheme. No-one can say the rational houses aren't needed now.'

'True enough, my love,' Jasper said. To Bates, 'Is it known yet how the fire started?'

'There's some idea that it began in the cotton store, sir, the one that butted onto Jackson's Court. It seems that a body was found there — I haven't heard all the details. Of course cotton is very combustible —'

'A body? Someone was killed?' Sophie cried.

'Yes, ma'am, I'm afraid so. More than one, I'm afraid.' He glanced at Jasper, and went on, 'Apart from the one found in the ruins of the cotton store, there were three or four — I don't know for sure — who died in the Courts. I suppose they were reluctant to leave their homes, and then got caught. The houses burned very briskly.'

Sophie was looking sick, and Jasper felt enough had been said. 'Well, thank you for coming up here, Bates. I shall be down myself tomorrow, but of course if anything arises that needs my attention, by all means send a message, and I'll come.'

'Yes, sir. Everything seems quiet for the moment. Good day, ma'am.'

Jasper would have liked to go to the club that evening to hear the latest reports, but he didn't like to leave Sophie, who was much distressed by the news of the deaths, so he remained quietly at home. Just after ten o'clock, however, Henry Droylsden walked in on his way home from his club. He was the brother of Percy Droylsden, who had married Prudence Pendlebury's sister Agnes. He was a sensible, intelligent man, and a great favourite with Sophie.

She had already gone upstairs, however, and on this occasion Jasper was glad, since it meant Henry could talk more frankly to Jasper alone.

'A bad business, this,' he said. 'I suppose you've heard there were lives lost?'

'I heard that, but I don't know the details,' Jasper said. 'What's the latest?'

'An entire family — father, mother and four children — died in one of the cellar rooms. Apparently didn't know there was a fire. It was one of those inner rooms that lead off another cellar, so there were no windows, just a black hole within a hole. They were killed when the building collapsed in on them. And two others died in their rooms — old people, probably too weak to get out of bed.'

'It's shocking,' Jasper said gravely. 'I'm glad Sophie doesn't hear this.'

'The oddest thing is this business of the body in Olmond-royd's mill. It was found on the site of the shed where they store bales of raw cotton. I say on the site — there was nothing but a heap of ashes where it had stood, so completely was it consumed. They didn't know at first that there was a body there — it didn't look like one. Only when someone raked the ashes over they saw bones.'

'Good God! Does no-one know who he is?'

'There isn't anything left to identify him by — assuming for

20

the moment it was a man. But Olmondroyd's employees are all accounted for, so it seems it was someone who shouldn't have been there.' Henry cocked his head at Jasper curiously. 'Olmondroyd hasn't been here, I take it?'

'Been here? No, why should he?'

'No reason, probably,' Henry said thoughtfully. 'I dare say there's nothing in it. But the word is that Olmondroyd has been saying that you set fire to his mill deliberately, and that the body is that of your agent who started the fire and then got caught by it before he could get out and report back to you.'

'You can't mean it,' Jasper said, aghast.

'As I said, it's probably a false rumour. I dare say he said something hasty, and it got exaggerated as it was passed along. You know how these things happen. I just thought it right to warn you, in case you should feel you need to consult somebody.'

'Consult somebody?'

'An attorney,' Henry said gravely. 'Accusations of that sort, if repeated, amount to serious slander, actionable in law.'

Jasper was at breakfast the next day when there was a knocking at the front door, loud enough to be heard even in the morning-room.

'Who can be calling so early?' Sophie said in surprise. 'I hope it isn't bad news.'

'Probably someone from the mill, my love,' Jasper said, throwing down his napkin. 'I'll go and see them downstairs, so as not to disturb you.' And he got up and left her before she could protest.

He intercepted the visitors in the hall, where they were still being received by the butler, and was glad that he had. John Whitworth was a gentleman with whom Jasper had a slight acquaintance, but he was also a magistrate, and that he had called in the latter capacity was indicated by the presence of the second visitor, George Spicer the attorney.

Jasper took them to his business-room. 'Well, gentlemen, what can I do for you?'

'Mr Hobsbawn, I have come here in my formal capacity of Justice of the Peace, accompanied, as you see, by Mr Spicer

21

who is Mr Olmondroyd's man of business,' Whitworth began. He looked slightly ill at ease. Spicer looked, to Jasper's mind, as he always did — weaselly. He didn't like him and never had, and the fact that he acted for Olmondroyd was a further point against him.

'A rather curious allegation has been made, Mr Hobsbawn,' Whitworth went on. 'A very remarkable allegation indeed,' he amplified, 'which, while I feel sure it cannot — that is to say — I beg your pardon, but it is my uneasy duty to make some enquiries about it. It has been put to me, and I cannot pretend that it has not, as I'm sure you will understand —?'

Jasper's mouth was set in a grim line. 'Please don't make yourself uneasy, Mr Whitworth. Pray tell me what has been said, and we will proceed from there.'

'Thank you, sir. Thank you. It is not something I care for, but Mr Spicer has come to me —'

'On instructions, sir,' Spicer interrupted. There was something eager and unpleasant about him, Jasper thought, like a stoat smelling blood. 'On specific instructions from my client, Mr Olmondroyd —'

'Mr Olmondroyd, yes,' Whitworth hurried on, 'who seems to think — or at least has alleged — in short, Mr Hobsbawn, he accuses you of deliberately setting fire to his mill and burning it down.'

Jasper looked from Whitworth's handsome, sweating face to Spicer's narrow, grinning one, and felt a strange calm come over him.

'A remarkable accusation, as you say, sir,' he said. 'Does he give any reason for it?'

Whitworth looked more uncomfortable than ever. 'Spicer, perhaps you — ?'

'Certainly sir, certainly sir. The well-known enmity between yourself and Mr Olmondroyd over the question of the land adjacent to Mr Olmondroyd's mill —'

'Enmity?' Jasper queried. 'I bear him no ill-will, I assure you.'

'But you were desirous of seeing the land cleared in order to further a building scheme of yours, and Mr Olmondroyd was not in favour of it. To that end he believes that you, or

22

agents acting on your instructions, started the fire deliberately.'

'It is the sheerest nonsense,' Jasper said. 'You do see that, don't you? If I wanted the courts cleared, why didn't I set fire to *them*? What would it serve to burn down the mill?'

'The bad feeling between you and my client —'

'There is none. Or at least, if there is it is all on his side.'

'My client has spoken — not exactly uncivilly, but let us say sharply — to your wife, sir, on the subject of her charitable activities —'

'I'd say it was uncivilly,' Jasper said judiciously, 'but let us not quibble over an adjective. I assure you neither my wife nor I was disturbed by Mr Olmondroyd's *sharpness*.' He was enjoying himself now. 'I do assure you most sincerely that we pay not the slightest heed to anything Mr Olmondroyd says.'

Whitworth gave a snort of laughter which he converted hastily into a cough and smothered with his handkerchief. Emerging from it, he took over the reins from Spicer, who was looking annoyed. 'Mr Hobsbawn, you are being very frank, sir, for which I thank you. May I ask your indulgence to put one or two questions to you, as I must in my official capacity?'

Jasper assented.

'Do you know anything about the origin of the fire at Olmondroyd's mill last night?'

'Nothing at all.'

'You were in the vicinity at the time?'

'I was in my office in Number Two Mill. I had been at the mill all day. The first I knew of the fire was when the nightwatchman of my Number Three came and told me about it.'

'And your actions then, sir?'

'I closed down my operating mill and sent the hands out to try to fight the fire.'

Whitworth shot a triumphant glance at Spicer. 'And you yourself also helped with this noble task?'

Jasper bowed his head. 'We did our best, all through the night, but we weren't able to save Olmondroyd's mill.'

'You may have heard that a body was found in the ashes of the mill.' Jasper bowed again. 'Do you know who the unfortunate man was?'

'No, sir.'

'Or anything about him?'

'No, sir.'

Whitworth smiled broadly. 'Then I am happy to say that that is all I have to ask you, and I am grateful to you for your patience and courtesy, sir. I shall leave you in peace now, Mr Hobsbawn.'

Spicer was not happy. 'Is that all you can —?'

'Come, Mr Spicer,' Whitworth said sternly. 'We must not take up any more of Mr Hobsbawn's time.'

Spicer subsided, and Jasper escorted them to the door himself. Whitworth donned his hat with the express purpose, it seemed, of raising it to Jasper in farewell, and walked down the steps like a prisoner set free.

Spicer turned in the doorway to say in a low, urgent voice, 'You have not heard the last of this, sir. I can safely say that my client will not be happy with your answers or your attitude. This is not the end of it.'

There were many things Jasper might have said, but he preferred to maintain a dignified silence. Olmondroyd must have been beside himself to instruct Spicer and take his ravings to the magistrate. When he had calmed down and had time to reflect, he would doubtless feel the fool and knave he had acted, and if he were man enough he would apologise. Jasper was keenly aware of what the loss of his mill would mean to Olmondroyd, and seeing a man down he had no desire to dance on the body, however much he had been provoked.

CHAPTER TWO

Saying goodbye to Farraline left Rosamund feeling weak and empty. It was a hard thing to part each time, never knowing when they would meet again.

'Why don't you just stay in London?' she said peevishly as she sat on the bed in his rented rooms, watching him pack. 'Why do you have to go back to Manchester at all? There's nothing there.'

'Nothing except the mills,' he agreed genially.

'Damn the mills!' she said.

'By all means,' he said genially. 'But I have a curious notion that my brother would stop paying my allowance if I refused to look after his factories for him.'

'No he wouldn't,' she said, and then, meeting his eye, she shrugged and said, 'Oh well, even if he did —'

He sat down beside her and took hold of her hands. They were strong and beautiful and sparkled with diamonds. He loved her hands, but they reminded him of unpalatable truths about their situation.

'Don't say it,' he said. The tone was playful but his eyes were serious. 'You can't really think I would let you pay out of Marcus's purse for me to live in idleness here. Credit me with some pride, my darling!'

'I would pay out of my own allowance,' she said, annoyed. 'Credit me with some sense!'

'It would still be his money,' Farraline said. He saw the light of battle in her eye, and said smilingly, 'Besides, you wouldn't respect me if I hung around you like a pet dog, at your beck and call. And if you didn't respect me, you wouldn't love me.'

25

'Oh Jes,' she said, putting an arm round his neck. He bent towards her and kissed her, long and sweetly. 'It's not fair!' she cried when he released her.

'Not at all,' he agreed. 'But it's all we have. We must make the best of it.' It was strange now for her to be the supplicant; at the beginning of their relationship, it was always he who wanted more than she would give. He watched her face for a moment, following her thoughts because he knew her so well. 'And no, it wouldn't do for us to run away together and think the world well lost! You wouldn't be happy living in a hovel — and frankly, my darling, neither would I.'

She sighed, knowing it was true, and said nothing.

'There's nothing we can do about any of it,' he concluded, 'except to take our love where and when we can.'

She let him go, and watched him as he moved about the room, packing with the economic movements she knew now, and loved. She loved the grave cast of his features when he was thoughtful; the long, thin scar down one cheek, where once she had held a sword-gash together with her own fingers until the surgeon came to stitch it. She loved his tall, male body, tenderly white except for his hands and forearms, face and neck, and a triangle at the base of his throat where sometimes in summer he worked with his shirt open. She loved the pleasure his body gave her, and the pleasure it took of her; their ease with each other; the simple feeling of rightness that everything seemed to have when she was near him.

'When shall I see you again?' she asked, though she knew the answer.

'As soon as possible,' he said. He rolled his brushes into his housewife and looked around to check that nothing had been missed. 'It will be a busy time now for some months. Can't you come to Manchester — visit your cousin Sophie?'

She frowned. 'I don't like making use of her like that. She's a dear creature, and I hate deceiving her.' She met his eyes, and knew he was thinking of Marcus: did *he* deserve to be deceived?

'I'll write to you as soon as I get back,' he said. 'The same arrangement? Address it to Moss at the Post Office?'

'Yes; and I'll write to you. Oh my love —'

'I know.' He caught her outstretched hand and lifted it to his lips, laid a kiss on the palm, folded the fingers over it. 'We'd better go now. I don't want to miss the coach. Will you come with me to Snow Hill?'

'Of course I will.'

It was after five when Rosamund got back to Chelmsford House, but there was still no relief from the baking heat of the day. Pall Mall lay exhausted under it, a glaring battery of windows and railings — even the pavements seemed to glitter. By contrast the great hall of the house, with its black and white marble floor, was as cold as an ice-house. Rosamund shivered, though there was a sheen of moisture on her upper lip.

After the blinding light in the street, she could only just see that the butler, Beason, was waiting for her in the gloom of the hall. His presence was ominous. She had inherited him from her late mother-in-law, and he disapproved of her.

'Oh Lord, am I very late?' she said lightly, heading straight for the stairs. Beason, who was being a monument of reproach in the exact centre of the hall, had to move quickly to keep up with her.

'His lordship has enquired for you, my lady.'

'Is Moss in my room?' she asked, starting up.

'Yes, my lady.'

'Order the carriage in ten minutes, then.'

She and Marcus and Barbarina — Marcus's unmarried sister, who lived with them — were to dine with his cousins. The Greyshotts would not mind if their guests were late, but Marcus had a strict military code of punctuality learned in his days as a staff officer under the Duke of Wellington — his great hero. She would have to move fast if she was not to annoy him.

By the time she reached the top of the stairs she had stripped off her gloves and was tugging at her hat-ribbons; but she found her maid hovering outside the bedroom door like Sister Anne.

'Not you as well, Judy,' Rosamund said, with terse humour. 'Yes, I know I'm late, but you shall see how quickly I can be ready.'

27

Moss's eyes were urgent. 'His lordship asked me to leave the room, my lady.'

Rosamund glanced at the door as if it might speak. 'Is he in there?'

'Yes my lady.'

Rosamund drew herself up. There was no avoiding it, then. 'Wait here until I call you,' she said. 'I shan't be long.' She turned the handle and went in, stitching a smile of contrition across her face.

Marcus was standing by the window, staring moodily out at nothing. He was already dressed, and she thought how well the black and white of evening clothes suited his fairness. The tightly-fitting smallclothes and stockings clung to his well-muscled legs, the cut of the tailcoat emphasised his broad cavalryman's shoulders and trim waist. Marcus Morland, Eighth Earl of Chelmsford, young, handsome and wealthy: he was a maiden's dream, she thought ironically. He had been her dream once. She didn't want to quarrel with him, but as he turned towards her, frowning, she felt sure she was going to.

'Now don't scold me,' she said lightly in the vain hope of deflecting him. 'I know I'm horribly late, but I shall change like lightning. And I'll say it was all my fault when we get there — own up and take it like a man!'

Vain hope. 'Where have you been?' Marcus demanded.

'To my mantuamaker, as you know very well. Bertoril was so slow today, the fitting took for ever. She had to keep stopping to dip her hands in cold water: that new silk marks horribly. I'm not sure it will —'

'You haven't been at Madame Bertoril's all this time. You went out at eleven this morning; and you came home in a common hackney. I saw you from the window.'

'Are you setting up to spy on me?' she said, trying to make it sound playful. 'I sent the carriage back from Bond Street because I didn't know how long I'd be. You mustn't be so Gothic, Marcus. This is 1821: a married woman can ride in a hackney without damaging her reputation.'

'Perhaps I need to spy on you, if it's the only way to find out the truth,' he said grimly.

She went on fighting the rearguard action, though she knew it was hopeless. 'It was the truth,' she said. 'I went to

28

Bertoril first, and she did take ages —'

'You've been with *him*, haven't you?' Marcus demanded; and then, as though the name hurt him to pronounce, 'You've been with Farraline.'

Well, that was that, she thought. Faced with the direct question, she drew herself up straight and said, 'Yes.'

Marcus, by contrast, seemed to crumple a little. 'Oh God,' he said quietly. It sounded like a private appeal. 'Why do you lie to me?'

'I didn't,' she said. 'I don't lie. I just — don't tell you everything.'

He snorted. 'The merest quibble!'

'No, it's not. I'm not trying to deceive you. I just try to arrange things so you won't know about it.'

He was staring just past her ear, his mind obviously — ominously — working. 'How long has this been going on?' he asked at last.

The question surprised her. It was over a year since he'd found out about her and Jes. Since then she'd done her best to be discreet, but had he really thought it was all over?

'What do you mean?' she said.

'Have you been seeing him all this summer? I suppose he came up for the Coronation?'

He wasn't invited. He's only a younger son —'

'All those fittings for robes you had. The State banquet when you felt faint and went home early. Those riding expeditions when you refused to take Bab along —'

Guilt made her angry. 'Bab didn't want to come,' she broke in. 'She hates riding, as you know perfectly well. It was only you that wanted her to come with me, for some God-knows-what reason. To spy on me, I suppose.'

He moved his head in a gesture of impatience and pain.

'Oh what does it matter? You've been having a clandestine affair all summer and all you can do is to argue about petty points —'

'Clandestine? What do you mean, clandestine? Would you prefer me to see him openly, and tell you about it afterwards?'

'What kind of question is that? I don't want you to see him at all!'

29

'Marcus, I'm just trying to do the best I can — to hurt you as little as possible, that's all.'

'And I'm expected to be grateful for that, I suppose?'

'No! I don't want you to thank me —'

'Oh good, because I shan't!'

She looked at his angry, averted profile. It was all so awful, she thought, biting her lip. In the schoolroom she had adored him: he had been her hero, the golden, godlike cousin she had planned one day to marry, as little girls say *one day* about things they know will never happen. She had never meant it to be like this. She had been brought up to be straightforward and honest, and it hurt her to do anything that smacked of the underhand. But now there was Jes, and what was she to do about that? If she were honest about her feelings for him, as she wished to be, she hurt Marcus. If she tried to keep it secret, it hurt them both.

'Oh Marcus,' she said at last, 'why must you mind so much?'

His face still turned away, he said, 'How can you ask me that?'

'Lots of other people have lovers. Most of Society, I should think. Look at Lord Egremont, Lord Uxbridge — why, even your precious Wellington always has some female or other in tow.'

'It's different for men,' he said. 'You know that.'

She shrugged. 'Well then, what about your own Cousin Helena? Or —'

'What about Caroline Lamb?' he suggested bitterly. 'I suppose you have me marked down for the part of the complacent husband, like poor William Lamb.'

'Oh come, Caro Lamb's behaviour is outrageous. I would never shame you like that —'

'*You do shame me!*'

They looked at each other in silence for a long moment.

'Give him up, Ros,' he said quietly. 'I'm asking you now — I'm begging you.'

'Marcus, don't —'

'I thought after what happened last year — Mother dying — and everything else — that it was all over with him. You've been so nice to me —'

'Oh Marcus!' It sounded awful, so seedy, she thought.

'You're my wife,' he went on relentlessly. 'We can forget all this. I'll never hold it against you, I swear, if only you'll give him up.'

'I can't,' she said despairingly.

He stared. 'You mean you don't want to.'

'If you like,' she said with difficulty. She tried to smile, but felt it going all wrong, and stopped, not sure why she had tried. A defence, perhaps, like a cat purring when it is threatened.

He stared at her, thinking again. 'I could stop you, you know,' he said at last. 'I could lock you up, keep you prisoner in your room. I could beat you every time you try to see him. The law allows. I could do it.'

She said nothing, meeting his eyes steadily. In a way, she wished he would. Anger and violence might have been easier to bear than the blackmail of his pain.

His shoulders sank helplessly. 'I couldn't really. I love you. That's what makes it all so hard. I wish I didn't care about you, but I do.'

She had to say it. 'You could divorce me.'

'No,' he said quickly. 'I don't want to do that.' He looked at her hesitantly. 'Do you want me to?'

'No,' she said. She saw him take hope from her answer, and hated herself for the answer and what she meant by it. But Jes could not have supported her, and she had no money of her own. There was nowhere else she could go. What she was asking was for Marcus to keep her while she cuckolded him — that was the brutal truth.

'You do care for me, then?' Marcus said. 'A little?'

'Of course I care for you —' she began harshly, and he cut in.

'But you care for *him* more. Damn it all —' a little weak spurt of anger — 'you're my wife! It makes such a fool of me that I can't stop you!'

He stepped closer and took hold of her shoulders and shook her; but even as he began, his own inner restraints curbed him, and it became a gentle, token shaking.

'I don't want you to see him any more!' he said hopelessly.

She detached herself from him gently. 'He's going back

31

home tonight,' she said, hating herself for offering him the poisonous false hope. 'Back to Manchester.'

But for once he saw it for what it was. His hands went down to his sides and he looked at her numbly, like a punch-drunk fighter.

'You won't give him up?'

Rosamund sighed and turned away. 'There's no point in going on with this conversation. Besides, we're going to be late for dinner. You'd better let me call Moss in, and get changed.' He didn't move, and she said gently, 'No more now please Marcus. When we get back tonight, I promise you may say anything you like to me, and I will sit and listen to it all.'

'What's the point?'

'I don't know. Perhaps you might find a way to convince me.'

He quivered. 'You treat everything as a joke.'

'I assure you this is not a joke to me,' she said. 'Do you think I enjoy hurting you?'

He opened his mouth to reply, and then closed it again, and walked out of the room.

Rosamund stood quite still for a moment, breathing carefully; as in a hiatus in battle a soldier may pause an instant to see where he has been wounded and whether he can go on. Then she raised her voice and called for her maid.

The silence in the carriage was uncomfortable. Barbarina was never much of a talker at any time and probably thought her brother was angry with Rosamund for being late home. She sat with her hands in her lap and her eyes turned politely towards the side window. She was a mouse-like creature, with a pink and white complexion, fine pale-gold hair that would neither curl nor stay up, prominent eyes and a receding chin. Having spent the first twenty-four years of her life in thrall to a dominant and capricious mother she had not learned in the single year since that parent's death to be confident or assertive.

Since Marcus had taken the backward seat, Rosamund had either to look directly at him, or out of the window on her side. She chose the latter, watched the passing scene and explored her feelings. On the debit side the pins of her head-dress were sticking into her scalp, her busk was biting into her ribs, and there was the suspicion of a trickle of sweat under her armpits. On the credit side, there was a pleasant smell of new fabric inside the carriage, which had just come back from being re-upholstered; and the evening sunlight outside was gilding the trees in St James's Square rather prettily. It was a trick she had learned in Brussels, when she was helping her mother tend the wounded after the battle of Waterloo: to keep her mind from unendurable thoughts by concentrating on her physical sensations.

They hadn't far to go. The Greyshotts' house was in Hanover Square, as ancient and inconvenient a mansion as Chelmsford House. Helena Greyshott would probably have pulled it down long ago, or at least have sold it, if it were up to her. But Cedric, Lord Greyshott, was quietly firm about his heritage as he was indifferent about almost everything else.

Helena was probably the person most calculated at that moment to make Rosamund feel at ease with herself, for she had notoriously taken lovers from the very beginning of her marriage. Greyshott was considerably older than she, and a man of indolent good humour. He had as notoriously refused to mind about Helena's misdemeanours; and all the duels fought over her — there had been six that Rosamund knew of — had been fought by and between her lovers.

Of recent years, however, Helena had settled down in near domesticity with a Captain Twombley, a plain and pleasant man some years her junior whom nobody but her found in any way extraordinary. Twombley had rooms in Albany — paid for by Helena — but everybody knew he lived more or less permanently at Greyshott House, where, indeed, he and Helena often entertained like man and wife.

Greyshott had his own suite there separately from his lady's, and lived a contented bachelor life migrating between clubs, racecourses, and the country houses of his old friends, exactly as he had done since inheriting the title in 1779. He squired Helena to certain formal or court functions, and received at her side on family occasions, and thus respectability was served. If he met Twombley by accident on the stairs or in the hall of his own house, he greeted him vaguely and

33

cheerfully as he might an acquaintance on the street.

It was an extraordinary arrangement, but it had been going on for so long that Society had come to accept it, and the usual comment upon it was 'If Greyshott don't mind it, why should anyone else?' Which all went to show, Rosamund thought as the carriage drew up, that one could do absolutely anything in London, provided one knew how to carry it off. Why, *why* couldn't Marcus be like Lord Greyshott, accept the situation, and save them all so much misery?

The Greyshotts had two children: a daughter Thalia, who was eighteen and had just had her first Season, and a son Maurice who was almost seventeen, and was between Eton and the university. They were both present that evening, and there were two other guests. One was Helena's widowed brother Viscount Ballincrea, an urbane and pleasant man Rosamund liked very much. The other was Fitzherbert Hawker.

He rose to his feet as the Chelmsford party came in, a faint smile on his handsome, piratical face. Rosamund felt herself blushing, and her eyes flew to Helena with a questioning look: had she invited Hawker simply out of mischief? It was not unknown for Lady Greyshott to amuse herself by discomfiting her guests. But she looked innocent enough, welcoming Barbarina and ushering her to a seat. Rosamund was intensely aware of Marcus by her side, and wished she dared take a glance at his face. Hawker was Farraline's intimate friend — indeed, it was he who had first introduced Jes to her — and Marcus must think there was something pointed about his being invited along with them.

But no, Marcus was going forward to shake Hawker's hand, and there was nothing but plain friendliness in his face or voice.

'How d'ye do, Hawker? I didn't know you were in England.'

'One of my flying visits. This Greek business is looking increasingly dangerous: Castlereagh's thinking of sending me out there next, so I'm home reviewing my wardrobe. Lady Rosamund, your servant, ma'am!'

Of course, she thought, as Hawker bent over her hand, he and Marcus were old acquaintances too — they had been in

34

Paris together in 1816 with the Army of Occupation. Evidently Marcus had made no connection in his mind between Hawker's presence in London and Farraline's, though Rosamund knew, because Jes had told her, that Jes and Hawker had dined twice in the last week. The dichotomy between what she knew and what she was supposed to know made her feel dizzy; and the look of amused complicity in Hawker's eyes started up in her a simple ache of longing for Farraline. He would have left for Manchester by now. She missed him already, and God knew when she would see him again.

The servants were handing tall glasses of iced champagne — just what was wanted this sticky, stifling evening. Hawker had taken a seat beside Barbarina, and was being nice to her. Rosamund found herself between Greyshott and Ballincrea.

'And when does your mama mean to return?' Greyshott asked her, turning a little sideways and stretching out one elegant leg. 'I thought she would have been back for the Coronation.'

'She did mean to come back for it,' Rosamund answered, 'but they had to change their plans at the last minute.'

'She was missed, you know — Prinny looked about for her at the banquet,' Greyshott drawled. To those of his generation, King George IV would probably always be *Prinny*. 'Quite put out she and Theakston hadn't come. I hope it was somethin' important that kept her away.'

'It was,' said Rosamund. 'Can't you guess? They heard of a stallion for sale at one of the best studs in Spain, and nothing would do for Mother but to go and see it.'

Ballincrea laughed. 'Ha! That sounds like Lucy! Did she buy it?'

'No, as it happens she thought it had a mean eye. But she said that in the natural course of things there was bound to be another coronation soon, whereas an Andalusian stallion might come along only once in a lifetime.'

'Poor Prinny, snubbed for a horse!' Ballincrea said.

'So when is she to come home?' Lord Greyshott persisted. 'London ain't the same without her.'

'They should be on their way now,' Rosamund said. 'She wrote from Gibraltar, where she was going to visit my Uncle Harry — his squadron was refitting there. She said they would take passage on the *Camilla*, and hoped to be back in England by the end of October.'

'They'll have some tales to tell,' Ballincrea remarked. 'They've been away quite some time, haven't they?'

'More than four years,' Rosamund said. 'I suppose I shall hardly recognise my brothers. They were just schoolboys when they left —'

'And they'll come back grown men,' said Greyshott. 'At least, that's the idea, isn't it. I suppose I shall have to send my sprig on a Grand Tour soon, what d'ye say, Ballincrea? Shall it be that or the university for young Maurice, d'you think?'

'The Grand Tour every time, for my money,' Ballincrea said good-humouredly. 'Oxford teaches a young man nothing but vice and idleness.'

'And how to hold his wine and his cards,' Greyshott protested mildly. 'A gentleman's education, y'know.'

'But it would be Cambridge for Maurice, anyway,' Helena put in, catching the end of the conversation.

'Even worse,' Ballincrea grinned. 'They allow Methodists in at Cambridge.'

'You, I take it, were an Oxford man?' said Hawker pointedly from across the room.

'He was at the House, weren't you, Uncle?' said young Maurice. 'I must say, Papa,' he added, taking the opportunity, 'that I'd rather not go to Cambridge, if I might have my choice.'

'My dear boy, *I* don't mind what you do,' Greyshott said, raising an eyebrow at the thought of so much particularity.

Maurice took hope. 'Well, sir, it's just that Roland and Tom wrote me such *interesting* letters from their Grand Tour, I'm sure something like that would do me much more good than grinding away at Latin and Greek and such stuff.'

'Learning at the university of life, eh?' Hawker said teasingly. 'I can certainly recommend it, Lady Greyshott: it made me what I am.'

Helena, who knew perfectly well what he was, laughed. 'That's no recommendation to a mother, Mr Hawker!'

'Ballincrea's shall be the deciding vote,' Greyshott said, 'since young Maurice is to inherit his title as well as mine.'

'No, no,' Helena said quickly, 'he will marry again — won't you, brother?'

'I can't go courting again, Nell. I'm too old,' Ballincrea said sadly.

'Nonsense. Prinny means to marry again, and he's fifty-nine! If he can do it, so can you!'

'He might say he means to, but he won't,' Greyshott said. 'He only says it to annoy, because he can't bear the idea of the Duke of Kent's daughter inheriting the crown.'

'But surely,' Barbarina said, her light and hesitant voice only just carrying across the wide room, 'surely she won't? The Clarences will have another child, I'm sure. It was only bad luck that their poor little Princess Elizabeth died.'

'Extremely bad luck,' Rosamund remarked wryly.

Barbarina looked flustered. 'I meant that she was a perfectly healthy baby. An accident like a twisted bowel could happen to anyone. It isn't likely to happen again.'

'Mother had a horse once died that way,' Rosamund said. 'Well, she shot it, of course: I suppose they let the baby linger on in pain.'

Hawker looked darkly amused. 'You recommend shooting in every case, Lady Rosamund? Horse or princess, it's all the same to you!'

'It's an agonising condition, Mr Hawker,' Rosamund said severely.

'I agree with you,' Helena said to Barbarina, firmly ignoring this aside. 'My money is on the Clarences. The Duchess is not yet thirty, and there's no doubt about the Duke's ability to get children, with all those Fitzclarences running about Bushey. They'll produce an heir within the year, I guarantee.'

'They had better, my dear,' Greyshott said. 'Prinny hates the Kents worse than a cook hates mice.'

Marcus joined in. 'That's true, sir. You remember back in February when Lord Liverpool begged him to give the Duchess of Kent a pension to support herself and the child, and the King simply said he'd be damned if he would.' Greyshott laughed at the memory, but Marcus was grave. 'If the Duchess's brother hadn't taken it on himself to give her money, they'd both have starved to death by now.'

'Prince Leopold has enough English gold in his pockets from his pension,' said Helena sourly. 'He can spare a few sovereigns to support his own sister and niece.'

'That's certainly the King's point of view,' Greyshott said.

'And of course Germans are very unpopular at the moment,' Ballincrea added. 'I dare say the Commons would like to revoke Leopold's pension if they could.'

'But it would reflect badly on us abroad if the child were brought up in want,' Hawker pointed out.

'That's right, sir,' Marcus agreed. 'The Duke of York swears he won't marry again, and until and unless the Duchess of Clarence produces a live baby, like it or not Princess Alexandrina of Kent is heir to the throne of England. She ought to have a proper establishment.'

The butler came in at that moment and caught Helena's eye. 'Dinner is served, my lady.'

'Very good. Shall we go in, everyone?'

Tea was brought in when the gentlemen returned to the drawing-room, and there was a general movement as everyone went to fetch their cup and change their seat. On Ballincrea's polite insistence Thalia was persuaded to sit down at the pianoforte and play, and under cover of this circulation and sound, Hawker came to stand beside Rosamund at the tea-table.

'You seem to be surviving the separation very well so far,' he said. 'Six hours already, isn't it? I had expected paler cheeks and wilder eyes.'

'If you've come just to torment me —' Rosamund began indignantly, but Hawker smiled his most annoying smile, gazing across the room and stirring his tea.

'Don't scowl at me, dear girl. You'll ruin the illusion I have carefully created that we are chatting idly of nothing in particular.'

'I'm not your dear girl,' Rosamund growled, but she unbuckled her brow and tried to look pleasant.

'Very well, you're not mine, but you are dear to me,' Hawker said agreeably.

'Am I?' Rosamund said shortly. 'I know you don't approve of Jes and me; though God knows you're the last person —'

'The very last,' he agreed. 'But one must back the right horse for the right race. I know all three protagonists in this little drama very well, and you are the last three people in the world to take it lightly. Now if you had waited a year or two and had an affair with *me*, Lady Rosamund, as I suggested when you first married —'

'*Before* I married, as I remember,' Rosamund said, smiling in spite of herself. It was impossible to stay angry with Hawker for very long; and besides, she felt badly in need of a friend. 'You made your reprehensible suggestion while the wedding was still only being planned.'

He grinned. 'But you see I knew you could never fall in love with me. We could have had fun together, and no-one the worse off.'

'Fun? Outrageous man!'

'As it is —' He became serious. 'I hate waste, and here you are ruining three lives in this profligate way.'

'Why is it to be my fault?' Rosamund asked indignantly.

'When a man makes love to a married woman, I hold it is always her fault. Men are opportunists, you see — like cats. They obey their instincts and take what they can, where they can: one can hardly call it stealing.'

'Nonsense!'

'Besides,' he smiled darkly, 'you know perfectly well that you are by far the most intelligent of the three. You think more deeply than the other two put together.'

Rosamund looked bleak. 'If I think more, it only means I suffer more.'

'I agree,' he said, and the unexpected warmth in his voice made her turn to look at him. His smile was no longer mocking. 'I think you are in need of a friend, Lady Rosamund. But you mustn't cry here, you know. There are eyes on you.'

She flicked her head round and saw Marcus looking at her across the room, his head a little lowered, a troubled expression on his face.

She turned back to Hawker. 'What am I to do?' she asked helplessly.

'You won't give Jes up?' Hawker said without hope.

'I love him,' she said, and then, because that sounded so

inadequate, 'He gives meaning to my life.'

'Ah, is it like that?' Hawker said. He turned his back to the room under cover of putting down his cup on the table, and Rosamund turned a little towards him. He was frowning. He took the whole business very seriously, she thought.

'Why do you mind about what happens to us?' she asked suddenly.

'I've told you, I hate waste,' he said. 'It's what makes me useful to my diplomatic masters. In international affairs, as in affairs of the heart, there is rarely a simple situation where everyone is happy and the budget balances perfectly. What one has to do is to make the best use of the resources; make sure all parties have the modicum to keep them happy. And looking at your situation, there seems to be one person who is paying for everything and gaining nothing.'

'You mean Marcus. Do you think I don't know that?' Rosamund sighed. 'It doesn't make me happy, knowing it.'

'I see that it doesn't,' he said kindly.

'But what can I do?' Rosamund went on, and she added quickly, 'He doesn't want to divorce me, even if that —'

'You could give him a child,' Hawker said quietly.

'*What*?'

He touched her elbow, turning her away from the table as Helena approached with an empty cup and a question in her eye; walked a few steps with her to pretend to examine a painting on the wall.

'Do try not to look as though I were saying stirring things, dear Lady Chelmsford,' he complained smilingly. 'I don't wish to be suspected of making love to you — at least until I really am.'

'You are utterly impossible!' she exclaimed, goaded almost to laughter.

He grew serious. 'Has it occurred to you how unfair you are being to your husband? He is an earl: he needs a son to pass the title and the estate to. If he won't divorce you, he can only get that son from you. Have you the right to deny him?'

Rosamund suppressed a shudder. 'I don't want a child — anyone's child.'

'I don't in the least blame you. Nevertheless,' he went on relentlessly, 'you married him, and bearing your husband's children is part of marriage — a consequence you may be assumed to have accepted along with his hand, his fortune and his protection. It is your duty —'

'Duty!'

'Yes. A spiky, uncomfortable sort of word, and not fashionable these days, but there it is, you know.'

She met his eye unwillingly. 'But if I did — what you say — how would it help?'

Hawker returned her look steadily. 'Probably it wouldn't help you or Farraline. But you will take what you want of each other anyway, and more or less suffer the cost. I was thinking of Marcus. Shouldn't he have something? The modicum, at least, that he might be entitled to expect from having married you?'

Rosamund stared at him, unable to speak; the dinner she had just eaten seemed to churn restlessly in her stomach. Damn you, she thought, for giving form to my own unease. And then they were interrupted: a tall shadow, a warm voice and firm hand coming between Rosamund and her self-appointed conscience.

'I can't let Mr Hawker monopolise you all evening.' Lord Ballincrea drew her gently away and into the company, saying, 'Don't I remember that you were a notable performer in your schoolroom days? Let me persuade you to play and sing for us now! Thalia is beginning to look rebellious.'

Rosamund responded brightly, too brightly perhaps, but she hadn't yet quite re-established control over all her parts. 'If you remember that, sir, your memory is sadly at fault! I play tolerably well, I suppose, but I sing like a corncrake. If you would care to sing, however, I am willing to accompany you.'

Ballincrea laughed. 'My singing days are long over! Well, perhaps you will just play for us, if you don't care to give voice.'

She could hardly refuse, now that everyone was looking at her; and at least playing she would not be expected to converse, which she might have found difficult just then. She sat at the pianoforte, took a piece of music from the pile at random, and began to play. Ballincrea stood politely nearby to encourage her; and after a moment he was joined by

41

another more interested observer. Marcus came to stand at the other side, and to stare at her face while she played.

At first she avoided his eyes; but the music soothed her thoughts, and after a page or two she was able to return his gaze. It was, after all, a very familiar face, one she had known from childhood. He had been kind to her when she was a ragamuffin brat always in trouble; he was more gentle and patient with her now than she had any right to expect. She looked at him and played, and saw the love and longing in his eyes; and for once it filled her not with irritation and a desire to escape, but with affection — even with a sort of tenderness, albeit a sad one.

In the carriage going home, Marcus made an effort, for Bab's sake, to be conversible.

'I think poor Greyshott is going to have trouble with young Thalia. If ever there was a young woman of spirit —!'

'Oh, but she's a good girl, I'm sure,' Bab said quickly. 'And she's very good-natured. Look how she played and sang the moment she was asked, without making the slightest complaint. When I was her age it was the worst trial in the world to me to be asked.'

Marcus laughed. 'Not everyone is as shy as you, dearest! Don't you know young ladies like Thalia love to show off?'

'Still, I don't know why you think she will be troublesome,' Bab insisted. 'She didn't do or say anything to upset her parents tonight.'

'I didn't mean it like that. But don't you remember when Helena was talking about arranging a marriage for her, Thalia announced very firmly that she would marry for love.'

'All girls say that,' Bab said.

'But I think she meant it.'

'Perhaps she did when she said it, but it doesn't mean that she will defy her parents, or that she'd even want to.'

Marcus looked at his sister tenderly. '*You* did, meekest and gentlest of all creatures! You wanted to marry Bobbie Chelmsford, even though Mama was dead set against it.'

Barbarina blushed. 'I didn't mean to upset Mama. But Papa was for it, and you were too. And if Bobbie hadn't — hadn't died —'

42

'Oh Bab, I'm sorry! I didn't mean to make you cry. I was only teasing you a little, out of affection. We all miss Bobbie. It was the worst thing in the world, his dying that way.'

Barbarina blew her nose and subdued her own interests firmly in favour of those of her brother. 'It was very sad, to be sure. But after all, there is always some good in everything, however bad it seems at the time. And if Bobbie hadn't died you could never have married Rosamund.' She turned a shy smile on the silent onlooker in the corner of the carriage. 'And I'd have missed the best sister-in-law who ever lived.'

Rosamund could feel that the smile with which she responded was not entirely successful, but she did her best.

Rosamund wasn't surprised when there was a scratching at her bedchamber door after Moss had left her. She didn't want a confrontation with Marcus tonight, but given the stirring his emotions had undergone, she had steeled herself for it.

He came in in response to her call, and walked across to stand in front of her almost at attention, but with a hesitant look about his face — half supplicant, half tax collector, she thought, looking up at him.

'You said —' he began defensively.

'Yes, I did,' she interrupted. 'I said I would listen to you for as long as you liked.' She pushed back the chair and stood up. 'Well, we might as well be comfortable about it.' She led the way across to the sofa in front of the fire. There was a small table there with a decanter and glass. 'Would you like something to sustain you?'

'What is it?' he asked.

'Madeira. But I have a little flask of whisky in my dressing-table drawer, if you prefer.'

'Have you?' He almost smiled. 'That doesn't seem like you. Are you a secret drinker?'

'It's my hunting flask,' Rosamund said. 'I haven't used it since last winter, but it was full when I put it away.'

He sat down. 'Yes, well, thanks. I'll have whisky.'

She fetched it and poured him some into the glass, and used the cap of the flask to take a little for herself. Sharing the whisky seemed a companionable thing to do, and a treacherous little warmth seemed to spring up between them. Or was that the spirit? She risked a look at him. He didn't seem in any hurry to begin the interview, sitting forward with his forearms resting on his knees, staring into the arrangement of dried flowers and pine-cones in the grate as though it were a flickering fire. His hair was uncharacteristically ruffled, and that and the brown silk dressing-gown made him look younger. He looked rather like the schoolboy whom she had sneaked out of the schoolroom to stare at over the banisters, when he had come to visit her stepfather. She felt fond of him, and yet completely detached, as though he were a character in a story, nothing to do with her at all. She didn't feel as though she shared her life with him, or had ever agreed to. The idea seemed preposterous. She didn't feel married. She was Lady Rosamund Chetwyn still, seventeen years old, mad about horses, and without the faintest idea what she meant to do with her life.

She thought suddenly, and for the first time in years, about her father. How different would things have been if he hadn't died? She hardly remembered him — she was only nine when he died, and he had never been much at home — and yet she felt sure that he must have influenced her life had he lived to see her brought out. She might have come to know him, and he might have given her guidance and love. I've lacked a father, she thought; and Hawker's face sprang unbidden into her mind. That's why everything is so difficult for me: I've never learnt what men are *for*.

Marcus looked up and spoke at last. 'Do you think I've treated you unfairly?'

She was so far away with her own thoughts that it took her a moment to get back and absorb his question. 'No,' she said, startled. 'Of course not. Why do you ask that?'

He looked at the fire again. 'I don't know. I don't seem to be able to understand how you feel about things — think about them. I want to understand. If I've failed you in some way —'

'It isn't that,' she said patiently. 'How can you think it? It isn't anything to do with you —'

'But it ought to be! Don't you see that that's the problem? Sometimes I think you don't believe you're really married to me at all.'

She stared at him, unable to answer. Was it pure chance that he had come so near the truth?

'I have tried —' she began at last.

'I wish you didn't have to,' he interrupted. 'I wish it came naturally to you. I don't know what to do, Ros. I don't know how to make things better. I thought when Mother died you would — feel able to make a new start, perhaps. I know you and she didn't get on. Perhaps I was wrong not to take your side more, but —' he spread his hands helplessly — 'I grew up with her, you see. Under her shadow. It isn't easy to change your feelings towards a parent.'

Rosamund felt the rise of the familiar irritation. 'I wish you wouldn't be so humble. You haven't been unfair to me — I've been unfair to you. For God's sake, you've every right to be angry! You shouldn't be apologising to me.'

'I can't be angry. I love you too much.' He looked at her. 'Ros, what are we going to do?'

Hawker's face, Hawker's voice in her head. Father, advise me! Her mind was full of wry, ironic, bitter thoughts. All decisions will have to be made by me, she thought. I must place my own head upon the block; I shall probably even have to sharpen the axe myself.

'Marcus, I haven't behaved properly by you. I know you would like to have a child.'

He looked surprised. 'But you said —'

'I know what I said. The thing is that I hadn't considered it properly from your point of view. Unless you divorce me, I am the only one who can give you a legitimate heir.'

'I don't want to divorce you,' he said quickly. His face was full of hope now. She observed it sadly.

'I can't be so selfish as to deny you a child. That would be cruel, and I don't mean to be cruel. But if I give you your heir, will you then let me go?'

The hope began to fade. 'What do you mean?'

'You know what I mean,' she said steadily, holding his gaze. 'If I give you your child, will you let me have Jes?'

For a long time he said nothing, and she watched realisation sink in, thoughts develop, resignation, despair, and finally a kind of cunning. She felt mean, miserable, desperate, cornered. But which of them was the fox, and which the pack?

45

At last he answered. 'I understand,' he said. 'But if I agree to that, I must make a condition of my own.'

'Yes?' she said warily.

'It's only fair,' he said defensively. 'If you are to give me an heir, there must be no doubt, no possible doubt, that it is my child. Do you understand what I'm saying?'

'You want me,' she said slowly, 'not to see Jes — for how long?'

'From now,' Marcus said, 'until the child is born. So that we both know. It is fair, isn't it?'

'Yes,' she said absently. She looked down a long corridor of empty days. Nine months of gestation, and how long before she conceived? Not to see him for all that time?

'Or write to him — communicate with him in any way,' Marcus went on. She focused on him. 'I want you to behave as my wife for that time — in fairness to the child, if not to me.'

'Oh Marcus —'

'Surely it's not too much to ask — one year of your life?'

'One year?'

'More or less.' He blushed suddenly, surprising her. His fine, pale skin showed it clearly, the rush of blood, and the almost instant ebb. 'We must make sure first of all that you're not already — that he hasn't —'

'I'm not,' she said starkly.

'But you can't know for certain. We must be sure,' he insisted.

She bowed her head in assent. What must be done, must be done; but it all seemed so calculated, so joyless.

'So you agree?' he pressed eagerly. 'To my conditions? You will be a real wife to me?'

'Yes,' she said at last. 'I agree to it all.' She looked up, and caught the tail end of the smile he quickly suppressed. For a moment she didn't understand; and then she thought, he hopes that if I don't see Jes for a year, or however long it takes, I'll forget him. He thinks that if I play the loving wife as agreed, I won't want my half of the bargain when the time comes.

'Marcus —' she began, but he forestalled her.

'Don't say any more now,' he said. He picked up the flask

46

from the side-table and poured the last of its contents. 'Ought to be champagne really,' he said, 'but this will have to do. A toast, my darling — to our child!'

She looked at him blankly, but could not refuse to touch glasses or drink. 'Our child?'

'Oh my love,' he said, 'don't worry. Everything will be all right now. We're doing the right thing, I know we are. And I'll make you happy, Ros, you'll see! You've never given me the chance before. I'll show you how good it can be. Everything's going to be wonderful!'

He looked so happy, flushed and bright-eyed like a boy; so why did she feel like both fox and pack simultaneously? Hawker, this was all your idea! she thought fiercely. But it wasn't, of course. Whatever this was, for good or ill, it was her own work.

CHAPTER THREE

It was the moonlight which woke Benedict. The night
nursery at Morland Place was a large, long room with a row
of latticed windows along the east wall, and these windows
were not curtained. The moon was full tonight, and since the
night was also cloudless, there was nothing to stop it flooding
into the room like blue-white water, throwing a sharp black
shadow of meshes from the window leads across the ceiling.

Bendy — as he was usually called and as he thought of
himself — turned onto his back and stared upwards, enjoying
the sensations of being wide awake when the rest of the world
was asleep. He had the bed to himself — oh luxury! Usually
he slept with his brother Nicholas, who even at the best of
times was a restless and noisy sleeper; but Harry Anstey, who
shared their lessons with Father Moineau, was staying the
night at Morland Place, so he and Nicky were sleeping in the
larger tester bed on the other side of the room.

Harry and Nicky were the same age — they had been born
within days of each other in fact — and were best friends.
Bendy was only nine, four years younger, and they often left
him out of things. He wished he had a best friend, or any
friend at all, really. If only he could have gone to school, he
might have made friends with one of the village boys; but
Mama said they didn't do hard enough lessons at the school,
so he had to be taught at home by Father Sparrow. He liked
Father Sparrow, and he quite liked his lessons, but he wished
he had someone to do things with, the way Nicky had Harry.

He could hear Nicky's snoring from across the room.
Nicky was 'delicate', as the maids put it: he had a weak chest,
sometimes suffered asthma attacks, and had a weak stomach

48

too, which meant he was often ill. That, together with his being the eldest, meant that everyone had to make a fuss of him all the time, and not cross him in anything.

Nicky would inherit Morland Place one day, the whole estate, every stone and blade of grass and animal and tree, which would make him very rich and important. Bendy, who understood many things he was not yet expected to, quite saw that the servants and tenants and tradesmen were anxious to keep in with Nicky, against the day when he would have the making or breaking of their fortunes. Bendy didn't blame them. It seemed as natural to him as that he should try to keep in with Father Moineau to avoid being beaten.

Down the far end of the room Matty, the junior nursery maid, had her bed. She had been Nicky's wet nurse, so she was especially devoted to him. Sarah, the senior nursery maid, slept upstairs in the servants' quarters now. She had only become senior last year when old Jenny died, and she was very proud of her position, and very strict. Bendy had cried a lot when Jenny died, though Mama said he ought to have rejoiced that she was past her pain and gone to dwell with the Blessed Saints in Heaven. He supposed that was true, but he missed her all the same.

It just seemed to him that he never had anything of his very own to love. Papa had given them a puppy once, but it had died of distemper; and anyway, Nicky had always claimed it was really his dog, because he was the eldest, even though he hadn't really liked it. Nicky had his own pony too, while Snowball, the one Bendy rode, belonged to the estate and was used to go down to the post office and to fetch parcels and things from the staging inn. Papa said he could have a pony of his own when he was eleven, but that was so far away it was like saying 'never'. It was hateful sometimes to be the youngest.

The moonlight had moved across the ceiling now: Bendy could tell because the edge of the window-shadow had started to go down the wall opposite. Then, as he watched, a black shadow of broad wings fluttered across the mesh, and a moment later he heard the harsh shriek of an owl from somewhere above. It shrieked twice more, and then the shadow beat softly across the ceiling again. It must have landed on the roof for a moment before resuming its hunt.

Bendy was suddenly filled with a desire to see more. He sat up and slipped carefully out of bed, feeling down with his bare toes from the high bedstead for the polished wooden floor, listening for a moment for the regular breathing of the other inmates. The casements were quite high up, but there was a bench along most of the wall, and standing on that he would be able to see out perfectly.

The lattice leads spoiled his view, so he unlatched the window and swung it wide open. At once a wonderful warm smell flooded in with the moonlight, a smell of grass and trees and summer-baked earth, hay and harvest and apples. He drew a huge, rapturous breath as he stared out over the landscape, magically spread out and illuminated for him. It was a beautiful night, warm and still. The moon sailed clear above the trees, looking small and hot, pouring down a light so intense that he could see everything almost as clearly as by daylight. The sky was velvet black up above the house, but nearer the moon it lightened to violet and then to cobalt blue.

Below him, at the foot of the house, the moat lay like a narrow strip of polished silver. He could see the drawbridge from the back door just below to the right, and from the end of the drawbridge a path ran pale in the darker grass, branching one way towards the orchard, and the other way skirting the trees of the copse towards the village. Above the orchard wall the fruit trees stuck up their branches towards the sky, and the light was so bright Bendy could see apples hanging amongst the topmost leaves, little silver globes like harness bells. If there had been a wind, he imagined they might have chimed softly, like the the bells on the ponies that drew Mama's phaeton.

Resting his elbows on the sill and his chin in his hands, Bendy gazed out, content just to stare. The moment was his and his alone. No-one else was awake, no-one else was seeing what he saw, and that made it special to him, his own. He would never tell anyone about it, he decided, not ever in his life. And even though Nicky would one day own Morland Place and everything about it, he would never own this secret moment under the bright, white moon.

Then the magical thing happened. A shadow detached

itself from the darkness under the copse; a fox came trotting out. Bendy drew a breath of excitement and kept very still, afraid it might see him, but the fox seemed quite fearless, coming straight towards the house as if it knew exactly where it was going. It was a big dog-fox, Bendy saw: its sharply pricked ears were rimmed with moonlight, and its white breast-mark, shaped like a flame, and the white tip to its tail seemed to burn silver. It trotted not on the path, but just beside it, following it straight down to the moat.

Just beside the drawbridge on the far side there was a place where the bank had been worn away, probably by rain running off the side of the bridge. Bendy knew it well — it was a place where you could get right down to the level of the water, and he had often crouched there to look at the carp. He'd had a plan once to teach them to feed from his hand, but they were not as tame as the ones in the fish pond, and they wouldn't come close enough.

The fox knew the place too: he took one quick glance around him, and then stepped down onto the broken part and lowered his head to drink. Bendy watched, entranced. A delicate ripple of silver rings spread outwards from the dipped muzzle. The fox seemed so close to him, he felt as though he were sharing its sensations, the coldness of the water and the pleasure of thirst relieved. It's my fox, he thought; my very own. My friend. The fox finished drinking, stepped back up onto the bank, shook itself briskly, sending a spray of silver drops flying from its muzzle, quite visible in the moonlight; and then for an instant it raised its head.

It looked straight at Bendy, as though it had known all along he was there; looked at him quite unafraid. The pointed, beautiful face, the sharply pricked ears, the fine golden eyes, all drawn so clearly in the bright moonlight, were lifted towards him. It looked at Bendy and he looked back, and then its jaws parted in what seemed to Bendy unmistakably a smile. He smiled too, and the fox, as though satisfied, turned and trotted away, crossing the shining grass with its own short shadow keeping close beside it, and disappeared into the trees again.

Bendy stayed where he was, long after the fox was gone. The moon moved round, trailing a fine wisp of cloud, now,

51

like a gauzy scarf; and the light, moving down the walls, finally reached the eyelids of the least sound sleeper in the room. There as a whimper, and then a wail. Sophie and her husband had come to stay at Morland Place; Bendy had forgotten the baby was sleeping in the nursery with them.

He was caught fair and square before he had the chance to get back into bed. First the baby's nurse, Janet, woke, and then Matty, and the two of them set up an uproar. It was the moonlight which had woken the baby, and the moonlight wasn't Bendy's fault; but he had opened a window wide, and everyone knew night air was dangerous to all human beings, and possibly fatal to small babies. How could Bendy be so thoughtless, so careless? Janet cradled small Fanny Hobsbawn against her breast defensively as Matty rushed over to slam the offending window and smack Bendy sharply.

Now Harry and Nicky woke too, and sat up sleepily, wondering at the commotion. Bendy couldn't help noticing the smirk on Nicky's face as Matty promised to report his iniquity to Sarah in the morning. Nicky was hoping he'd get a beating; but when Bendy climbed back into bed at last, he found he didn't much care about any of that. In his mind, small and clear and silver, was the image of the fox — *his* fox. That was something that was all his, and no-one could take it away from him.

James came home just after noon. It was the hour of the servants' dinner; the stableyard basked in the sunshine, innocent of movement. There was the wholesome smell of hot tarred wood and clean straw; the contented sounds of horses munching and a pigeon somewhere croodling to its mate. James loved Morland Place at this hour and this time of year. The warm bricks smelled faintly of caramel and the upstairs casements stood open on the sweet, cool darkness of the bedrooms. Everything was safe and good and welcoming: everything said *home* to him.

Unwilling to spoil anyone's dinner, he stabled his own horse, enjoying the simple pleasures of it: Victor's sigh of comfort as he unbuckled the girth; the kindly smells of warm leather and hot horse; the sense of vicarious satisfaction as the bay plunged his muzzle into his water-bucket and sucked greedily. All's well with the world, James thought. He checked that the hayrack was full, slapped Victor companionably on the rump, and went out into the sunshine.

They would be in the rose garden on such a day, he thought, turning away from the house. The roses were in their third flush of bloom, their colours drained by the strong light, their scent almost too heady. The gravel felt hot under his feet, the cloth of his breeches scratchy, his riding boots unbearably heavy; but everything gave way to a feeling of refreshment at the sight of his wife and daughter sitting in the shade of the arbour, peacefully sewing.

Héloïse looked up at him. 'You look delicious,' he said, bending to kiss her upturned lips. 'Cool and serene, like the inside of a cathedral.' She laughed at his absurdity, and he turned to Sophie, such a perfect little matron in her frilled cap, sewing away at a baby-shirt. 'Is that for my granddaughter? Where is she, by the way?'

'In the nursery, asleep, to be sure. Where did you think she would be, Papa? It isn't for Fanny, anyway,' Sophie added, holding the miniscule garment out critically at arm's length. 'It's for Mathilde's new baby. Can't you tell by the size?'

Héloïse laughed. 'Now you expect entirely too much, my Sophie! If a man can remember a baby's name it is remarkable, never mind its age!'

James sat down on the deliciously cold marble of the bench beside them, and stretched out his legs luxuriously. 'Be thou as chaste as ice, as pure as snow, thou shalt not escape calumny! Mathilde's offspring are called Mary, Harriet and Jemima in that order, and Jemima was born in May, so that makes her — hum — three months old, nearly four months. Now then!'

'Bravo, Papa! I'm astonished!'

'None of your impudence, child — you must know I take a great interest in my family. I have the firm intention of becoming a patriarch — perhaps even an ancestor! Though it would help if one of you would try to produce a male sprig. Not that the females aren't attractive little brutes, but —'

'Babies come in their own good time,' Héloïse said peacefully. 'In God's time.'

'I don't seem to remember such exemplary patience on

your part, my wife, when you were waiting for babies,' James teased her. 'You fretted yourself to a fiddle-string, in spite of all I could say.'

'Did she?' Sophie said with interest. 'Did you, Maman?'

'A little, perhaps,' Héloïse was forced to admit. 'But you see how foolish it was. Along came Nicky and Bendy all in good time. Don't be in a hurry, my Sophie. It's better to have a little space between babies.'

'But I do so want to give Jasper a son,' Sophie sighed. 'If Fanny had been a boy, I wouldn't mind waiting for the second. Of course, I love Fanny dearly, but we do need to have a son to follow us.'

'You don't think a female could run the mills?' James asked with a detachment which fooled no-one.

'I know what you're thinking, Papa — that my sister Fanny meant to run the mills herself. Probably she would have managed very well; but she was different from other females.'

'Yes, she was,' James said abruptly. 'Well, I wouldn't want my granddaughter to be too like her namesake. My Fanny had too much spirit for her own good. Very well, Sophie, you may wish for a boy if you like.'

'Poor Mathilde must want one even more than me, after three disappointments,' Sophie said. 'A female can't be a builder, after all.'

'Talking of which,' James said, 'here comes the builder — and the philanthropist too. Well, gentlemen, have you changed the world for the better this morning?'

Jasper came into the garden with John Skelwith behind him. James's natural son — a youthful indiscretion — looked very like a younger, taller James. He had married Héloïse's ward, Mathilde, which made it easier for Héloïse to treat him like a real son, and to think of his children as her grand-children as well as James's.

'I hope at least we haven't changed it for the worse,' Jasper replied cheerfully.

'Mathilde sends her respects,' Skelwith told Héloïse, 'and begs to inform you that she believes Jemima may be about to cut her first tooth.'

'At three months? But that is astonishing!'

'Almost four months,' Skelwith corrected, 'but yes, it is

astonishing. Jemima is more advanced even than Mary was at that age, and Mary is the most remarkable child in the world.'

'I'm sorry to contradict you so directly, Skelwith,' said Jasper, 'but Fanny is the most remarkable child who ever lived. There cannot be the slightest doubt about it — I'm her father, so I must know.'

Skelwith grinned. 'They are both paragons without equal. I shan't quarrel with you, especially as you mean to introduce me to so many influential men in Manchester.'

'Oh, is your scheme really to go ahead?' Héloïse asked.

'That must depend on finances,' Jasper said, 'and finances depend on our being able to persuade other mill masters to invest in it.'

'You have a strange way of ingratiating yourself with mill masters, from what you were saying last night,' James said drily. 'Did you know, John, that Jasper has become an arsonist?'

'So he has just been telling me.'

'But surely no-one believes it?' Héloïse said quickly.

'I shouldn't think so,' Jasper said. 'Probably not even Olmondroyd, once he'd thought about it.'

'It's a serious slander,' Skelwith said. 'I wonder you don't take him to court.'

'Our attorney wanted us to act,' Sophie put in, 'but Jasper was against it.'

'Whetlore likes nothing better than a court case, like all these attorneys. But it wouldn't be the thing at all. The sooner it's all forgotten the better. I won't be the one to kick a man who's already down.'

'But he has influence,' Sophie said anxiously. 'Even if people don't really, truly believe, they'll still side with him against us.'

'My love, they would anyway,' Jasper said. 'Taking Olmondroyd to court wouldn't make them change sides.'

'The fire ought to facilitate the building scheme, at all events,' Skelwith said thoughtfully. 'There's the site cleared and ready: no reason not to go ahead.'

'I'd like to be able to begin before anything else is built on the site,' Jasper said restlessly. 'Already there are rough shelters going up. If we leave it too long, we'll be back where we started.'

'Then why not begin?' James asked.

'We haven't discovered who owns the land yet. And more importantly, we haven't raised enough capital.'

'Have you investors in mind?'

'I shall ask absolutely everyone,' Jasper said, 'on the principle that the wider you cast your net, the more likely you are to catch a fish. But my main hope is with one or two of the more liberal mill masters. There are enough who care about the condition of the workers —'

'Those who agitate for laws to limit factory hours, I suppose?' James asked.

'Those, and others,' Jasper said. 'Concern takes many forms. Our friend Farraline, for instance, disagrees forcefully with me over the need for factory laws, but I'm sure he'll see the necessity of decent housing.'

'But he hasn't any money of his own,' Sophie pointed out. 'The mills really belong to his brother the Earl.'

'I know, dear; but I'm sure Farraline can find a way to persuade his brother to invest, if he wants to. That's for him to decide, anyway. I shall put the project to him as soon as we get back.'

'Mr Farraline is a very nice young man,' Héloïse said. There had been a time when she had thought he was interested in Sophie, but it had come to nothing. 'Do you see much of him in Manchester?'

'Yes, Maman,' Sophie said. 'He and Jasper belong to the same club. He dines with us quite often and has tremendous arguments with Jasper. But he's been in London all summer. I don't know when he returns.'

'He went for the Coronation, I suppose?' Skelwith asked.

'I suppose so,' Sophie said. 'It was such a pity Rosamund didn't have the house-party she planned for the Coronation. I so looked forward to it.'

'I suppose it was because of her mother not coming home after all,' Skelwith said.

'But she could still have had it, even without Aunt Lucy.'

'Never mind, love,' Jasper said, as one who hated his wife to be cheated of any pleasure, 'we've had a much nicer time here than we would have in London. And it would have been difficult for me to get away in brisk-time, you know, in July.'

'Farraline seems to have managed it,' James observed.

'The cases are very different,' said Jasper.

A servant came out to tell them that a nuncheon of cold meat, fruit, and pastries had been laid out for them in the long saloon, and they all repaired indoors. The long saloon's windows looked over the inner courtyard, which was almost always in shade, so it was cooler in there than in the drawing-room, whose windows faced south.

The long, handsome room was used mainly for large parties and for dances: sixteen couples could stand up there with comfort. It had a large fireplace at either end, and the walls were partly covered with bookshelves and partly with family portraits. It was furnished with chairs all around the walls, sundry tables, a couple of large sofas bracketing the fireplaces, and at one end the old pianoforte which had belonged to James's first wife.

Polly was in the long saloon when they arrived, sitting at the pianoforte and coaxing a Beethoven sonata out of its elderly strings, while Father Moineau leaned against the piano lid and watched her face. They were an incongruous pair: the small, cheerful-faced, almost circular priest — growing even more circular of late under the influence of good Yorkshire food and little exercise — compared oddly with the slender form of James's beautiful niece. Everything about Polly exuded grace and elegance: she wore her simple gowns with an air that made every other woman in her company seem either over- or under-dressed. To James she always seemed the image of her mother, his sister Mary, who had had that same porcelain skin, those violet-blue eyes, and that black silk hair, pinned up above a long, lovely neck.

She looked up and blushed surprisingly as they came in.

'Don't stop, *ma chère*!' Héloïse said. 'You play so nicely.'

But she closed the piano lid firmly. 'I was making a nonsense of it.'

Moineau straightened up. 'I found this lovely creature in a dark corridor, pining like a linnet in a cage,' he said to Héloïse, 'so I insisted on setting her free, in spite of all her protests.'

'Thank you, Father,' Héloïse said. 'I begged her to come out of doors with us. It was not necessary to go through the linen cupboard, Polly dear. Mrs Thomson and I would have done it tomorrow.'

'I've sorted it all, anyway, Aunt,' Polly said. 'Father Moineau came just as I was finishing.'

She looked at him as she said it, and he glanced towards her at the same moment. It struck Héloïse suddenly as odd, as if there were some sort of complicity between them. It was the sort of look that might pass between intimate friends. She had noticed before — how could she not? — how well they got on together. It was no wonder Father Moineau should enjoy Polly's company: her education was superior, and she was loveliness itself to look at. But she wished Polly were more interested in proper men — no, of course she didn't mean quite that, but it did seem such a waste of Polly that she remained single. It was four years since the tragedy, but though Polly seemed to have recovered completely, she shewed no desire to alter her state, or even to want to be courted.

They all moved over to the table where the nuncheon was laid out. Father Moineau spoke the grace, and conversation broke out again.

'How is Bendy this morning?' Sophie asked him. 'From what I heard from Janet, it was all a to-do about nothing. I hope he wasn't upset?'

'Not at all,' Moineau said cheerfully. 'I asked him to draw me something from fancy this morning while I heard the older boys in their construe, and he drew me the most beautiful picture of a fox. That was not the work of a grieving soul, I assure you.'

'I'm glad. I shouldn't want him to be punished for opening a window. It was such a warm night, it couldn't have harmed Fanny.'

'It is not the warmth or otherwise that makes the night air dangerous, I understand,' Moineau said gravely, 'but the evil humours which arise from the earth during the dark hours. So I was told this morning at great length by the good Sarah. She was most indignant to learn that I had not beat him for endangering everyone's lives.'

58

'You don't beat him enough, and that's a fact,' James said, sampling his cook Barnard's breathtaking game pie. 'Now with Nicky I could understand it, him being so delicate, but Benedict wants the dev — pardon me Father — the *deuce* beating out of him.'

Father Moineau, delicately spearing slices of pink, fragrant ham onto his plate, turned a serene face to him.

'I beg your pardon,' he said calmly, 'but you are wrong. It is Benedict who is the sensitive one. Nicholas never minds what is said or done to him. He goes on in his own way, sufficient unto himself, hardly acknowledging anyone else's existence. But Benedict notices everything, and cares very deeply.'

A chorus of protest met his words.

'It is true,' he insisted. 'If anyone says a reproving word to Nicky he sulks and pouts, but it only confirms his belief that he is right and everyone else wrong. But speak harshly to Benedict, and his soul sickens under the blow. He carries the reproof away, and goes over and over it, examining it and blaming himself bitterly.'

James shook his head in sheer disbelief. 'I can't believe you're talking about my two sons. Nicky, who's as good as gold, and Bendy, who's always up to mischief?'

'Yes, Father,' Héloïse put in, 'after all, it is Bendy who is *méchant*. Nicky always minds what he is told.'

'And since you admit that you beat Nicky more than Bendy,' James added triumphantly, 'it proves the value of it. Good God, we were all beaten when we were boys, my brothers and I!'

Father Moineau did not smile, but Héloïse noticed he had a very satirical eye. James had not been such a very good advertisement for beating, she acknowledged inwardly. In his time he had been a noted sinner.

'In fact,' Moineau said, 'I beat both of them very little — Nicky because it would do no good, and Bendy because it would do much harm. But you must not worry about them,' he added with a kindly smile. 'There is nothing much amiss with either of them. They will grow up to be fine men.'

James turned to Sophie with a wry smile. 'Perhaps I should not be urging you to have boys, love. You see what a trial they are.'

59

Sophie caught Jasper's eye, and blushed in a way which still made his pulses race, even after two and a half years of marriage. 'I'll take the risk, Papa,' she said.

'I wish you took more after your mother, Polly,' James went on with mock severity to his niece. 'To be sure she didn't marry your father until she was nearly thirty, but she never tried to make a nun of herself. She always had dozens of young men hanging round her, and she loved dancing and parties and going out into society.'

Polly narrowed her eyes shrewdly. 'Didn't my mother refuse an offer from the Earl of Tonbridge, Uncle?'

James laughed. 'Several, I believe! But still she used to let him drive her in the Park, and escort her to the theatre. Now I know York isn't London, but —'

'Don't tease her, James,' Héloïse intervened. 'She's old enough to choose for herself. If she does not care to go to balls —'

'My uncle thinks I should be made to,' Polly said. 'For my own good, is that not so, sir?'

'Certainly,' James said, unabashed. 'And if your father were at home, he'd say the same thing. He'd take you himself, and pick out your partners for you.'

Polly smiled. 'You have given me the only possible reason for being glad of his absence.'

'Have you heard nothing more from him?' Sophie asked.

'Nothing from Papa since he wrote in May to say that Bonaparte was dead. But I had a letter from my sister two weeks ago telling me they were coming home.'

'That's good news! You must be pleased,' Sophie said. 'Will it be a visit only, or for longer?'

'Papa is coming home for good,' Polly said. 'When Bonaparte died, the defences of St Helena were reduced, you see, so it's no longer a vice-admiral's command. Papa's tour was almost finished anyway, and as soon as it ended he was to come home. Africa says he doesn't mean to seek another command. There are so few of them anyway, with the navy shrinking and ships laid up every week, and Papa's nearly seventy now. Africa says he fancies a few quiet years in a cottage somewhere — Southsea or Bath or some such place.'

'Will he not be bored, after such an active life?' Héloïse asked.

'He has his plans,' said Polly. 'He means to make a garden. He's never had one before, having been at sea since he was ten years old. And he means to introduce Africa into Society before it's too late, and make a civilised creature of her.'

'There,' said James triumphantly,' I told you he'd agree with me! As soon as he's settled, he'll send for you, and tame you both, you and your sister. He'll have you both married off within a twelvemonth!'

'I assure you, Uncle —' Polly began, half cross, half amused, but James interrupted airily.

'Oh, he'll manage you, I've no doubt at all. After a shipload of pressed sailors, daughters will be a mere nothing to him.'

'When will he be back?' Héloïse asked.

'They were to set sail at the end of July, so they should be in England some time in October, depending on the speed of their passage.'

'It will be wonderful to see Africa again,' Sophie said. She and her cousin had been at school together for a time. 'I wonder if she'll find me changed? What will she think of Fanny? I suppose she'll think me very dull to have married and had a baby, considering all the exciting things she must have seen and done.'

'Each of us does what is in our nature,' Father Moineau said. 'But I must admit an eagerness to meet this wild woman I've heard so much about.'

Polly looked at him sharply. 'She is not at all what you approve of in a woman — or, at least, what I gather you approve of.'

'Yet I shall enjoy hearing about her adventures,' he said.

'Your own must have been much more exciting,' Héloïse said, but Moineau's attention had changed. She turned her head to see what the priest was looking at, and saw her son Benedict hovering in the doorway, looking wistful. 'Yes, *mon petit*, what is it?' she asked. She would not normally have allowed him to interrupt a grown-up gathering, but just then he looked so like James in one of his wheedling moods that it softened her heart towards him.

Benedict sidled over to her cautiously. There were raspberry and cherry tarts on the table and he couldn't help looking at them briefly, though he dragged his eyes firmly away. His dinner of boiled beef and rice pudding had been sustaining but inelegant, and there was in him a longing for the finer things of life. But his present business was more important.

'Where is Nicky?' Héloïse asked before he could speak. 'Why are you not with him?'

'He and Harry are playing a game. They didn't want me,' Bendy said simply. He wished he were alone with his mother. There were too many people to hear his question and perhaps guess his secret. '*Maman, puis-je vous demander quelque chose?*'

'In English, *p'tit*, since there is company,' Héloïse said, defeating his purpose.

Bendy looked round the circle, rubbing one foot thought-fully against the back of the other leg. Sophie and Father Moineau were looking at him; the others, he saw, were only waiting for him to go away again. There was nothing for it.

'Maman, where would a fox live?'

'In its den, of course,' Héloïse said, puzzled.

'No, I mean where would it live *here*? Somewhere near this house?'

'It would not live near the house, I think, because of the dogs,' Héloïse said. 'Do you think there is a fox nearby? If there is we must get rid of it, before it gets into the fowl yard.'

This was as bad as it could be. Benedict wished he had never brought up the subject. But Father Moineau was watching him with those all-seeing eyes. 'I think I understand your question,' he said. 'You want to know what kind of place foxes live in?' Bendy nodded gratefully. 'Woods are their favourite haunts. A vixen may dig out an earth amongst tree roots, or she may take over a deserted rabbit warren or badger's sett. Does that answer you?'

'Yes, sir, thank you,' Bendy said. He was anxious now to make his escape. 'I'm sorry I disturbed you, Maman.'

Héloïse pushed the dark hair out of his eyes, wondering what trouble he was brewing up now. If only he were more like Nicky — and yet she couldn't help imagining that James must have been very like this when he was the same age. 'Run along, then,' she said. 'Don't get into mischief.'

The servant had come to escort Harry Anstey home. The Ansteys lived in a large and rambling house of mediaeval grandeur and inconvenience in the Lendal in York, with gardens that ran down to the river; and cellars through which the river ran in flood-time.

The Anstey fortune came from coal, but Harry's father, the second Baron, was far enough removed both historically and physically from the mines at Garforth to be accepted anywhere in society. He had held an uncontested seat in the House of Commons until his father's death had elevated him to the Lords. The seat was now being nursed for the second son, Alfred. Harry's eldest brother, Jack, had gone into the navy at a very early age at his own passionate request, and would not be parted from his chosen career.

There had always been a close friendship between the Ansteys and Morlands. Harry's mother had been a Morland before her marriage, and Harry's father in his youth had been in love with Mary Morland, James's sister and Polly's mother. But Mary would not have him; and his marriage to her cousin Louisa had proved a successful and happy one, with eight surviving children, of whom Harry was the seventh.

Harry's friendship with Nicholas Morland was a matter of satisfaction for all parties. Harry had not at first relished the harder lessons, and being so directly under the tutor's eye: at school discipline had been much looser and he had managed to while away many a dishonourable hour in the back row with pleasantly useless activities. But now at thirteen he was beginning to understand that as a younger son he must have some gentlemanly career to support him in adulthood. To that end, the education he was receiving at Morland Place would prove invaluable, and he did his best to work hard and benefit from it.

He liked Morland Place, and the fresher air and greener spaces around it; he liked Father Moineau and Lady Morland; and the food was better than at home. He liked being with Nicky, who was his friend from infancy; and if Nicky was sometimes overbearing, or demanded more homage or service from him than was comfortable — well, it was only what was due to his position. Nicky was heir to Morland Place, after all, and would one day be rich and influential; while Harry as fourth son and seventh child would have nothing but what he could earn with his own skills.

Nicky liked the arrangement too. Harry was the perfect companion, uncritical, easy-going, always willing to concede the best part of everything to Nicky as his right. The only thing Nicky didn't like was when Harry went home, for that left him to his own devices, and he was not a boy to relish his own company. He had asked over and over again for Harry to come and live permanently at Morland Place; but Lord and Lady Anstey had refused to consider it. Even Harry himself had expressed, cautiously, a desire to see his parents and sisters and brothers with what Nicky considered unnecessary frequency.

'What do you need them for?' he had asked impatiently. 'If you come and live here you'll have me, and my mother and father. And Bendy,' he added as an afterthought. 'It's much better here than in that nasty old house of yours. And next year we'll be able to have our own room, instead of sleeping in the nursery.'

But Harry, though apologetic and evidently hating to disappoint his friend in anything, had refused to give up wanting his own family. The times when he stayed overnight at Morland Place continued to be infrequent, and when they happened they only made Nicky mind his departure all the more.

So when Harry had been whisked up by the Anstey carriage and driven away, Nicky felt himself very hard done by. He hung around the yard at first, at a loss for something to do, or someone to talk to. The grooms went about their work, ignoring him as far as possible. He was aware that their attitude towards him was subtly different from that of the indoor staff. They treated him with politeness rather than respect, and though he could not have put a name to the difference, he knew it existed and resented it.

After he had been put out of someone's way twice with great firmness, and almost knocked down by a hay bale swung on someone's shoulder, he removed himself to the bottom of the house steps and watched the activity broodingly under his brows, occupying himself with kicking at a loose cobble. He had succeeded in lifting it completely, breaking the earth around it and making quite a satisfactory hole, when the door to the buttery opened and the cook, Monsieur Barnard, came out carrying a wooden chair.

It was Barnard's habit in the afternoon to take a rest from his labours and sit in the sunny corner of the yard to enjoy a cigar. Nicholas eyed him with caution. He knew Monsieur Barnard didn't like him, and he was the one member of the household who did not have to pretend. A cook of his genius might express himself freely without fear of retribution. Nicky knew that even his mother would not take his part against the old Frenchman.

Barnard placed his chair with exactitude, sat down on it, drew out his cigar, and then fixed Nicky with a look of disapproval, staring deliberately at the hole he had just made, and then lifting his hostile black eyes to Nicky's face. Nicky met the stare defiantly for a moment, but he could not hold it, and was forced, red-faced and furious, to lower his own eyes and take his departure.

He went out through the barbican, trying to look as though he had meant to go that way anyway, and slouched along the path beside the moat, wondering what to do with himself. Round the first corner there was a pair of swans sitting on the water and dipping their necks in turn to feed. They both straightened up when he came into sight, eyeing him from hostile black eyes just like Monsieur Barnard's. He called to them, and even twiddled his fingers, making believe to have some bread for them, but they wouldn't approach. After a moment they turned and glided away, seeming quite casual about it, but rapidly putting a distance between themselves and him. Even the swans don't like me, he thought morosely, and stooping down, searched for a stone to throw at them. It missed them and hit the wall harmlessly, but speeded their disappearance round the next corner.

He walked on in the same direction; and when he rounded the corner he saw his little brother descending from the orchard wall, evidently having taken a short-cut through the orchard from somewhere. He had a purposeful look about him as he dropped to the ground and headed for the back door to the house. When he saw Nicky he halted in obvious dismay, hesitated a moment, and then carried on, trying to appear casual but still to reach the house before Nicky caught him.

Nicky covered the ground faster. He jumped in front of Bendy just as he reached the drawbridge, blocking his path.

'Where've you been?'

Bendy eyed him cautiously. 'Nowhere.'

'Yes you have. You've been up to something. What is it?'

'Nothing. I haven't done anything,' Bendy said, and tried to dodge past under his arm. Nicky caught him. 'Let me go,' Bendy cried.

'Where've you been?'

'It's a secret.'

Nicky's eyes gleamed. 'Tell me,' he demanded.

'No, I won't!'

'You'd better,' Nicky said. He shifted his grip, got hold of Bendy firmly by both shoulders. 'You're not to have secrets from me! Tell me where you've been this minute, or it'll be the worse for you!'

'I can't. Leave me alone. I won't tell you.'

'Here's for you, then!' Nicky said, and with a quick twist put Bendy face down on the grass and sat on him, holding his wrists to stop him hitting out. Bendy wriggled, dragging his head round sideways so that he could breathe.

'You tell me! You tell me now!' Nicky growled. One eye rolled up towards him: it infuriated him that he saw no fear in that eye. 'I'll make you sorry!' he said, gripping the wrists harder, twisting the loose skin on them to make it hurt.

Bendy went on writhing. Though he was only nine, he was sturdily built, a strong little boy, while Nicky, though older and taller, was puny. But Bendy was hampered by the respect he had always been taught to shew his elder brother. Nicky was the heir, and was delicate: Nicky must not be harmed; Nicky must be humoured. So Bendy didn't use all his strength against him, though he was unaware that he was holding back.

'Are you going to tell me where you've been?' Nicky demanded.

Bendy felt tears rising, of frustration, and fear — not for himself, but for his secret. 'No,' he sobbed.

'You little rat!' Nicky dragged Bendy's arms behind his

back so that he could hold them with one hand, and used the other to tear up handfuls of grass and stuff them into Bendy's mouth. Tears rolled down Bendy's grimy cheek as he writhed and spluttered, and Nicky was satisfied. The next time he heaved, Nicky let himself be thrown off, and stood a safe step or two away as Bendy sat up slowly, rubbing his hands over his face to remove the grass and tears.

'And it's no use you telling on me, because no-one will believe you,' Nicky said with satisfaction.

But just as Bendy couldn't fight him freely, he could not defend himself either. 'I don't tell,' he said in a low voice. 'I'm not a tattle.'

Nicky stared a moment longer, and then turned and walked off. Bendy sat where he was, dolefully hooking grass and mud out of his mouth with a forefinger. He felt shaken, bruised more in spirit than in body. But he hadn't told. He had that to comfort himself with: his secret was still his secret.

CHAPTER FOUR

The stifling August and September was followed by a long spell of cold, rainy weather. Low clouds rolled across a dull, gun-grey sky, and a mean little wind tugged the billows of rain this way and that, just to make sure no hastily-sought shelter would really serve. Rosamund's daily rides in the Park were now soaking affairs.

Parslow, the groom, followed her glumly, contemplating the work that lay ahead of him with two wet horses, eight muddy legs and two sets of dirt-splashed tack to clean. But her ladyship, like her mother, would never be deterred from riding by mere bad weather, and Parslow thought she was probably staying out even longer than usual from sheer perversity. He knew a great deal about her, having cared for her all her life, and he knew this self-punishing mood of hers. He wished she were not so unhappy. He wished her mother were home, for everyone's sake. If her mother had not gone away, she wouldn't have got into trouble in the first place — so Parslow believed.

By rights he was her mother's groom, but Lucy had decided by a narrow margin that the horses she was leaving at home needed him more than she did. Parslow had not wished to stay behind — not that he had been consulted, of course. He had been with Lucy since she was a new bride of fifteen, and this recent Grand Tour was the only time they had been apart. In her service he had become a famous figure: everyone in London knew the name of Lady Theakston's groom, and many had been the offers he had had to change service. At one time even the Prince of Wales had tried to coax him away from her with an offer to double his salary; but he would never leave her.

She was a generous employer, of course: his salary was handsome; and being of the old school she would always see him right, with a pension to come if ever he became too old or infirm to do his job properly. But he was of the old school too, a horseman, with a horseman's pride. What he gave to his mistress no amount of money could buy. He served and obeyed her not from servility or even from necessity, but because it pleased him to do so.

He didn't think that when Lucy had decided to leave him behind in England she had been thinking of Rosamund. It was her precious horses she was worried about — Magnus Apollo and Hotspur and the others. But Parslow believed that Lucy was a better mother than she knew, and that subconsciously she had been uneasy about leaving Rosamund so soon after her wedding, to face the unknown hazards of wedlock all alone. There was nothing Parslow could have done, of course, to stop Rosamund from getting into trouble; but he was there all the same to represent Lucy — not really *in loco parentis*, but to keep the spirit of her, and of her (too often unspoken) love for her daughter.

They had crossed the carriage road onto the tan again. Rosamund touched her heel to Magnus's side and put him into a canter, and the big chestnut laid his ears back sulkily, and fly-bucked as the cold rain pattered on his loins. His drenched chestnut coat was the same colour as the wet autumn leaves which were scattered over the grass. It was going to take hours to get him dry, Parslow thought, and he was a thin-skinned, chilly sort of horse, not one you could leave to steam dry by his own body heat. They were going away from the Stanhope Gate now, and Parslow saw his lady push the reluctant Magnus on, evidently intending to do another circuit — another half-hour at least. His heart sank, and his hat brim overflowed in sympathy with his mood and sent an icy stream down inside his collar.

Suddenly Rosamund pulled up and turned Magnus to face him. He halted his own horse before her. Her face was pale and set under her tall hat; a ribbon of fox-dark hair had escaped her net and was plastered to her cheek like a strand of seaweed; her jacket was soaked through at the shoulders and the forearms, and was sticking to her like sealskin. She's drowning, he thought painfully; and I can't reach her.

Magnus surged restively, and Rosamund checked him automatically, feeling him swing his weight from foot to foot — a sensation like a large wave passing under a small boat. She looked through the pouring rain at the patient face of her companion, saw that the tip of his nose was red, and that there were bluish patches on his cheeks.

'You're cold,' she said. The dark eyes came alive for an instant in the bland, polite face. This capacity of his for obliterating his personality, unless it pleased him to let it show, always puzzled and disarmed her. She felt he was a match for her, though she could not have said in what possible sense. He did her bidding without question, but somehow that only made him stronger than her. It was as though his obedience were a game they played, of which he alone knew the rules.

'Yes, my lady,' he said. He might just as easily have said, 'No, not at all.' Both answers meant the same thing she reflected, which was 'Go ahead and make a fool of yourself if you like. I understand.'

Two could play at that game. 'You must be wet through,' she said. 'I've been a bad mistress to you, haven't I? You'll be so glad to go back into my mother's service.'

'I shall be glad when her ladyship is safe at home again, my lady,' Parslow said unfathomably.

The rain intensified for a moment, falling in an oblique and hissing sheet. The horses hunched resentfully, but Rosamund didn't seem to notice. 'What will you say to her about me?' she asked. The rain ran over her lips, and she licked them automatically.

'Her ladyship would not ask my opinion, my lady,' Parslow said.

'No,' she said slowly. 'No, not about people. Only about horses, I suppose.' But even as she said it, she wondered. She remembered how when her mother went away she had said goodbye to Parslow last. She remembered the look which had passed between them.

Still he waited patiently, not reproaching her by so much as a lifted eyebrow, nor hurrying her by the flicker of an eye. She

70

thought again of Papa, and wished suddenly, foolishly, that Parslow had been her father. She imagined a small groom's cottage, everything neat and plain and horsemanlike about it; herself making it comfortable and homelike; helping him in the stable when times were busy; drying his coat before the fire when his selfish mistress kept him out too long in the rain.

Why couldn't she feel any desire to do such things for poor Marcus? Well, because there were servants to do them, of course. All the easy ways of showing affection were used up, and only the hard ones remained for her. Rich people who marry, she concluded, need to love each other a great deal more than poor people. Either that, or not at all.

'I'm doing the right thing now,' she said. He held her gaze, but said nothing. 'You know what I mean. What you suggested — last year when you talked to me about — about everything.'

'My lady.'

She strained through the rivering rain to read his expression, to find a hint of approval or support — anything so as not to be alone with the decision and its consequences, and the awful, aching loneliness of being without Jes, and with Marcus.

'The silver charm you gave me for my wedding — do you remember? The little horseshoe — I carry it with me all the time now.'

Still no answer, but the eyes were warm. *I am yours to command, my lady* — he had said that once, in deep disapproval. But it could be said with approval too, and had been.

'There was a time when I couldn't,' she went on desperately, 'but now — I'm trying to make the best of things.'

'It can be hard to do one's duty, my lady,' he said. 'But there is One who sees every struggle, and gives credit where it's due.'

For a stupid moment she thought he meant himself; and then she understood. But God seemed far away in that bleak moment. If God knew everything and arranged everything, couldn't He just as well have arranged it so that Jes's brother died instead of Bobbie? Then Jes could have married her,

71

Bobbie could have married Bab, and Marcus would have fallen in love with some nice, gentle girl who would have worshipped him. Everyone would have been happy and good. Instead there was this mess, and everyone unhappy. That wasn't very clever of God, was it?

She suddenly realised how cold and wet she was. 'We'd better get the horses in,' she said abruptly. 'I've made a lot of work for you. I'm sorry.'

'It's my job, my lady,' he said comfortingly. But he was blue-grey with cold, she saw, and she felt guilty all the way home.

As soon as they reached the end of Pall Mall, they could see the coaches drawn up outside Chelmsford House. Rosamund peered through the driving rain: a shabby and very muddy berlin, with post horses, and a job-chaise behind, both piled with luggage.

'What on earth —?' Rosamund began; and then a glance at Parslow's face told all. It seemed all planes, as tense and eager as a pointer scenting a pheasant. There was a light of joy in his eyes she knew she was not meant to see. She looked away, feeling suddenly very cold and very alone.

'It's them,' she said. 'Mother's home.'

When they reached the house Parslow dismounted quickly and held Magnus's head while she jumped down.

'Come in,' she said generously. 'Someone else can take the horses back. Mother will want to see you straight away.'

But his face was at its most impenetrable. 'She'll send for me when she wants me, my lady,' he said expressionlessly. 'I must see to the horses myself.'

That, Rosamund thought, as she walked up the steps, hearing the two horses clattering away to the stables, was true devotion.

But there was no more time to think of Parslow. The hall of Chelmsford House was full of people and noise. Beason managed to get to her side as she came in through the open door, but he didn't manage to seize her attention. Rosamund saw Marcus red-faced with excitement standing over the slender, pin-neat figure of Papa Danby, who was shedding his greatcoat with the help of his man, Bird — a thin and crowlike figure in black. That great tall young man, chatting so pleasantly to Bab — could that possibly be her brother Roland? He had gone away a gawky schoolboy, painfully shy and terrified of everyone and everything. The Grand Tour had plainly done wonders for him.

And there was Tom, unmistakably Tom, though he was also a young man who had been but a child. He had seen her, and was smiling at her across the room, a sly, beguiling, enmeshing smile that tugged at her lips even before she had assembled her thoughts. Good God, he was handsome! Though he was only eighteen, there was nothing of the boy in him — he looked twenty-five if a day. How many broken hearts had he left behind him in Europe? she wondered. London had better look out next Season.

There was dear old Docwra, her mother's woman, twice as fat as when she went away, if that were possible; brushing with the flat of her hand against the pile to shake the rain from the fur collar of a pelisse; throwing non-stop directions at the servants who were hovering on the fringes of the group, torn between curiosity and the fear of Beason's disapproval.

And there, oh there, was Mother, in a smart coral-coloured travelling dress trimmed with black braid, just taking off her hat and shaking her head to loosen her compressed hair. Rosamund felt a pang of love and fear at the sight of that curly head, now brushed here and there with grey, held so high above the slight shoulders and the straight back. What you love is so easily lost to you: there were a thousand accidents which might have prevented Mother from coming home. Rosamund wanted to be noticed by her, but could not speak or move, stricken by the absurd and belated realisation of human frailty.

But Lucy's eyes were never far from Tom, and now she looked to see who he was smiling at. Rosamund saw the smooth, weather-tanned face turn towards her, saw the cool, grey-blue eyes widen a little, saw her own name formed by her mother's lips. Then she was walking forward, hurrying a little, a path opening up for her to that slight figure by the fire. For one moment she thought Lucy might fling wide her arms and gather her in; but that was foolish — that was not Lucy's way. Now as Rosamund arrived before her, she pulled her lower lip in under her teeth a moment — a gesture of shyness, but it looked as though she were preventing herself from smiling. She surveyed her tall daughter quickly, and then said, 'You're soaking wet. I hope the horses haven't caught cold.'

Rosamund could either have laughed or cried: she felt equally like both, longing for love and being baulked of it at the last moment, like treading up a step that wasn't there. Oh Mother, Mother! But Papa Danby stepped in, smiling, and gave Rosamund the hug her mother couldn't give.

'My dear girl! Wet or dry, I'm glad to see you!'

His fair whiskers tickled her face, his cheek was warm and firm against hers, and a clean and familiar smell hung around him, of starch and lavender and a hint of bay rum. Affection surged up in her, and her arms went quickly round him. 'I've missed you, sir. I'm glad you're home.'

And now the others crowded round her, greeting and explaining, bubbling over with disjointed details of the journey and the arrival. Her mother in the middle of it all, the smile apparent in her eyes at last, flicked a quick glance of approval from Rosamund to Marcus; then back to Rosamund with the hint of a question in it. It was a subtle change — from 'It's all right, isn't it?' to 'It *is* all right, isn't it?' — but Rosamund saw it. With Marcus's eyes on her, she felt obliged to smile reassuringly for them both: 'Yes, it's all right. Everything's all right.' Doing my best, Parslow, she thought far away in the back of her mind. Trying to do the right thing.

But there was someone else here, someone they were wanting her attention for. A stranger, but not quite a stranger: a young woman dressed all in black; a foreigner? — very brown of face, with curly black hair, rather wild and unruly, and an air about her of being not quite tame — as though wearing clothes and being inside a house were something of a surprise to her. The strong face and bright eyes were turned keenly towards Rosamund; she was holding out a brown hand which Rosamund found, when she took it bemusedly, was as hard as a plank and endowed with a leathery callous at the base of each finger.

It was the callouses which convinced her. A grin spread across Rosamund's face as she returned the hard grip with

74

enthusiasm. 'Good God, is it possible? Is it really you?'

'Who else,' laughed Africa, 'would have such an unladylike hand? Dear cousin Rosamund, what a lady you've become! Last time I saw you, you still had plaits. You wanted to run away and join the army.'

'And you did run away, and joined a circus! I can't tell you how much I envied you your adventures!'

They embraced affectionately. Was it her imagination, or did Africa smell of salt and wide ocean winds?

'Aunt Lucy's right, though,' Africa said as she released her. 'You are soaking wet. It makes me feel at home — no-one on board a ship is ever really quite dry.'

'But what are you doing here? I mean, how do you come to be here? Did you arrive with Mama? Well, I suppose you must have —'

'They found me kicking my heels in Gibraltar, driving Uncle Harry to distraction. I'd never met him before — have you? He's such a dear! Exactly the crusty old sea-dog you'd expect: said "Harrumph!" and called me m'dear, and worried over me as though I were a piece of fine old porcelain — *me*, can you imagine! I think he was afraid he might have to adopt me permanently, so when Aunt Lucy and Uncle Danby arrived and said they'd take me off, he was as grateful as could be.'

'But what were you doing in Gibraltar?' Rosamund asked. 'Surely you weren't all alone? Where's your father?'

The bright, almost feral eyes filled surprisingly with tears, one of which welled over her eyelashes with the ease and grace of a natural spring. 'Oh dear, I'm sorry, but still whenever I think of him —' Africa said. Too late Rosamund realised the significance of the black clothes. Had it been anyone else, she would not have been so slow, but Africa was too full of life for death to come naturally to mind. 'Papa's dead. He died in August of a fever. The day after my birthday, it was, in fact.'

'Oh Africa, I'm so sorry,' Rosamund said, dismayed. Africa stood in the middle of them all and spilled tears with the unselfconscious ease of a child; looking so alien and out of place that it seemed to Rosamund almost as though weeping were a strange skill learned in a foreign place, something so arcane and exotic that it was impossible to judge how well she might be doing it.

Dinner that evening was late, and went on for a very long time. The travellers were to stay that night at Chelmsford House, though Lucy had wanted at first to go back to her own house in Upper Grosvenor Street. But Danby and Marcus between them had persuaded her that it would be more convenient for everyone to stay where they were for the time being.

Rosamund had given orders for rooms to be prepared, and for the extra covers for dinner; and then for immediate refreshments to be brought to the green drawing-room, where she, Marcus and Bab usually sat when they had no visitors. Rosamund liked it as little as any of the other rooms, but the fire was already bright there.

'And now, darling, you must go and take off those wet clothes,' Marcus urged her when everything had been arranged. 'You'll catch cold if you stand around in them any longer.'

'Nonsense,' she said robustly, catching Africa's eye. 'If wet clothes were harmful, sailors would die young.'

'So they do, lots of them,' Africa said.

'Thank you, Cousin! Well, then, I can't leave now, with so many stories to hear.'

'The stories will keep,' Lucy said. 'Marcus is right. Besides,' she added, meeting Rosamund's rebellious eye, 'you can't possibly sit about in a drawing-room in your riding habit — *and* with a muddy hem. Think of poor Danby's sensibilities, if nothing else.'

Danby turned an unwinking countenance on his step-daughter. 'Quite right, dear girl. Once a dandy, always a dandy. Could bring on a fit, you know, seeing you in the wrong outfit.'

Rosamund couldn't resist him. She took her departure more or less gracefully. By the time she had washed and changed, the conversation in the green drawing-room had moved on to the travellers' experiences in Italy, and so it was not until they all met again at dinner that she heard Africa's story in full.

'Now tell me how you came to be in Gibraltar,' Rosamund said, glancing round the table to make sure everything was as it should be. The soup was already in the plates before each person, and there were two removes at each end of the table. Otherwise, except for the sideboard dishes, it was a case of 'You see your dinner'; but it was an informal, family occasion, after all. A single course was permissible.

Africa fortified herself with a robust draught from her wine glass before beginning. Rosamund thought blissfully how her forthright manners were going to upset Beason, and silently planned to ask her to stay here permanently as an ally.

'Well, Papa hauled down his flag in the middle of July,' Africa began, 'and we took passage on a cargo vessel, because it would get us home sooner than waiting for the next King's ship. We were only ten days out from St Helena when Papa got ill — some kind of gastric fever. The ship put into Ascension and put us off, and we took Papa to the Governor's house. The Governor and his wife were very kind to us, and a doctor came. Everything was done that could be done, but Papa died two days later. The doctor said his heart was worn out, and the fever was just the last straw.'

She paused a moment, her eyes were far away. Rosamund tried to imagine the place she was seeing — some exotic scene, perhaps, of jungle and creeper and high-coloured tropical flowers, with butterflies the size of birds, and monkeys and parrots swinging about in the branches. But Rosamund had never been out of England, and she couldn't make it real. In her mind it looked as flat as a drawing from a book of travels.

'I'd have liked to bring him home,' Africa went on, 'but it wasn't possible, so we buried him there. The burial ground was high up, overlooking the sea, and the wind blows over it all the time, and the sea-birds cry. It was a good place for him, really. We couldn't have laid him next to Mama anyway, because she was buried at sea, so I suppose it didn't matter not bringing him back.'

'That's right,' said Lucy abruptly. 'But he's with her now, that's all that matters.'

Africa gave her a little nod of acknowledgement, and the servants came to remove the soup plates. There was a pause now, and for a while the talk was general as clean plates were

77

laid and each gentleman carved and offered the dish in front of him, dishes were passed up and down, and glasses were refilled.

'These pheasants are beautifully tender — can I carve one for you, mother-in-law?'

'How has the game been so far, Marcus? Have you had much shooting?'

'The made dish is a fricassee of capon and prunes, I believe. And that's a damson dumpling by you, Tom.'

'It's wonderful not to be eating goat. Horse and goat — I swear that's all foreigners ever eat!'

'A little of the red cabbage — ah, thank you.'

'Is it true, Mama, that Beau Brummell refused to marry a girl because he discovered she ate cabbage?'

When everyone was served and the servants had retired to the wall again, Rosamund prompted Africa to resume her story.

'So what happened then? How did you get to Gibraltar?'

'I stayed with the Governor and his wife for a while, because I didn't really know what to do next. But of course I had to come back to England eventually to sort out Papa's affairs, so I took a passage on the next possible ship, which was bound for Madeira and Gibraltar. I thought it would be easy enough to get home from Gibraltar, but the passage was so slow and we stopped in Madeira for so long that I ran out of money. When I got to Gibraltar, I was just a poor little orphan with a mound of luggage and not a penny to my name. There I was at the Port Admiral's office trying to persuade them to give me a docket for a King's ship and getting nowhere, when Uncle Harry walked in and rescued me — much to his own discomposure.'

'Nonsense, you know he loved having you,' Danby broke in. 'When we arrived, Rosamund m'dear, he was making feverish plans to escort her to every ball and party on the Rock, as proud as Punch of his pretty niece. No flattery on that subject was too gross for him.'

Africa grinned. 'Oh, is that how you remember it, sir? It's as well you did take me away, then, before his dreams were destroyed. No-one would have asked me to stand up with them, with a face as brown as mine.'

'You might have become betrothed to an Ethiop prince,' Tom suggested idly.

'Thank you, but I'm happy as I am. Betrothal doesn't fit in with my plans,' Africa said equably.

'What are your plans?' Lucy asked.

'Well, Aunt, I have to see to Papa's affairs to begin with. I suppose his estate will take some time to settle, since he died out of the country. But there should be enough at the end of it to set me up in a little business venture I have in mind. Half of everything will go to Polly, of course. Is she still staying at Morland Place?'

'Yes,' Rosamund answered. 'She seems fixed there for the time being.'

'I shall go up and see her as soon as I can,' Africa said, frowning in thought. 'Once Papa's man of business has furnished me with some ready money.'

'Don't worry about that, child,' Lucy said. 'I can see to your immediate wants. But you will be back in time for Christmas, won't you? I want everyone to spend Christmas at Wolvercote — the whole family. All that's left of the family, I should say,' she corrected herself. 'We do seem to be shrinking at an alarming rate.'

'Never mind, Mama,' Tom said. 'The next generation will be coming along soon. The numbers will go up again.'

It was a comment fraught with peril in all sorts of ways, Rosamund thought; and to judge by his teasing smile, typical of Tom to have thrown it out to trip them all up. She made a face at him across the table, and then straightened it hastily as Marcus looked across at her.

'Have you tried the baked ham, Mama?' she said quickly. 'Roland, it's with you — do carve some for Mama. The glaze is our cook's special recipe.'

They did not sit up late, for soon after tea the travellers were plainly ready for their beds. As they left the drawing-room and clustered around the table where the night candles were set out, Africa caught Rosamund's eye and with a nod and a gesture invited her to stay behind for a private word.

'I wanted to speak to you about Polly. You say she's fixed at Morland Place?'

79

'Yes. It seemed best to begin with to get her out of London. Aunt Héloïse was glad to have her; and she was brought up there, after all, so it was like going home. I thought it would be a temporary thing, just until she had got over the shock, but now she doesn't seem to want to leave.'

'It was a bad business,' Africa said, studying Rosamund's face. 'For you most of all, I should think.'

'Me? Oh no,' Rosamund began automatically to disclaim.

'Minnie was your sister,' Africa stopped her. 'And if I know anything about people, it was you who had to bear all the trouble. Who else was there, after all, with Aunt Lucy away?'

'The trial was the worst thing,' Rosamund blurted, unable to resist the understanding eyes. 'The very idea that one's own sister might have been murdered. Her death was shocking enough, but *that*—'

'Do you think he did it, this Marquess of wherever it was?'

'Penrith. No,' Rosamund said hesitantly; and then more certainly, 'No. It was all a horrible mistake. I don't believe he was capable of such a thing. But —' meeting Africa's eyes frankly, 'I have an idea that Polly half believed it. At all events, she wouldn't marry him, even after it had all died down, even though —'

'Even though they had been lovers,' Africa finished without embarrassment. 'It's all right, I knew about that part. She hinted as much in her letters; and it's nothing to me what they got up to. I'm sorry, since it concerned your sister, but Polly seemed to think she didn't know about it.'

'I don't know what she knew,' Rosamund said bleakly.

Africa studied her half-averted face in silence for a moment. Then she said briskly, 'Well, I think its time Polly stopped hiding away and feeling sorry for herself. I shall go up and see her as soon as I can; and when Papa's estate is settled, I shall make her come back with me to London and join in my business venture.'

Rosamund brightened. 'Yes, what is this idea of yours? I noticed at dinner you very cleverly avoided speaking about it. Is it something we'll disapprove of?'

'I should think your mother, at least, will approve of it wholeheartedly! No, I just didn't want to discuss it then, not until I have worked out some of the details. I would be obliged if you wouldn't mention it just yet either.'

'You haven't told me anything yet to mention,' Rosamund pointed out.

'Oh I don't mind telling you, if you'll keep it to yourself. I mean to start up a riding school, somewhere near the Park for preference. A fashionable one for elegant young ladies and gentlemen. Nothing shabby about it, you know — the very best of horses and the very highest of fees.' Rosamund's eyes were widening as she spoke. 'Polly will be quite an asset. She'll set the tone. She's so very elegant and beautiful, and she rides extremely well.'

'She should do,' Rosamund said faintly. 'She had the best teacher — my mother.'

'Well then,' Africa nodded approvingly, 'she can teach the timid young ladies, and I can teach the wild young men who are bent on breaking their necks. We'll make an excellent team.'

Rosamund stared at her, fascinated. 'I'm sure it's a very good idea. There's certainly a need for a fashionable school in the centre of London. What riding schools there are seem to be in places like Kensington, and their standards are not very high, to judge by some of the seats I see in the Park every day.'

'Yes, that's what I thought,' Africa said with a brisk nod.

'But how can you know? You've been in St Helena for five years, and out of England for I don't know how many.'

'I have a correspondent,' Africa said, 'a very faithful, observant one.' She smiled suddenly. Her teeth looked very white in her brown face. 'And that's another secret.'

When she reached her bedchamber, Rosamund found Marcus there. He must have changed like lightning, she reflected, for he was in his night attire and dressing-gown, and there was a pleasant fragrance of verbena toilet-water about him. He looked up with an expression half-hopeful, half-doubtful as she came in, as one who has presumed, and fears he has presumed too much.

'I sent Moss away,' he said. 'I hope that was all right.'

Rosamund realised with a flash of insight that he had seen her wait behind to talk to Polly, and had taken the opportunity to present her with the *fait accompli* of his presence in her room. She was both touched and annoyed by his trickery. That he should feel it necessary, when she had already agreed to receive him and acknowledged that it was his right, made her feel guilty, and she disliked very much to feel guilty.

'Of course,' she said shortly, crossing to her dressing-table and unclasping her bracelets. She couldn't even pretend it was the wrong time, for he knew her times now better than she did herself.

Marcus seemed relieved at her acquiescence. 'I can help you with any difficult hooks and laces,' he said lightly, trying to generate a little warmth. 'I think I can manage that much for you.'

'I'm sure you can.' Warmth was the last thing Rosamund wanted. If she was to survive the experience at all, she must regard what they did together simply as breeding, a dispassionate act undertaken for the good of the family; but she knew that was not what Marcus wanted, or what he intended. She kept her back to him, continuing with her preparations for bed, putting off the moment of contact.

'I'm so glad your mother is home again,' he said after a minute. 'For your sake most of all — I know you've missed her. She doesn't seem to have changed at all, does she?'

'Mother never changes,' Rosamund agreed.

'But the difference in your brothers is astonishing,' he tried next. 'Roland is so very much improved. I think he will make a sensible and valuable addition to the House.' No answer. 'Your mother will want to see him married soon.'

'I suppose so.'

'And Tom — I should think he'd grace any profession he turned his hand to. We must see what we can do for Tom.'

'Papa Danby will do whatever needs to be done. There's no need for you to be troubled,' Rosamund said.

'It's no trouble, I assure —'

'You forget Papa Danby has influence in the highest places,' she snapped. 'He can place him creditably without your patronage.'

Marcus was crestfallen. 'I'm sorry. I didn't mean to annoy you. I intended no slight, I assure you. I've always had the greatest respect for Lord Theakston.'

Rosamund turned wearily. 'Yes, I know. I'm sorry I spoke roughly. I don't know what's the matter with me.'

She should not have shown softness. He rose and came across the room to her with a tender light in his eyes.

'Let me help you with your gown, my love. It's been an exciting day, and you're tired. Turn around and I'll undo you.'

You have already undone me, Rosamund thought. She felt his hands at her back, his fingers less skilful about the fastenings than Jes's, his breath gently disturbing the short, oose hairs at the nape of her neck as he concentrated on the task. How many women had he performed it for? She knew of only one besides herself, but that didn't mean there had not been others. He had been a soldier on campaign for four years before they married: there must certainly have been others. The laces undone, he helped her shrug out of her gown, pushing the short sleeves down her arms for her, and then running his hands lightly up to her shoulders again.

She felt the breath of a kiss on the base of her neck as he undid the buttons of her chemise. When that had dropped to the floor, he began on her stay-laces, and she knew from his breathing that he was growing excited. The cool air reached the bare skin over her spine, and she shuddered lightly, aware that she was becoming aroused in her turn, though she didn't want to, though it seemed wrong to her for all sorts of reasons. But she couldn't help it. Her stays fell to the floor and she stepped out of them, and now she was naked except for her silk drawers.

Marcus stepped up close behind her, kissed her shoulder and neck slipped his arms round her waist and brought his hands up to cup her breasts. Rosamund closed her eyes, feeling the treacherous longings of her body, struggling to remain cool and dispassionate.

'You're so beautiful,' Marcus whispered, moving his lips sensuously across her bare neck and shoulders. He leaned his body against hers, and she felt his heat, and the hardness of his rider's muscles. 'So beautiful, my love, my wife.' Rosamund ached with longing for Jes; but it was not Jes who was making her body tremble with desire.

The hands slid down her body to her waist and unbuttoned

her drawers. She had never been entirely naked with Marcus before, and the awareness and strangeness themselves were exciting. He buried his face between her shoulder blades and groaned, muffled by her flesh. 'Oh God, I love you! I love you, Ros.' He released her only to tear off his own clothes, and then naked as she was, walked her to the bed, gently turned her and laid her down.

He was tremendously aroused. Rosamund caught one glimpse of him before she quickly closed her eyes — one glimpse that seared on her mind his image, a well-formed, handsome, wholesome man, frightening in his male attractiveness. She felt her own excitement as though at a distance, detached from her mind: her body felt hot, her skin flushed and abnormally sensitive, aching as though she were in a fever. It was wrong, she thought despairingly, wrong and bad. Her mind and heart and soul may have been calling out for Jes, but right there and then it was Marcus that her body wanted.

He climbed onto the bed with her, stretched himself over her, and she locked her arms round him, drawing him close.

'Oh my darling,' he gasped, his mouth buried in her hair beside her ear. She heard her own rapid breaths, felt him enter her, and was pierced with pleasure and despair. Not like this, she thought, faint and far away through the storm of sensation: it was not meant to happen like this.

CHAPTER FIVE

The letter had come to Farraline like a bolt out of the blue. He had called at the Post Office as he did every day on his way past, but he had not expected anything from Rosamund, since he had written to her only the day before. The sight of her handwriting made his heart leap; it was only at second glance that he realised Marcus had franked it for her, and apprehension crept in. What excuse could she possibly have offered Marcus for writing to him? He knew she did not like to lie to him: the letter must contain something extraordinary and important.

Still, he couldn't stand there on the street and read it, so he put it into his pocket and continued on his way to Ordsall Mills. His father had bought the mills from old Samuel Ordsall, who had built them up from nothing, and promised him that they would never pass out of the Farraline family. They belonged now, of course, to his brother Kit, though Kit would have died a thousand deaths rather than set foot in them. Kit cared for nothing but hunting, drinking and gambling — he could never even be brought to interest himself in the fair sex, in spite of every endeavour of the Dowager Lady Batchworth, who feared for the succession. But Jesmond Farraline had learned the magic of the manufacturing process at an early age from his father. Machines fascinated him; the power of the steam engines thrilled him. He was happy to take care of the business, and though he would sooner have done it on his own behalf than on his brother's, it was at least better than the boredom and discipline of a gentlemanly career.

There were a number of matters requiring his immediate

attention when he arrived at the mills, and it was not until some time later that he was able to seek the solitude of his office and take out the letter which had been burning a hole in his pocket. On first reading he could not bring himself to understand the words. In time they were to become seared on his mind.

'. . . I have promised him I shall not see you nor communicate with you until this business is over. It was hard to say the words, but I conceded that the condition was a fair one. The most damnable aspect of all this, my Jes, has been that I do see his side, all the time, as well as my own, and yours, and ours. It is because I do that I have to go through with this, give him this one thing that he is entitled to. I wish I could be *more* wicked, *more* selfish, so that I need not mind about him, only about us, my dearest, dearest love . . .'

He read on, feeling sick, his hands cold and damp clutching the expensive paper which seemed — though perhaps it was his imagination — to smell faintly of her perfume.

'. . . He does not ask to see this letter before I send it. It is between us only — words for you alone. My spirits faint when I think of the time stretching ahead when I may not see you, or speak to you, or hear from you. But I believe it must be done if we are to have any happiness together. Try to understand, Jes. Wait for me — don't fail me. All that I am is yours, yours only, I swear it . . .'

He sat still for a long time when he had finished reading, the letter held before him still, his eyes fixed unseeingly on the wall opposite. He understood — oh yes! Only too well. She spoke as one who was to undergo an operation, frightening and painful but necessary for ultimate health; at the time she wrote the letter, she was thinking of it in those detached terms. But it took only an hour or two to write a letter; so much, much longer to conceive and carry and bear a child. She would not, could not, remain detached to the end. She thought she could have Marcus's child and then forget the whole business. She simply had not the experience, or the imagination, or perhaps even the will, to see what it would really mean.

From the start he had had to face the fact that she was

married to another, that she could never be his, that what little of her he had might one day be taken from him. In the beginning she had not loved him as much as he loved her, and he had thought that the time might come when she would tire of him. He had faced the thought of losing her that way, faced it and accepted it. But he had never thought of this.

With a desperation born of honesty, and a courage born of ignorance, she was going to sacrifice herself in the attempt to be fair to all of them. She simply had no idea what it would cost her, and he could not tell her now: she had promised not to communicate with him, and if he wrote to her she would not open the letter, however much she wanted to.

At least he was able to lose himself in work. After the summer slack, the early autumn brought a brisk increase of trade. The problems of the immediate post-war years seemed to have disappeared, and things looked set for a period of prosperity. The mills took care of his days and some of his evenings, too. Once a week he rode out to the family seat at Grasscroft to pay his respects to his mother and to report to the utterly indifferent Kit that all was well at the factory. He dined at his club once a week and sought oblivion in masculine company, sound claret, and the mental discipline of piquet. He avoided anything or anyone who might remind him of Rosamund, and managed so well that his waking hours were mostly free from anguish. Only when he lay down to sleep was his guard lowered. His dreams were full of her, and he woke every day to a renewed awareness of loss.

One evening in November he was invited to dine with the Hobsbawns. He had been doubtful about the wisdom of accepting the invitation, for he could hardly hope to pass a whole evening with Sophie without hearing something of Rosamund. But Jasper Hobsbawn had caught him on his way out of his club when he had dined rather lavishly, and he had not been quick-witted enough to think of an excuse. He hoped that perhaps there would be a large company at dinner in which he could lose himself, but when he arrived at Hobsbawn House he found only Henry Droylsden and one other guest, John Skelwith.

He knew Skelwith slightly, having met him in York when he

had gone there for the races a few years back, and knew he was a connection of Sophie's, the husband of Lady Morland's ward, with whom Sophie had grown up as a sister. He seemed a decent young man, quiet and sensible — not the sort who could be relied upon safely to draw attention away from Farraline all evening.

And first of all there was Sophie herself to be got over. She greeted him warmly: he had been instrumental in bringing her and her beloved Jasper together, so she looked upon him with great favour. Farraline bowed over her hand, reflecting that there was no need to fear that her looks would remind him of his lost love. Rosamund was so tall and well-made, Sophie so small and thin, with hardly more figure than a child; Rosamund so fair, with her coppery hair and strong, handsome face, Sophie dark, sallow and plain, with nothing to recommend her but her large, expressive eyes.

But when he straightened up and looked into her face he was reminded inexorably of the first time he had met Rosamund, on the sands at Scarborough in company with Sophie. The only thing that occurred to his unready tongue to ask was whether she had heard from her cousin lately, and he curbed the desire sternly. It was left to Sophie to make some commonplace remark about the weather, and such dullnesses kept them all occupied until the servant came to announce dinner.

At the table, the talk turned to business. Droylsden enquired politely after the Ordsall Mills. Farraline returned an enquiry after the banking business, and repeated his recent thought that the troubles of the last few years were behind them at last. Jasper concurred and added that the harvest had been so good that they had no reason to fear social unrest that winter or next spring.

'Low corn prices mean peace,' he said, 'at least as far as people like us are concerned.'

'But peace has its drawbacks,' Farraline said. 'Without discontent, there is no impetus for change.'

Sophie looked puzzled at this. 'But if there is no discontent, why should you want change?'

Henry Droylsden laughed. 'Impeccable logic, Mrs Hobsbawn. Farraline, you must concede a touch!'

'Oh dear, am I being stupid?' Sophie asked.

'No, not at all,' Farraline said quickly.

'You see, love,' Jasper said, 'at the moment corn prices are low because the harvest was plentiful, and that means cheap bread and contented workers. But there's no way of guaranteeing that next year's harvest will be good, and if it fails, the Corn Laws will force the price up again.'

'I've never really understood what the Corn Laws do,' Sophie confessed.

'They protect the farmer's income,' Henry explained kindly. 'Back in 1815 Parliament decided that eighty shillings was a fair price for corn — a price that would allow the farmers to earn a decent living — so they passed a law to say that foreign corn could only be imported free of duty when the price reached eighty shillings.'

Sophie asked, 'Is that a very high price?'

Jasper answered. 'You remember in 1817 that we had all those strikes and riots? Well, the price of corn then was a hundred shillings a quarter. This year the price is already down to forty shillings.'

'Yes, I see,' Sophie said. She frowned a moment, and then resumed hesitantly. 'But if the Corn Laws are such bad things, why does the Government allow them?'

John Skelwith laughed shortly. 'That's easy enough to answer. Parliament is made up of landowners and farmers who want a high price for their corn — that's all! It's the landed interest that rules this country.'

'True enough,' said Droylsden.

'You know that, don't you, my love?' Jasper nodded to Sophie. 'There's no representation whatever for factory masters and others like us who want a low price for bread so that our employees can eat. Until we change the way Parliament is constituted, we shall never have our interest put forward —'

'And until there is sufficient unrest amongst the people to frighten the Government, we shall never be able to change the way Parliament is constituted,' Farraline finished for him.

'Yes, I see,' Sophie said, concentrating hard. 'But exactly what would you do, if you had representation in Parliament?'

'Abolish the Corn Laws, of course,' Farraline said promptly.

Sophie looked at him doubtfully, remembering, as he did not, where the discussion had begun. 'So you want the harvest to fail, so that the mill hands will be hungry, so that they will riot, so that the Government will let you be a Member of Parliament, so that you can abolish the Corn Laws, so that the mill hands won't be hungry any more. Have I that right?'

The other three men laughed, while Farraline said ruefully, 'I have the feeling, Mrs Hobsbawn, that you are making fun of me.'

'Oh no,' Sophie said, shocked. 'You've made it all quite clear for me now. I'm very grateful. Jasper has mentioned the Corn Laws when he talks about the factory laws he would like to have passed, and I've never properly understood.'

'You think it is all the sheerest nonsense, don't you?' Henry said, grinning. 'Your feminine wisdom rejects it all as simply something men worry about, because they haven't enough to keep them occupied.'

'No, for shame!' Sophie protested. 'I know very well you are all much cleverer than I. I don't expect to be able to understand all your concerns.'

'And that's the way you keep us enslaved,' Farraline said, 'through the grossest of flattery! Applied with a skilled hand, it has us all purring like tea-kettles.'

Sophie laughed at that. Jasper looked at her wistfully, thinking how lovely she looked and wishing he could be more lively and witty so as to make her laugh more often. It was foolish in the extreme for him to be jealous of Farraline, especially when it was he who had finally prodded Jasper into proposing to Sophie; but Farraline was so tall, handsome, witty and urbane, while Jasper knew himself to be undersized, plain and dull. He suffered from a deep seated and unspoken fear that Sophie might one day regret that she had married him instead of Farraline, especially as Farraline had remained single, against general expectation. It was partly for that reason that he brought Sophie into contact with Farraline as often as possible. He knew it was irrational, but if the worst was going to happen, he wanted to get it over with.

He cleared his throat. 'I wonder, Farraline, if this might be a good moment to bring up the subject I wanted to address to you.'

Farraline turned his attention to him. 'You mean your rational housing for factory hands?'

'How did you know it was that?'

'My dear man, the subject is canvassed at great length every time I meet a fellow mill master!'

'Especially Olmondroyd and his bosom bows,' Henry put in mischievously.

'Oh Harry, you aren't going to bring that up again,' Sophie said reproachfully.

'It's hard to leave it out, when you belong to the same club,' Droylsden said easily. 'He hates you quite desperately, Hobsbawn. He's still convinced you burned down his mill a-purpose. Oh, no-one believes him of course,' he added hastily, 'but your ideas are not universally liked, and he makes a focus for the opposition.'

'I wonder you don't do something to stop his mouth,' Farraline said. 'Don't you sometimes feel you are taking patience and understanding too far? Forgive me, but when you do not take the trouble to punish the slander, there must be some who wonder if there is not some truth in it.'

Jasper's face tightened. 'Have you heard that said?'

'No,' said Farraline. 'But I don't keep company with the sort of people who are qualified to be Olmondroyd's friends.'

'Then what have you heard?' Jasper demanded.

Farraline glanced at him, and tried to introduce a lighter tone. 'You mean about your scheme? Opinion seems to be evenly divided between those who think you are quite mad, and those who think you might go ahead with their blessing but emphatically without their money.'

Droylsden laughed. 'The same goes for anything that's proposed of general benefit. "Yes, I should like to have a public garden to stroll in, provided I don't have to pay for it."'

'And which school do you belong to?' Jasper asked Farraline.

'Neither,' he said. 'I prefer to make up my own mind about things.'

'Well then —?'

Farraline spread his elegant hands. 'If it's capital you are after, you know perfectly well that I have none. Ordsall Mills

91

belong to my brother — and to save you trouble I can tell you it's no use your applying to him for money.'

'I shouldn't think of it, of course,' Jasper said. 'But I hoped you might apply to him —'

'On your behalf?'

'On behalf of the factory workers,' Jasper corrected.

'Oh, that's your argument is it? No, let them apply for themselves. It is not my business to house them.'

Jasper said indignantly, 'Have you seen the conditions they live in?'

'Yes, I've seen them,' Farraline said shortly.

'Especially along Water Lane. Since the fire, half of the homeless have crowded into the remaining houses, which were crowded already. The other half are living in the ruins, sheltered by whatever scraps of wood and rags they can drag together. Do you mean to tell me you find that satisfactory?'

Farraline laid down his fork with an air of being pressed into something he didn't like. 'Each man must live according to his condition,' he said. 'The rich man in his castle, the poor man in his hovel.'

'And which men must live in filth and degradation?'

'Those who can do no better for themselves. You or I, Hobsbawn, would not tolerate it. We would do something about it. So must every man better his own lot or suffer the consequences.'

'Mr Farraline,' Sophie broke in gently, 'have you no compassion?'

He looked at her thoughtfully. 'Compassion? Well, I don't know. Where it is appropriate, perhaps. Do you think it is compassion they need?'

'Don't you?' Sophie returned.

'I think that if you take away the incentive for man to improve himself, he will never improve himself. He will be condemned to subsist on whatever level of charity it pleases his masters to bestow on him.'

Henry Droylsden had been following the argument with interest. Now he said, 'Hold hard, do you mean to tell me you disapprove of charity altogether? The Church teaches us to be charitable. Do you think that's wrong?'

Farraline sighed inwardly as he felt himself being sucked

92

further in. 'Charity where it relieves an unusual, unforeseen hardship is one thing. But constant charity to provide the basic necessities of life — that takes away a man's free spirit.'

'Free spirit?' Jasper exclaimed. 'What freedom do they have, but the freedom to starve?'

'That is the first and only freedom of man's condition: to starve, or to strive.'

'All I want to do is house them. You talk as if I mean to imprison them!'

'But if you house them, what then? They will come to you for the next thing they need instead of finding it for themselves, and in compassion you will give it to them. Little by little you will take away their need to fend for themselves, and with it their ability to do so. In a generation or two they will have become nothing more than domestic animals, kept like cattle for your purposes. Your new workers' houses will be barns and stables in which to shelter the dumb beasts who work your tread-mills. Is that what you want for mankind?'

'Oh no!' Sophie exclaimed before Jasper could answer. 'Surely it would not be like that?'

'Tremendous ideas, Farraline,' John Skelwith said, 'but exaggerated surely?'

'You have only to look at the operation of the Poor Laws,' Farraline said, turning to him. 'There are thousands dependent on the Poor Rate who have neither will nor hope of ever escaping its charity.'

'By Jove, yes!' Skelwith exclaimed. He had often complained about the drain of the Poor Rate on his pocket. 'You have a point there.'

'But you can't leave people to starve,' Jasper cried, exasperated. 'The Poor Laws may not work as well as one would wish, but —'

'What is the point in keeping a man alive if he is without hope, without dignity, without purpose?' Farraline said inexorably. 'He is no longer a man.'

Sophie looked at her husband doubtfully. 'It's what Maman says, Jasper. You know she had the same sort of doubts about our scheme.'

'Mr Farraline is putting an extreme case, my love,' Jasper said, trying to speak patiently to her, though his face was working with passion. 'There some truth in what he says, of course, but all we propose is to build decent houses for the poor to live in. What could be wrong with that? Someone must build houses, or how would they ever exist at all?'

'I simply say that it is not our business,' Farraline said. 'And it is certainly not the best way of using our capital.'

'Not the best for *us*, perhaps,' Jasper said pointedly.

'Not for the poor, either,' Farraline said. 'If you'll forgive me, you are thinking rather too much like a mill hand and not enough like a mill master. Our proper business is to prosper, to make profit so that we can expand our operations. Thus we provide more jobs and better wages, to benefit the poor by providing them with the means to support themselves honestly and with dignity. Let those, like Skelwith,' with a polite nod in his direction, 'whose business it is, build houses.'

'Thank you, I shall,' Skelwith said with a smile.

'But for profit, I hope,' Farraline responded, scenting an ally.

'I should not think of doing anything else,' Skelwith said. 'I have a wife and three children to think about.'

'Charity begins at home, eh?' Farraline grinned. 'How did you get yourself in amongst philanthropist company, Mr Skelwith? Hobsbawn, you are the best of fellows, and I hope you will not take it amiss that I disagree with your views wholeheartedly. That I express myself so freely while at your very table,' he went on with a mock bow, 'is proof of how well known you are for your just and liberal mind.'

'Hear, hear!' Droylsden said, thumping the table. 'Well said, that man!'

Jasper had no desire to smile, but in Sophie's presence he could not be the one to turn the conversation into a quarrel. He began to regret having broached the subject in front of her. He had hoped she would help him persuade Farraline, but instead she had sided against him. He felt a resurgence of his old jealousies and uncertainties.

And why had this fair, aristocratic, damnable man said that Jasper thought like a mill hand? Was he referring to Jasper's origins, the fact that he had gone into the mills at the age of eight as a piecener and worked his way up to foreman? Well, in justice, Jasper didn't think Farraline meant that at all. If he

94

knew it, or remembered it, he would be too much of a gentleman ever to mention it; but that was the most damnable thing of all, for it gave Jasper no decent reason to hate him.

'So you won't come in with us?' he said at last, when he had command of his tongue.

Farraline smiled. 'For profit, yes — for charity, no. I would only recommend it to my brother if you could convince me it was a good investment, likely to show a decent return.' As he said it, he cast a covert and considering glance in Skelwith's direction. If there were going to be any profit at all in the venture, he had a shrewd idea whose pocket it was going to end up in.

After a protracted search, Africa found her sister in the brew-house where, with the help of one of the kitchen-maids, she was making pauper soup in one of the coppers.

'Monsieur Barnard doesn't like his kitchen to be used for this,' Polly said at Africa's enquiring glance. 'It's my fault. I was foolish enough to remind him to crack the shin bones before he boiled them, and he took mortal offence. It took my aunt an hour to placate him. He offered to leave if she preferred a female cook in her kitchens.'

The kitchen-maid giggled, though rather nervously. She was only twelve, and was so in awe of the irascible Frenchman that she half believed he had supernatural powers and could see and hear her wherever she was.

'I'd like to talk to you, Polly,' Africa said, with a significant jerk of the head towards the child.

Polly regarded her sister for a moment as though weighing the desirability of a tête-à-tête, and then said to the maid, 'Now Emmie, I want you to go and pick some more herbs for the soup. Winter savory — do you know which one that is? — and thyme.'

'Yes, miss,' said the child. 'How much, miss?'

'An apronful will be about right,' Polly said. 'Off you go, and don't hurry back.'

Emmie looked intelligent. 'Yes, miss. I understand, miss.'

When she had gone, Polly said, 'Bright child, that one. I think Aunt ought to start training her for a housemaid. She won't do in the kitchen — too much imagination.'

Africa sat on the edge of the table and eyed her sister curiously. 'Is this what you do all day? Occupy yourself about household matters?'

'Not all day. I read, I walk in the gardens, pick and arrange the flowers. And I'm studying —'

'With Father Moineau?'

Polly looked away. 'Under his guidance. Who is better qualified to teach me theology?'

Africa studied her averted face for a moment. 'You know that Aunt Héloïse doesn't want you to busy yourself in this way?' she said, waving a hand at the soup.

Polly looked at her, her cheeks pink. 'She says I don't need to trouble myself. But it's no trouble, and I wish to earn my keep.'

'You're her niece. You dont need to earn your keep. Aunt would far sooner you enjoyed yourself —'

'And found myself a husband,' Polly finished for her. 'I'm well aware of the keen interest everyone has in *that* aspect of my life. It makes me feel like a prize breeding mare,' she added indignantly. 'And if you have come to add your voice to theirs, sister, I can tell you that you're —'

'It is the priest, isn't it?' Africa interrupted as though she had not been listening. She was studying Polly's face keenly. 'You are in love with Father Moineau.'

Polly grew scarlet. 'How dare you suggest such a thing!'

'I thought from the first it was that,' Africa went on, unmoved, 'but then I told myself it couldn't be. He's such an odd little man — and a *priest*, after all, a Catholic priest that you couldn't even hope to marry.'

Polly moved away. 'I won't listen to any more of this,' she said, her eyes filling with tears. 'You've no right to say such things to me. I shall —'

Africa moved casually to block her exit. 'But the more I see of him the more I understand it. He is the sort of man one might easily fall in love with, especially after what you've been through, my poor Polly.'

The unexpected sympathy was too much to bear, and the tears spilled over. Polly put her hands over her face. Africa stepped close, put her arms around her sister and drew her against her shoulder.

For a while nothing was said; and when the first paroxysm of weeping was over, it was Polly who spoke. 'You don't know how awful it has been,' she sobbed, still muffled by her sister's neck. Africa, she found, was a very comfortable person to cry on: strong and steady, with a shoulder at exactly the right height; and she stayed still and didn't pat or fuss, just let one get on with crying. 'All those years living with Minnie — the tedium — shut up in that dark house in the middle of the wood and never seeing anyone.'

She drew away at last, and found a large, sensible handker-chief ready for her in Africa's hand. She began to mop. 'And then — and then Minnie died. I felt so bad about it — so guilty. The worst of all was finding myself thinking, just for a moment, that now I'd be able to marry Harvey.' The drowned blue eyes, like rain-drenched violets, fixed Africa's with desperate appeal. 'It was only for a second, I swear it! But then came that terrible accusation, and he was arrested for murder, and I never knew — I never knew —' The tears spilled over again.

'Do you really think he did murder her?' Africa asked quietly after a moment.

Polly shook her head, mopping again. 'I don't know. He was acquitted under the law, so that makes him innocent, doesn't it? But that isn't the point. The point was — is —'

She didn't seem to be able to go on, so Africa finished for her, very gently. 'The point is that you shouldn't have been in any doubt about his innocence. And when you found you were in doubt —'

Polly nodded. 'That destroyed it.' A quivering gulp. 'It almost destroyed me. I felt guilty now on both sides. For all sorts of things. I wanted to die — so badly, Africa, you can't imagine!' Africa nodded encouragingly. 'And then I came here, so completely without hope — and Father Moineau saved me.'

'Yes, I do see,' Africa said. 'And given all that, it must be maddening for you to have kindly people urging you all the time to marry, especially since your Harvey is such a good catch and hasn't married anyone else.'

'He still writes to me from time to time. He still wants to marry me. But I couldn't,' she added with a shudder.

97

'No, I see how that would be impossible,' Africa said thoughtfully. 'But now, Polly dear,' she went on briskly, 'you must also see that it won't do to stay here making a nuisance of yourself about the house and embarrassing that good man with your unwanted love.'

'My —!' Polly stopped, almost open-mouthed, staring at her sister in a mixture of indignation and hurt.

'You have been through a perfectly dreadful time, and you had a right to a period of convalescence, just as if you had been ill. But enough is enough. You're well again now, and it's time to move on. That nice Father Sparrow, as Aunt calls him, has done all he can for you, and you ought in simple gratitude to leave him alone now.'

'And if he doesn't want to be left alone, as you so vulgarly put it?' Polly said, her eyes bright with anger.

Africa grinned. 'Do you find me vulgar? Oh dear, I'm afraid it must be living with sailors for so long. Well, I should warn you from the beginning I am not a great diplomat. I speak as I think, and you will always find me honest with you — but that may be no bad thing. Just put the question to yourself, sister, if you will. What do you want of him? Do you want him to love you back? Because if so, what would become of his vows? Is it kind to tempt the poor man with something he can't have, or at least can't have without a dreadful struggle of conscience?'

'I don't —' Polly began, and stopped, baffled and furious.

'Don't you? What then? I think you haven't really thought about it at all. You've been lingering in a perfumed garden far from the noise of the world: very nice for a vacation, but it won't do for a permanency. The real world awaits you, dear Polly. Come with me, and try it on for size.'

She cocked her head with such an expression of mischief mixed with affection that Polly felt herself, quite against her will, beginning to smile and relent.

'I don't want the real world,' she said, but it only sounded sulky. She changed it for, 'What could I do in the real world anyway?'

'Join in my scheme, of course; come and live with me and be useful and independent. I promise you *I* will never urge you to go to balls and find a husband. We will have a great deal of hard work and a great deal of pleasure, keep good company and a good table, be respectable and respected, and live honestly by our own efforts. What more could any woman want?'

Polly laughed at last. 'You really are absurd! Well, what is this scheme of yours?'

'I mean to open a fashionable riding school, to teach ladies and gentlemen of good *ton* to ride properly without disgracing that noble animal, the horse. I mean only to allow the very best families to enrol in my classes, and I shall charge them such exorbitant fees that they will be proud to boast to their friends how much it is costing them to have Miss Georgiana taught to sit on a horse. The friends will then feel obliged to send their Misses Charlotte and Augusta along; and thus you and I will become ever more exclusive, fashionable, successful, and finally rich.'

Polly stared. 'You want me to become a riding-mistress?'

'Who better?' Africa agreed, unintimidated. 'You are so very beautiful, Pol, and you ride so well. Every mother must want her daughter to look as good upon a horse as you. By the by, we must have nothing but very handsome animals, and we must both dress in the very latest shriek of fashion — not showy, of course,' she added hastily, 'but with the sort of elegance that makes every other woman want to tear her hair with envy. Oh, *you* know — you do it as naturally as breathing, and, unpromising material as I am, I'm sure you can make something of me.'

'You wouldn't be trying to confuse me with flattery, would you?' Polly asked, narrow-eyed.

Africa opened hers wide. 'I mean every word of it, I promise you. Now Polly *do* say you'll come in with me! You've had such a miserable life, and we could be so happy together with our little school!'

'If I say no —?'

Africa shrugged. 'I shall go ahead on my own. I've marked down exactly the right piece of land — just at the end of the Park, next to St George's burial ground, almost opposite the Cumberland Gate. So handy for all the fashionable houses! Now, with my share of Papa's money I can build the stables and buy enough horses to make a start; but if you come in with your share, we could build a manège too, for bad weather, and for those too shy or timid to take their first lessons in public view. It would be in all ways better, you see.'

'Yes,' said Polly thoughtfully.

'So will you come with me?' Africa fixed her with her most beguiling look. 'Can't you just imagine it? The Miss Haworths' School for the Equestrian Art.' With one hand she sketched a huge sign above their heads. 'By appointment to His Majesty, instructresses to all the little princes and princesses to come. I wouldn't be surprised,' she added matter-of-factly, 'if we ended up with a peerage apiece for our services to the Crown.'

Polly laughed. 'You do say such foolish things! Well, I can't make up my mind about it in an instant. I need time to think.'

'That's all right. It will be some time before Papa's will is proved and the money released. But you are tempted by the idea, aren't you?'

'Yes,' said Polly, and sounded as if her answer had surprised her. 'I think you're a madcap, but — yes, I am tempted.'

'Then that will do for now,' Africa said with a satisfied nod.

CHAPTER SIX

The ball at Wolvercote on the day before Christmas Eve was a very grand occasion, with most of the county in attendance. Everyone was eager to refresh their memories of the notorious Lady Theakston, who had been away for long enough to make her an object of curiosity. All those whose futures were directly affected — tenants, neighbours, and mothers of unmarried daughters — were also naturally eager to see how the young Earl of Aylesbury had turned out.

Rosamund, not dancing for the moment, studied him across the ballroom as he worked his way up the set and listened patiently to his partner, who was being (probably on her mother's orders) rather too sprightly for his comfort. It was strange to think that Roly was twenty-two now. Rosamund was used to the idea of his being a child, a pale and puny schoolboy, frightened of everyone and everything.

He had been only seven when Papa died and he came into the title, and it had always seemed too great a burden for his spindly shoulders. But he had had his twenty-first birthday last September in Vienna, and was now in full control of his fortune. Effectively, Wolvercote was already his: he could turn them all out and lock the gates after them if he wanted. But from the way Lucy had arranged the Christmas house-party and issued the invitations to the ball, the Boxing Day meet, and various other festivities, it was clear she still looked upon it as her own. When Roly married, Rosamund thought, there would be some stormy scenes between her and the new countess.

When he married? The words sounded so odd in her mind, she tried to look at him with the eyes of a stranger, to decide if he were marriageable. He would never be thought of as handsome, with that strange pale face and reddish hair; but since he'd been away he had grown taller and filled out a little, and his sensible air and quiet, dignified bearing did him no disservice. He was certainly what one might call personable, Rosamund decided. And then she smiled at herself. Personable? Roly was Earl of Aylesbury and in command of a considerable fortune: he must be near the top of every mama's list. He would be able to take his pick of next season's beauties, if he wanted.

And what of Tom? Rosamund scanned the room for him, and spotted him just as he began to dance down his set, his hands linked through the slender fingers of Thalia Hampton. She was laughing, her eyes bright, her chestnut hair flying. She was the prettiest and most vivacious girl in the room, but she had eyes for no-one but her partner. When they reached the bottom of the set and fell into line again she burst at once into lively chat, to which Tom responded with lazy amusement. But even as Rosamund watched he turned his dark head and looked across at her. Their eyes met, and he smiled a smile of wickedness and complicity to which she found herself irresistibly responding. And she was only his sister! He was heart-breakingly handsome, and at eighteen had the mature and self-assured air of one twice his age.

The Grand Tour seemed to have served him well — not that Lucy had taken him abroad to improve him, because as far as she was concerned Tom was and always had been quite perfect. He was her love-child, son of a Captain Weston, who had died at Trafalgar. Rosamund thought it a gauge of her stepfather's magnanimity that he had not only accepted Tom into the household, but had lately adopted him as his own son, in order to regularise Tom's position and give him security and a name.

But then, Rosamund thought, Papa Danby was a remarkable person. No-one else had ever been able to keep a rein on her mother. He had courted her long and patiently, remaining in the background as a faithful and undemanding friend through her marriage with Rosamund's father and her affair with Captain Weston. Rosamund did not underestimate the strength of character it must have taken to wait so long and with so little hope for the one woman he wanted. God send me such a friend, she thought. Oh Jes, be patient! Be faithful!

Marcus was suddenly at her side. It was almost as if he had heard her thoughts.

'Not dancing, my darling?'

'I'm resting. I've danced the last three.'

'That's right,' he approved. 'Best not to overdo things. I don't think you should stay up late tonight.'

'Oh, for God's sake —!' Rosamund muttered, trying to push down the irritation which rose at the suffocating words. 'I'm not an invalid, Marcus,' she said, trying to speak calmly.

'But we mustn't take any chances,' he insisted.

'We don't even know for certain yet,' she retorted. She had missed last month's flux; the date for this month's was only just past. 'It could happen at any moment.'

'All the more reason to be careful,' Marcus said.

A pregnancy which could be jeopardised by the exercise of dancing down a set or two, Rosamund thought, was unlikely to produce anything very sturdy by way of a child; but she didn't say so. To speak of such matters in a ballroom would upset Marcus's sense of propriety. In any case, Rosamund didn't want to think about it at all, and particularly not when she was trying to enjoy herself. So she said, almost at random, 'I'm glad Africa brought Polly back for the Christmas season. It's good to see her enjoying herself.'

Marcus watched her as she moved up the set, talking to Lord Ballincrea, who was partnering her.

'I think she's the most beautiful woman I've ever seen. I remember when she came out, with Minnie and Cousin Fanny — everyone said she was the most beautiful girl of the Season. She was much admired.'

Rosamund frowned. 'Is that how you remember it? I thought Fanny was more popular.'

'You don't remember. You were too young,' Marcus said. 'Anyway, Harvey Sale was quite nutty on her. It's a great pity he didn't marry her instead of poor Minnie.'

'That comes perilously close to criticising my mother,' Rosamund said.

'Oh, I meant no disrespect. All the same, I think your mother would be glad to see Polly marry him now. I wonder why she didn't invite him down here too?'

Rosamund gave him an exasperated look. 'Don't you think that would have been tactlessness on a rather large scale even for my mother? I seem to remember a few years back *you* refused even to have him in the house.'

Marcus flushed. 'You know it was my mother who objected to him.'

'She called him a murderer, and you agreed with her.'

'Only for Bab's sake — the scandal was so fresh then. It was a long time ago — things have changed,' he said defensively. 'Besides, I took him to dine with me in my club, don't you remember?'

'Yes, I remember,' Rosamund said shortly. 'Don't let's argue about it.' She really didn't care about it; it just seemed impossible to talk to Marcus these days without quarrelling with him. He was so defensive, and she was so irritable. Her nerves were always on edge. If he had hoped that being apart from Jes would make her settle down into happy domesticity, he had missed his guess. She found his attentions suffocating, his conscientious efforts in her bed embarrassing.

For the first two months she had waited in hope and dread, to experience a mixture of regret and relief when the flux came. Now she was waiting with a different mixture of emotions, half of her mind thinking it would be glad to have it over with, the other half white and numb with terror and revulsion at the idea. She couldn't believe that she might at this very moment be pregnant. When she tried the words on for size, they became meaningless gibberish. Under her rose-coloured silk ballgown her slender white body was hers still, *must* remain so, *could* not change. And yet while it remained so, she could not be freed from Marcus's attentions.

'Are you all right, my darling?' His tender enquiry broke through her fevered thoughts. 'You aren't feeling faint?'

'No — no, of course not.' She shook the mental images away, and spoke briskly. 'I'm perfectly well, Marcus. Don't fuss.'

The music had come to an end. The sets were breaking into their component couples and scattering, ladies being escorted back to their protective groups, new liaisons being negotiated for the next dance. Her mother came up to join them, looking magnificent in a dress of lilac-coloured silk boldly trimmed with black lace, her hair dressed *à l'espagnol* with a mantilla brought back from Seville. Rosamund noted with secret amusement that she was wearing a magnificent parure of amethysts and diamonds which formed part of the Aylesbury family jewels. Well, they looked better on Mother than in a bank vault, Rosamund thought; but she didn't envy Roland's future wife the task of asking for them back.

'It's going well, don't you think?' Lucy said, scanning the room judiciously. Roland came into view, having returned his partner to her mother and made his escape. Lucy beckoned him over. 'Who are you dancing with next? Did you do as I told you and ask Thalia Hampton?'

'Yes, Mama. I was just going to find her,' Roland said patiently.

'Very good. And you will be taking her in to supper?'

'Yes, Mama. It's all arranged.'

Lucy nodded. 'Go and find her, then, before she changes her mind. Not a very steady girl,' she added thoughtfully as Roland disappeared into the glittering crowd, 'but she's young enough to change.'

'Do you suppose Roly fancies her, then, Mama?' Rosamund asked in surprise.

Lucy raised an eyebrow. 'What sort of talk is that? He must marry, and as soon as possible, to get an heir. Thalia Hampton is the right age and of suitable background. Helena and I have discussed it, and Greyshott's in favour. I expect we shall have it all arranged before the house party breaks up.'

'Arranged?'

Lucy frowned. 'Oh, you needn't worry. Roland has no strong feelings on the subject. Danby had a few words with him, and he said he had no objection.'

'I should think not, indeed,' Marcus said, trying to bridge the chasm between them. 'She's the prettiest girl of her year. He'll be a lucky fellow if she accepts him.'

'Who, accepts whom?' Lord Theakston said, strolling up at that moment.

'Roland,' Rosamund said. 'Did you really speak to him, Papa Danby?'

'About the little Hampton chit? Well, she's very young of

course; but it's a good match for her,' Theakston said. 'The Aylesbury fortune must be quite a temptation — not to mention the jewels,' he added with a suppressed smile, looking at his wife's glittering head and neck.

Lucy missed the joke. 'It's a case where I think mother and daughter will agree for very different reasons,' she said. 'Helena wants to get the child married before she gets into trouble; and I dare say Thalia would like to be out from under her mother's thumb.'

'Oh Mother, poor Roly!' Rosamund exclaimed. 'You aren't choosing him a very comfortable wife.'

'Nonsense!' Lucy said stoutly. 'I was a little wild as a girl, but I settled down as soon as I was married. I'm sure your father was perfectly comfortable.'

Theakston considered the notoriously unsuccessful history of that marriage, and the scandal Lucy and her husband had provoked when he left her to live apart while she shared the matrimonial home with her lover, and felt it prudent to say only, 'Quite so.'

Marcus thought it was high time to change the subject. 'It's a splendid dance, ma'am. What a pity your brother's family couldn't come. It would have been good to have everyone together for Christmas.'

'Wouldn't come, rather,' Lucy said. 'But James was always selfish. He'd prefer to stay home at Morland Place and have his children around him.'

'Monstrous!' Danby said. 'The unnatural villain!'

Lucy smiled reluctantly. 'Oh, very well! But I have been away a long time. I thought he might make an exception on this occasion. There are so few of us left now; and I wanted to tell him about meeting Harry in Gibraltar.'

'We'll go down to Yorkshire after Christmas,' Danby suggested. 'Before the hunting finishes.'

'That will be nice,' Lucy said. 'Speaking of hunting, did you talk to Pole about stopping that earth in Godstow Holt? It will be the shortest run in history if he bolts in there on Boxing Day.'

'Yes, my love, it's all attended to,' Theakston said.

Lucy looked at Rosamund consideringly. 'You will have to think about buying yourself some horses, now that I'm home again. I must say you've taken care of mine very well.'

'Thank you,' Rosamund said, 'but it was all Parslow, you know.'

'You rode them,' Lucy pointed out. 'Would you like to have Hotspur on Boxing Day? I'm going to hunt Magnus, and the Rector is lending Roland something.'

Rosamund felt Marcus draw breath to say something on the subject of her hunting, and she flashed him such a quelling look that it actually stopped him. 'Thank you, Mama,' she said, and then turned quickly to Lord Theakston. 'What about you, sir? Are you going to risk the mud and dirt? Do you remember when Mr Brummell had those riding boots with white tops made for him, so that he could refuse to hunt for fear of getting them dirty?'

Theakston smiled. 'I wouldnt dare aspire to those heights of dandyism. Only George could carry it off without makin' himself ridiculous.'

'Poor George!' Lucy said automatically. 'Did we tell you, Rosamund, that we saw him in Calais on our way home?'

'I meant to ask you if you had,' Rosamund said.

'Yes, he called as soon as we arrived in town, and had dinner with us that night. And then the next day we called on him in his rooms.'

'How was he? I have fond memories of Mr Brummell. He was always very kind to me, in spite of my freckles.'

Lucy sighed. 'He pretends to be cheerful, but even I can see how the situation wears him down. To be continually in debt, with no prospect of getting out; creditors pressing all the time . . . He's grown very thin, and there's almost something — shabby about him.'

'I just can't imagine the great Mr Brummell shabby,' Marcus said. 'What does he do in Calais?'

'Just what he did in London,' Theakston said economically. 'Gets dressed and strolls with his friends.'

'But what friends!' Lucy said. 'We walked with him on the ramparts the second day, didn't we, Danby, and he nodded quite civilly to people he would never have noticed in London.'

'He has to cut his coat according to his cloth, love,' Danby pointed out.

107

'Is there nothing to be done for him?' Rosamund asked.

'What he needs is an income,' Danby said. 'Some kind of post abroad with a salary to it. But I'm not really on the right terms with Castlereagh to ask. What about you, Marcus? Do you know anyone useful in the Cabinet?'

Marcus frowned. 'I'm afraid not, sir.'

Lucy looked as though she found that barely credible. How could an earl, living in London, not have useful friends in the Government? 'Canning's out of office again, isn't he?' she pondered. He and George were at school together. I'm sure he'd do something for him, if he were in.'

'What about the Duke of Wellington, Mama?' Rosamund asked. 'Wouldn't he help, as a favour to you?'

'You should know better than that,' Marcus intervened sternly. 'You know the Beau hates jobbery.'

'That's right,' Lucy nodded. 'I'm afraid poor George will have to wait for a change of government. Well, I shall send him a few little things to make life more comfortable. Silk handkerchiefs, for instance — I know he needs them — and his favourite snuff; and that elixir for hair, Danby, that you mentioned.'

'Good idea,' Theakston said. 'The poor chap did mention he was afraid the thatch was wearin' thin. We're none of us gettin' any younger.'

Rosamund slipped a hand under his arm. 'I'd believe that of anyone except you, dear Papa Danby. I'm sure you take a year off each birthday, instead of putting one on.'

'In that case,' he said, capturing her hand and lifting it to his lips, 'I must be somewhere near the right age by now to ask you to dance. Dear Lady Chelmsford, will you tread a measure with me?'

Rosamund curtseyed, fluttering her eyelids. 'Dear Lord Theakston, you are all condescension! How could I refuse?'

They went off, laughing, to join the nearest set, to stand below Maurice Ballincrea, who had just led Barbarina in to join it. Lucy and Marcus watched them go in disapproving silence.

'It must be very pleasant for you, ma'am, that Lord Theakston gets on so well with your children,' Marcus said gloomily.

108

'It's well past time you and Rosamund produced an heir,' Lucy replied in kind. 'Four years married — what are you thinking of, Marcus?'

Marcus flushed a little at the directness, but had to find something to say. 'I think she has felt rather unsettled, with you being away, ma'am. Things will be better now you're back.'

Lucy turned her attention from the dancers to study Marcus's expression carefully. There were things she wanted to know, but simply hadn't the vocabulary to ask. At length she said, 'You were always her hero, from the nursery onwards. I used to think it was just childish nonsense when she said she would marry you when she grew up.'

Marcus understood the unspoken question mark at the end of the sentence, but had neither words nor wish to answer it. He watched the bright, multicoloured movement of the dancers and said nothing.

Rosamund knew that the trouble had not gone away, only been postponed. It came when the company retired on Christmas evening to dress for dinner. Marcus followed her into her room, and Moss, taking one look at his face, backed tactfully out.

'Ros, you don't really mean to hunt tomorrow, do you?'

'Of course,' she said, trying to sound casual about it. 'Mama's offered me Hotspur — how could I refuse?'

'Your mother doesn't know about — well, that you might be with child,' said Marcus awkwardly.

'If she did it wouldn't make any difference. You should know her well enough by now to know that.' She turned away from him and fiddled with things on the dressing-table. 'It isn't even certain yet. For heaven's sake, don't fuss so!'

'But dearest —!'

'If you had your way you'd lock me up in a cage until it was all over, I know that. Well I'm not a dumb animal, I'm a rational human being, and I'm not going to be told what I can and can't do. I shall decide for myself!'

When he spoke again, it was in a quiet, puzzled voice. 'Why are you so angry with me?'

She whipped round on him with a retort ready on her

109

tongue, but it died in the face of his undemanding patience. She wanted to scream and break things, and that was just silly. Instead she dug her fingernails into her palms, and muttered, 'Oh, this is Hell!'

The next question cost him dearly to ask. 'Do you regret your decision? Do you want to go back on it?'

To what purpose? she thought. Then I would be back where I started. 'No,' she said at last. 'I want to do it. It is my own decision.'

'If it's so painful to you —' he said hesitantly. 'You seem all the time to want to make it bad for me. If it hurts you so much to do this, then perhaps —'

'Oh Marcus!' I have no right, no right. I chose this when I married you, and to say that I didn't know then what it would cost is beside the point. I must not make you suffer when you have no choices at all. 'I'm sorry. I have been unkind to you. It's my wretched temper. I shall try to do better.'

Hope warmed his eyes again — absurd, unquenchable hope. Would he never learn?

'Then, tomorrow —?'

She felt herself begin to scowl and dug her nails further into her palms to regain control. 'You really mustn't worry about that. It won't do any harm.'

Marcus persisted. 'But you know how your mother hunts — neck or nothing — and you'll go with her whatever she does.'

'I'm not going to give up riding and spend nine months lying upon a sofa, so you may as well save your breath.'

He tried to smile. 'Of course not. I'm not so foolish as that. But an ordinary ride through the park is one thing. Hunting — particularly in company with your mother — is quite another. You must see that?'

'I see nothing of the sort. For heaven's sake, Marcus, do you think I would do anything to harm the outcome? I want it as much as you do.' More, perhaps — oh, but for different reasons!

Marcus bit his lip. 'Well, will you at least promise me to take care — not to compete with your mother — not to jump anything difficult or dangerous. Please, Rosamund. I can't

110

help worrying, when I remember —'

Her eyes narrowed, and he stopped himself from mentioning the unmentionable.

'Just ride like a lady,' he went on, trying for lightness of tone, 'instead of like a Hussar, and I shall be content.'

She continued to stare at him stiffly for a moment, and then turned away. 'Very well, if it will please you. You had better let Moss come in now, or I shall be late for dinner.'

The scene in the open courtyard before the house was all colour and movement: the glossy horses, the smart grooms, the well-dressed people laughing and talking, the footmen carrying round trays of glasses, the maids with their offerings of hot patties and cold pies for those not invited to breakfast within.

In the breakfast room, the hunting party sat down to a substantial breakfast against the rigours to come. Lucy packed sausages and cold beef and mutton chops and buttered eggs away inside her slender frame; Papa Danby, neat as a pin, carved ham with as much dedicated concentration as if he were painting the Sistine Chapel; Roland helped Thalia to oyster puffs and devilled kidneys and put the same on his own plate to show how much he approved her choice; Helena and Africa together accounted for most of a magnificent raised pork pie.

The young people talked excitedly about what they meant to do, the older people spoke languidly about what they had done on other occasions, and all agreed that the weather was perfect, and that the scent would be breast-high, the going firm but without the least 'bone'. Those who were not hunting — Barbarina, Tom and Lord Ballincrea — looked on with that air of puzzled amusement elicited by the sight of people about to risk their necks for some incomprehensibly esoteric pleasure, and Ballincrea invited Bab to take a civilised stroll with him through the succession-houses and talk about anything except horses.

At last Lucy and Roland led the way outside. All heads turned, there were smiles and greetings to exchange, and a general movement began as people mounted up and the grooms came forward with the family's horses. Parslow came round from the side of the house leading Magnus Apollo, who looked fresh and full of himself. When Lucy went down the steps to greet him and slid a tidbit under the enquiring chestnut muzzle, her slight form made the gelding look as big as a house.

Another groom brought Hotspur, and as Rosamund was about to mount, Marcus appeared at her side and bent with linked hands to throw her up. He stood looking up at her as she settled herself, so obviously trying not to speak that she took pity on him, smiled and said, 'No, I shan't forget my promise, and yes, I shall be careful. Go and get mounted, Marcus, or you'll keep us all waiting.'

He left her reluctantly, and Rosamund walked Hotspur forward a little to clear space for others. In a moment Helena Greyshott came up beside her, her handsome grey champing his bit and digging at the cobbles in his excitement.

'Is Marcus being solicitous? Men are such sentimental creatures! I know just how you feel, my dear — my poor Captain Twombley fusses like a mother hen whenever I go out on Thunder, despite the fact that he's as gentle as a ewe lamb, and I've been riding him for five years.'

'How do you calm the Captain's fears?' Rosamund asked with interest.

Helena smiled her most wicked smile. 'I don't. The more he believes he'll never see me alive again, the sweeter the reunion when I come home unscathed.'

Rosamund smiled. 'I wonder you could bear to be without him for the whole Christmas season, ma'am.'

'So do I. If it weren't for the need to settle Thalia's future — and even so, I have half an idea that I might be called back to London on urgent business as soon as the engagement's agreed!' She checked Thunder's restless surging, and looked at Rosamund keenly. 'Your honest opinion, my dear cousin — what sort of husband would your brother make for my daughter?'

Rosamund met her eyes. 'Kind and self-effacing, I should think. But what sort of wife would your daughter make for my brother?'

'Touché!' Helena laughed. 'But she will give him his heir and look very pretty on his arm on formal occasions, and I

don't know what more an earl could want of his countess.'
She cocked her head at Rosamund thoughtfully. 'You need
not think, however, that your mother and I would force the
thing upon them. We both agreed long ago that we wanted
our children to be happy in their marriages. That's why she
agreed to your marrying Marcus, of course.'

'Yes,' said Rosamund. She was saved from having to
pursue the topic because just then, heralded by a sudden rise
in the emotional temperature, hounds appeared. They
rushed into the picture in a white and tan flood, gay sterns
waving, mouths smiling, eyes shining. The horses suddenly
came awake; their ears shot forward and they began to fidget;
the air seemed full of electricity.

Thunder was swirling on the spot in excitement, and
Helena sat him with difficulty. 'He'll settle down once we've
had a run,' she said. 'I have it on good authority that we'll put
up a fox at Wytham Mill Copse, and if they can keep him out
of Marley Wood we shall have a three-mile point of it.'

Rosamund felt her spirits rise. If only I can keep out of
Marcus's way, she thought, I should have a good day. The last
stragglers hurried to get mounted as the huntsman gave a
couple of toots on his horn and led the way out into the park.
Thunder went up and down on the spot like a rocking-horse
as Helena held him back for hounds to pass her; and infected
by this wanton spirit, Hotspur fly-bucked foolishly as though
he were half his age.

Tom did not hunt. In that respect he took after his father, the
sea-captain, who regarded the horse as nothing more than a
means of transport from point A to point B where there was
no water in between. Having ascertained that Barbarina was
happy in Lord Ballincrea's company and didn't need him, he
slipped a book of poetry into his pocket and went off in search
of a sheltered and secluded spot in the park where he could
read in peace.

He returned at one o'clock expecting to meet them in the
saloon for a nuncheon. The fire was lit and briskly blazing, and
the tray of sherry, madeira and claret was laid out, but the room
was occupied only by a stranger, a fair-haired man with a
weather-beaten complexion who looked about ten years Tom's

113

senior. He was seated in a deep chair by the fire perusing a quarterly review, but he stood up and flung the paper aside when Tom came in and greeted him with a ready smile.

'I say, I am glad to see you! I was beginning to feel like that chap in the ghostly house — "where nought but spirits bound", you know. Are you Lord Aylesbury, by any chance?'

'Not by any chance,' Tom answered cheerfully. 'I'm his brother Tom Weston. Everyone's out hunting.' The stranger, in rising, had revealed that he wore his hair in an old-fashioned *queue*, which together with the tanned faced put him down as a sailor. Tom eyed him with interest. 'Have you been here long?'

The stranger recovered himself. 'I'm so sorry, I should have introduced myself at once. My name's Morpurgo. I arrived about half an hour ago, and the servant showed me in here and said someone would be along in a moment.'

'That should have been me; or Lord Ballincrea, who's somewhere about with Bab. I expected to meet them here for a nuncheon. Did you come to see my mother — Lady Theakston?'

'Yes — well, in a way. I wanted to pay my respects to her, of course, though I don't know whether she'll remember me. But I really came to see her niece, Miss Haworth.'

Tom snapped his fingers. 'Now I remember why your name's familiar! You're Africa's friend, aren't you? The one who found her and brought her back when she ran away to join the circus. I should just about think my mother would remember you! She couldn't have been more grateful to you for preventing a scandal.'

'Oh, really? Well it's very kind of you to say so. I hesitated to presume on so slight an acquaintance, but I did want to see Afr — Miss Haworth to express my condolences on her father's death. I knew the Admiral very well — served under him for several years when he was a captain.'

'Yes, I know. That's how you met Africa, wasn't it?'

Morpurgo nodded. 'I was like an older brother to her. But I haven't seen her for a long time, not since before she went to St Helena. I had a shore post then; I was at the admiralty for four years. We corresponded — with her father's permission, of course,' he added hastily. 'Then last year I got a cruise out to the

114

Bahamas on the *Hydra* — only arrived back two days ago. It was deuced bad luck my being out of the way just when I might have been of use to her; but of course Africa's the most sensible person in the world, so I don't suppose she felt the slightest need of me.'

The last part of the sentence sounded almost wistful. Tom smiled, thinking that if Mr Morpurgo had hurried straight to Wolvercote to see Africa almost before he'd got the roll out of his walk, so to speak, he must be very strongly attached to her.

'I'm sure she'll be very glad to see you,' he said kindly. 'And since you must have had a long journey, I think I should ring for refreshments without waiting for the other two. They'll come when they're hungry, I dare say.' He pulled the bell.

'Africa's out hunting too, is she?'

'Yes, and her sister. You remember Polly?'

'I know of her from Africa's letters. I only met her once, many years ago.'

The butler came in, followed by two footmen bearing a handsome collation on trays. Tom caught the butler's attention and said to Morpurgo, 'You will be staying, I hope? I'm sure I can speak for my mother in saying she will want very much for you to join the party.'

Morpurgo looked pleased and flustered. 'Thank you — if it is not an imposition — that is, I should like very much —'

'That's settled, then. Have a room made ready for Mr Morpurgo, will you, Savage?'

'Very good, sir.'

The servants withdrew, and Tom ushered Morpurgo towards the food. 'I'm glad you've come. There are too few of us non-hunters to counterbalance the sporting influence! I look forward to an afternoon of rational conversation with you, with no mention of horse, hound or fox. But first, what will you drink?'

Ballincrea and Barbarina did not return for the nuncheon. In the middle of the afternoon, when Tom and Morpurgo were happily discussing the situation in Portugal, the door to the saloon burst open and Thalia came in, wild of hair and liberally mud-splashed.

115

'There you are! What a day you've missed! Oceans of grief, loose horses, bodies everywhere, and guess what? Even Mama bought some land! Thunder was behaving like a demon and she put him at a double oxer to try to settle him down, but he slipped taking off and away she went, right over his shoulder, and landed in the mud!'

'You dreadful little ghoul,' Tom said equably from the depths of his comfortable armchair. 'I hope she wasn't hurt?'

'Of course not! Mama never gets hurt. But she was wild as fire — she hates parting company in front of strangers!'

Tom looked her up and down. 'And did you "part company" too? You're muddy enough for it. Is that why you're back early?'

Thalia looked scornful. 'I never come off! This is just splashing from the horse in front. No, I just thought Jupiter had had enough, so I slipped away.' She took in at last that there was a stranger present, and bestowed a brief glance on him. 'Hullo! I'm Thalia Hampton. I suppose you must have arrived while we were out.'

'How do you do? My name's Morpurgo.'

'Do sit down. You don't need to keep standing for my sake. I say, is there going to be some tea? I'm almost starved. Do ring the bell, Tom. I must have something before I go up for my bath.' She sat down on the sofa nearest to Tom, addressing him so exclusively that, despite her invitation, Morpurgo felt no inclination to be of their company.

'If you'll forgive me,' he said hesitantly, 'I would like to go to my room and tidy myself before everyone else arrives back.'

Thalia hardly noticed he had gone.

An hour later Young Maurice came in. 'So this is where you've got to,' he exclaimed, seeing his sister, still in her dirt, chattering to Tom over tea and the second dish of muffins. 'Why did you dash off like that? We had a wonderful run after you'd gone.'

'Jupiter was tired. I don't overface my horses.'

'He didn't look tired, the way he was taking hold during that last point,' Maurice said bluntly.

Tom was smiling cynically, and Thalia blushed with

116

annoyance. Brothers could be so tiresome! 'Well he was all the same. For that matter, why are you home early? Or are the others here too?'

The last thought seemed unwelcome to her, so it was as well that Maurice said, 'No, it's just me. Copper's lame — put his foot down a rabbit hole just after you left us. I've had to walk him home.'

'What *horrid* luck,' Thalia said with perfunctory sympathy. 'I hope it isn't bad. Hadn't you better go and see?'

'Rogers is bathing it now. I came to see if you were all right — but I see you are,' he added with a significant glance at the muffin dish.

'Won't you have some tea?' Tom asked politely.

Maurice looked down at himself. 'Not like this, thanks all the same. I'll go and have my bath first. You should do that too, Thalia, before it sets on you,' he added pointedly.

'Yes, I will in a minute,' she said crossly, making a face at him. 'Do go away, Maurice. You're interrupting me.'

On his way upstairs to the bachelor wing, Maurice saw Lord Ballincrea coming in through the passage from the back hall with Barbarina. He paused, meaning to greet them over the banisters, but before he could speak he saw his uncle stoop to kiss Barbarina's hand in a very tender way. Maurice froze on the stair as a wonderful idea struck him. The kiss was obviously a farewell, for in a moment Barbarina had withdrawn her hand and come running up the stairs — in itself an unusual thing for a young woman taught from childhood to move slowly and with dignity. She saw Young Maurice only at the last moment, glanced into his face with a gasp and a blush as she passed, and ran on upwards.

Ballincrea down in the hall, was looking up at him too with an expression of wry amusement.

'I say, Uncle,' Maurice began in tones half eager, half apologetic.

'So much for country-house dalliance,' Ballincrea said, mostly to himself. 'Are you back early, or do you herald the general invasion?'

'I'm early — Copper went lame. I say, sir, do you think I might have a word with you?'

Ballincrea started up the stairs towards him. 'Don't you think a change of clothes might be beneficial — on artistic if not hygienic grounds — before you begin your inquisition?'

Maurice blushed. 'I wouldn't dream of — that is, I beg your pardon for being here, sir, but I couldn't help —'

'You couldn't help noticing a passage of more-than-cousinly affection between myself and Lady Barbarina, damn your impudence, which leads you to wonder whether your inheritance is safe?'

Maurice was now scarlet. 'I wouldn't dream of asking — saying — I didn't even *think* anything so — so —'

'Good for you! In that case, what was it you wanted to say to me? Something about the day's sport, I apprehend.'

'I'm sorry, sir, I didn't mean to annoy you,' Maurice said rather stiffly. His very young dignity had been wounded. 'I had better follow your advice and go and take my bath.' He started on up the stairs.

Ballincrea grinned, and put a restraining hand on his arm. 'Don't flounce off, young stiff-neck! I didn't mean to hurt your feelings. It's just that when a fellow gets to my age, he feels rather foolish when he's caught in the act of making love to a lady.'

Maurice turned back, his face lighting up. 'Oh Uncle, is it love, then? I beg your pardon, I don't mean to be impertinent, only — well, you're absolutely my favourite uncle, and — and I have your interests at heart, you know!'

Ballincrea chuckled at the choice of words. 'Have you now! I'm glad to hear it. But seriously Young Maurice, I feel I owe you something of an explanation, or perhaps an apology. It's been understood for a very long time now that you were to inherit my title and my estate, and if I *were* to —'

'Oh no, Uncle, please! I've always said I didn't want it, and I meant it. I shall have Papa's title one day, and whenever that happens it will be too soon for me. All I want to do is to go travelling, like Roly and Tom did, and be an ordinary person. I don't want wealth and titles and estates.'

Ballincrea patted his shoulder affectionately. 'Then you're a young jackass: those things are important, as you'll discover one day. But I like you the better for saying it, however wrong-headed it is. So I have your permission, have I, to address the lady?'

Maurice gave him a blissful smile. 'I think it's a *splendid* notion!'

'Thank you for those kind words. But I must ask you to be discretion itself for the time being. I have hardly so much as put my toe into the water: at my age, one must proceed with caution and dignity. Please say nothing to anyone — anyone — until I tell you so.'

'Of course I won't, sir.' Maurice said stoutly. 'You may rely on me.'

'I thought perhaps I might,' said Ballincrea.

Dinner that evening was particularly merry, and the lively talk went on into the drawing-room, so that it was late before everyone retired. Rosamund found Moss not only waiting for her, but wide awake for once, and disposed for conversation as she helped her mistress undress.

'It was a wonderful thing, my lady, to see the meeting between Miss Africa and Mr Morpurgo! I remember when he found her in the circus that time and brought her back, and as careful of her as if he was her brother! But don't you think, my lady, that it was a sweet thing to see them together — so frank and open as Miss Africa's manners always are, and the pleasing way she has of showing when something is agreeable to her. She never was one to hold back praise, as I remember when she was a little girl and living with you and the other young ladies in your mama's house; and to see the way her eyes lit up when she saw Mr Morpurgo — such a nice young gentleman, my lady, and your mama always so favourable to anyone with a *naval* connection! They do say one wedding brings on another, don't they, my lady?'

'Why, who is getting married?' Rosamund asked absently, staring at her reflection in the looking-glass, white face, red hair, smudged eyes. It looked unreal to her, like a painted image, almost ghostly. Moss came up behind her and began taking out the pins, letting down the long coils of hair to lie like snakes over her shoulders and down her back. Medusa head, she thought.

119

'Why, my lady, they were saying in the servants' hall — Mr Savage was saying, my lady, that there's an engagement planned between his lordship your brother, my lady, and Miss Hampton, and that's why Lord Greyshott came down to Wolvercote for Christmas, instead of going to Windsor with the King, like he usually does. A wonderful thing that would be for his lordship, don't you think, my lady? A very pretty, lively young lady indeed, Miss Hampton, so everyone thinks in the servants' hall.'

'You all gossip far too much,' Rosamund said, but not unkindly. 'I suppose there's nothing anyone can do to stop you; so you had better tell me what else is being canvassed. Miss Hampton to marry Lord Aylesbury, Miss Africa to marry Mr Morpurgo — a lieutenant without a commission in a peace-time navy that shrinks hourly, by the by: hardly a prudent choice for her on your part. And what else?'

'Well, my lady,' Moss leaned closer and grew confidential as she loosened the snakes with her fingers, 'it hasn't escaped notice that Lord Ballincrea walked the whole day with Lady Barbarina in the orangery, and they never even went up to the saloon for a nuncheon when they were expected.'

Rosamund was amused. 'Lord Ballincrea and Barbarina? Now you really are spinning moonbeams! Lord Ballincrea will never marry again, and even if he did think of it, he'd never choose —' She broke off abruptly as though something had occurred to her.

Moss nodded wisely. 'You see, my lady, it isn't so impossible when you think about it! His lordship was heart-whole for her late ladyship, as everyone knows, but she's been in her grave six years now, poor good lady, and life must —'

Rosamund's hand came up and gripped her wrist like a vice, and Moss stopped in mid-sentence, startled. The hard fingers closed tighter, and Moss gave a little sigh of pain. The hairbrush dropped with a clatter on the dressing-table top and slid off onto the floor. Rosamund's face looked as white as paper; her eyes met Moss's in the looking-glass, wide and frightened.

'Oh, what is it, my lady?' Moss gasped.

The lips moved, but no sound came. And then the iron grip relaxed, and Rosamund closed her eyes and lowered her head; her hands dropped into her lap defeatedly. 'Oh Judy,' she said quietly.

'My lady? What is it? Is it —? Oh no, please God! My lady?'

Her eyes still shut, Rosamund nodded. 'It's come,' she said; and after a long moment she added, almost to herself, 'How will I be able to tell him?'

CHAPTER SEVEN

It was said of the Exchange in Manchester that if you strolled there long enough you would meet everyone you knew. Sophie must have left just too early, for it was in the street outside that she encountered Jesmond Farraline. He was walking very fast down Cross Street as she emerged, and encountered her so hard he almost knocked her down.

'Indeed, indeed, I don't mind in the least,' Sophie protested as he retrieved her basket for her and apologised for his brutality. 'There's no-one I would sooner be trampled by than you, Mr Farraline.'

He grinned at her. 'And that's what you call forgiveness? You have a wicked tongue, Mrs Hobsbawn, for all your mild and gentle mien! I hope there was nothing breakable in your basket?'

'Only ribbons for the baby and some twilled braid for trimming. Nothing important at all, but it was such a lovely day I wanted to be out. It's a great pity, don't you think Mr Farraline, that we have nowhere nice to walk in Manchester?'

'I feel the lack daily,' he said solemnly. 'Are you going home? May I walk with you and carry your basket? It's the least I can do after bowling you over like a ninepin.'

'If it does not take you out of your way —'

'No more than a step. I was going down to the mill. Let me have the basket — that's right. And now if you will oblige me by taking my arm, so — now we are comfortable.'

'*I* am, certainly,' Sophie said. 'The streets are so crowded. It is very pleasant to have a man to make a passage for me.'

'You should have brought a footman with you.'

'That's what Jasper says; but they have enough to do at

home, and the poor creatures do so hate dawdling after me that they spoil all my pleasure.'

'Then perhaps you should have gone in the carriage.'

'But I wanted the walk. Going round and round the garden is well enough, but one does not meet one's acquaintances there. I wish we had public walks and gardens, as York does.'

'York is an old-established city, Manchester a very new one. But wait until I am Member of Parliament for Manchester: I shall — no, why do you laugh?'

'Only because it seems all you men have your hobby horses! But I'm sure I see no reason why Manchester shouldn't have a Member,' she added politely.

'No reason at all,' Farraline nodded, 'except the great body of people who think any change in our ancient institutions will lead us straight to revolution in the French style. But Parliament as it is now is a nonsense. Do you realise, ma'am that since the middle of the last century the population of England has *doubled*, and yet there has been no increase in the electorate?'

'You mean, those who vote?' Sophie frowned in thought. 'But I don't really see why there should have been. Wouldn't most of the extra people be of the lower orders, who don't vote anyway?'

'Many of them, no doubt. But still, the largest increase in population has been in the new towns like Manchester, which have no representation at all. Think of this: the total population of Manchester, Leeds and Birmingham is about five hundred thousand, and they haven't a Member of Parliament between them. Yet Cornwall, with much the same population, has forty-four seats.'

'That does seem a little unfair,' Sophie murmured obediently.

'And there's the case of Old Sarum, which is nothing more than a ruined castle, quite uninhabited, and yet it has two Members of Parliament. Twelve of the votes that elect them are attached to empty fields.'

'Well, yes, I can see that you might find that absurd,' Sophie said. 'But my Uncle Ned used to say that each Member represents everyone in the country, not just those who vote for him, so it doesn't really matter how they get into the Commons.'

Farraline looked down at her. 'In an ideal world, that would be true. But a Member must look to the interests of his own voters, otherwise the next time they won't elect him.'

'Is that really true?' Sophie said doubtfully. 'It sounds — dishonest.'

'I'm afraid so. And besides, our parliamentary system was devised in ancient times when the population was small, the country was entirely agricultural, and there was only one interest. But now we have towns and crowded cities, factories and factory workers — interests quite different from the agricultural. Things are changing rapidly, and we must have a new system to reflect our new society. The future is with us, the manufacturers, and we must be given the power to shape the laws which will govern us.'

Sophie looked mischievous. 'When you offered to accompany me home, I didn't realise you meant to practise your speech for the next meeting on me. But it was very good — quite stirring.'

'My deepest apologies, ma'am,' Farraline grinned. 'You are quite right to rebuke me. I don't know what I deserve for boring you with my political nonsense!'

'You know we women can't understand such things,' Sophie returned demurely. 'All we can talk about is babies and hats.'

'Of course I knew that; I must have forgotten! So, Mrs Hobsbawn, how is your own baby? Let me see, didn't she have her first birthday recently?'

'Not so very recently,' Sophie said severely. 'She was born in March, you know, and it's now June.'

'I beg your pardon,' Farraline said humbly. 'Time flies, doesn't it? But how is this elderly daughter of yours?'

'She is bonny and blooming, thank you. She runs about everywhere now, and chatters away about everything she sees. Jasper tells her all about the mills when he comes home, and she sits and listens to him so gravely! He swears she understands every word. None of the other mothers I speak to,' she finished proudly, 'have babies as advanced as Fanny. She was talking in proper sentences before she was a year old.'

'She is plainly the most remarkable child that ever lived,' Farraline agreed.

124

'Well, you may tease, but I really think she is. Though of course,' with an unconscious sigh, 'I have no other yet to compare her with. But,' she brightened again, 'we hear she is soon to have another cousin to play with when she's older.'

'Is Mrs Skelwith to add to her husband's joys again, then?' Farraline asked unwarily.

'No, not Mathilde. I should have said second cousin, of course: Rosamund writes that she is expecting a child! Isn't that splendid news? Especially after her sad experience at Christmas — a miscarriage must be the worst thing in the world for a woman, don't you agree? I felt so sorry for the poor Duchess of Clarence back in April — and it was worse still for her, for it was twins, and her child would be heir to the throne. The poor lady must begin to fear she will never have one.'

'Yes,' Farraline said absently.

'And although she never said as much to me, Rosamund must have been worried too, for she and Marcus have been married five years this month. But it all looks well for her this time. We must pray that everything goes right.'

'Yes indeed, we must,' Farraline said. His voice was so devoid of expression that Sophie looked up at him curiously. He was staring blankly into the middle distance, a slight frown puckering his brows. She thought she must have been boring him and determined to say no more on the subject, though it was dear to her heart. The next best thing to becoming pregnant herself, in her mind, was the news that Rosamund was with child at last; but she would not wish to harp on a subject he didn't care for, so she walked on in silence.

But after a moment Farraline said, 'It is very good news indeed for your cousin. When does —' He cleared his throat and began again. 'When is the happy event to be?'

'At the end of November or the beginning of December; they are not quite sure within a week or two,' Sophie said. 'They had guessed it was so some time ago, but after the last disappointment they didn't want to say anything publicly until matters were a little further along. Well, everyone says the third and the fifth month are the dangerous ones, and she has one of those behind her already.'

'Three months!' He didn't know whether to be glad or sorry. If there were to be any hope of his ever seeing her again, it must lie in her bearing the child whose existence would tear him to the heart. Yet to think of her being three months pregnant already — and he hadn't known about it, he had known nothing! It was a bitter thing. He struggled to thrust it out of his mind so that he could continue a normal conversation with Sophie. There were a thousand things he wanted to ask her about Rosamund, but all of them were impossible.

He drew a breath, and almost at random asked, 'How is your husband's housing scheme coming along? Is there any progress yet?'

It was such an abrupt change of subject that Sophie decided she had been right in thinking that babies bored him. She answered cheerfully, 'Yes, we think there is at last. Our man of business —'

'Whetlore, isn't it?'

'Yes, of Whetlore and Cass. Jasper doesn't much like him, but he was old Mr Hobsbawn's attorney, and he is very good, and understands the business. And the news is that he has finally managed to find out who owns the piece of land where the tenements were burned down. Will you believe me, it is the Church!'

'I am not particularly surprised. It owns quite a lot of land along that part of the river.'

Sophie nodded. 'Mr Whetlore thinks there may have been an ancient foundation of some sort thereabouts — a monastery or something. At all events, it must favour our scheme, don't you think? Jasper is to see the Bishop tomorrow.'

'I don't suppose Olmondroyd will be happy about it,' Farraline said.

'No. He has a particular interest in the land because it adjoins his own. I think he would like to use it to build a bigger mill.'

'He would sooner see it used for anything other than your scheme,' Farraline said frankly.

Sophie sighed. 'I know. I wish he would get it out of his head that Jasper had anything to do with the fire. It's such a wicked delusion. We were both so pleased when we heard Mr

126

Olmondroyd was able to start rebuilding — that he hadn't been quite ruined by the fire. Jasper tried to tell him so after church one Sunday, but he wouldn't listen. In fact, he spoke so abusively that Jasper had to hurry me away. I think perhaps,' she added tentatively, 'that the shock of it all has turned his brain.'

They had reached Hobsbawn House. 'Won't you come in, Mr Farraline?' Sophie asked. Farraline hesitated, and to persuade him she added temptingly, 'Come and see Fanny. She will have woken from her nap by now, and she's always at her liveliest when she first wakes.'

'No, thank you Mrs Hobsbawn. I have so much to do — I really must get on,' he said firmly, bowed, and made his escape.

Little Fanny Hobsbawn, from what he had seen of her, was the prettiest and most delightful child he had ever come across, and he didn't think he could bear that just now.

Jasper came into the house in a fury, or as much of a fury as it was possible for such a restrained man to show.

'He won't agree! He absolutely refuses to consider the scheme.'

Sophie looked up from her sewing. 'You can't mean the Bishop?'

'I can and do. He said that the Church would not make the land available to me.'

'But why? What could his objection be?'

'He told me that they had other uses in mind for it, but when I pressed him he refused to say what they were.'

'You're sure he understood the nature of the scheme? That it was housing for the labouring poor?'

'I explained it all to him in considerable detail. I emphasised the benevolent aspect of it. I even pointed out that it would give him a large and grateful addition to his flock, and hinted that we would drive them to church like sheep if need be —'

'Oh Jasper, you didn't!' Sophie looked reproachful. 'A great many of them are Irish, you know. You couldn't make them go to an Anglican church.'

'He didn't listen anyway,' Jasper said, pacing up and down the room in his agitation. 'He just put his fingertips together and stared at the ceiling as though he were praying for patience. Patience! It's I who need it! Here's the Church, supposed to care for the poor, won't let me use the land, won't say why not, won't say what they want it for!'

Sophie put down her work. 'Perhaps they mean to rebuild the houses themselves. Perhaps that's what he meant by "other uses".'

'I don't know. I asked him directly if the Church was going to rebuild the houses, but he wouldn't answer. I told him these people are living on the site anyway, in conditions of great squalor and distress. I pointed out that to use the land for any other purpose they would have to evict them, but all he said was "No doubt that had been taken into account."' He parodied the Bishop's fluting tones.

'It's a great shame,' Sophie said feelingly.

'Shame!' Jasper plainly felt the word inadequate.

'But if that's the way it is, there's nothing to be done about it,' she went on. 'We'll just have to find some other land. After all, it doesn't matter, does it, where the houses are?'

'But what about the people living in the ruins?'

'They can live in the new houses when they're finished,' Sophie said.

Jasper shook his head. 'You don't understand. If we move one lot out, another will take their place. And with the famine and typhus in Ireland, there are thousands flocking over here, all as poor as weevils, and even the rough shelters built in the ruins are attractive to them. As long as such places exist, the poor will live in them.'

'But dearest, you can't do everything yourself,' Sophie said reasonably. 'There must be hundreds of such dreadful places all over England. You aren't responsible for them all.'

Jasper ceased his pacing and began slowly to smile at her.

'What a logical little person you are,' he said. 'I'm sorry, Sophie my love. Of course you're right. I lost my sense of proportion for a while. It's just that I had my heart set on the scheme exactly as it was. The sin of vanity, I suppose.'

'The Church is bound to move slowly,' Sophie said comfortingly, 'and it may well be that they intend to build new houses on that land, so then there'll be two lots, and that will be even better.'

128

Jasper laughed. 'Ever the optimist. Shall we have dinner soon, my darling?'

'We were only waiting for you. I expect Fenby will announce it at any moment.' As if on cue, the door opened. 'Ah, here he is!'

The butler entered, but instead of announcing dinner he coughed in an embarrassed way and said, 'I beg your pardon, madam, but there is a visitor. He insists on seeing the master immediately.'

'A visitor?' Sophie said in surprise. 'I wasn't expecting anyone — were you?'

'I *showed* him into your business room, sir,' Fenby said, but his doubtful tone suggested he wasn't sure the visitor would stay there; and even as he spoke, he was thrust ungently aside and the large, red-faced figure of Olmondroyd appeared in the doorway, glowering at them.

'I know a put-off when I hear one, and I'm not taking it, Hobsbawn, so you might as well listen to what I've got to say!' He intercepted the glance which passed between master and man, and curled his lip contemptuously. 'No use in looking to that whey-faced mealmouth to throw me out! I could make four of him; but I've no wish to make a mill in your house, and I doubt you want that either.'

Jasper nodded to the butler. 'It's all right, Fenby. I'll hear Mr Olmondroyd. You may wait until I ring for you.' Fenby backed out, looking doubtful, and Jasper hoped he'd have the sense to wait within earshot in case of trouble. He wasn't entirely sure the visitor was sober; and he felt he had never been completely rational. 'What is it you want, Olmondroyd? Put it briefly, if you will — we are about to dine.'

'Oh, I can be brief all right,' Olmondroyd said. The note of triumph was plain in his voice. 'I can be as brief as you like! You've been to see the Bishop today, Hobsbawn. Aye, I know you have! I know all about it. And I know what he said to you.'

'How can you? It was a private meeting,' Jasper said stiffly.

'Because t'was me as told him what to say. Aye, you may well look blue! But I've come to tell you one thing only: you'll never get that land, and that's all about it!'

'What do you mean? What have you got to do with it?'

129

'Everything. I warned you not to cross me! Isaiah Olmondroyd makes a bad enemy, anyone'll tell you that. I don't forget those that do me down. I've got influence you've never even thought of, and I shall use it to scuttle your plans, my fine young cockerel!'

'For God's sake, man,' Jasper cried, exasperated, 'can't you understand that the fire was nothing to do with me? I assure you —'

'Oh, you *assure* me, do you?' Olmondroyd sneered. 'Well I assure you that if I find you sniffing about my land, I shall have you taken up for trespass. And as for your crack-brained scheme, you can take it somewhere else, for you'll never have that land next to mine, I've seen to that!'

With that he turned and left them, flinging open the door and almost tripping over Fenby, who was lingering outside with his ears on stalks. Olmondroyd flung a curse at him and marched off down the stairs with the butler hopping along behind him, torn between his outrage and his training.

Jasper turned slowly to Sophie. 'I'm sorry you should have been witness to that.'

Sophie made a gesture of negation, though she was trembling with distress. 'It wasn't your fault. I really think he must be ill —'

Jasper hardly heard her. 'By God, I'd dearly love to know how he did it, though,' he muttered through clenched teeth. '"I have influence," he says. What influence could he have with the Church? What pressure did he bring to bear on the Bishop? Or what did he pay him?'

'Oh no,' Sophie said in automatic protest. 'Surely not!'

'I tell you one thing, Sophie,' Jasper declared, resuming his pacing, 'he's not going to best me on this! Going behind my back — bursting into my house — I'll show him who's master! I'll find a way to exert influence myself, and it will be a greater and better influence than his. He says I'll never have that land, and I say I will! We shall see who's the better man.'

'I know who is,' Sophie said anxiously, alarmed at his frowning brows and grim determination. 'Surely it doesn't matter where we build the houses? I don't think we should go on trying to —'

'I'll build them on that land and no other,' Jasper said.

'Don't you see, my love, I can't let him get away with that? It's a matter of principle now.'

Sophie wondered afresh what had happened to his sense of proportion. She concluded sadly that the sin of vanity he rejected earlier had transmuted into the sin of pride.

Benedict had been still for so long that every part of him was aching to move. He was lying on his front, propped by his elbows, and shielded by a thick tangle of elder bushes, right in the heart of Harewood Whin. Somewhere behind him and to his left he could hear the small sounds of the brook, a murmur like a conversation going on just too far away to make out the words. From time to time a small breeze moved the leaves at the top of the wood canopy. Otherwise, the Whin was silent.

It was not an oppressive silence, but the mild, sweet, dreaming silence of a sunny wood on a summer afternoon. The ground he lay on, though in the shade, was warm, and the smells that came to him were of grass and earth, of leaf-mould and mushrooms, of sweet woodruff and just the faintest tang of wild garlic. Before him was a natural gully, a stream in winter but now at midsummer only a damp-bottomed ditch; and where the ground rose on the other side was the beaten earth-mound and smooth-edged holes of an old badger sett.

Everything was still: it was one of those moments when even the birds are suddenly silent. Benedict carefully eased one leg and then the other. Between the leaves of the beech tree beyond the sett, the sun gleamed suddenly, throwing glittering specks of gold across the ground and in his face, and he screwed up his eyes against them. He flexed his fingers carefully, and then his shoulders. It wouldn't be long now. He settled himself again, alert and relaxed.

He had found the setts by accident two months ago while he was looking for hares. They lived on the north side of the Whin, and taking a short-cut through the dense mass of elder at the heart of the wood he had come upon this place. There was often elder near badger setts. Badgers liked to eat elderberries, and the seeds, enriched by the badgers' dung, flourished where they were dropped.

But there were no badgers here now. The sett had been deserted by them some years ago, by his guess; it was occupied by a family of foxes. Bendy came often to see them. So far he had managed to keep them a secret, using hare-watching as an excuse whenever he wanted to slip away alone. No-one on the Morland estate would ever harm a hare. Apart from the country superstition surrounding them, they were special to the Morland family, whose badge had been a hare since mediaeval times.

But foxes were a different matter: everyone's hand was against them. Poultry-maids feared for their hen-houses, and gamekeepers for their young pheasants. If anyone found out about this family, it would not be long before they came with dogs and guns a spades and destroyed them all. Bendy couldn't let that happen. They were *his*, he thought fiercely. No-one was to harm them. Fortunately no-one ever came to this part of the Whin — no-one except him.

Something was happening. A muzzle appeared, raised in the entrance hole of the main sett, testing the air. Bendy grew even stiller, his body sinking closer to the scent-disguising ground. What little breeze there was was towards him — he had made sure of that. After a moment the pointed head emerged, the golden, bright eyes gazing round, the sensitive nose still questing. It was the vixen. She walked a few steps from the hole and then sat down to scratch herself vigorously, like a dog.

The young vixen — one of last year's litter — appeared at the entrance next, but the cubs thrust past and emerged before her, trotting out and sniffing the ground and the air eagerly. They had been born in mid-March, and were now half grown and at their most playful. Bendy had learned so much about foxes since then, and had come to love them. He watched entranced as the cubs explored the world which was still so new to them, and then sat down to wash and groom each other, a process which soon turned into horseplay and sent them rolling about the bare ground opposite, locked in mock battle. The dog-fox emerged last, and after a protracted bout of scratching — he was moulting heavily and loose fur flew from his claws — he began snuffing about the ground for beetles and earthworms.

Then suddenly Bendy stiffened, and the hair rose on his scalp. Someone was behind him. A second afterwards he heard the breathing which told him it was his brother; and a second after that the foxes heard it too. Vixens and cubs shot back down into the earth, while the dog disappeared into the elder. Bendy turned in mingled fury and alarm, scrambling to his feet defensively as Nicky came thrusting through the thicket with a noise and clumsiness which must have driven away every creature in the Whin. Bendy wouldn't have minded that, if only he could have escaped notice. He wouldn't have had Nicky find him here for worlds, but there was no time to hide.

'Well, this is very nice, very nice indeed,' Nicholas said as he arrived. 'What's this, I wonder? A badger sett?' Bendy said nothing, watching his brother cautiously, trying to gauge the danger. 'You shouldn't have kept it to yourself, though,' Nicky went on with an unkind smile. 'There's good sport in badger-baiting. I'm sure there's lots in the village would like to join in.'

'No!' said Bendy before he could stop himself. Better never speak, for fear of giving something away; but the thought of men coming here with dogs and spades bent on some bloody 'sport' was more than he could bear.

'No what?' Nicky asked. 'No, you won't share them? But I'm sure I don't have to remind you that I am the eldest, and that everything on this estate belongs to me — or will do one day.'

'There aren't any badgers,' Bendy said desperately. 'They deserted the sett long ago.'

'And you've been lying here watching nothing?' Nicky said. 'You've been coming here several times a week to look at an empty sett? Oh, don't look so surprised. I've followed you before, but I've always lost you in the trees until now. I've been wondering what it was that so fascinated you about the Whin, and now I know.'

'It — it's not badgers,' Bendy said.

'What then?' Nicky insisted. 'I'll find out — I'll bring some men up here with spades if you don't tell me.'

'It's foxes,' Bendy said, his eyes urgent and appealing. 'And it isn't hunting season.'

133

'Papa will be glad to know about them all the same,' Nicky said, eyeing his brother with interest. 'Foxes are vermin, and these are too close to the house for the hunt.'

'No, please —!'

'Please?'

Bendy swallowed. 'Please don't tell. They're —'

'They're what?' Nicky said tormentingly. 'They're not yours, if that's what you were going to say.'

'They're beautiful. I love them,' Bendy blurted out foolishly.

Nicky smiled. 'Then it must be worth something to you for me to keep your little secret.'

Bendy stared at him, burning with resentment, cold with fear. 'What do you want?' he asked at last.

'I'll have to think about that. A good bit, I should think, for keeping such a big, difficult secret!' Nicky paused, toying with his victim. 'Well, to begin with, you can do that Latin exercise Father Sparrow gave me this morning. You're much better at Latin than me, and I can't be bothered with it. I've better things to do than his old ekkers.'

'He'll recognise my fist,' Bendy said doubtfully. It seemed a small enough price to pay, to do his brother's imposition to keep his foxes safe.

'Oh, I'll copy it out afterwards, once you've done it,' Nicky said. He had been thinking this out for some time. 'Then there's that knife of yours with the ivory handle — I think I'd like to have that,' he added thoughtfully.

'But Old Tom gave me that.' Old Tom, the gamekeeper in Acomb Wood, had been a special friend, and was dead now. The knife was one of Bendy's dearest treasures.

Nicky turned away as if indifferently. 'Oh well, of course, if you'd sooner I told Papa —'

'No! No, you can have it,' Bendy said hastily.

'And you'll do my Latin impot?'

'Yes. And then you'll keep it secret, about the foxes?'

'Oh yes — for the moment.' Nicky grinned at Bendy's baffled expression. 'That will do for now,' he explained, 'but I don't suppose it will keep me quiet for ever. You'll have to bear it in mind from now on, that *I know*. So you'll have to be careful in future not to upset me, won't you?' He turned and walked away, calling back over his shoulder casually, 'You can give me that knife tonight, in the nursery. And be sure to get the impot done before teatime. Father Sparrow's sure to ask for it. Don't make any mistakes in it, will you?'

The garden of Chelmsford House was the nicest thing about it, Rosamund always thought; especially now that the close heat of August was with them again. Her favourite place was at the bottom of the garden, a rather wild corner where there was a stone bench under the cherry trees. Here she could sit out of sight of the house, with the cool, dappled shade on her head and her feet deep in the long grass. It was blissful to go barefoot, here where there was no-one to see her, and dress in the simplest, loosest gown. Now that she was five months along, stays were an agony if she wore them for longer than an hour or two; but she couldn't bear anyone to see her without them.

So she spent most of her time in this tangled spot, watching the birds, eating cherries, reading novels that Moss fetched for her from the library, and trying not to think about the future. Marcus had asked her weeks ago if she wanted to go out of Town — he was everything that was considerate towards her — but she had refused. She didn't want to go down to the country because the country to her meant horses. Not to be able to ride in London was bad enough, but just endurable; not to be able to ride when surrounded by green fields *calling out* to be galloped over would be a torture. Besides, she didn't really want to see anyone, not even her mother, who was as uninterested in babies as it was possible for a woman to be.

It had been bad enough last month when Mr Brummell had returned for a brief visit to London, hoping to advance his ailing fortunes. Lucy had come up to Town to entertain him. She had given him the run of her house, and had naturally invited Rosamund and Marcus to dine with them. Rosamund had believed that nothing was yet showing, but at the first glance from Mr Brummell she knew he had noticed, and blushed scarlet. All evening she had felt huge and ungainly; and her sensibilities were not soothed by Marcus's veiled hints about his proud fatherhood, which Mr Brummell had politely affected not to understand.

One of her worst trials since the pregnancy was announced had been her sister-in-law, who was so thrilled with the idea that she could talk about nothing else. An heir to the title — a new little Chelmsford — the patter of feet and the sound of childish laughter about the gloomy old house — a darling nephew for Aunt Barbarina to spoil: this was the substance of her chatter, and threatened to drive Rosamund mad. Until she entered the fifth month she had been feeling ill most of the time, and Bab's wholehearted rejoicing had seemed to her the depths of tactlessness. But of late Bab had been otherwise occupied: Lord Ballincrea had come to London on some business or other, and had been taking her out driving or walking most days. Rosamund wondered vaguely if he had guessed the situation and was bent on rescuing her; she couldn't imagine any other reason he would seek out Bab's company.

As it turned out, it was as well that they hadn't gone down to the country for a crisis had blown up in August which would have necessitated Marcus's return: Viscount Castlereagh, who had only recently succeeded his father as Marquess of Londonderry, had committed suicide, and the Government was in turmoil.

Castlereagh had been Foreign Secretary for as long as anyone could remember, through the most difficult years of the war and the most nervous years of the peace: a uniquely respected man in the field of world diplomacy. No-one could begin to think how they would do without him. The circumstances surrounding his death were mysterious and unpleasant. It seemed a gang of blackmailers had laid a trap for him, luring him into a homosexual brothel in the company of a young man dressed as a woman. They then threatened to charge him publicly with the vice and produce the evidence, and, overworked and in failing health, Castlereagh had been unable to bear the situation. On the twelfth of August he had shut himself in his library and shot himself.

It was as odd as it was distressing, for there had never been any hint before that Castlereagh was vicious. He was a happily married man, and was very attractive to women — indeed, his friendships with Princess Lieven and Mrs Arbuthnot, though probably quite innocent, had caused Lady

Castlereagh many pangs of jealousy. Rosamund heard about the strange blackmail plot from Marcus, though his delicacy was such that she had to piece it together from his oblique references and euphemisms. It seemed that a few days before his death Castlereagh had gone to see Wellington to tell him about the threats. Wellington had told Harriett Arbuthnot, his latest flirt, who was also an intimate friend of Castlereagh's, and she had told Marcus.

Rosamund would have been happy to think that Marcus might be having an affair with Mrs Arbuthnot: it would have taken some of the guilt from her own shoulders. But Harriett Arbuthnot was a noted political hostess who had close but platonic friendships with many men, and Marcus had dropped in on her on that occasion because he was expecting to meet Canning there. No doubt the details of the Castlereagh business were discussed openly enough in *that* company, Rosamund thought, with the annoyance of one who has been shown only the tip of something inexplicable, and left to wonder about the rest.

The birds she had been watching took alarm and flew off, and turning her head she saw Marcus coming towards her across the garden.

'I thought I would find you here,' he said. 'It must be the coolest place in London.' There were beads of sweat running down his face. He stooped to kiss her.

'You smell of damp wool,' she said, wrinkling her nose. 'Like a hot, wet sheep. Men's clothes are madness in this weather.'

'I can think of more comfortable things than a starched collar and neckcloth,' he agreed, sitting down beside her.

'At least take off your coat,' she suggested, but he wouldn't. He had a code of propriety which she sometimes felt was taken to extreme.

'I shall be cool by and by,' he said. 'How are you feeling?'

'Bored.'

'You should go out more. Or have people to visit.'

'And have them see me like this? No thank you.'

'I think you look beautiful,' he said sincerely.

'Yes, I expect you do.' She didn't want him to start being sentimental with her this early in the evening. 'Tell me the

137

news. Have you seen Wellington?'

'Yes, I caught him at the club. He was with Lord Liverpool this morning. They both think that Canning must be brought in.'

'Canning? Good God, there's a turn-around! The last I heard was that he was so sure he'd never hold office again, he'd accepted governor-generalship of India.'

'That's right, only he couldn't bring himself actually to leave, and was lingering on in England for as long as he could.'

'Mother will be pleased,' Rosamund mused with a private smile.

'Yes, I've never understood your mother's attachment to him,' Marcus said. 'I wouldn't have put her down as a Canningite.'

'I dare say if she knew what Canning believes in she would be one, for she's a born free-trader. But it's nothing to do with politics. She didn't use to approve of him — thought he was "too clever" — but he bested her in an argument one day over the bloodlines of a horse. When she looked into it, she found he was right and she was wrong, so she decided she had to like him after that.'

Marcus shook his head wonderingly. 'I will never understand your mother.'

'No-one does except Parslow and Papa Danby. But tell me more about Canning. Why is he suddenly back in favour?'

'The Beau thinks, and Liverpool agrees, that they can't hold the ministry together without him. So they're going to ask him to be Foreign Secretary in Castlereagh's place —'

'They couldn't do better,' Rosamund said. 'He has a first-rate brain.'

'— and Leader of the House. That will bring in all his cronies and keep them quiet.'

'I suppose we shall see some changes, then,' Rosamund said, bending down to flick an ant off her shin. 'He's bound to —' She broke off abruptly, straightening up.

Marcus, who had been idly watching her bare toes twiddling in the grass, looked up, and saw that a strange, preoccupied expression had come over her face. 'What is it? Is something wrong?'

She didn't answer. She was staring ahead of her with an extraordinary look he couldn't define, and he grew alarmed. 'Darling, is it a pain? What's the matter?'

Still she said nothing; but after a long moment she closed her eyes and drew a shuddering sigh. Her hands had been resting on the rise of her belly, and now she lifted one to pass across her brow, though there was no moisture there. It was as if she were trying to wipe away a thought or a memory.

'It's all right,' she said at last. 'Don't worry, Marcus. It's nothing.'

Fear made him angry. 'Don't say "nothing" to me like that. Something happened. What was it? *Tell* me!'

She turned to look at him unwillingly. 'It was the baby. I felt it move.'

At first he didn't seem to understand her bald words; but then a slow joy spread across his face. She didn't want to see it. 'You call that nothing? It's a miracle! Oh my darling —!'

'It's not a miracle, it's perfectly normal. Don't *fuss* so,' she said. She saw him gathering himself to protest, and stood up. 'If you go on talking about it, I shall go indoors.'

He stood too. 'Darling, please, don't speak in that way. Why are you so angry with me? This is a wonderful moment in our lives.'

'In your life!' she said, goaded. 'It's all right for you, thinking everything's so wonderful and exciting! You don't think what it's like for me to have to go through with it. What have I got ahead of me? The agony of childbirth — and women die, Marcus! They *die*!'

He was stricken by her words; and before he could find a reply, or move to comfort her, she had turned and left him. She ran towards the house, clumsily through the grass in her bare feet, her hands cradling her belly, her head tilted down so that he knew she was crying.

In the hall the next morning as she prepared to leave the house, she was faced by Moss, small and round and determined, like a rubicund sheep-dog.

'I'll come with you, my lady. His lordship doesn't like you to go out alone.'

'His lordship needn't think he can order my every waking

moment, and nor need you,' Rosamund retorted.

Moss looked reproachful. 'Oh my lady, don't talk so. You know he only has your best interests at heart. Suppose something was to happen to you when you were out all alone?'

Rosamund softened a little. 'I know what *you* worry about. But you needn't. I'm only going to take a little air and look in the shop windows. And as for being all alone, I shall be in Bond Street surrounded by people and hackney carriages, not in the middle of the Dark Continent. If I feel unwell, I promise I'll come straight home — does that satisfy you?'

Moss was not entirely convinced. 'I don't see why I can't come with you, just the same. Who will carry your packages?'

'I don't mean to buy anything. I just want to be out on my own for a while. Come now, Moss, let me go, before my good sister-in-law hears the riot and comes and adds her pleas to yours!'

Moss softened. 'Oh, but didn't you know, my lady, Lady Barbarina went out an hour since for a drive. Lord Ballincrea called for her in a curricle.'

'How very dashing of him! I am gone, then. Give me my parasol. And don't worry, Judy, I shan't stay out long.'

She had reckoned without the heat. At first the walk was pleasant, through the garden of St James's Square, up York Street and through the leafy shade of St James's churchyard. But the traffic in Piccadilly was heavy as always, and the noise and dust, added to the glare of light from the flagway, made her begin to feel tired and nervous. When she came opposite the end of Bond Street and had to cross the road to reach it, her courage almost failed her. She felt large and awkward, very conscious of the life she was carrying inside her; and as she looked at all those dashing wheels and flashing legs between her and the other side, for the first time in her life she was afraid of falling.

A stranger stopped beside her, a middle-aged, gentle-manly-looking person in a tall hat which he was lifting politely as he offered her his arm.

'Your pardon, ma'am — if you will permit me. Such a difficult road to cross at the best of times! I hope you do not

140

think me impertinent. My own dear wife always has the greatest fear of traffic when she is in the same condition.'

He so plainly meant nothing but kindness by it that Rosamund could not take offence; and yet having her condition noticed and her helplessness underlined made her feel almost tearful. She suppressed her weak rage and allowed him to escort her across, between the rushing vehicles. On the far flagway when he doffed his hat again to enquire gently if he could be of any further service, she shook her head and thanked him meekly, and then turned away up Bond Street with a scowl between her brows and her lip stuck out rebelliously.

It was very hot, though, and the crowds jostled her unpleasantly. Dawdling about the shops was not, in any case, her favourite occupation, and she had only chosen it out of boredom and the desire to get away from Marcus's tender solicitude. It was not long before her stays began to cut into her in a most unpleasant way, her back began to ache, and her feet to feel as though they were crammed into someone else's shoes. She would have been glad to sit down, but she simply refused to go into a shop and demand a chair by virtue of her "condition". So she walked on up Bond Street growing hotter and crosser with every shop-window she stared into.

She had just passed the end of Maddox Street when someone's footman on an errand bumped into her and trod on her foot. He was a heavy man with large feet, and he trod hard, plainly so insensitive himself that he was not aware he had walked on anything but the flagway, for he hurried on without pausing or apologising. Rosamund reeled back against the wall of the nearest shop, fighting with tears of anger and pain. The other pedestrians trod past her unheeding; her foot throbbing and her back aching, Rosamund began to feel dizzy. She reached behind her and tried to get a fingerhold on the brickwork. If I faint here, she thought grimly through the pounding in her head, I'll probably be trampled to death, for none of *these* will ever notice.

And then there was someone standing before her, a dark shape blocking out the sun. There was a feeling of pressure behind her eyes and she could not see clearly. She tried to speak but her lips were dry. And then there was a strong male hand supporting her, and a familiar, welcome, teasing voice said, 'Every time I meet you you seem to have got yourself into another scrape! My dear Lady Rosamund, if you can manage *not* to swoon away for a few more moments you will find it a great deal more convenient. Breathe deeply and keep your eyes fixed on the ground. That's right: lean on me.'

Putting one foot in front of the other — he was quite right, it did help to keep looking down — occupied all her breath for the next few moments. Then they were suddenly out of the flow of pedestrians and there was more air around her, and she was able to look at him and say, 'Thank you, I am feeling better now.'

'Not better enough,' said Hawker tersely. She stumbled slightly. 'Keep walking — unless you would sooner I carried you?'

'Not at all,' Rosamund said hastily. 'Where are you taking me?'

'Never mind. You'll find out.'

Despite her plight, Rosamund felt a smile tugging at her lips. 'Are you always so dictatorial, or only with maidens in distress?'

'Only with wooden-headed little numbskulls who don't look after themselves properly,' he told her pleasantly.

Her head was clearing a little, and she saw they were coming into Hanover Square. She tugged on his arm, and he paused and looked down at her searchingly. 'I really am feeling better now,' she said. 'It was an ass of a footman stepping on my toes that overcame me for a moment.'

'Is that all?' There was a mixture of tenderness and amusement in his expression.

'It did *hurt*,' she assured him.

'What were you doing out on your own, you little fool?' he asked rhetorically, moving on again.

'Where *are* we going?'

He smiled, though not to her. 'Lady Greyshott's house. I've been staying there for the last few days. You will be able to sit down and refresh yourself.'

'Why are you staying with cousin Helena?' Rosamund asked suspiciously.

'Do you mean why am I staying with her, or why am I in London at all?'

142

'I think I can work out the latter for myself,' she said. 'Your instructions used to come directly from Castlereagh, didn't they?'

An expression of pain crossed his face. 'The world has lost a great statesman; and it could hardly have come at a more awkward time. With the Greek rebellion weakening Turkey, the Tsar toying with the idea of intervening, trouble brewing in the Spanish colonies, and the Congress of Verona only two months away —'

'At least Canning isn't an unknown quantity,' Rosamund said. 'Though I suppose there will be changes.'

'One change may be in the offing that you will approve of,' Hawker said with a faint smile. 'I understand the Duke of York intends to petition Canning for a post for your old friend Mr Brummell — consular agent or something of the sort.'

'Do you think Canning will agree? Might he not think it's early days yet for granting favours?'

'He'll do what he can for an old school friend — ah, here we are at Greyshott House. And not a moment too soon. You are looking fagged to death. No need to knock — I have the run of the house.'

The hallway was blissfully cool after the damp heat of the day outside, but even as she went in, Rosamund felt that the house was oddly quiet. It didn't seem right to her not to announce herself. Lady Greyshott was not of her generation; it was not like calling on an intimate friend who might welcome a lack of formality.

'Is no-one about?' she asked nervously as Hawker led the way towards the stairs.

'A servant or two, I dare say. Helena went down to the country this morning with Harry Twombley, and she left only the minimum of staff.'

Rosamund drew back. 'Oh, but —'

He turned to looked at her with raised eyebrows. 'My dear Lady Rosamund, what do you fear? That I have evil designs on you?'

She reddened. 'Of course not. But it might be thought —'

'Do you think I would risk your reputation? Lord Greyshott is somewhere about the house; and Lord Ballincrea has been staying here too, though I believe he is out at the

143

moment. I wouldn't have thought you needed a chaperone in your own cousin's house.'

Rosamund shrugged and let him lead her on upwards. 'I had better not stay long, however, or Moss will have the Runners out after me,' she said. 'But I would be grateful for a dish of tea before I go, if there is anyone about to make it.'

'You shall have it, and a carriage to take you home,' Hawker said, his hand on the knob of the morning-room door. 'But first —' He opened the door and stood back to usher her in. 'We have been using this as our sitting-room. More pleasant and informal than the drawing-room.'

She had walked past him as he spoke, and had not even had time to wonder about that 'we'. The room was not empty. Her eyes flew to the occupant, who was rising automatically to his feet before he realised who she was. Her senses seemed to come adrift from her body; she took a faltering step forward, stretching her hands out and heard herself make an incoherent but vaguely a interrogative sound. *Now*, she thought, *would be quite a good time to faint*. If she had been the heroine of a three-volume novel she would probably have done just that. As it was, she found herself caught as she swayed by the hands she knew best in the world, and was swept, almost carried across the room to an armchair. When her poor brain stopped reeling she found herself enthroned there with Jes on his knees beside her, his dear head pressed to her shoulder and his tears soaking through the thin sprig muslin of her gown.

Caroline Lamb used to wet her muslins to make them cling, she thought bemusedly; *I hope not with her lovers' tears*. She didn't, of course, say anything so frivolous and pointless. What she did say, as she stroked his head over and over, was, 'Jes, oh my Jes, oh my dear, oh my Jes —'

Hawker backed quietly out of the room and closed the door soundlessly behind him.

Neither of them had any idea how long he was gone. They probably didn't use the time very wisely: they both cried a little and smiled a lot, gazed at each other wonderingly, hugged, and made foolish and tender and sad little sounds, dumb in their love as any animals that have been parted

144

without understanding why. He kissed her hands and pressed them against his cheek; she touched his face with her fingertips with a reverence of love she had not felt before.

If she had had any doubt that she truly loved him, it was resolved in those moments. She saw that what she felt for him had been refined in the fire of their being separated: it was bright steel now, a sword with which to fight the world, or destroy themselves. As for his love for her, she saw it undisguised in his face, and it made her feel both humble and exalted. As he held her hands, she felt as though he were inside her and all around her, part of her that she had lost and mourned like her own soul; not complete without him; not *human*.

Only when Hawker came back to join them did they slip out of that wordless stream of fire and communicate in ordinary words again. Hawker had brought tea: wonderfully prosaic, wonderfully restoring. They both fussed over her, bringing her cup, moving a footstool, drawing the curtain a little; and she let them, and even enjoyed it. When they were settled, Hawker lounging elegantly on the sofa opposite, Jes sitting on the floor and leaning on her lap so that she could touch him whenever she needed to, which was almost all the time, then she asked, 'What are you doing here?'

'Fitz came back because Castlereagh was dead; I came to London to see Fitz,' Jes answered simply.

'Helena Greyshott is an old friend of mine, as you very well know,' Hawker added, 'and she offered me the run of her house. When I mentioned that Jes was coming to see me, she invited him too. And that's all there is to it.'

'Not quite,' Rosamund said pointedly.

Hawker looked grave. 'If you mean, did I bring you here deliberately to see him, I have to say yes. At the very first instant, when I found you fainting in the street, I thought only of shelter for you. It crossed my mind to take you to your mother's house to rest; but at the second glance I saw how truly miserable you were, how drawn and uncomfortable, and there was no more doubt in my mind.' He looked at the couple opposite, their hands intertwined as though that was all that kept them from plunging into oblivion, and he said, 'I have done you a grave disservice, Rosamund. I have to

145

apologise for that, though apology must be meaningless in the face of the harm I think I have done you.'

He had always called her, teasingly, Lady Rosamund — because she had once said she didn't like to be called Lady Chelmsford — and now his use of her forename *tout court* startled her, sharpened her attention.

'No,' she began foolishly, and then stopped because she didn't yet understand him.

'Yes,' he countered. 'I interfered where I had no right — gave advice where I had no expertise — harried you where I had no understanding. In my defence I can only say that I had always believed your attachment to Jes was lighthearted, and the result of discontent rather than a serious preference. I thought absence would wear it away — and on your side too, Jes. But I have seen how wrong I was. I never meant to make you miserable. I beg you to forgive me.'

Rosamund was too shocked to speak at once. She felt Jes tighten his fingers around hers, giving her strength; and at the same moment she felt the baby move inside her, and it was a good feeling, not alien, but part of what she was, and what they were. He had not referred to it by look or word since she had entered that room, but she knew it was not because he had not thought about it, nor — miraculously — because he hated or rejected it. Simply, it was part of her, and he loved her, therefore he loved it, too.

So when she spoke to Hawker, it was in an unexpectedly strong voice. 'There's nothing to forgive you for. You haven't harmed me. You didn't make me do anything, or even persuade me. What I did I chose for myself, because I thought it was right.'

'But if I'd realised how much you love each other —' Hawker began.

Farraline answered, 'It wouldn't have made any difference. She would have thought of it for herself; she would still have done it.' He looked at her. 'And I think you were right. It has been a living hell being without you, but now I've seen you, I know it's right. Afterwards, we can be together without regret or guilt. Nothing will come between us.'

She pressed his hand in assent, and said to Hawker, 'I'm glad you brought me here. I know it means I have broken my

146

promise to Marcus, but I needed so much to see Jes.' To Jes, 'That's what was wrong with the arrangement. I needed to know you consented; that you would wait for me. Now I know, I can go through with it calmly. And afterwards —'

Farraline didn't speak; but he thought that probably Marcus had made his rules for that very reason.

She refused the carriage home. Someone might see her getting out of it, she thought; and she would prefer to walk.

'If you find yourself getting tired, you will take a hackney?' Farraline asked her anxiously.

'Yes; don't worry. But it's only a step — less than a mile. I shall walk slowly and do very well.'

They both walked with her as far as Conduit Street; parting was hard, but they spoke calmly, hiding what they felt, each for the sake of the other.

'You'll send for me as soon as the time comes?' Farraline said.

'Yes, the very first moment.' She turned to Hawker. 'Thank you. You have been a friend to me.' She touched his hand, held Farraline's for a moment, and then turned away. She didn't look back. She knew the pretence of calmness would not survive that.

It lasted almost all the way home. By the time she reached Chelmsford House, she was beginning to feel footsore and weary, and with the weariness came sorrow and longing for Jes. But it would not be long now. Only a few more months to endure.

Beason came out of the shadows like a spider as she entered the hall. 'His lordship is in the blue saloon, my lady,' he intoned, taking her umbrella and gloves with an air of handling them with the tips of his fingers. She mounted the stairs slowly, anticipating a chiding for going out alone, preparing to face his solicitude and smothering affection. The first sight of him woke her from that dream as though she had been dipped in icy water.

'Where have you been? And don't tell me you've been shopping — I heard *that* from Moss!'

Barbarina was in the room too. Rosamund glanced at her with surprise. She was pale, her eyes pink as though she'd been crying. She avoided Rosamund's eye, twisting her hands together as though they were trying to escape the coming confrontation.

Rosamund turned her gaze calmly back to Marcus. 'I felt faint in Bond Street,' she said. 'I went to sit down for a while in Cousin Helena's house.'

'Is that all you have to say to me?' Marcus's voice was soft and deadly. 'I suppose you were all alone there? Helena is not in Town — or didn't you know that?'

'I didn't know it then. I know it now.'

'I'm sure you do. You didn't know Ballincrea was staying there either, did you?'

'Yes, I —' At the mention of his name, Rosamund remembered what Moss had said as she left, that Bab had gone driving with Ballincrea. The connection was made at last in her mind: Ballincrea had taken Barbarina back to the house for some reason. She had been seen.

'You've been seen, my fine lady,' Marcus said, and there was hatred in his eyes. 'Bab was driven into the square just as you were walking off down George Street with your two gallants! Caught fair and square!'

'No, Marcus —' Rosamund began, but he crossed the room in two strides and caught her by the throat. Bab let out a squeak of alarm, but Rosamund made no sound.

'Oh you slut!' he cried, and his voice broke hoarsely on the hateful word. 'Oh you miserable liar! You couldn't keep yourself pure for a few paltry months! You broke your word to me!'

His hands were tightening, but she managed to gasp out a few words, holding his eye with a terrible calm above his throttling fingers. 'No. It wasn't — as you think. I didn't — know he was there. We spoke — a little — nothing more. I swear —!'

She shouldn't have said that. He made a terrible noise, like a sob, and his fingers closed convulsively, shaking her. Her words were cut off with a gurgling sound.

'No Marcus, stop it! Stop it!' Bab flew at him, pounded him punily, clawed at his hands. 'You're killing her! Stop it I say!'

He let go suddenly, and Rosamund collapsed to the floor,

148

retching for breath. Bab flung herself down beside her.

'You're right,' he said, 'I mustn't kill her. That would be too easy. I want her to live and know the suffering I've felt. I want her to live and know her lover is dead.'

He turned away. Bab half rose, torn between the two emergencies. 'What are you going to do? Marcus, don't go!' She stood and caught at him, but too late. 'Don't do anything foolish! Marcus, *wait* !'

He was gone, slamming the door behind him. Bab wavered, her hands fluttering futilely, taking a step or two towards the door, and then returning to Rosamund, still crouched on the floor, who was now being sick.

CHAPTER EIGHT

It was chance alone which determined that Marcus found Hawker and not Farraline. The two men had gone back to the house after parting from Rosamund, but at the door Farraline halted.

'I need to be alone for a while,' he said. 'I think I'll just walk around, while I settle my thoughts. You don't mind?'

'Not at all. I understand,' said Hawker. 'Will you still dine with me tonight?'

'Yes, of course. Shall we meet here later?'

'At about eight,' Hawker said. 'We'll change and go to Fouberts, shall we?'

They parted and Farraline walked off in one direction while Hawker entered the house to change his neckcloth before going off to visit Mrs Arbuthnot. Thus when Marcus called, no-one was able to tell him where Farraline was; but since his air was agitated, Hawker's manservant, who was passing through the hall at the time, thought the matter might be urgent and respectfully suggested Mr Farraline might have gone with Mr Hawker to Mrs Arbuthnot's and that Lord Chelmsford might try there.

When Marcus reached Harriett Arbuthnot's Hawker had already left. He was told that no, Farraline had not been with him, but that Hawker had said he was going on to his club: Chelmsford might find him there.

Thus by the time Marcus ran Hawker to earth at Brooks's his temper had been long simmering and was ready to boil over. The club was unusually full for that time of year, largely because Castlereagh's suicide had roused Whig hopes that the government might fall, and a great many gentlemen whose interests were political had come back up to Town. Hawker was in the smoking-room talking with a group of his acquaintances. Whatever his emotions on seeing Marcus, he concealed them behind an air of pleasant normality.

'Hullo Chelmsford! Come to see the fun? What are you doing in this nest of Whigs? You're a White's man by rights, aren't you?'

'I came looking for you,' Marcus said, managing just to sound polite. 'Will you oblige me by telling me where I can find your friend Farraline?'

Hawker's steady gaze did not waver, but Marcus could not miss the swift glances exchanged by others of his group, and it infuriated him further. So it was common knowledge, was it? He wondered bitterly whom he could thank for making his private business public.

Hawker viewed Marcus's tense face and flaring nostrils with exasperation. When a married man comes seething with barely suppressed rage and demanding in a trembling voice the whereabouts of a handsome bachelor, any witness might well write the rest of the story for himself. He answered in a light, casual tone, hoping Marcus would take the hint and modify his own manner. 'I'm afraid I have no idea where he is at present. Won't you —'

'Don't prevaricate with me, if you please!' Marcus interrupted, only just in control. 'I am quite sure you know where he is — and what I want to see him about!'

The other members of the group now looked away in embarrassment, and began politely talking amongst themselves, hoping to shut out the sound of whatever was to come. Marcus viewed their tact with fury, convinced that it proved everyone in London knew by now how he had been cuckolded. Hawker stepped forward, trying to guide Marcus away from them.

'I assure you, I am not prevaricating. I really don't know where he is. But perhaps I can help you in some way. Won't you step aside with me, and continue this conversation somewhere a little more private?'

'It is your friend I have business with, not you!'

Hawker risked taking his arm. 'Please — let me persuade you —'

Marcus shook him off, but Hawker fixed him with a determined eye and gestured towards the door, and after a moment's hesitation, Marcus obeyed. Drawing a breath of relief, Hawker ushered him to the library, which as he expected was deserted at that time of day. Facing Marcus, Hawker said steadily, 'I think you had better tell me what has happened.'

Marcus narrowed his eyes. 'Don't pretend you don't know! You were with Farraline today when he was seen in company with my wife, coming out of Greyshott House — where I happen to know you are staying.'

'I assure you, you are quite mistaken if you think anything happened today which —'

'What happened today is none of your business,' Marcus interrupted. 'It is between me and Farraline, and I mean to seek him out and have satisfaction of him. If you will not tell me where he is —'

'At this moment, I truly do not know. But you must not call him out! I beg you to listen to me, Chelmsford — you are mistaken about this whole business!'

'You would naturally defend him,' Marcus said with a curl of the lip. 'It is to his credit, I suppose, that he can command the loyalty of a friend.'

'I do not defend him,' Hawker said quietly. 'I tell you that your business is with me, not with him.'

That stopped Marcus in his tracks. He whitened, and stared at Hawker in desperation to understand what had been said, but was unable to frame the question.

Into the silence, Hawker spoke. 'Farraline made no attempt to see Lady Chelmsford, and meant to make none. He came to London only to see me. And I need hardly tell you that her ladyship likewise did not attempt to contact him. Indeed, I believe she did not know he was in Town.'

Still Marcus stared, his senses straining to understand. 'What can you mean? What are you saying?'

Hawker's hands down at his sides clenched into fists, not in aggression, but in an unconscious reaction to the presence of danger. In the same way during a battle he might have waited for the first salvo from the approaching enemy infantry.

152

'I met Lady Chelmsford by chance in Bond Street,' he said. 'She was fainting from the heat. I took her back to Greyshott House to rest.'

'Knowing Farraline was there?'

'Yes.'

The next question was more difficult. 'Knowing what they are to each other?'

'Yes.'

'In God's name, man, *why*?' Marcus cried in anguish. 'She had promised me not to see him, and I believed she was keeping her promise.'

Hawker looked at him despairingly. He knew Marcus very well, well enough to know that he would not understand the reason, that it would not be possible to explain it to him in any way that would make sense to him.

'I acted in what I thought was everyone's best interest. I believed that the separation from Farraline was making her ill and that —'

Marcus shook his head in despair. 'No. That was not why she fainted. Oh God, why did you interfere? It was not *that* making her ill: she is increasing!'

'I know,' said Hawker softly.

'You know?' The anger was rising again. Hawker saw it with relief: it was better than the pain. 'But why did you interfere? Why? Because Farraline is your friend?'

'Because I felt responsible. Because it was I who persuaded her in the first place to give you an heir.'

He saw the words go home like knives. The silence was like an act of violence. Slowly Marcus worked it out for himself. 'That dinner party a year ago at the Greyshotts'. You were there. And it was after that that she —' He shook his head. 'You persuaded her? *You*?' Hawker said nothing; stood almost to attention, waiting for the shot. 'Dear God, man, did you think I needed your help to manage my own marriage? Perhaps you offered to perform the office for me? Am I so much of a jest to you?'

Still Hawker said nothing. What was there to say? Suddenly Marcus roared. 'By Christ, I will have satisfaction for this! I will show you what mark of man you have insulted!'

'No,' said Hawker. 'I won't meet you.'

153

Marcus struck him; an open-handed blow across the cheek. It caught Hawker off-balance, and he staggered one step before recovering. 'You coward! Name your friend!'

'I won't fight you,' Hawker said desperately.

Marcus boiled over with fury. 'I say you will! You have insulted me, and you will give me satisfaction, or I shall brand you a skulking coward in every club and drawing-room in the country!'

'I won't —'

Marcus struck him again, and this time Hawker's eyes flashed for an instant before he controlled himself. But Marcus had seen that flash. He said triumphantly, 'Name your friend, or I will pursue you everywhere you go, Hawker. I will strike you in front of every company you seek.'

Hawker deliberately unclenched his hands. 'Very well,' he said at last. 'I will meet you.'

'Tomorrow morning,' Marcus said. 'I will send someone to Greyshott House this evening.' With that he turned and left.

Hawker stood a moment in thought. His face was stinging from the blows. Then he lifted his hand slowly and held it out in front of him. 'Steady as a rock,' he said aloud. The observation didn't seem to give him much pleasure.

'For God's sake, you can't do it!' Farraline cried. He had been sitting since they parted in the Hanover Square garden, only yards from the house. If Marcus had known that . . . 'He has no quarrel with you.'

Hawker shrugged. 'He thinks so.'

'But you have none with him.'

Hawker tenderly fingered his cheek. 'He has made one,' he said coolly.

Farraline was red with anger. 'If you think you can protect me from the consequences of my own acts, than I have to tell you that I am man enough to meet my own challenges. What the deuce —'

Hawker interrupted wearily. 'Not you as well. Please, Jes, don't thrust any more outraged manhood on me.'

'But —'

'Chelmsford had accepted your affair with his wife. If he had been going to call you out, he would have done so two

154

years ago. Credit him with a little consistency.'

'But — then, why?'

'That is between him and me,' Hawker said. 'He finds sufficient reason for which to require satisfaction.'

Farraline lifted his hands in desperate appeal. 'Please, Fitz! You can't have considered —!'

Hawker smiled tautly. 'Oh, don't worry! I shan't kill him. I intend to delope.'

Farraline stared as the full implications came home to him. 'But he might kill *you*!'

'I don't think so.'

'I don't know what kind of a shot he is, but he's a soldier, and at that distance —'

'Yes, I know. But when he sees that I mean to fire into the air, he will be content with drawing a little blood for his honour's sake.'

'You mean to stand there and let him shoot at you?' Farraline shook his head. 'By God, you're a cold devil! Why, Fitz?'

Hawker met his eyes steadily for a moment, and then turned away. 'Like Chelmsford, I find sufficient reason,' he said quietly. He walked over to the side table and poured a measure of brandy into a glass. Farraline watched him, baffled and suspicious. He still had an idea that Hawker was attempting to protect him from Marcus. Or could it be — horrible thought — that he meant to kill Marcus in order to free Rosamund to marry him? No, that was nonsense of course. And yet — how to account for it?

'You will let me act for you?' Farraline said at last.

Hawker turned from his slow sipping and grinned at his friend, looking for a moment like his old self. 'Now you have reached the dizzy heights of absurdity! I have no wish to insult the poor man further by presenting his cuckold as my second. Now do oblige me, old fellow,' he went on quickly as Farraline opened his mouth to protest, 'by dropping the subject for the moment. I would like to make a good dinner tonight, and I don't wish to spoil it with rancid thoughts.'

Hawker was no in the mood for Foubert's, so they dined at home. When they returned to the morning-room they found Ballincrea waiting for them.

'Hawker, this is the deuce of a business,' he said gravely.

Hawker headed for the side table. 'Brandy, I think. Jes, you'll join me. Ballincrea?'

'No, thank you. Look here, is there nothing that can be done?'

'I should be willing to give up the fight on almost any terms,' Hawker said lightly, 'but I don't think Chelmsford will be satisfied without my blood. However, if you would care to try, I should be happy to name you my friend. If anyone could persuade him, I suppose it would be you.'

But Ballincrea shook his head. 'Marcus has already asked me to act for him. Little as I like it, I could not refuse.'

Hawker smiled faintly. 'Yes, you're courting his sister, aren't you?'

Ballincrea looked embarrassed. 'That was the most unlucky thing! I tried to distract her attention, but once she'd seen you, I couldn't ask her not to tell Marcus without telling her why. I could only trust that she would find it of too little interest to mention. She hadn't the slightest suspicion, of course, that there was anything to hide. She is,' his tone softened, 'the most innocent of creatures.'

'Hanged for a sheep, by a lamb,' Hawker murmured. 'Ah well! I suppose you have tried to talk him out of it?'

Ballincrea nodded gravely. 'I have. He won't be moved.'

'Oh God, can nothing be done?' Farraline cried out.

'I'm afraid not,' Ballincrea said. He looked at him with pity: *I would not be in your shoes for all the world.* 'I have come to settle the details with your second, Hawker. Have you anyone in mind?'

Hawker shrugged. 'It hardly matters, except that it cannot be Jes, of course.'

'Is Greyshott in the house? Perhaps he will act for you.'

Again the faint smile. 'There would be a certain pleasing irony in that,' Hawker mused. 'Certainly there cannot be a man less likely to be surprised by the whole business.'

Rosamund came to Marcus's room while he was dressing himself.

'How did you know I was up?' he asked her. 'I haven't even called my man.'

'I asked the housemaid who does your fire to call me as soon as you stirred. Marcus, I've come to ask you — *beg you* — not to do this. There's no reason for it. Mr Hawker has been a friend to us both. He's done nothing that you need to meet him for.'

'That's for me to decide,' Marcus said coldly. 'I wouldn't expect a female to understand matters of honour.'

'It's murder, then, plain and simple.'

'So solicitous for his life, madam?'

Rosamund made an impatient gesture. 'Oh, don't be so pompous! Of course I don't want you to kill him! You know perfectly well that there is nothing between me and Mr Hawker, and never has been. He's practically a relation; and he has always been very fond of you.'

'You don't know the facts. Why should you?' Marcus said, turning away to face the looking-glass as he tied his neck-cloth. 'This is not woman's business.'

Rosamund's face, dead white under the crown of dark red hair, swam like a drowned thing in the shadowed reflection behind him. 'It's *my* business,' she said quietly. 'Suppose he kills you?'

'Do you pretend that you would care?'

'Oh Marcus!' she said painfully. 'How did we get to this? I do care for you, of course I do! If I did not, do you think that any consideration in the world would make me bear your child?' She saw something quiver in his face, and pressed the advantage. 'If you won't give it up for me, at least think of the child.'

'I did think of it,' he said. His hands fumbled a little at his neck and he took a long breath to steady them and began again. 'I do think of it. That is precisely why I have to expunge the insult.'

A new thought crossed Rosamund's mind. 'You don't mean — you don't think —? The child is yours, Marcus! You must believe that!'

He turned to face her, and many thoughts passed through his mind. He thought how beautiful she was, the candlelight just touching the edges of her hair to gold, her face below a chiaroscuro hardly differentiated from the shadows behind it, as though she had been smudged in softly by a loving artist's

157

thumb. He thought of the terrifying joy of making love to her; he thought of the agony of discovering she had taken a lover. She had been too much in love to resist the dishonour of Farraline's arms; and yet too honourable to break her promise not to see him.

He thought of the child growing sweetly in the cradle of her bones, moving softly like a sea-anemone in the tides of her blood, and he loved it consumingly. He had no doubt that it was his child — their child. Yet its innocence was a sword which he might turn on himself if he did not protect it to the very limits of his power. And when he thought of Hawker, grinning devil Hawker with his insinuating ways, touching where he had no right and besmirching where he touched; thought of him proposing the bargain to Rosamund, a life for a life; thought that through Hawker's meddling he might have his child only to lose its mother; then he knew he must kill or die himself.

And all those things passed through his mind in the fraction of a second as Rosamund gazed urgently at him, waiting for his answer; and he had no words to explain it to her, any of it.

He said, 'Yes, I believe it. But it doesn't matter now. You must go back to your room — leave me. I need to be alone.'

The dark streets were almost deserted as the coach rattled its way north towards Primrose Hill. Sunrise would be at a quarter to five; by five o'clock, Marcus thought, I may be dead. The morning was chilly, with a slight mist over the open fields, and he was glad of Ballincrea's warm bulk beside him. He was even more grateful for the tact by which he kept silent. There seemed nothing to say and nothing to think. From the moment he had struck Hawker's face, the rest was as inevitable as the ride in the hangman's cart.

The appointed field at last. Another coach stood there, its lamps glowing yellow in the greyness of before-dawn; beyond it a hackney in which his own surgeon had come. As Marcus stepped out onto the cold grass, he heard one of the horses sneeze, and the clink of the bit as it rubbed its nose against its knee. Small, homely sounds: he realised suddenly that he loved his life, that he didn't want to die.

'There they are,' Ballincrea said softly.

A group of figures at a little distance, shadows in the growing light: the figure standing a little apart must be Hawker; the others were Greyshott and the two surgeons. He and Ballincrea walked towards them. The grass was white with dew, and Marcus made dark tracks in it. To the west the sky was still night, but to the east, even as he looked, a faint streak of pearl appeared. Dawn was coming, perhaps the last he would ever see. He longed for the sun with a clear fervour, as though he had never really appreciated it before.

Greyshott stepped forward, looking pinched with cold and older than his years. 'Well, Ballincrea,' he said, 'this is the last chance to resolve the matter. Does your principal intend to go on with this bloody business? Can there be no other form of restitution?'

Marcus felt rather than saw Ballincrea glance at him. His own eyes were fixed rigidly on the horizon. The dawn was coming in grey and blank, the sky veiled with cloud: there would be no sun.

'My principal will have satisfaction,' said Ballincrea.

'Then we'd better get on with it,' Greyshott said, and the tone of his voice said plainly what folly he thought it all. 'It seems level enough here. Will this serve? Very well. Doctor Vincent has the pistols.'

The butt felt cold in Marcus's hand as he took his weapon. He saw Hawker's hand close round the other, and looked up for a moment. Hawker met his gaze, but his face was blank, without recognition or expression, as though he were alone in this field and lost in his own thoughts.

Ballincrea took command, speaking quietly but briskly. 'Will you stand here, gentlemen? Chelmsford — Hawker. Just so. Now I shall count out the paces, and at the end of them I shall say "Turn, aim, fire", with those intervals. At the word "fire" you may fire as you please. Is that understood?'

Hawker said, 'Yes.'

Marcus licked his lips. 'Understood,' he said.

'Then we begin. One —'

Marcus had to force his legs to move for the first step, but once set in motion they seemed to march him effortlessly towards death, making nothing of the tussocky

159

grass, never faltering or stumbling. He tried to concentrate on the thought of Hawker, tried to feel hatred or even indignation, but he was walking towards a distant wood, and the edges of the trees framed against the lightening sky seemed astonishingly beautiful. He did not want to leave the world which he loved; but there was nothing now but the steadiness of hand and eye and the vagaries of a pistol between him and darkness.

'— turn,' said Ballincrea.

Marcus turned, a cold pain of fear gripping his heart just for an instant as he saw his enemy turn also to face him, a distance of cold dewy grass away. Not devil Hawker, but just a blank figure now, as featureless as the enemy soldier who presents himself for your shot, a thing of no personality and no importance.

'— aim —'

The pistol seemed to raise itself. He took it up too far in order to come down onto the target, as he had been taught since boyhood. He saw Hawker raise his own pistol, turning himself a little sideways as he did to present a smaller target. Marcus levelled the muzzle at Hawker's chest; but Hawker went on aiming upwards to the sky.

— 'fire!'

There was a fraction of a second of silence as Marcus absorbed the significance of Hawker's stance: he meant to receive fire unreturned — to delope. Then Marcus's pistol went off. He had no awareness of having pulled the trigger; he had not even accounted to himself for Hawker's action. His last thought was merely one of surprise as he heard the sound and almost simultaneously saw Hawker begin to crumple.

And then there was a second explosion, and a white blaze of agony streaked across his lower body like a meteor, searing his belly, groin and thigh. He doubled over, and then felt the cold grass under his cheek, so he knew he had fallen. *Shot*? he thought; but the agony was surging in tides of fire and blackness. He could hear screaming, thin and high like an animal in pain, but he had no idea who it was.

'We must get them to shelter at once,' said Tilvern, Hawker's surgeon. 'The farm's nearest — just beyond that hedge.'

Vincent demurred. 'Not both under the same roof.'

'For God's sake, man,' Tilvern cried, exasperated, 'shots have been exchanged. Honour is satisfied. Do you want your man to die?'

'Is Hawker alive?' Ballincrea asked. He felt dazed. He had known that Hawker meant to delope. He had hoped — assumed — that Marcus would be satisfied with wounding; but his shot had taken Hawker full in the chest, and in falling Hawker had somehow discharged his own weapon. Was it intentional, in anger that Marcus had aimed to kill after all, or simply the convulsion of agony tightening his finger on the trigger? Whichever it was, Hawker was lying as still as a stone on the grass, while Marcus whimpered with pain.

'He's still breathing,' Tilvern said, his fingers under Hawker's jaw, feeling the pulse.

Vincent, crouched over Marcus, lifted a haggard face. His hands were wet with blood. 'The ball missed the artery, God knows how, but his lordship will bleed to death unless I can get him somewhere where I can work on him.'

Ballincrea looked across the field, and saw the thread of smoke rising from the distant farmhouse.

'Chalk Farm, then,' he said. Even as he spoke he saw figures appear at the gate — the inmates presumably alerted by the sound of shots. It would not have been the first time, he thought grimly, that they had witnessed such bloody acts of gentlemanly folly. He waved to them, a wide, beckoning movement. 'Hi! Halloo! We need help!'

Farraline, forbidden to attend the bloody meeting, had taken a while to find where they had gone. Primrose Hill was the nearest likely ground, but it was all open farmland thereabouts, and there were many fields which might have done. A trampled space, wheelmarks and dung, and a group of labourers gawping at the blood on the grass told him he had found the right place, and a terse question or two elicited the information that both gentlemen had been carried to the farmhouse.

Greyshott met him at the door. 'Oh, it's you. Thank God — I thought it might be the magistrate. How long we can

161

'keep this secret I don't know, but the longer the better.'

'What happened? Are they —? I was told they were both carried here.'

'Yes. They're both still alive, but —' He shook his head. 'Hawker's struck in the chest. The doctor says he can do nothing for him. Chelmsford took a ball in the thigh. Tore his belly open. Both surgeons are trying to sew him together now.'

'Chelmsford struck?' Farraline said in bewilderment. 'But — but Fitz meant to delope. He said so.'

'He fired as he fell — probably accidentally. I don't suppose we shall ever know.' Greyshott made a face. 'It's a damn' bad business. Young fools, all this talk of honour and where has it got them? A grave tomorrow for one, and a trial for murder for the other — if he survives to face it. I've been called out half a dozen times in my life and refused every time, and no-one shuns me. Shooting holes in each other at dawn doesn't make you gentlemen.'

Behind the growling Farraline read a genuine concern, and so refrained from uttering the retort he first thought of. 'Can I see him — Fitz, I mean?'

Lord Ballincrea was sitting with Hawker, who seemed to be unconscious. Farraline was struck at once by the waxy whiteness of his face. He had seen it before, in battles, and any hope he had come in with quietly died.

'Has he spoken?' Greyshott asked.

'No.' Ballincrea yielded his place to Farraline. 'Any news of Chelmsford?'

'No. The sawbones are still with him.' He grimaced. 'He won't be fleeing the country, that's for sure.'

'Someone will have to tell his wife — and his sister.'

'You're the best candidate for that, Maurice,' Greyshott said with unaccustomed gentleness. 'Little though I like burdening you with the office.'

Ballincrea nodded. 'I suppose so. Though they must have guessed by now that all is not well. As soon as I have some news from Vincent, I'll go.'

Farraline had been sitting by Hawker, holding his hand and stroking it almost unconsciously. Perhaps the action aroused him from his stupor, or perhaps it was the sound of the voices;

162

at all events, his eyelids fluttered and opened, and he stared upwards in an unfocused but seeking way.

'Who's there?' he whispered.

'Fitz?' said Farraline gently. 'Can you hear me? It's me, Jes.'

'Jes,' he said. A long pause. 'It's dark. How long have I been here?'

'It's not dark, old chap. Can't you see me?'

There was no answer. The eyes wandered. Then the hand Farraline held tightened. 'Marcus?'

'He's alive,' Farraline said. He wanted to add more, but was finding it hard to speak. They had been friends a long, long time.

Hawker moved his head on the pillow, frowning with pain. 'Witness,' he whispered.

Farraline didn't understand. 'What is it, old man? What do you want?'

'You — witness. Not — his fault.'

Ballincrea came nearer. 'I think he wants to make a statement exonerating Chelmsford.' He took Hawker's other hand and pressed it. 'It's Ballincrea here, Hawker; and Greyshott is in the room. We will bear witness to anything you want to say.'

Hawker turned his head towards him, and then back to Farraline. 'Not his — fault. All mine. Acquit him. Write — down. *I — did not — name — my assailant.*'

'Yes,' said Farraline. 'I understand.'

And Ballincrea added gently, 'It shall be done as you say. Be easy.'

Hawker sighed a little as though with relief, and closed his eyes. Farraline watched him bitterly, thinking of the long years of friendship, all thrown away on a whim. If anyone had to meet Marcus, why should it not have been him instead of Hawker? There was no sense in it. At last he could hold it in no longer. He said, 'Why did you do it? Why?'

Hawker opened his eyes again, and stared sightlessly at the ceiling. Farraline thought he had not heard the question, but after a moment he said in the thread of a whisper, 'Debt — paid.'

And then he smiled: a strange, grim smile which did not

163

end, only faded imperceptibly like the light seeping out of a twilight sky.

Ballincrea faced the two women in the blue saloon with the courage of a soldier. He would sooner have faced enemy fire, but it was not his way to shirk a duty, however unpleasant.

'He is alive, but gravely wounded. Doctor Vincent has patched him up sufficiently to move him. They're bringing him home now, but I came on ahead — they have to move slowly, not to jolt him too much.'

They were both white but still in control. Barbarina had her knuckles in her mouth, perhaps to stop herself screaming, so it was Rosamund who spoke.

'Will he live?'

The bald question made Barbarina gasp; but she bit down on her fist again, and Ballincrea's heart went out to her, for her determination to be brave.

'It's possible. That's all that can be said at the moment. Vincent operated on him at the farm to remove the ball from his thigh and sew up the wound, but —'

'His thigh? He was wounded in the leg?' Rosamund said. Her voice had lifted with relief. She probably knew more about shot wounds, Ballincrea reflected, than he did, and knew all the odds: a ball lodged in the dense muscle of the thigh was survivable. He hated to disabuse her.

'The inner thigh. The ball tore across his groin and lower abdomen —'

Barbarina let out a dreadful cry, sank into a chair with her hands over her face. Rosamund stared ahead of her like a soldier, her face working with pain. 'How — how much damage?' she managed to ask at last.

'I don't know. Vincent will have to tell you that when he comes. But he lost a great deal of blood.'

Rosamund nodded, unable to speak. Loss of blood, shock, and above all mortification — these were the hovering fates which might — probably would — carry him off.

Ballincrea, remembering the child she was carrying, said, 'Won't you sit down? It will be better —'

Rosamund shook her head. She could think better standing up; and she needed to think. 'What of Mr Hawker?'

'He died about half an hour later. There was nothing that could have been done. But he did regain consciousness for long enough to speak, and — this is important. I must implore both of you to listen to what I have to say.'

Rosamund looked towards her weeping sister-in-law and said sharply, 'Bab, stop crying and pay attention. This is important.'

Ballincrea winced at her roughness, but Bab's sobbing did check for a moment, and she lifted a sodden face from her hands. 'You know, don't you,' he said, addressing Barbarina rather than Rosamund, 'that duelling is against the law, and that if one gentleman challenges another and kills him, it is considered to be murder, and he must stand his trial. If Marcus had not been wounded, he would probably have to flee the country. As it is —'

'Don't ask me to be grateful on that account,' Bab cried passionately. 'Don't ask it!'

'Hush, love. Listen,' said Rosamund.

'I was with Hawker when he regained consciousness. So were two other gentlemen. He asked us to bear witness that he did not know his assailant.'

'What? But —'

'Hush, Bab,' Rosamund said again. 'Go on, sir.'

'If anyone asks you, you must simply say that you know nothing of this matter.'

'But that would be a lie,' Rosamund said doubtfully.

'Not so. You have no knowledge *of yourself* as to what happened, since you were not there. You are perfectly entitled not to speculate — indeed, you are bound in justice not to do so. Hawker's dying testimony must be accepted, and if there is no-one else to accuse Marcus, he cannot be indicted. So you must both be very brave, speak to no-one about this, make sure your servants do not gossip, and above all, answer no questions.'

'I understand,' Rosamund said. 'Bab?'

Barbarina nodded tearfully. Ballincrea was longing to take her in his arms and comfort her, but all he could do with propriety was to give her his handkerchief, which was more serviceable than her own. Seeing that she was weeping more quietly now, Rosamund nodded to Ballincrea to step aside with her for a private word.

'You are a good friend, sir,' she said feelingly. 'You have been placed in a terrible position —'

'No need for that,' he said briskly. 'What is it you want to know?'

'Was Mr Farraline there?'

'He did not witness the duel. He arrived in time to speak to Hawker. He was one of the witnesses I mentioned.'

'And now?'

Ballincrea looked at her with a terrible pity. 'He is bound to be questioned if he remains in London. He is — was — Hawker's closest friend. I advised him to leave London immediately, and he agreed. I'm sorry, but it was for the best.'

She nodded. Her promise to Marcus still stood, in any case, though Ballincrea knew nothing of that. Would Jes remember it? She wished she knew how he was feeling. Did he blame her for Hawker's death? Did he blame himself?

'Tell me truly, do you think Marcus will survive?' she asked at length.

Ballincrea hesitated, thinking of the child. 'I'm not a doctor,' he said at last.

She took that to mean no; but given what she already knew of his wound, she expected it.

'He will have the best nurse, at any rate,' Ballincrea said kindly. Then, 'I'll wait below, to be on hand when they arrive. I think you had better look to Lady Barbarina.'

He left them alone, and Rosamund turned back to Bab, thinking less of comforting her than shaking her out of her hysterics, for there were things to be done, orders to be given for the preparation of a room and medical supplies. Bab had stopped weeping, and as Rosamund approached she looked up, red-eyed and swollen-faced, from Ballincrea's handkerchief.

'I hope you're satisfied now!' she said fiercely. 'When you see your handiwork, I hope it makes you sick!'

'What are you talking about?' Rosamund said wearily.

'Come, there's no time for this. We've work to do.'

'I should have let him kill you!' Barbarina hissed. 'Why did I stop him? If you were dead, he'd still be alive.'

'He *is* alive; and we have things to prepare —'

'You've killed him! You never loved him, and now you've killed him, you evil, wicked woman! I hate you!'

Rosamund looked at her with grim self-control. 'No doubt you do, but while he lives, we must do what we can to help him, and that means preparing a room and a bed and other things. You can help or not, as you please, but I won't waste time arguing with you.'

She turned away towards the door, but Barbarina jumped up and ran after her, catching her by the arm. 'Do you think I'd let you *touch* him? I'll look after him! I'll do everything for him! You just keep away!'

Rosamund looked down at the hand gripping her arm, and then up at Bab's sodden face. 'Don't be a fool. Who do you think is the better nurse? What did you do in Brussels?'

Bab opened her mouth, but no sound emerged. She flushed scarlet, and removed her hand as though it had been stung, and without another glance Rosamund opened the door and went out. She left the door open behind her, however, and after a moment, Barbarina swallowed her passion and followed quietly.

BOOK TWO

Secret Joys

Sweet babe, in thy face
Soft desires I can trace,
Secret joys and secret smiles,
Little pretty infant wiles.

William Blake: *Cradle Song*

BOOK TWO

CHAPTER NINE

The front yard of Miss Haworth's School of Equitation was always immaculate, so that even the most fastidious of ladies might enter it without fear of dirtying her boots or her hem. Here the nervous, shy or merely young were helped onto their mounts and taught how to sit elegantly and safely, and there were ample oak benches arranged along the sides of the yard so that nurses, chaperones or even doting mamas could sit and watch their darlings' first lessons.

The stables were ingeniously designed so that the gleaming heads of the handsome horses gazed out innocently upon the customers over their half-doors, while any disagreeable substances they produced were removed discreetly through a second set of doors at the back, which led onto another yard where all the real work went on. Such thoughtful arrangements for the comfort of the customers had already brought the Misses Haworth a great deal of business and the venture promised to be a tremendous success. The exquisite features and heavenly blue eyes of the elder Miss Haworth convinced papas that she must be the best teacher for their little ones, while the fact that no-one looked better on a horse persuaded the mamas of the same thing.

'In fact,' said Thalia Hampton to Polly one day in November, 'this is becoming a tonnish place to be seen. You've only to open a tea-room and a circulating library, and you'll be the most fashionable lounge in London.'

Polly smiled and said, 'You do talk nonsense!' She was preoccupied with teaching Lady Mary Penshurst how to hold two sets of reins without either dropping them or breaking her horse's jaw. Lady Mary, daughter of the Earl of Tonbridge, was to be married in the spring to Sir Henry Hope, an extremely wealthy man-about-town. She had never much cared for horses, but he was a notable horseman and a Dandy of the second generation, whose ambition seemed to be to outbrummell the Beau himself.

As Lady Mary herself had said when she first arrived at the school, 'I *must* be able to accompany him out riding without offending his sensibilities, or I shall always feel he has married beneath him. Please help me, Miss Haworth.'

Now Polly said, 'That's right, I think you have it now. But sit up straight, Lady Mary. If you bend forward like that you give your horse the office to walk on, which confuses him.'

'And it makes you look as though you're going to be sick, Mary,' Thalia added helpfully. She and Lady Mary were good friends, and Thalia always liked to accompany her for her lessons because a chaperone was not considered necessary while she was at the school, and she never knew who she might meet here.

'It is true that Mary's papa was once going to marry your mama, Miss Haworth?' she asked idly.

Polly looked across at her warily. 'Now what makes you say that?'

'Oh, I've just heard it said. She was very beautiful, wasn't she?'

'Mama says she was the most beautiful girl of her Season,' Mary said shyly. 'She says you look a great deal like her, ma'am.'

'I'm sure that's why they sent you here to learn, isn't it, Mary?' Thalia added irrepressibly. 'And they're going to send her sister Psyche too, Miss Haworth — aren't they, Mary?'

'Yes, Miss Haworth. Psyche's twelve now and she can ride anything — she's not a bit afraid — but Papa says she rides like a hoyden, and he said what was wanted was something of Miss Haworth's ethereal look on a horse.'

'I think you've paid me enough outrageous compliments for one day,' Polly laughed.

'Oh, but we're only repeating what we hear,' Thalia said pertly.

'Well you shouldn't,' Polly said firmly. 'We'll change the

172

subject, if you please.' The groom led Lady Mary on a circuit of the yard while Polly watched critically.

Suddenly Thalia asked, 'Is your aunt coming back to Town soon, Miss Haworth? Lady Theakston, I mean.'

'I hadn't heard that she was. Why do you ask?'

'Oh, only that I heard Papa say that when she came up he would talk to her again about a wedding date.'

Polly looked sympathetic. 'You must be eager to have it settled. It was very unfortunate that it should have to be cancelled in that way, because of the accident.'

'Oh, I didn't mind that,' Thalia said easily. 'In fact, I don't really want to have it all settled — not too soon.'

'Why, don't you want to marry Cousin Roland?' Polly asked in surprise.

Thalia looked uneasy. 'It isn't that. At least, one has to marry, and I like Roland, and I'll be Lady Aylesbury and tremendously rich. But I just wish —'

She trailed off, biting her lip. Polly sent the groom round again and said gently, 'You may speak to me in confidence if you wish. I will not repeat anything you say.'

'I know you won't,' Thalia said gratefully, and then it came out in a rush. '*You* understand, which a great many people wouldn't. You see, I can't help thinking that once one is married — and then one has to have *babies*,' with an indescribable grimace, '— and then all one's fun is over. Now I should like to have fun for a year or two first, but it seems to me that Mama's whole purpose in getting me married is to *stop* me having fun. It isn't fair!'

Polly repressed a smile.

Thalia went on, 'But you're very beautiful, Miss Haworth, and you managed not to get married right away when you came out. You do just as you like — and now you've even made staying single and having a business respectable. How did you do it?'

Polly thought of the years of miserable dependence at Stainton, and the hideous tragedy which had haunted her life, and wondered at the innocence of the pretty girl before her. What could she possibly tell her about the other side of love and flirtation, the dark and poisoned side that withered everything it touched?

173

'Things are hardly ever the same on the inside as they appear from the outside,' she began rather helplessly. 'What seems simple can be complicated and difficult —'

'Yes, I know that,' Thalia nodded quickly. 'Everyone seems to have secrets, don't they? Do you know, I think Papa had something to do with poor Lord Chelmsford's accident. I hear the most peculiar stories about it — oh, I don't mean people tell me, but I overhear things, and the servants gossip when they think I'm not listening.

'You shouldn't be listening,' Polly said severely.

Thalia smiled. 'Now don't put on that governessy look, dear Miss Haworth, for it doesn't suit you at all! And how is a girl to find things out if no-one will tell her? But I've heard it said that Lord Chelmsford fought in a duel, and that's how he got injured, and that the other man was killed! Don't you think that's the most exciting thing you've ever heard? Of course, I'm terrible sorry for Lord Chelmsford,' she added hastily, 'but I must say that it makes him terribly brave and romantic, don't you think? I wonder what it was all about?'

'Don't wonder,' Polly advised, and Thalia leapt on the words.

'You mean the story's true? That there was a duel?'

'I mean nothing of the sort! I mean that it is very unladylike to wonder about what doesn't concern you, and very unhealthy to dwell on subjects like that. As far as I know, it was a shooting accident, and you ought to remember, before you repeat rumours like that, that Lady Chelmsford will be your sister-in-law when you are married, and that any scandal will reflect on you as well.'

'Oh I wouldn't say anything to anyone but you,' Thalia said easily. 'You're family too. Anyway there's nothing so very disgraceful about a duel, is there? Mama's had *dozens* fought over her.'

'That was in the olden days,' Polly said quickly. 'Times have changed, Miss Hampton. It is not considered respectable any more.'

Thalia shrugged. 'Oh well, I dare say I shall find out all about it one day. And anyway, I still mean to have a great deal of fun while I can, so I'm in no hurry for Papa to settle things with Lady Theakston.'

Lady Mary, reaching them at that moment, heard the last words and said, 'You should be careful, Thalia. Lord Aylesbury's what Mama calls an eligible *parti*, and if you delay too long you might lose him to someone else.'

'I don't mind,' Thalia said. 'There are plenty of other young men. Or I might just remain single like Miss Haworth. I think she and Miss Africa have the *best* fun.'

'That child is a minx,' Polly said to Africa that evening over supper. 'All the same, I'm sure there is some truth in what she says. I don't believe it was a simple shooting accident. Have you heard anything?'

'At first my young gentlemen could hardly talk of anything else,' Africa said. 'Rumours were bound to fly about, but whatever it was, they must have done a very good job of covering it up, for I've never heard anything but the most tentative speculation.'

'But *was* it a duel?'

Africa looked at her cannily. 'You don't really want to know, Pol. If they want it kept secret, we should respect that. And if you knew the truth, you couldn't deny it to impertinent questioners, could you? Not with any conviction, anyway,' she added with a smile as Polly began to protest. 'I know you, my good sister, and you can't tell a lie without blushing like a furnace.'

'That's true,' Polly sighed. 'And yet one can't help wondering. There must have been something in it, for everyone to leave Town just at that moment. I don't suppose Lord Greyshott has spent so much time in the country in his life, and for Aunt Lucy to miss the Season —'

'She hasn't any daughters or nieces to bring out or take to parties,' Africa said logically. 'Why should she come up?'

Polly smiled. 'That excuse might do for public consumption, but you and I know better. Besides, with Rosamund expecting her baby at any moment, she ought to be hovering over her instead of hiding down at Wolvercote.'

'I don't think Aunt Lucy cares for the idea of becoming a grandmother,' Africa said; and then, 'It's Barbarina I feel sorry for. There was definitely a tendresse beginning between her and Lord Ballincrea — I noticed it last Christmas at

Wolvercote — and now he's hundreds of miles away up on the Borders. I had the idea he was going to propose to her, you know, before all this happened.'

'Then she'd have to go and live up there,' Polly said. 'Sooner her than me. It must be like going to the end of the world.'

'If she loves him she won't care,' Africa said with a private smile which was not lost on Polly. 'Well, perhaps by Christmas things will be back to normal, and everyone will meet at Wolvercote again. Rosamund will have had her baby —'

'But Marcus will still be a helpless invalid,' Polly said soberly. 'I can't imagine joy being unconfined in those circumstances.'

Shortly afterwards they left the dining-table and withdrew to their comfortable parlour. They had just settled themselves when their man came in. Polly looked up.

'Yes, Mansell, you may bring the tea in. We're quite ready.'

'I beg your pardon, miss, but there's a gentleman to see you — Mr Weston, miss.'

'Tom? Well, that's a surprise. Show him up, Mansell.' And when Tom appeared she greeted him with, 'You didn't need to be so formal. You're practically a brother to us. You should have come straight up.'

'There are those,' Tom smiled, 'of the opinion that two ravishingly handsome young women living alone without a chaperone cannot be too careful of their reputation.'

'Tom, I'm twenty-eight years old,' Polly said reproachfully. 'I'm perfectly old-cattish, and quite able to chaperone my little sister.'

Africa laughed at that. 'It's quite the other way round. You may be older than me in years, Pol, but I've more worldly wisdom in my little finger than you have in your whole beautiful head!'

'You can squabble about it all you like,' Tom said peaceably, 'but the world regards you both as young and eligible, and to prove it I have some gentlemen with me who wish to call on you, if you don't think it's too late. That's why I had myself announced. They're waiting below. Shall I call 'em, or send 'em away?'

'You are absurd,' Africa said. 'Call 'em, of course! Who are they?'

176

'I like the order in which you put those two remarks,' Tom grinned. 'They are three friends, very handsome and proper gentlemen, I may say. There's a Mr Morpurgo —' Africa gave a cry of pleasure. Tom nodded to it and continued, '— and a Mr Paston who went to school with him, and who swears he danced with you in your London Season, Polly —'

'Yes,' Polly said with an interesting colour in her cheeks, 'I remember him.' Mr Paston was an extremely wealthy and urbane man-about-town who had been the object of every mama's baited hooks for years, and had avoided them all with dexterity and indifference. She *had* danced with him during her Season, and remembered having felt disappointed that he talked such intellectual sense to her, instead of the flirtatious folly which most gentlemen offered to girls who had just come out. She had felt it proved what her cousin Fanny had often said to her, that though she was very beautiful, the gentlemen just didn't take to her.

'— and finally,' Tom said, 'there is Sir Henry Hope, who by virtue of his great age (because he's thirty-five if he's a day) and the fact that he's thoroughly betrothed to Lady Mary Penshurst who is your pupil, guarantees to give respectability to the whole proceeding, and to keep the rest of us in order. And if you think that my being almost a brother to you constitutes enough of a chaperonage,' he concluded in fine style, 'I shall be happy to bring them up and present them to you.'

'You shall do no such thing,' Polly said with dignity. 'Mansell shall bring them up.' She rang the bell. 'And he can bring tea at the same time.'

'Peter must only just have got back,' Africa said, following her own line of thought.

'Yesterday,' Tom said. 'Why do you say so?'

'Because he would have sent me a note, or come to see me, of course,' Africa said with confidence. Polly looked at her warily.

'I met him at Paston's house — he's staying there,' Tom explained 'When I saw him he was so freshly back from sea he was still scraping the barnacles out of his hair.'

'It was only a six-month cruise, of course,' Africa said. 'Did he mention whether he has another yet?'

177

'Not to me,' Tom said.

Polly interrupted. 'You can ask *him* that in a moment. More importantly, what are you doing in Town, Tom?'

'Oh, I couldn't stand the gloom at Wolvercote any more, so I escaped. Told Mama I'd get the house opened up for her. She'll be coming up next week, I fancy.'

There were many things Polly would have liked to ask about that statement, but there was no time, for the door opened and Mansell announced the three gentlemen. Morpurgo got in first, and crossed the room in two strides to clasp Africa's hands, saying, 'How comfortable this is! But elegant, too. Just as I've imagined it all this last trip.'

But for once the sight of his preference for her sister didn't make Polly feel nervous, for her attention was completely taken up by the other two gentlemen, who were very properly addressing themselves to her first, apologising for the intrusion and hoping that she would not consider it impertinent of them to have hoped that they might visit her.

'But really, you know,' Sir Henry Hope said, 'there are so many connections between the Tonbridge family and yours, Miss Haworth, that I really feel I am almost a relative.'

'A transparent fiction,' Polly laughed, 'but a pleasant one. I am happy to receive you, with or without excuses. I hope I am not one to forget old friends, though it is a very long time since my London Season when I danced with you, Sir Henry — and with you, Mr Paston.'

Mr Paston bowed over her hand. 'When I look at you, Miss Haworth, I really find it impossible to believe how long it has been.'

It was precisely the sort of nonsense that he didn't speak to her when she was a debutante, Polly thought. How *odd* that he should offer it now to an old maid of twenty-eight.

If Rosamund had thought before that Chelmsford House was like a tomb, how much more so was it now! She rarely ventured out of doors, and never into public, and no-one came to the house. It was as if they had ceased to inhabit the real world. They might have been sealed up in the heart of a glacier, separated from the rest of humanity by walls of ice.

178

She was large with child now, and found moving about difficult, resting uncomfortable, sleep almost impossible. She didn't want to see anyone while she was like this yet she was lonely, hungry for warmth and companionship. She didn't want to do anything, yet she was so bored she wanted to scream. The combination of lethargy and restlessness was particularly hard to bear; and it did nothing to keep her from the thoughts and speculations which nagged constantly at her mind.

And it did nothing to distract from the thought of Marcus, lying in bed upstairs, immobile and suffering. He bore it silently, and yet it seemed to Rosamund that the whole house throbbed with him, that his pain was transmitted through every wall and floor, that it ran into her through every chair, table, doorknob she touched. *My fault*, her mind hissed at her every day. There had been times when she had wished, bitterly, that Hawker had done his business better. There had been times, too, when she had hoped that she might die in childbed, only to escape the consciousness of Marcus's plight.

But he was getting better. There was a long time when they thought — believed — that he would die. The wound was too extensive, mortification was bound to set in. Now the doctor said he would probably one day walk again, though whether he would regain other functions was unknown. It made the child she carried all the more important; it made it harder to live with herself, with her feelings and longings, with her pity for and anger towards her husband.

They had had a scare in October when he had caught a chill which had settled on his chest, and the doctor had feared it might turn into pneumonia. But he had come through it. He was amazingly strong, the doctor said, and he fought for life with tremendous determination. Rosamund had helped Bab nurse him through it. He had had to be watched day and night, and the exhaustion caused by the constant attention had made her feel detached, as though she were hovering in the air and witnessing the scenes from above. She saw then how his death would be much the best thing for them all — yes, even for him, for what could life hold for him as he was? Yet he clung to it and survived, fought his way back to the

179

bedridden pain that was now his norm.

And soon it would be her turn. The agony of childbirth; and if she survived it, what then? She would have fulfilled her half of the bargain, but could she really demand his half from Marcus as he was? Would she even have the heart for it? Just at the moment she wanted most of all to get away from everyone, to go and live in the middle of a moor with none but birds and wild deer for company. She knew with some distant part of her mind that she loved Jes, but she didn't really feel it. It was something that had been locked away to keep it safe from the rest of experience. She was glad in a vague, numb sort of way that he was far away in Manchester, out of reach and out of sight. The time when she wished she knew what he was thinking was long past.

She was on her way upstairs to relieve Bab at the bedside when Beason came to tell her that there was a caller. It had been so long since anyone had come to the house that she didn't understand him at once; and then, understanding, hurried down to the morning room to receive Lord Ballincrea.

'I didn't know that you were in Town,' she said, offering her hand.

'I only came up yesterday. I had some business to attend to.' Ballincrea looked at her searchingly. 'You don't mind my calling? How are you? You look tired.'

'It has been a struggle sometimes. But I am very well.'

'And Marcus?'

'He is improving, slowly but daily. I don't know,' she faltered, 'whether he will be well enough to see you.'

'I don't suppose he would want to see me,' Ballincrea said frankly. 'It might remind him too much of past events. But Greyshott says there was no further trouble — magistrates and so on?'

'Nothing of that sort, thank God. I suppose there has been a lot of gossip, but we don't hear it. No-one comes near us.'

He frowned. 'That's very bad. You should not have been left all alone. Surely members of your family —?'

'It was better that we were left alone,' Rosamund said hastily. 'We would have had no time or inclination for outsiders.'

180

'At first, perhaps — I can understand it. But now, if you say he is improving, surely others can help you carry the burden?'

'My mother will be coming to Town soon,' Rosamund said, though not as if the prospect gave her any pleasure.

'Helena is back, with Thalia and Maurice — that was another reason I came up. May I tell Helena that you will receive her? I know she would love to call on you.'

Rosamund thought of Helena and her quick mind and sharp conversation, and felt exhausted at the prospect. 'Not yet,' she begged. 'Perhaps after the baby is born. I don't think I could bear anyone to see me like this.'

He smiled gently. 'Aren't I anyone?'

Rosamund met his eyes frankly. 'In a way, I suppose not. You know everything about this wretched business. You know the worst there is to know about me. It can't signify any more how I appear to you.'

Ballincrea took her hand. 'I am very fond of you, you know,' he said. 'I wish there were — something — anything I could do to make matters better for you.'

Unwelcome tears jumped to her eyes. 'Don't,' she said. 'I can't bear it if you pity me.' She removed her hand. 'But thank you all the same.'

He hesitated. 'Would it seem monstrous of me —? If there is nothing I can do for you, perhaps there is something you can do for me.'

Rosamund looked surprised. 'Anything,' she said. 'You have only to name it.'

He nodded, still pursuing his thoughts, and after a moment seemed to make up his mind. 'You may have wondered why I didn't ask after your sister-in-law.'

'She's tolerably well,' Rosamund said, taking it for a question. 'The confinement tells on both of us, I fancy.'

'Yes; I'm very conscious of that. Rosamund, my dear, you may have noticed — you're a noticing person — that I have grown very fond of Barbarina.'

Rosamund smiled slowly. The exercise was so unaccustomed she almost felt the muscles of her face creak. 'I did — wonder, shall we say?'

'She reminds me so much of my dear Mary — though she

181

is very different,' he added, as though the confession surprised him. 'I think she has never been properly appreciated,
never given the environment in which her qualities could
shine out. I don't mean to be impolite to you, my dear, but
I imagine Barbarina is not the sort of woman you would
naturally choose as a friend.'

'Perhaps not,' Rosamund said shortly. She remembered all
the things she had done for Bab, how she had made her
welcome in her home, taken her to parties and balls, tried to
bring her out of herself, defended her against her mother and
life in general. But had she ever cared for her? Not really —
only in the sense that one cared for a dependent child or
servant. She had never confided in her or regarded her as a
friend. 'But what is it you are trying to say to me, sir?'

He smiled ruefully. 'In my roundabout way, that I want to
marry Barbarina. If this dreadful business had not intervened, I would have asked her long ago, back in August. But
I think the time is right, now. I would not expect her to marry
me at once, of course — I don't suppose she would want to
leave Marcus — or you — until he is further on the road to
health. But I think it could only be a good thing for her to
know of my feelings, and to have that security to look forward
to.'

He paused as if he wanted an answer, and Rosamund
looked at him rather blankly. 'I'm sure you're right. But what
is it you want to ask me? You said there was something I could
do for you.'

'You,' said Lord Ballincrea, 'can give your permission.'

'My permission? I don't have any right of veto over Bab's
decisions. She is over twenty-one. She may marry whom she
pleases.'

'I know that, of course. But if I marry her, if she marries
me, I will be taking her away from you. She may not be the
sort of woman you would choose for a friend, but I know she
must be a valuable companion to you, and in circumstances,
now more than ever, when you must need a companion very
much. I'm very fond of you, as I said, and I would not even
ask for her hand unless I knew you were willing to let her go.'

Rosamund looked astonished. 'Do you mean to tell me
that if I said no, you wouldn't ask her to marry you?'

He smiled ruefully. 'Not now. Not yet. I would wait until your circumstances were better before putting my proposal to her.'

'You would be willing to wait?'

'She is worth waiting for,' he said simply.

Rosamund shook her head. 'It passes me. But if you love her as much as all that, I couldn't possibly stand in your way. Have her with my blessing, as soon as ever she'll have you.'

'You are generosity itself. But don't you want to think about it before deciding?'

'There's nothing to think about. I have no right, and no wish, to keep you apart. There's not so much happiness in the world that I can bear to be responsible for another lessening of it,' she added bleakly. She saw that he was about to say something kind and sympathetic to her, and she moved away from it as she would have moved away from a touch. 'I was just about to take her place at Marcus's bedside. I'll send her down to you, and you can put the question at once.'

She managed to get as far as the door. As her hand reached the knob he said gently, 'Things will get better. I know that at the moment you can't believe it, but it's true. I remember when Mary died I thought I would feel as miserable for ever. But the human heart has great resilience. Things will get better, I swear to you.'

She had paused to hear him, but didn't turn. He had made her cry after all, damn him. 'I wish you luck,' she managed to say, and ran out.

As she closed the door, she heard him say softly, 'God bless you!'

She called Bab out of the room to give the message that Ballincrea was downstairs and wished to see her, and saw her run off with joy and apprehension in her face. Then she went in to Marcus's room, to the smell of sickness and putrefaction, to the grey fog of boredom and pain which seemed to fall through the air and gather on every surface like the dust of eternity. Marcus lay against his rumpled pillows, his face grey and lined with suffering like an old man's, his eyes remote and yet anxious, like those of a prisoner glimpsed at a small, barred window.

'What were you saying to Bab?' he demanded as soon as she came back in.

'Just that there was someone to see her. We've had a visitor today, the first for a long time.' She had to build up to it, so as not to agitate him. 'Lord Ballincrea came to see how we all were.'

'Ballincrea?'

'It's the first time he's been in London. He asked after you, of course, the first thing, but I said I thought you would not be well enough to see him.'

'Ballincrea?' He brooded on the name. 'I haven't seen him since — of course, he was my second. I should perhaps have seen him for a moment.' His mood changed. 'But he has been no friend to me. If he had not taken Bab to Hanover Square that day —' He scowled. 'I won't see him.'

'So I told him,' Rosamund said soothingly. She crossed to the bed and began to shake up his pillows to make him more comfortable.

'I can't see anyone anyway,' he went on pathetically. 'Only you and Bab. I'm too ill to see anyone.'

'I'll keep them all away,' she said. 'You won't be disturbed.'

'He might have come sooner, if he wanted to know how I was.' Another change of mood. 'No-one comes near us. No-one cares about us. I might just as well have died, for all the interest anyone shows in me. Never even a card left. When was the last time anyone left a card?'

'We decided it was best to have no callers, don't you remember. It was either that, or go away, and you were too ill to go away. We disappeared in the middle of London.'

'Yes, so we did. I was very ill, wasn't I? But the rumours have been quashed, haven't they? It was worth it — no-one talks about us, do they?'

'No,' Rosamund said. She imagined they did not. Out of sight was out of mind, which had been the whole point of it. True friends might have stayed close to them, but they had proved not to have any true friends. Except those, like Ballincrea, who had stayed away out of kindness. Round in circles. She shook her thoughts away.

'Let me sit you up a little. You've slipped down. You can't be comfortable.'

He smiled up at her, a travesty of a smile which dragged at her heart. 'You're a good nurse, Rosy. You nursed me once before remember? In Brussels. You were so good to our soldiers, you and your mother. When is your mother coming here?'

'Next week, probably. But she won't be staying here, you know.'

'Won't she?'

'I told you. She'll be staying in her own house.'

'I'd forgotten.' He took hold of her arms, and she passed her hands behind him and tried to lift him, but he cried out in pain. 'No, don't! It hurts me!'

'Draw up your knees and push with your legs, the way I told you before,' she said patiently. 'Try again.'

'It will open the wound again. I'll bleed again.'

'No you won't. Just do as I tell you.'

She managed to lift him on the second attempt, but as she did she felt something happen inside her, a dragging feeling, as though something had broken loose. In terror she stayed still, exploring her inner sensations, waiting for dissolution or pain to follow. She remained just as she was, bent over him, her face fixed and staring, until at last even Marcus noticed.

'What's the matter? Have you hurt yourself? Ros, what's the matter?'

Nothing had happened. Nothing seemed to be happening. Slowly she straightened, and no pain followed.

'It's all right,' she said automatically to his repeated question. 'I thought I'd pulled a muscle, but it's all right.'

No it wasn't, though. As she moved away from his bedside to fetch him a drink, she felt that something inside her had changed. She didn't know what, and it didn't hurt, but it was different, and she didn't like it. As soon as she could get away, she thought, she would send someone for Knighton.

She lay in a world of agony, trapped at the centre of a glassy globe of pain like a fly in amber, trapped for ever, unmoving, unchanging. From time to time she was aware of people moving on the other side of the glass. Bab she saw quite often, her chinless, surprised face drifting in and out like an anxious mother mouse; and Judy Moss with tears running down her face — now what was she crying for? — and Sir William, looking comfortable and comforting as always. But she was worried that she couldn't communicate with them through the glass to tell them of the pain. She was afraid they didn't know she was there, and would go away again and leave her for ever. She struggled to move or to cry out, but the pain was too big for her, and too strong. It had been inside her, but now she was inside it. She had been swallowed whole by it, like Jonah by the whale. They would never find her.

Bitter tears ran down her face, and a hand wiped them away. She knew that hand. She tried to think whose it was, but it was hard to concentrate through the pain. A brown hand; a smell of camomile. The hand slipped under her head and lifted it, and the rim of something hard was put to her lips.

'Try to drink a little. It will help with the pains.'

'Mother?'

The face swam into focus before her, firm brown skin, fine lines about the eyes, a little frown of concentration between the fair brows.

'Mother?' She heard herself say it that time.

'Yes, it's me. They sent a message for me yesterday. Didn't you know?'

'How long —?'

'Have you been in labour? Fifty hours, I suppose. Drink some more, it will help you along.'

Rosamund sipped, and it was bitter and tasted green. 'Am I going to die?'

'Of course not. Don't be silly.' It sounded all right, but Rosamund looked deep into her mother's eyes as she said it, past her eyes into her brain, past her brain into her soul, and she saw an empty space, a space where someone had been and was no longer. And so she knew. She was going to die after all. Well, that was all right. Here, at the edge, she discovered she was not much afraid. And if she died it would be the end of the pain. She was only sorry to put everyone to so much trouble.

'I'm sorry,' she said; and her voice was tiny and far off, very far off, like a dragonfly sitting on a rock at the other end of the universe.

Barbarina went into Marcus's room with a tray, and he looked towards her eagerly. 'News? Is there news?'

'Nothing yet,' she said, crossing to him to put the tray down beside the bed. 'I've brought you some tea.'

He didn't seem to have heard her. 'Oh God, why isn't anything happening? How long can it go on? Is Knighton with her?'

'Not at the moment. He was here earlier.'

'He should be with her. God knows, his fees are high enough!'

'He has done everything he ought. It's just a matter of time now. Let me give you some tea.'

'But how long can she bear it?' He ignored the cup she held out to him. 'She'll die if it goes on like this! Oh God, if she dies, I'll never forgive myself!'

Bab hated it when he talked like that. 'She won't die. Take your tea.'

'Tea? I don't want tea!' he said wildly. 'Oh Ros, oh my love, don't die! If she dies I don't want to live, do you hear me, Bab? If she dies I'll find a way to kill myself!'

'You mustn't talk like that, Marcus. It's a sin, and God will punish you.'

He laughed savagely. 'How much more do you think I can be punished? Bab, who's with her? She's not been left alone has she?'

'Of course not. Her mother's with her.'

'You go too. Stay with her, and come and tell me when anything happens. Go, I tell you!' She decided it was best to leave him. As she reached the door he shouted, 'And get Knighton back! He should be here!'

She didn't go back to Rosamund's room. There was nothing she could do there. In truth she thought Rosamund was going to die, and she knew Knighton did too, though he hadn't said as much. Barbarina went to her own room and sat down on the window seat, staring out into the grey rain. It was the first of December. She thought of her interview with Lord Ballincrea, and felt tears rising again, as they had then. In the morning-room that day with her hands in his she had wept, for her long imprisonment, for Bobby who had died;

for the chance of escape which she had lost without ever knowing it existed.

If she had not told Marcus that she had seen Rosamund that day with Hawker and Farraline — told him in all innocence — he would not have fought the duel, and she would have been married to Lord Ballincrea by now, married and away and free. He had come back to her to give her a second chance, but she was so afraid that something would happen to snatch it from her. If Rosamund died, would she ever be able to leave Marcus, widowed and crippled both? She didn't think she could. There had been so much to weep for lately, but just for once she wept for herself, for poor Bab who had never had anything of her own.

There was sunshine in the room, thin, frail sunshine without the power to warm, only to gladden. Rosamund had been watching it for some time as it moved across the wall, without realising that she was awake, conscious, back in the world again. Now she became aware of those things, and explored her sensations cautiously. Had she been ill? She felt very weak. She could move her head on the pillow, but she couldn't lift it; move her fingers, but not lift her hand. But she didn't really want to move. She felt languorous with the pleasure of pain removed.

She had suffered pain, she knew that — the memory of it was drifting just beyond the edge of her mind, in the golden mist there — but she didn't remember when or why. There were questions to ask, difficult things to learn and come to terms with, but not yet. There was still time to drift a little on this sea of peacefulness . . .

A moment or a thousand years later she drifted back to hear her mother's voice saying, 'Are you awake, then? I thought I saw your fingers move.'

Slowly Rosamund turned her head, frowning with concentration. Her mother was sitting beside her bed. 'I couldn't remember . . . I thought I was a child again. I was playing the piano in the schoolroom and there was someone else there . . .' She drifted again. 'I can't remember.'

'How are you feeling?' Lucy asked patiently.

'I'm not sure. Tired, I think. Or weak.'

'Yes, that's to be expected. No pain anywhere?' Rosamund considered. 'I feel as if I ought to have, but I can't find it.'

'That will be the laudanum. I expect you'll notice when it wears off,' Lucy said with spare humour. 'Anything else?'

'I can't remember what happened to me. I suppose I must have been ill, because I remember Sir William Knighton was here —' Her eyes widened suddenly and she tried to sit up. 'No, no, lie still,' Lucy said, pushing her back down. 'You remember now?'

'I was having a baby. I thought I was going to die.'

'So did we all,' Lucy said grimly. 'But we cheated you.'

'But Mother — what happened? Did I have it?'

'Yes.'

'What was it?'

'A girl.'

'A girl?' That took some thinking about. She had never considered having a girl. It had always been a boy in those few imaginings she had spared herself. A girl. A daughter. The words were strange and exciting and absurdly pleasant. She had a daughter. She was a mother. Mother was a grandmother. Then a hideous thought struck her.

'Alive?'

'Yes, she's alive.'

'Can I see her?'

'Yes, of course. Let me sit you up a little.' Propped further up, Rosamund saw for the first time the crib on the other side of the room, a very old wooden rocking-cradle hung with fresh muslin drapes. 'Where did that come from?'

'Family heirloom. Bobby slept in it, and his father before him it seems. Moss put new drapes on it for you — it looked rather hideous before.'

She had crossed the room and now dipped her arms deep into the white gauzy clouds, to come up with a woollen bundle. Rosamund gazed with painful eagerness as Lucy brought it across to her, and a moment later it was laid in the crook of her arm, astonishingly small, unexpectedly heavy. She reached with a terrified finger to draw back the fold of the shawl from the face, and there was her daughter, new and real and alive, eyes tightly shut, flesh of her own flesh. Her eyes filled instantly with tears, and there was such an ache in her

189

chest that she could hardly draw breath. She looked up at her mother with astonishment and fear and hope.

'Oh why does it hurt so?' she asked desperately. 'Does it always hurt like this?'

Lucy smiled for the first time, and it was a smile Rosamund had never seen before — not directed at her. 'It's only love,' she said. She reached down and touched the tiny petal of a face with the back of one finger, as though any more robust caress might take off the bloom. Her mouth trembled. 'Nature does that to us,' she said softly, 'so that we will never part from them.'

Rosamund gazed at her, sharing with her for the first time something so profound that it could not be spoken of. *Did you love me like this, Mother, when I was born? Did you feel this gasping, consuming pain of love when you first looked at me? And will she one day look at me as I look at you now, and know what I am feeling at this moment?*

She returned her gaze to her baby, and after the love now came concern. 'She's so small,' she said. 'Is she really all right? Does she sleep all the time?'

'She's very new,' Lucy said. 'Remember the birth was hard for her, too. She'll sleep for a long time yet.'

'But she is all right?'

'As far as one can tell.'

It was not ungenerous. To Rosamund, living on the trembling edge of a new and perilous experience, it seemed as much as could be hoped for. This love, unlike any other, had made her humble and grateful. She gazed and gazed at the face of her child, memorising her, learning what she looked like. 'I never knew what she looked like,' she said aloud with new surprise. 'She doesn't look like anyone I know. She doesn't look like me.'

'She will,' said Lucy, godlike from the heights of experience.

'She's so perfect. Look at her hands — her tiny nails.'

'Let me know if you feel tired, and I'll take her from you.'

Rosamund's arms tightened without her volition. 'Oh no! I'm not tired. I feel as though I just want to look at her for hours and hours — for ever.'

Lucy sat down again, patiently, at the bedside. After a

moment, Rosamund said, 'I wonder what her name is? I suppose Marcus will want to choose it.' Her mouth drooped as she remembered. 'My God, Marcus,' she said softly. 'I'd forgotten. Has he seen her? Is he pleased?'

'He's seen her,' said Lucy.

'What did he say?'

'He cried a great deal. I think he was pleased.'

'Poor Marcus.'

Lucy hesitated, and then said, 'His first question was for you. He was very much concerned about you. Of course, we tried not to worry him, but you were in labour for so long he could hardly help knowing it was not going well.'

Rosamund looked up. 'I thought I was dying,' she said, remembering the strange, supernatural experience she had had. 'There was a moment when I thought I looked into your heart and saw an empty space there, and I knew you were thinking about death. You were thinking about someone dying. I thought it was me.'

Lucy looked startled, and then a little afraid. 'What foolishness,' she said unconvincingly.

'Did you think that, Mother?'

For a moment she met Rosamund's gaze, wide-eyed. 'I thought I'd lost you,' she said at last.

There had been many times in her life that Rosamund had doubted whether her mother cared for her at all, still less felt anything as positive as love for her. But now she knew: the knowledge was made flesh in the person — *person*! — of this child lying in her arms. She knew exactly how, and how much, her mother loved her, and therefore what such a loss would mean.

'You won't lose me, Mother,' she said. Never again.

Jasper Hobsbawn met Jesmond Farraline in the doorway of their club as he was coming out and Farraline was going in. He had not seen Farraline for some weeks, and thought with surprise how very ill he was looking, drawn and pinched as though with constant pain.

'Are you well, old fellow?' Jasper asked with quick concern. 'You're looking quite fagged.'

Farraline shrugged it off. 'Well enough, thank you. I've

been working rather hard, that's all.'

'I thought I hadn't seen you about.'

'I hope everything goes on with you,' Farraline said with an obvious effort. 'Mrs Hobsbawn well?'

'Yes, thank you. She's very excited at the moment because she's had some good news. Her cousin Rosamund has been safely delivered of a daughter.'

Farraline seemed to sway on his feet. 'She — she's all right?'

'Yes indeed! Mother and child doing well,' said Jasper, and grew, for him, unusually expansive. 'Sophie's delighted that it's a girl, because she thinks she and Fanny will be great friends when they are a little older. I thought it was particularly hard luck on poor Chelmsford, especially after that tragic accident, poor man — and I believe there is some doubt whether he will be able to have any more. But Sophie learns from her mother that the Chelmsford title can be passed to either a male or a female successor — a special grant by Charles II, apparently — so it seems that it will be all right after all.'

'When — when was the child born?' Farraline managed to ask.

'Last week, on the fourth. I say, old man, are you all right? You look quite ill.'

Farraline pulled himself together. 'Yes. Yes, thank you. I haven't eaten all day, that's all. I was going in to dine now.'

'I won't keep you, then. You must come and dine with us again soon,' Jasper said.

'Thank you. I'd like that,' Farraline said faintly. 'My regards to Mrs Hobsbawn, if you please. Tell her — tell her that I'm very glad of the good news.'

CHAPTER TEN

The next few weeks were a respite, a holiday from reality. Rosamund lay in bed watching the sky change beyond her window, taking nourishment, nursing the baby, thinking of nothing beyond the healing of her body and the humble, tender love which grew in her day by day for her child. It was like a tree which had sprung up inside her, and when a breeze rocked the outer branches — when she looked at the baby or the baby looked at her — she could feel the deep roots tug at her soul.

The baby was to be called Charlotte. The decree had gone forth from Marcus's bedroom: Charlotte Georgiana Annunciata — after the King, and her ancestress in whose honour the title had first been granted. Marcus sent also a tender message to Rosamund, of congratulation and gladness that she had survived the ordeal. 'As soon as you are able to leave your bed, I hope that you will come and see me, so that I can satisfy myself you really are well.'

Rosamund tried not to think about that. That lay in the future, beyond the safe bounds of this chamber, a hazardous place where things would be demanded of her and decisions would have to be made. She shut her mind resolutely to what lay beyond the door of her bedroom. Meals came in through it, and at regular intervals Charlotte was borne out through it to be shown to her father, but Rosamund looked always towards the window and the patch of December sky.

After two weeks Knighton and, more importantly, her mother decreed that she could have visitors, and though she would really rather not have had them, they came anyway. Papa Danby was welcome, bending over her with a pleasant whiff of lavender and bay rum to kiss her cheek, murmur a few heartfelt words of relief that she was looking so well, and press into her hand a gift for the baby, a pretty silver ornament to hang over the crib.

Roland came, embarrassed and tongue-tied, congratulated her, and then found nothing to say for the rest of the allotted ten minutes of his visit. Tom, looking as always as sleek and privately amused as a dairy cat, didn't mention the baby at all. He chatted lightly about London doings, and Rosamund gained the impression that he was beginning to set up quite a complex web of social life all his own, breaking away from their mother at last. She thought it would be good for him, but wondered how her mother would feel about it.

Polly and Africa came. Polly enthused over the baby and Africa asked some probing questions about the experience of childbirth, and then they told her about their school and how fashionable it was becoming, and about the soirées they were giving and all the charming people who came to them.

'I'm sure it's Tom's doing,' Africa said with a sly look. 'He seems to be taking a perverse delight in making us the *succès fou* of the year. It amuses him to see the *ton* scrambling after two obscure girls living above a stable as though they were duke's daughters.'

'I'm sure it's not that at all,' Rosamund said politely, though it sounded very like a portrait of her wicked brother. 'People wouldn't come if they didn't enjoy themselves.'

'That's what I tell her,' Polly said. 'And after all lots of them are people I knew from my London Season —'

'Her former beaux,' Africa said provokingly. 'Lord Petersfield and Lord Somercott —'

Polly rose to the bait. 'You forget they married girls that I went to balls with — Lady Somercott was Corinna Tulvey, and Petersfield married Lady Mary Fleetwood.'

'That was during the Waterloo Season,' Rosamund remembered. 'What a year it was for marriages! Mrs Fauncett even managed to get Lavinia off her hands at last, though Alfred Fleetwood wasn't much of a catch.'

'Son of the Earl of Southport,' Polly pointed out.

'Second son. And Southport's all to pieces. He won't have a penny,' Africa said. 'But Tom brings all his unmarried friends along too, to look at Polly. They sit and gaze at her by the hour, you know, while I chat and smile and do everything but acrobatics to get their attention. Not the least use! I might as well be the drawing-room fender for all the notice they take of me.'

Charlotte continued to thrive, and Rosamund's fear that she would be snatched from them began to fade. On her mother's advice she fed her at her own breast.

'Just for the first few weeks. Once you're on your feet, you won't want the bother of it, but it gives the child a good start. Their stomachs are so delicate just at first.'

Rosamund was not convinced she would ever find it a bother. It seemed such a privilege to know she was able to do something of real importance for this tiny and perfect creature.

She was allowed out of bed at last, and found her head and her legs very weak. Once up, there was no putting off the duty of visiting Marcus, and on her second day out of bed Moss dressed her in a silk dressing-gown, put a fresh cap over her hair, which was showing a lack of attention, draped a heavy shawl about her shoulders, and helped her along the corridor to Marcus's room.

She had forgotten how depressing it was. Though she had spent more than a fortnight in bed, she had not been ill; this was very much a sick-room. Marcus looked grey and old, but his eyes lit when he saw her.

'Come and sit down. You mustn't tire yourself,' he said, holding out a hand to her. A chair had been placed ready at his bedside.

'How are you?' she asked.

'Going along,' he said. 'The wound is really healing now, I think. There's hardly any drainage. Knighton says that, barring any more setbacks, he thinks this time we are on the mend.'

'I'm very glad,' Rosamund said, suppressing an unworthy feeling of revulsion at the thought of his wound. She ought to pity him — she *did* pity him — but the contrast with the fresh new body she had been nursing was rather unnerving.

'But we don't want to talk about me,' Marcus said. 'More importantly, how are you? Are you quite recovered? We were all very worried about you.'

'I'm still rather tired, but otherwise there's nothing wrong with me,' she said. 'I'm sorry you should have been alarmed.'

Marcus reached out for her hand, and she could not refuse it. 'I thought I'd lost you. I can't tell you how badly I felt. I knew you had never wanted to bear a child, and I thought if you died it would have been as though I had killed you.' She could think of nothing to say; and he went on brightly, 'But here you are, and now that you have seen our dear Charlotte, I think even you must feel it was worth it.'

'She is lovely,' Rosamund agreed. She could not speak of her love for the baby to Marcus. She did not want to think about the fact that Charlotte was his as well as hers. It was too complicated, too painful.

'Lovely?' Marcus seemed to find the word inadequate. 'She's — miraculous! The first time I held her in my arms —'

'I'm sorry it wasn't a boy,' Rosamund interrupted desperately. She didn't want to see the rapture in his face.

'I'm not. I wouldn't change her for all the sons in Christendom. She's perfect and beautiful, and she will inherit everything I have. Our daughter will be Countess of Chelmsford in her own right. Ah, here she is!'

The door had opened, and Barbarina entered with the baby in the crook of her arm. Rosamund had never seen Bab's face so alight. She came across to the other side of the bed, and presented the bundle to Marcus, who took it carefully, but already with a certain accustomedness. Bab had brought her to him every day of her life so far.

'There's my little countess,' he murmured, beaming down into the tiny face. Charlotte pursed her lips and blew a thoughtful bubble, her eyebrows twitching as though she were solving complicated mental puzzles, far too busy to waste precious minutes of her life on parental sentiment.

Bab gazed too. 'She's wonderful, isn't she? I think she has a look of you already, Marcus. She's going to be fair — you can tell.'

Rosamund smiled to herself at the expertise Bab had suddenly found in these matters; yet she felt oddly left out, as though having performed the essential task she was to be paid off and sent away. She wanted to snatch Charlotte back and shout, 'She's *my* baby, not yours!'

196

'She's going to be fair and beautiful,' Marcus said. 'She shall have silk dresses, and pearls, and a milk-white pony. I'll have a little carriage made for her to drive around the Park, and a boy in livery to lead it, while I walk beside. She's going to be clever, too. We'll have a new pianoforte for her when she's a little older, one all her own. And she shall learn the harp, too, don't you think, darling?' He looked at Rosamund, smiling like a young man again. 'The harp is a graceful accomplishment for a young lady.'

'Yes, of course,' Rosamund said blankly. 'Anything you say.'

He kept on smiling at her. 'You've made me very happy, Rosy,' he said, oblivious of Bab's presence. 'I'm sorry things haven't always been quite right between us, but from now on everything will be different. I'll make it up to you. We'll be happy from now on, I promise you.'

Rosamund managed to smile, aware that Bab was watching her. It didn't seem the moment to mention the agreement.

They were alone for Christmas. Lucy went down to Wolvercote where there was the usual gathering, taking Roland and Tom, and Polly and Africa with her. She confided in Rosamund that she was a little worried about the proposed wedding between Roland and Thalia Hampton.

'It doesn't seem to get any further forward. Helena's for it, but Thalia seems reluctant to come to the point, and Greyshott says he won't press her against her will. And now it looks as though Roland's having second thoughts as well. I don't know what's to do. I'm hoping that if I can get them all together again over Christmas I may be able to settle it finally.'

She offered to transport Rosamund's household down there, and when that was refused, to have her own house party in Chelmsford House instead. Rosamund knew how much that offer cost, and refused it with a smile.

'Don't worry about us. We're not ready for company yet. We shall be quite all right staying quietly on our own. I wish you would take Bab down, though — she needs a break from the sick-bed, and she doesn't see enough company.'

'Certainly I'll ask her. Ballincrea has been asked, too. I

have an idea he's interested in her. It will be a shame for young Maurice to lose the title, but a good establishment for Barbarina if anything comes of it.'

Bab was reluctant to leave Marcus, and in the end would consent to go down only for a few days. She returned, however, much refreshed and looking radiant, and Rosamund assumed that Ballincrea had been making love to her. He brought her back to Chelmsford House in order to enjoy her company a few hours longer, and while she ran upstairs to see Marcus, Ballincrea gave Rosamund some news which startled her out of the dream she had been living in.

'I heard something from one of the guests at Wolvercote — some news which I wondered if you had heard,' he said. 'It's about Kit Batchworth.'

'Kit Batchworth? No, I've heard nothing.'

'It seems he has broken his neck at last, just as everyone predicted he would.'

Rosamund stared. 'Good God! You can't mean he's dead?'

'It was a hunting accident. He always was something of a crammer, so I'm told, and it seems he overfaced his horse, took a crashing fall, and was taken up dead. His brother was out with him and saw the whole thing. I imagine he must be very upset. The dowager took to her bed at once.'

'Poor Jes,' Rosamund said. 'How dreadful for him. Even if he had always feared it —'

'Yes. One never really believes anything of that sort until it happens. Of course,' Ballincrea added, looking at her carefully, 'he will inherit the title now, won't he, since Batchworth never married?'

'Yes,' said Rosamund, 'but it wasn't a thing he ever wanted. Though I imagine he will make a more careful steward than his brother. The tenants might well be pleased.'

'Quite so,' said Ballincrea, as though a question had been answered. 'I believe Batchworth was a reckless gambler as well as a reckless rider.'

Rosamund had written briefly to Farraline, as she had promised she would, telling him that the baby was born and that she was well, but she had had no reply. She thought now that his silence was amply explained. Apart from his own sorrow and the grief of his mother to cope with, he would

198

have been inundated with the business of the estate, now all falling to his part. Kit had probably left things in a fine muddle.

She wrote again, offering her sympathies and saying that in view of the situation she would not expect to hear from him for some time; but he replied by return, thanking her, telling her he loved her, and saying that he would be in London at the end of January on legal business and would hope to be allowed to see her.

This presented her with a problem. She longed to see Jes, but she had no wish to upset Marcus, especially since Knighton had hinted that his happiness over the baby was helping enormously in his recovery. 'The mind is a great healer,' Knighton had said. 'A cheerful disposition mends more quickly, as I have often noticed.'

She might, of course, see Jes secretly without mentioning it to Marcus; but she hated subterfuge, and it was precisely not to have to do that that she had agreed to give Marcus his heir. To go back to furtive meetings would put her back exactly where she was before. Besides, supposing someone saw them and Marcus found out? That would be worse than if he had known all along.

On the other hand, telling Marcus that she was going to see Jes would not be easy or pleasant. He was so happy since Charlotte had been born, and liked nothing more than to plan her future with Rosamund, as though they were a happily married couple without any shadows in their past. She believed he thought she had given up Jes in her heart, that she would not want to see him any more, and it would be dreadful to have to disabuse him.

But after long consideration she saw no other way. She could not live a life of deceit; but if she were allowed her moments of happiness with Jes, she would be able to be a good wife to Marcus, and to put all the rest of her energies into making him content and cherishing his child.

Deciding to do it was one thing; carrying it out another. She put it off from day to day, waiting for the right moment when she knew that there could be no right moment to shatter his dreams. She planned the careful, tactful words, the slow, cautious approach that she would use; but at last when time ran out she simply blurted it out in the most stupid way.

She was taking a nuncheon with him, and he was talking quite amusedly about what Tom had been telling him of Polly Haworth's romance. Tom had taken to calling on Marcus quite often, and his visits always cheered him.

'So it looks as though George Paston has really taken a tumble at last. Tom says he firmly expects him to make an offer before Candlemas, which will dash the hopes of a whole new generation of debutantes and their mamas! But here's the best part: Tom plotted the whole thing from the beginning with Africa, because Africa wanted to marry her sailor, what's his name, but she knew even the thought of it would upset Polly, so she asked Tom to bring along lots of hopeful suitors to prove to Polly that she was still marriageable herself. What do you think about that? Of course they couldn't know it was going to work as well as this, but in my view she's exactly right for Paston, and a mature man like him needs —'

Rosamund had scarcely been listening, her mind occupied with her own problems. Finally she interrupted. 'Marcus, I've got something to tell you — something important.' He stopped in mid-sentence and looked at her with surprise. 'It's about Jes Farraline.'

Marcus's face closed up. 'I don't want to hear it. I don't want to talk about him.'

'But I have to tell you,' she blundered on. 'You see, he's coming to Town tomorrow, and I must see him, but I didn't want to do it behind your back, so to speak —'

'Behind my back? What are you talking about? How can you possibly see him any other way?'

'But — but our agreement,' she stammered. 'You said —'

'I know what I said, but for God's sake, hasn't that all changed now?' he asked piteously. 'I thought all that dreadful business was behind us. We've both suffered so much, and now I thought we'd reached a — a haven. You don't mean to spoil it all now, surely? Please, Rosy, don't let's talk about him any more.'

'I have to,' she said. 'I have to see him; and you agreed to it. It was our bargain, and I've kept my part. I'm sorry if it upsets you, but —'

In his pain he reached for anger as the best defence. 'What kind of woman are you?' he demanded fiercely. 'You're a mother now! We have a child! Does that mean nothing to you?'

'Of course it does. I love my child —'

'You have a strange way of showing it! Here she is, not yet eight weeks old, and you want to cuckold her father and give her a whore for a mother!'

'Marcus *please* —!'

'I thought the experience of motherhood would arouse your decent instincts, make you give up what you must know to be wrong. But perhaps you haven't any decent instincts. How you can come here to me like this, boldfaced, and tell me you want to take up with your paramour again, when our child is sleeping a few rooms away — our innocent child —'

'You mustn't blackmail me like that,' Rosamund said with quiet desperation. 'I love Charlotte, more than you can possibly imagine, and I will be a good mother to her and a good wife to you, but I have to see Jes sometimes. That's the price. It won't be very often and I'll be very discreet, but it's what we agreed between us before we —'

'*You* agreed!'

'You did too. It was a bargain freely entered into.'

'Freely?' he said bitterly. What choice did I have? You presented me with a *fait accompli*.' Rosamund didn't answer that. His anger began to slither away from him. 'Please, Ros, don't insist on this — arrangement. It will destroy everything. We've been so happy these last weeks.'

'We can go on being happy,' she said, 'but only if you keep to your part of the bargain.'

'There would be no happiness for me in that,' he said flatly. 'How do you think I would feel, lying here helpless, as I am, knowing you were — in God's name, have you no humanity?'

Rosamund turned her head away so that he would not see the tears in her eyes. Did he think she hadn't thought of that? 'You're taking advantage of me,' she said quietly.

'*I'm* —!' He choked on his rage. 'I forbid you to see him! I forbid it!'

Oh, this was agony! 'You can't stop me,' she said, standing up. He was trembling all over, and she looked down at him with terrible pity. 'I don't want to hurt you,' she said. 'I never wanted to hurt you.'

He turned his face away. 'Leave me now,' he said. 'I don't want to talk about it any more.'

She hesitated. 'I'll send Bab in to you.'

'No! I want to be alone. Just go.'

She went. He managed to hold on to himself until the door closed quietly behind her. Then he put his arm over his face and cried quietly, in case a servant passing the door might hear.

She met Jes in the end in the tea-room in St James's Park. For such a public place it was almost private on a January afternoon before the hour of promenade. He was there before her, and stood up as she came towards him. They stared at each other hungrily for a long time.

'You look wonderful,' he said at last. 'I was afraid it would change you, but you look just the same.'

'You look older,' she said.

'I feel a hundred years old,' he said. They sat down.

'Have you been ill?'

'No, only anxious for you, and harried almost to death by Kit's creditors.'

'I was sorry to hear about him. It must have been a terrible shock for you.'

'Not so much, really. We'd all said for years that's what would happen to him. At least he was killed outright. He'd have hated to linger on year after year a helpless cripple.' He bit his lip. 'I'm sorry, that was a stupid thing to say.'

'No,' she said.

'Yes it was, and if I weren't so damnably nervous, I wouldn't be talking to you like a stranger anyway. Oh Ros, I can't tell you what these past months have been like.'

'I know anyway,' she said. 'It was bad for me, too. But we seem to have killed the scandal at least. Most people think Marcus had a shooting accident, and those who don't have got something else to talk about now.'

'That's one thing to be grateful for.' He looked at her searchingly. 'And now you're a mother. Is your baby nice?'

'Very nice,' she said solemnly. 'You shall see her one day.'

'And Marcus?'

'He's much better. The baby coming seems to have worked a miracle for him. He adores her, and Knighton says that being happy helps him to recover.'

'Did he take it well — your coming to see me today?'

The maid brought the tea and bread-and-butter, and they waited until she had placed everything within their reach and gone away. Then Rosamund leaned forward a little and said, 'Oh Jes, it was horrible! We had such a quarrel about it yesterday. I reminded him about our agreement, and he was dreadfully upset, and then he flew into a rage and forbade me to see you.'

Farraline looked grave. 'I was afraid of this.'

'Were you?'

'Even before the duel, I believed he was hoping that parting us for a time would make you forget me —'

'You mean he never had any intention of keeping his side of the bargain?'

'He didn't think it would ever come to that. But now, since his injury, how much more desperately must he have hoped it. Look at it from his point of view —'

'I do,' she interrupted bitterly. 'Don't you think I do?'

'My dearest, it isn't your fault —'

'Isn't it? I don't know whose else it is.'

Farraline spread his hands flat on the table, trying to keep his spirits from quaking. 'Do you want to end it, then? Is that what you've come to say?'

She looked surprised. 'No!' Then she laughed shakily. 'No, my God, no! Is that what you were thinking? Oh my Jes, it's only thinking about you that's kept me alive since last August. I've got to have you — my reward!'

He did not smile. 'But what about Marcus? If he won't consent to the arrangement —'

She grew grim. 'He'll have to, that's all. But, oh Jes, I didn't want it to be this way! I didn't have to give him the baby, but I wanted to be fair to him. Why can't he be fair to me?'

He took hold of her hand and held it across the table. 'I don't think he can be. I don't think you ought to hope for that.'

'Then —?'

'There's an alternative now.'

She grew afraid. He was going to say something difficult. 'Tell me.'

'I'm not plain Jes Farraline any more, my love. I'm Jesmond Aubrey Cavendish Farraline, Eleventh Earl of Batchworth and Baron Blithfield, of Grasscroft Manor in the County of Lancashire — and incidentally of Ordsall Mills, Manchester, also in the county of Lancashire.'

'No, Jes —' she knew what he was going to say now.

'And since my poor late brother proved as inefficient at wasting his fortune as in every other of his dealings with money, I shall find myself moderately well-to-do, even after paying his debts and settling my mother in a pleasant house as far away from me as possible.'

'Oh my dear —'

'Before I had nothing to offer you. I could not even have supported you if you had left your husband's protection and come to me. But now I can give you everything — including my dearest and most constant love. You have done your duty by him. Come to me now.'

'I can't.' It seemed dragged out of her like a wail of pain. 'How could I leave him? You know I can't. He is much better than he was, but still he is bedridden and in pain. He may never walk again. He may get worse and die. I love you with all my heart, Jes, but what sort of woman would I be if I were to leave him like that?'

He pressed her hand, and after a moment he nodded. 'I was afraid you'd say that. Well, I won't try to press you. You must decide for yourself. But the offer is there, if things get worse, or if you change your mind. I shan't change mine.'

She licked her lips. 'You might marry someone else,' she said bravely.

He grinned. 'Fool!'

'Oh Jes!' she laughed shakily. 'It's so good to be with you again. If I can just see you from time to time, I think I can bear it.'

He nodded comfortably. 'We'll see. I think you may find that you need more, and that it does no-one any good for you to sacrifice yourself on an altar not of your making. But for now we'll leave it.'

Seeing him restored her spirits so well that she arrived back at Chelmsford House feeling quite cheerful. The short January day was drawing in and it was growing dark, and with the darkness it was turning much colder. There was a hint of snow in the air, and the glowing lights in the hall looked warm and welcoming. The great door was shut, presumably to keep out the cold, and as she trod up the steps she was surprised that the door was not opened before she reached it. It was with some annoyance that she found herself in the undignified position of having to knock.

It opened almost at once and Beason stood before her. Her brows drew together, and she was about to utter a reprimand when she realised that he was standing in her way as though he didn't mean to let her in.

'Well, Beason?' she snapped. 'Do you mean me to walk through you like a ghost, or duck under your arm like an urchin?'

'I beg your pardon my lady,' he said, still not moving, 'but I have strict instructions from his lordship not to allow you to enter.'

The words didn't make any sense. 'What on earth are you talking about?'

'His lordship does not wish you to enter this house, my lady,' Beason intoned. 'He has instructed me not to admit you upon any occasion or any pretext whatever.'

Rosamund stared a moment longer and then, as the cold wind whistled round her ankles, tried to walk past him. 'Get out of my way, and stop talking nonsense!'

But he was large and implacable, and moved to stop her. 'I assure you, my lady,' he said with barely concealed relish, 'that I have no wish to be forced to restrain you physically.'

'You would not dare —!' Rosamund began in fury; but she saw that he was enjoying this, and that indeed he would dare. He had always hated her. She bit her lip as she tried to keep her temper. 'Let me see his lordship. There's some mistake.'

'His lordship will not see you, my lady.'

'Oh, this is ridiculous! You can't keep me out of my own house!'

'I take my instructions from his lordship, my lady, and they are quite plain.'

'But what am I supposed to do?' Rosamund cried, still more angry than upset.

'I am instructed to say, my lady, that a letter from his lordship awaits you at Lady Theakston's house. And now, if you will excuse me, I must close the door. The cold is penetrating the house.'

He did actually close it, and for a moment Rosamund had the greatest possible difficulty in restraining herself from beating on it and screaming in rage. But she knew it would do no good. He wouldn't even open it again, and in the mean time she was growing colder. She turned away. The carriage had gone, of course, back to the stables: she would have to walk. It was not very far, probably not more than a mile, but she was not dressed for it, and it was almost dark and very cold.

She set off, putting one foot in front of the other while her mind seethed with rage and *chagrin*. Little as she wanted to face her mother in this situation, she saw that she really had no alternative.

The walk seemed very long, the flagways cold and hard under her shoes, the whole world empty and hostile. She felt people were staring at her as she passed, in amusement or speculation. Once a young man with a ribald grin began to tip his hat to her, but moved on hastily as he encountered her glare. When she reached her mother's house at last, the door was opened to her by dear old Hicks, who had known her from childhood, and his astonishment as he looked past her at the road, innocent of any vehicle, could not have been greater.

'Why, Lady Rosamund,' he said, entirely forgetting himself, 'what can have happened?'

The sight of his kind face almost broke her control. 'Don't ask me that now,' she said, hurrying past him to the hall fire. 'I'm almost starved of cold. Is my mother at home?'

'No, my lady, she hasn't come back yet. But his lordship's above.'

'I'll go up to him in just a moment. First — was a letter delivered here for me?'

'Yes, my lady. I have it here, my lady. It says "To be called for" on the outside, or of course we would have sent it round.'

'Thank you, Hicks. You did just right. I'll read it before I go upstairs.'

Her hands were so cold she had difficulty unfolding it, and when it was open it shook so much she had difficulty reading it. But there weren't many words. It was short, to the point, and bitter. When she had stared at it long enough, she folded it carefully and put it in her reticule, and said to the patient butler, 'Very well, Hicks. You may take me up now.'

Her control lasted all the way up the stairs to the drawing-room, where Papa Danby was reading the newspaper by a brisk fire. He stood up as Hicks announced her, folded his paper and threw it down, and stepped forward. The sight of his dear face made her lips quiver, but she managed to hold on just long enough for Hicks to withdraw. Then she said, 'Oh Papa Danby!' and ran to his waiting arms.

He held her close and stroked her head while her hot tears soaked through the superfine of his coat and wet his shirt beneath.

'It's all right,' he said. 'I know all about it. Moss is here with a bag of your things. I got it out of her. Oh my poor, poor darling.'

Lucy came in, tearing off her hat and flinging it onto the sofa. 'It's no use,' she said, ruffling her already disordered hair. 'I got in to see him this time —'

'How did you get past Beason?'

'The butler has not yet been born who can keep me out,' Lucy said darkly. 'I was able to see Marcus, but he won't change his mind. I tried every argument, but he said you have made your own choice and must abide by it. Oh, it's outrageous!' she went on angrily, flinging herself down beside her hat. 'Ring the bell, Rosamund. I must have some tea. I know the poor man has a terrible affliction to bear, but he is behaving like a monster!'

Lord Theakston came in, his expression eager. 'I thought I heard you come in. Did you see him?'

'He won't change his mind. He won't have her back on any account,' Lucy answered.

207

'I was afraid of that,' Theakston said gravely.

'I don't know what he hopes to gain!' Lucy said wildly. 'It's not as though he wants to marry anyone else, or even as if he *could*. It's not as though she were behaving badly, making him uncomfortable or causing a scandal. And even if he wanted a separation, to go about it like this is pointlessly cruel.'

'I think we have to accept, my love, that his mind may be disordered,' said Theakston.

'But not enough to have him shut up, more's the pity,' said Lucy.

'Oh Mama!'

'And to see Barbarina hovering about him, like something half nun and half gaoler — and behaving so insolently to me, the ungrateful little minx, after all I've done for her!'

'Did you ask him about Charlotte?' Rosamund asked.

Lucy came down to earth. 'He says he won't let you see her,' she said gravely. 'My dear, I'm so sorry.'

Rosamund stared into the fire for a long time. Theakston sat down in the chair opposite her and leaned forward, resting his forearms on his knees. He looked at her averted profile for a while, and then said quietly, 'You will have to decide what to do with yourself, my dear.'

Rosamund looked up, and sighed — a shuddering and final sort of sigh that seemed to come up from the bottom of her life. 'I think I had better go to Jes.'

'Oh no,' Lucy said sharply. 'If you do that he'll never take you back.'

'He won't anyway.'

'You don't know that. He's angry at the moment, but his anger will wear off, and he'll be sorry and want you back.'

'But Mother, you don't understand. We had an agreement that he would let me see Jes without making a fuss —'

'A very foolish agreement,' Lucy said rather stiffly.

'The only way I could go back to him would be if the arrangement stood. Don't you see, the first time I tried to see Jes, it would all happen all over again. I can't live a life like that. Better get it over with at once.'

'You will make yourself an outcast,' Lucy said.

'Your mother's right,' Theakston added quietly.

Rosamund looked from one to the other. 'But it's only

what you did. You and Papa lived apart, and you lived with your lover. It didn't make you an outcast.'

'It was different.' Lucy looked uneasy at talking about it, but made herself go on. 'Your Papa had separate lodgings in London, and there was quite a scandal about that. But we were never officially separated, and all you children were safely down at Wolvercote where we both visited you. But in your case — if you go off with your lover everyone will think Marcus was justified in casting you off. You will be blamed for it all. You will be pariah.'

'Times are different now,' Theakston added his weight. 'In our young day people did a great many wicked things, and no-one thought anything of it; but they could not do the same things today.'

'You said young people were more censorious nowadays,' Rosamund said, looking at her mother. 'I remember that. But Marcus will divorce me and I'll marry Jes and people will forget.' Her mother shook her head, and Rosamund added, 'If they don't, I don't care. I love Jes, and I want to be with him. It's all I ever did want really — oh Mother, please don't cry!'

Lucy had put her head down into her hands. To her deep distress Rosamund could see the tears seeping through her thin fingers in the rosy firelight.

'I just don't understand any more. I think all my children must have been cursed,' Lucy cried. 'First Minnie was murdered, the poor little idiot, and now you've been thrown out of your house by a mad husband.' Theakston went to her and put a hand on her shoulder. She reached up a blind hand for him. 'Roland says he doesn't want to marry Thalia Hampton, when the whole of London's expecting it! If it weren't for Tom, I don't know what I'd do. And if you leave Marcus, what will happen to Charlotte?'

'I'm not leaving him, Mother; he's cast me out,' Rosamund reminded her.

'It's the same thing.'

Rosamund crouched down at her mother's knees and thrust her handkerchief into her hand, desperate for the tears to stop. 'He'll let me see Charlotte,' she said. 'He must do — I'm her mother. Oh please don't cry!' Occupied as she was, she didn't see the expression of grave doubt on her step-father's face over the last statement.

Ballincrea was not a superstitious man, but there was something dreadful about the house, something dark and cold and curst, which made him shiver as he waited in the morning room for Barbarina to come. Of course, there was no fire in the room, which might have had something to do with the shiver; but then what sort of household shows a visitor into a fireless room in February?

Barbarina came at last. He was surprised to see that she was wearing a cap, which made her look much older, and that she didn't smile. The interview was as cheerless as the room, unsatisfactory and frustrating. He had the feeling that he was speaking to her in a foreign language, or that she was answering in one. The two halves of what was said didn't seem to marry up, and yet there was no doubting what she was telling him. She would not marry him; she could not possibly leave Marcus alone; she did not wish to hold Ballincrea to his offer.

'You might change your mind,' he said desperately. God forbid he should say 'Marcus might die', but it was in his thoughts.

Barbarina shook her head. Her expression was one of immutable nobility which made him want to shake her hard. Whatever curse was on this house had infected her with its madness. She was not speaking like a rational woman, but like the heroine of a Gothic novel. He could not reach her.

At last she indicated that the interview was terminated, and that she had business which required her upstairs. He could only bow his head to the inevitable and take his leave.

But as she placed her cold hand in his, he said, 'I shan't give up, you know, Bab my dear, I shan't withdraw my offer. As soon as you change your mind, just send me word. I'll be waiting for you. And don't be afraid — arrangements can be made for Marcus's comfort. He won't be neglected.'

When he had gone, Barbarina drew a sigh of relief and resignation. It had been the hardest interview of her life; and she felt a bitterness against the woman who had made it necessary. She walked upstairs, brooding on the character of

210

her sister-in-law, in whom she had been so mistaken. The anger and bitterness were sustaining, a black food to keep her going through the dark days and darker nights.

She opened the door of the room next to her own and went in; walked across to the crib and looked down into it. Without her knowing it, her expression softened. This was the other thing that sustained her, of course.

Marcus had said, 'As far as we are concerned, as far as the world is concerned, the child has no mother now. That woman's name is never to mentioned in Charlotte's presence. I want every memory of her expunged. My daughter is to be brought up as though her mother died giving birth to her.'

The baby woke and murmured, and Barbarina bent down and scooped her up out of the crib and settled her in her arms.

'Poor little motherless baby,' she crooned. Charlotte gazed up at her, and her mouth moved as though she were trying to smile. Barbarina touched a finger to a pearly fist, and it opened and closed tightly around it. A vast, protective tenderness flushed through her at the feeling of that small grip and the sight of the perfect, rose-petal face gazing trustfully up into hers. Nothing, she swore fiercely, would ever harm this little creature if she could help it. 'You haven't got a mother any more, poor little baby, but you have an aunt, haven't you? Yes, that's right, my Charlotte, you have an Aunt Barbarina to take care of you. And Auntie will always keep you safe, my precious one.'

She smiled, rocking the baby to and fro in her arm, and Charlotte, gripping tightly onto the forefinger gazed up and blew bubbles, and almost smiled.

CHAPTER ELEVEN

'This is pleasant,' Héloïse said, though she had to catch at her bonnet as the phaeton jolted over a bump in the track.

Lucy cursed briefly but graphically. 'This road is the devil,' she observed. 'It wouldn't have been like this in my father's day. Doesn't James do *anything* about it?'

Héloïse thought this a little unfair. Under Lucy's direction the two normally docile little chestnuts were scorching along with their heads up, and the speed made the bumps and ruts seem worse than they were. She wondered whether her elderly phaeton would survive the experience intact.

'James works terribly hard,' she defended her husband. 'You saw yourself how early he went out. Before we had even finished breakfast he had ridden out to look at the merinos before going up to Twelvetrees.'

'What's he doing there this morning?'

'He is schooling a pair of bays for Mrs Chubb's new phaeton. She is very particular, but a good customer, so he sees to them himself.'

'He has completely taken over Edward's role, hasn't he?'

'He has almost taken over Edward's character,' Héloïse said, faintly smiling. 'He works so hard from dawn to dusk, determined that Morland Place shan't miss him. But *he* misses him. Edward was almost more like a father than a brother to James.'

Lucy nodded, concentrating on putting the phaeton through a track gate without slowing. Héloïse trusted her implicitly, but could not help knowing that she was driving rather more aggressively than was necessary, probably to take her mind off things. Héloïse would have liked to talk about them, but she would not press Lucy before she was ready. So she said again, 'This is very pleasant. It is kind of you to take me out for a drive.'

'You should get out more often,' Lucy said. 'You spend too many hours shut up indoors. Let your servants do their own work. That's what you pay them for.'

'It isn't quite as simple as that. Morland Place is not just a house, it's the centre of a whole universe.'

Lucy snorted. 'Don't I remember! It kept my blessed mother so busy she never had time to bother with me. That's how I managed to get into so much trouble when I was a child.'

A faintly wistful tone developed in the last sentence, but nothing more followed, so Héloïse said, 'I miss Polly's help, too. She took a great many tasks off my hands. But it's wonderful that she is going to be married at last.'

'As Mrs George Paston she'll have a handsome fortune to dispose. No household cares for her!'

'Her experience here won't be wasted,' Héloïse said. 'It's important to know how a thing should be done, if one is to see the servants do it properly.'

'That's what my mother used to say. I prefer to hire a good butler.'

'The wedding will make a great deal of work for you,' Héloïse observed.

'That's why I wanted to have a quiet few weeks here beforehand, to set myself up. And I must say it is quiet!'

'Too quiet without my boys. Do you know, I keep looking around for them without realising what I am looking for. It was like that when my old dog died. I missed the sound of his claws behind me.'

'You'll have to get used to it, if you really mean to send Nicholas to school in the autumn.'

Héloïse sighed. 'I wish I could be sure it is the best thing for him. He's such a sensitive boy, and everything I hear about Eton makes me fear for him. And he's delicate too — who will look after him?'

'The dames,' Lucy said briefly. 'They'll see he's all right. It would reflect badly on them if they lost one.'

'Lost one?' Héloïse laughed. 'Oh, what a comfort you are,

Lucy! Well, Father Moineau is quite determined that it will do Nicky good to mix with other boys of his own sort, even if only for a few years; and James agrees with him, so I must be content.'

'You'll still have Benedict to brood over.'

'One can't brood over Bendy,' Héloïse said. 'He's too much like his father: off on his own for hours at a time, making the strangest friends, always happy in his own company. I do not understand Bendy at all, but he seems happy and healthy enough, grâce à Dieu.'

They had skirted Harewood Whin now and come out onto Low Moor, with the little huddle of buildings which was Hessay a mile or so ahead of them. It was a perfect summer day, and the sky above them was a deep, creamy July blue. Lucy halted the ponies to breathe them, and when their fidgeting and clinking had died away, the only sound in the world was the singing of the gentle breeze against their ears, and the high, thin ecstasy of the skylarks.

'How quiet it is!' Lucy said at last. 'It's something one needs, this absolute silence. One forgets it, with all the noise and bustle every day — particularly in London. Of course, even in London it's quiet sometimes — at night, for instance — but when you come to a place like this, the silence seems different.'

'More profound,' Héloïse offered.

Lucy's silvery brows were drawn into a frown, partly against the sun, partly as she struggled with difficult thoughts. 'Do you remember when I came to stay with you at Plaisir? When Thomas was born.'

'Yes, of course.'

'I said to you once, "You bring God into everything," and you answered, "But how can you leave Him out?"'

'Did I? I don't remember.'

'I do. I've often thought about it, and wondered how differently you must see things — just ordinary things. Sitting here now, for instance, looking across the moor on a nice summer day — I would wager that you see God out there.'

'Of course,' Héloïse said. 'And hear Him.'

'But I only hear the wind and the skylarks.'

'It's the same thing.'

Lucy turned her frowning gaze on her. 'That's too simple, surely?'

Héloïse shrugged. 'How difficult do you want it to be?'

'You can be so very French sometimes,' Lucy laughed. 'Even after all these years! But it's all very well being simple when one is happy. When things go wrong they go wrong in such a complicated fashion. Unhappiness isn't simple at all.'

'No,' Héloïse agreed. She looked at companion with affection and sympathy. 'Do you want to talk about it, my Lucy?'

Lucy hesitated only a moment. 'It's Rosamund, of course. The way Marcus has behaved is monstrous, even making allowance for his unfortunate condition. Casting Rosamund off without a penny, forbidding her ever to see her child again — it's simply inhuman! I've done everything I can think of to make him change his mind, but it's no use.' She turned her head. 'You and I, Héloïse — in our time we have done wrong, pretty much as Rosamund did. It was wrong, and I don't defend it; but to punish her like that — how can that be right? How can one ever forgive him?'

Héloïse said tentatively, 'But she is with Lord Batchworth now, and that was what she wanted.'

Lucy made an impatient movement of her head. 'Yes, and I could bear it better if I thought she could be happy with him. But she is separated from her child, and she really loves Charlotte. And not only that, but Marcus is refusing to divorce her. If he would divorce her the disgrace would be bad enough, but at least she could then marry Batchworth and achieve a kind of respectability. As it is . . .'

'Perhaps she will not mind it so very much,' Héloïse said painfully. 'After all, you were able to be happy with Captain Weston without — without being able to —'

'That was brave of you,' Lucy said with spare humour, patting Héloïse's hand. 'But the case was very different — I was not an outcast, cut off from my children, the object of my husband's hostility. And in any case, Rosamund is not like me.' She shook her head in a bewildered way. 'I used to think she was. When she was younger, I used to think she would be wild and wicked and careless like me, and I didn't like her very much. But there is a thoughtful side to Rosamund that

215

takes one quite by surprise. She is more like you,' with a nod and an appraising look. 'She minds about things, as you do. She is —' A pause while she searched for the word; and when she found it, it seemed to puzzle her. 'She is *good*.'

Héloïse did not challenge the epithet which on the face of it might be considered inappropriate.

Lucy went on, 'But though she's not like me, I can't help feeling that I have been a bad mother to her, and that what has happened is at least partly my fault. I haven't led a good life, Héloïse, I know that. I haven't ever meant to do anyone harm, but I've let them down — all my children. I've set a bad example, and I haven't taken proper care of them.'

She was glad when Héloïse did not immediately offer a polite denial. She looked back down the years and wondered about the little touches of chaos which had protruded through into the order of her life, like the outcrops of rock which break through the thin turf of the high moors. It was unpleasant to be reminded how close under the surface that desolation was. She could not be held accountable for Weston's death, it was true. But her first husband's death — had that really been an accident as she had allowed herself to believe all these years? And poor Minnie's? Now Rosamund, whom she had thought happily settled when she went away on the Grand Tour, had plunged into a complicated morass of misery and shame.

At last Héloïse spoke. 'But Roland and Thomas — you have no worries for them?'

Lucy sighed. 'I don't know. Not Thomas, of course — he is quite perfect, though I wish he would spend more time with me instead of dashing about all over the country with his new friends. But Roland — I've been trying and trying to get his marriage to Thalia Hampton fixed, and neither of them precisely refuses to marry, but neither of them will come to the point. I first broached the subject with Greyshott at Christmas 1821, and here it is, July 1823 and we're no further along. I just don't know what to do with him.'

'Perhaps you should not do anything with him,' Héloïse said gently. 'He's almost twenty-four years old. Perhaps he should govern his own life.'

'You think I interfere too much?' Lucy looked at her

doubtfully, and there was a shadow of age in her eyes which struck Héloïse to the heart.

'Don't take advice from me, dear Lucy,' she said quickly. 'I know nothing. All I meant was that — everyone has to do what is in them to do, and praise God through their lives by using what He has given them. He will not judge the horse because it cannot fly like a bird, or the bird because it cannot draw a burden.'

Lucy smiled faintly. 'There, now you're back to God again.'

'I was never away from Him.'

'He has been away from me.' She added lightly, 'But I dare say that's my fault.'

'One does one's best, that's all,' Héloïse said seriously, 'and that has to be enough.'

Lucy and Danby were staying at Morland Place for four weeks, including race week, for which they would be joined by Roland and Thomas. The two young men were not far away, for they were staying at Castle Howard with Tom's new friend George Howard, and some other lively young bucks including Maurice Hampton and Lord Ashley, son of the Earl of Shaftesbury. They would all be coming over to York for the races during race week, and at the end of the month Maurice would be departing on the much longed-for Grand Tour in company with Ashley.

It was an arrangement to please everyone, and had largely come about through Tom, who saw the opportunity of bringing the two young men together. George Howard was Ashley's best friend from Christ Church days, and it was natural that he should introduce Tom to him, and that Tom should introduce Maurice. Ashley was a handsome, clever, but underneath rather serious young man, and he and Maurice got on like a house afire. Greyshott and Shaftesbury knew each other quite well, and so it seemed the most natural thing in the world for the young men to share their Grand Tour together.

Tom was proving to be something of a manipulator. 'I wish you could do something for me, old fellow,' Roland said to him gloomily when he heard the news about Maurice's good fortune. 'I shall find myself married to Thalia Hampton before I'm much older, and I really don't want to at all. She's a very nice girl, but she doesn't care a button for me, and the last thing I want is an unwilling wife.'

'Then tell Mama you won't marry her,' Tom said logically.

Roland sighed. 'You know I can't. I'm not like you. I never could tell Mama anything. You'll have to help me, or I'm sunk.'

'Very well, I'll see what I can do,' Tom said obligingly. 'But it will have to wait until after race week. I can't concentrate on anything other than horses until then.'

'You don't like horses,' Roland pointed out.

'I don't care about riding 'em,' Tom said with a grin, 'but I've no objection to their making my fortune.'

On the day after her drive with Lucy, Héloïse was expecting her own children back from a trip to Northumberland under the care of Lord Anstey. She was looking forward to having them home again, for she was never happy unless all her loved ones were within reach.

To make it a family occasion, Mathilde and John Skelwith came over to spend the day, bringing their children with them. Since there were now four of them, it involved a great many nursery maids and considerable organisation, but Héloïse could hardly be happier than when Miss Mary and Miss Harriet, aged six and four, came up to her to curtsey and say 'Good day, Grandmama,' and offer up their faces for kissing. Dear Miss Rosedale had taught them beautiful manners.

Miss Rosedale herself, not looking a day older, though she must, Héloïse reflected with a startled thought, be over fifty now, came forward after them to claim her kiss. Even when she had been Sophie's and Fanny's governess, she and Héloïse had been much more than employer and employee.

The first thing she asked was, 'When are the boys to arrive?'

'I don't expect them until this afternoon,' Héloïse said.

'And Sophie? She is coming for race week this year, I hope?'

'Oh yes,' said Mathilde quickly, 'do say she is, dear Madame! I long to see her, and dear little Fanny.'

218

'She and Jasper have promised to come this year,' Héloïse said, 'so I'm sure they will.'

'And she hasn't seen my new baby yet,' Mathilde said, cleverly bringing the attention back to her own family. The baby, Lydia, born in January of that year, had to be admired and her astonishing growth exclaimed upon, but Jemima was Héloïse's own favourite, and at two years old she already knew how to play on it. She tucked her hand into gran'ma's and fluttered her long brown eyelashes and displayed her dimples, secure in the knowledge that they would inevitably bring a little something for her out of gran'ma's hidden pocket.

'That child is practising to become a siren,' James remarked to John as they stood on the fringes with Danby, watching the exclusively female scene.

'It must be some kind of benign punishment,' John said ruefully, 'that I can only seem to beget female children. They all wind themselves round my heart in the most damnable way with their smiles and soft little kisses, and promise me nothing but trouble, and large dowries to find.'

'Ah,' said James, 'but you wouldn't swap 'em.'

Lord Theakston smiled his most urbane smile. 'No use applying to me, gentlemen. Avoidin' the whole issue's my speciality. Fine-looking colt you were lungeing this morning, by the way, James.'

James laughed. 'Just by way of changing the subject! But how did you happen to see me with the colt? It was too early for you to have been out of bed.'

'Country times for country habits,' Danby said with faint indignation. 'Morland Place ain't London, you know! I walked up to Twelvetrees before breakfast.'

'*Meret qui laborat*! Having exerted yourself, you reap the reward: I was keeping Helios a secret for the big race. Now I suppose I shall have to let you in on it.'

'Surely, sir, you would have told me?' John Skelwith asked with an air of hurt.

James grinned. 'Not I! You're a damned, parsimonious, pawky sort of gambler, Jack, and I won't have my fine horse insulted with nip-farthing bets! It's a fortune or nothing on his handsome nose.'

Danby took James's arm. 'I'm your man, James! Come and tell me all about it. I'm the fellow you want! I stake my all, and stand or fall by it like a gentleman. Come to the drawing-room and open a bottle of your good madeira, and you can tell me all about Helios while we warm the coats of our stomachs.'

'What an excellent idea!' James said. 'But I think we'd better take poor John along with us. How will he ever learn, except by the example of his betters?'

Skelwith accepted the role of acolyte meekly, and the three men walked off together in the greatest of good humour.

It wasn't possible to be in any doubt when the boys arrived home: their voices preceded them into the house. Having not seen them for several weeks, James was struck anew with the difference between them as they bounded into the hall, followed by Harry Anstey and his father and Father Moineau. Benedict at eleven was tall and stout for his age, and of late he had even begun to be a little heavy about the face and neck. His thick dark hair curled vigorously, his high-coloured face bloomed with health, his dark eyes shone. He was the picture of suppressed energy.

Beside him Nicholas looked almost sickly. He was not tall for fifteen, but thin and pale which made him look like an overgrown weed. His face had a pinched look, and he moved and spoke carefully as though he had always to conserve his strength. There was nothing exuberant or outgoing about him. He hunched his shoulders a little about his concave chest, and kept his hands close to himself as though to guard giving away his vital resources.

How Moineau could claim that it was Bendy who was the sensitive one, James thought again with a shake of the head, was beyond him!

But all three boys were bubbling over with what they had seen. Lord Anstey had gone on a tour through Northumberland and Durham to study the improvements to mining in those areas, and since he had wanted to take Harry along to whet his appetite for the family business, he had offered to take Nicky and Bendy too. With Father Moineau along to take charge of the boys when Lord Anstey was engaged in business, they had been travelling for four weeks through lands as remote and strange to the inhabitants of Morland Place as India or far Cathay.

'It was wonderful, Papa! You never saw such mines! And there were tramways all over the place,' Bendy enthused, 'and waggons and waggons of coal going up and down to the water — thousands of them!'

'And such a noise and clanking and banging,' Harry said with boyish relish. 'Steam ships going up and down the river to the sea. And they had a steam winding-engine, too, at the top of one tramway, to drag the waggons up the slope. It has a rod and crank, you see, and the ropes pass round —'

'Oh that wasn't the interesting part,' Nicky interrupted loudly. 'Mama, I must tell you about the horses! You see, in one place where we were, the entrance to the mines is higher than the river where they load the coal onto the boats, so the loaded waggons run down the rails on their own, just by gravity; but they have to have horses to drag the empty waggons back up. When they get to the top they unhitch the horses and let them loose, and the clever animals rush round to the other end and jump into their own special waggon to be carried back down the hill! No-one has to tell them what to do, they just do it. They really seem to enjoy the ride!'

'How remarkable,' Héloïse said obediently.

'You have brought my sons back tramway-nutty, I see,' James smiled. 'Are you going to make mine-masters of them?'

'It certainly was very interesting,' Anstey said. 'There are as many ways of getting the coal to the water as there are mines, and some of those waggonways are marvels of engineering, what with the cuttings and embankments to even out the gradient —'

'And the turntables, Papa, to change the waggons from one line to another,' Harry added. 'And the rails are so cleverly made — the wheels have flanges, you see, which sit —'

'And did you learn anything to your own advantage?' James asked Anstey, interrupting hastily.

'Only that there's no reason at all why we shouldn't eventually have tramroads to connect every part of the canal system. Where the terrain isn't suitable for the digging of a navigation, it may still be perfectly possible to lay down a tramway and then — off one boat onto waggon, a short horse-haul along a track, and back to the water again! All those awkward little gaps in our great hydraulic enterprise filled in! Goods crossing England from coast to coast with ease and expediency!'

'And in your own case, sir,' John Skelwith added with interest, 'I suppose you are thinking of a tramroad from your mines — what, all the way to Selby, to pick up the navigation there?'

Anstey smiled. 'It would be quite an undertaking. That's twelve miles or more. I would not think of embarking on it alone.'

'I imagine not. You would need partners,' Skelwith said.

'But who would come in with you on such a scheme?' Héloïse said. 'Who else would it benefit?'

'Oh, the tramroad once built need not be used for coal alone,' Anstey said. 'Anyone might run a waggonload of goods on it, for a fee.'

'It would be a great improvement on the roads, I can see that,' James said. 'On smooth rails a horse can pull many times the load, and the permanent way does not deteriorate in bad weather as a road does.'

'Especially with iron rails instead of wooden ones,' Anstey agreed.

'But sir,' Bendy said eagerly, 'why stick to horses? Why not steam engines?'

Anstey smiled across his head at Héloïse. 'This one is not tramway-nutty, he is machine-nutty, I'm afraid.'

'As I understand it, from what I've read,' James said, 'the steam engines are only used on slopes too steep for horses.'

'That's right: it wouldn't be economical to use them on the flat. A stationary engine can only pull waggons a short distance, and then you have all the trouble of unhitching them from one and hitching them up to the next. And even so you have frequent trouble with fouling of the lines, and lines breaking, and so on.'

'True, sir,' Bendy said excitedly, 'but that's stationary engines. What about locomotive engines?'

'That's mere fantasy, I'm afraid, my boy,' Lord Anstey said.

Bendy was about to enter the argument with passion when he received support from an unexpected quarter. Lucy said, 'I *saw* a locomotive engine once.'

Bendy's eyes grew round. 'Did you really, ma'am?' he asked reverently.

'Yes, it was in the year 'seven — or was it 'eight? Do you remember, Danby? I think it was in Islington, or somewhere like that.'

'Eh?' Lord Theakston returned from the gentle doze into which all this engineering talk had sent him drifting. 'Ah, yes, m'dear, I remember it well. It was the summer of the year 'eight. Everybody went out to see it.'

'You took me, as I recall,' Lucy said with a fond smile for him. It was at a time when she was still deep in mourning for Captain Weston, who died at Trafalgar, and Danby had been her shadow, endlessly and patiently trying to find things to distract her from her grief. 'It was called the *Catch-me-who-can*, and it ran round and round on a circular track, and the man who owned it —'

'Trevithick,' Theakston supplied.

'He tried to get people to ride in the little waggons and be pulled around, but no-one would dare. I certainly wouldn't — it was quite frightening to see those waggons moving all on their own, with no horses in front! And the locomotive engine made a frightful noise and an even more frightful smell. It threw out sparks like a mad blacksmith! I wonder whatever happened to it?'

'Oh Father,' Bendy said eagerly, turning to Father Moineau for support, 'didn't we read something about Mr Trevithick in Rees' Cyclopaedia, under the section on canals? Sir,' to Lord Anstey, 'didn't he make a locomotive engine for a coal mine somewhere?'

'You certainly have a good memory,' Anstey said genially. 'Yes, it was a coal mine somewhere in Wales, as I remember, but it wasn't a success. The locomotive engine worked all right, and even managed to drag the waggons, but the rails couldn't take the weight. They shattered after just a few passages. Even iron rails can't bear the enormous weight of a locomotive engine, you know.'

'But perhaps —' Bendy began.

223

'In any case,' Anstey said gently, 'the engine couldn't pull the waggons as fast as horses could, and it cost a great deal more to run. I can't see the point of it. No, water is the natural means of carrying goods, depend upon it. But horse tramways have their uses.'

'Bendy talks nonsense, doesn't he, Papa?' Nicky appealed to his father. 'Nothing can ever replace the horse.'

'I certainly hope not, or I shall be a poorer man,' James laughed. 'So, Anstey, you fancy yourself as an undertaker, do you?'

'You haven't heard the half of my plans yet,' Anstey smiled, and it was plain that he was only half in jest. Not only would I undertake a tramroad from my mines to Selby; but what about from my mines right into the city of York itself?'

'No, now you really are dealing in fantasy,' James said.

'Perhaps I am at the moment. But I sell a great deal of coal in York, and look at the choice I have of transportation! Either I haul it by road over the ruts and bumps, and risk being bogged down permanently in the winter; or I haul it to Selby and pay the Ouse Navigation's wickedly high fees to bring it in to York by boat. It's no wonder coal is so dear in the city — and not just coal, either.'

'That's true, sir,' Skelwith agreed. 'Half the cost of timber is the cost of transportation — and brick, and stone. A tramway to give the Navigation Companies a little healthy competition would be a boon to everyone.'

'It's something to think about, certainly,' Lord Anstey said. 'Perhaps one day we might get together a group of like-minded investors to consider the possibility.'

The conversation thereafter grew dull, from Benedict's point of view, wandering off onto grown-up topics. The mention of Nicky's going to Eton provoked all sorts of memoirs from Lord Theakston and Lord Anstey, to which Nicky listened with eagerness and Harry with politeness. Bendy concentrated on moving himself inch by inch to the back of the group and thence to the door, and finally managed to slip out without anyone's noticing. He ran upstairs to the nursery to haul off his smart travelling coat and shiny boots, pulled on some brogues and a jacket, and in a few minutes he was down the nursery stairs and out through the back door to freedom.

It was bliss to run after being cramped in the carriage all morning. He climbed the orchard wall, took the short cut across it — gathering a few windfalls on the way — and on the other side set off at a dog-trot towards the Whin. This year's cubs would be almost grown up by now, he thought. He had enjoyed every minute of the trip up north, but he had hated missing any episode of the lives of what he thought of as 'his' cubs. Sometimes on a warm afternoon they would lie about in the clearing by the earth enjoying the sun, and play-fight and box with each other. He paused to test the wind direction, and then started off again, changing direction slightly. If he crept up on them from down-wind, he could get quite close without their seeing him . . .

Africa and Polly were both to marry from Upper Grosvenor Street, and Lord Theakston was to give them away.

'It really is most extremely kind of you,' Polly had thanked their aunt and uncle on behalf of both of them.

'Nonsense,' Lucy had said. 'You couldn't get married from that stable of yours, now could you?'

'Complete self-interest,' Danby had protested with a small smile. 'Couldn't ask all my friends to the weddin' breakfast otherwise, could I?'

Nevertheless, Polly felt privately that it was a great deal more kind than she deserved, and that without the kindness things might not have come to the satisfactory conclusion she was now within reach of. She was acutely aware of the cobwebs of unsavoury scandal which must cling to her because of Harvey's trial for murder and her own involvement in it. Somehow Africa and Tom between them had made the eccentricity of the School of Equitation a fashionable thing, but Mr Paston was not the sort of man to relish any sort of notoriety clinging to his wife.

With a shadowed past, an eccentric present, and no portion to speak of, she felt she would have been far below Paston's touch, had it not been that she was niece to Lady Theakston and first cousin to the Earl of Aylesbury. Polly had been through dark times, and was inclined to give too little

225

weight to her own attractions, her intelligence, and the fact that Mr Paston was madly in love with her and no-one else. Still, for Aunt Lucy to offer her patronage and protection, her home for the wedding, her husband for the ceremony, and to foot the bill for the whole thing into the bargain, was generosity of no small order.

They were at Upper Grosvenor Place one morning in September, opening replies to wedding invitations and ticking names on Lucy's list. They had been joined by Thalia Hampton, who had been to visit her friend Lady Hope — the former Lady Mary Penshurst — and had called in on them on the way home.

'His Grace the Duke of Wellington,' she read from a card she had just opened. 'I say, is he really going to come to your wedding, Polly? You are lucky.'

'Lord and Lady Theakston are friends of his,' Polly said.

'And the First Lord of the Admiralty?'

'Friend of Papa's,' Africa said, searching the list for the name to tick. 'You needn't be *too* humble, you see, Pol.'

'All the same,' Polly laid down the cards in her hand, 'it doesn't seem right that I should have all this and not you — Dukes and Admirals and a wedding breakfast for two hundred. I *wish* you would have made it a double wedding, sister.'

'So do I,' Thalia said. 'How romantic that would have been!'

Africa laughed. 'Not our style at all. St George's, Hanover Square? Peter and I will be poor as church mice, and you can't make a silk purse out of a sow's ear.'

'You are not a sow's ear. And you won't really be poor, will you?' Polly said, the first firmly, the second doubtfully.

'We'll get by,' Africa said, laughing. 'But think of poor Mr Paston! He wouldn't want a gypsy like me walking up the aisle beside his lovely wife, to say nothing of a half-pay lieutenant. He wants you all to himself, Hippolyta my dear. You shall have your moment of glory, and very lovely you will look too.'

Polly smiled at the thought of him. 'I still can't believe it's true, sometimes. For him to choose me, of all people —'

'When every mama in London has been after him for I

don't know how many Seasons,' Thalia agreed. 'But you are very beautiful, Polly; and clever too, and Mr Paston always was rather satirical.'

Africa laughed at the analysis. 'He adores you, and you will make him the perfect wife. After all, a man as rich as he is needs a wife who is elegant and beautiful and will grace his house and his carriages and be witty at the dinner table. I shall be very sorry to lose you, though, but one can see Mr Paston would not like his wife to go on giving riding lessons.'

'Lucky for you that Peter doesn't mind,' Polly smiled.

'But what *will* you do?' Thalia asked. 'Polly was such an asset, wasn't she?'

'Peter will help me. I suppose he will take over my young men and I'll teach the young ladies. But there was no-one like Polly for looking good on a horse. I shall miss her sorely.'

'Do you need another lady instructress?' Thalia asked casually.

'If I go on getting so many customers, I shall,' Africa said. 'I don't quite know how to go about finding one, though. I can't hope for another lady, or even a gentlewoman, and yet nothing less will do for *my* clients.'

Thalia dropped her mask. 'What about me?' she gasped. And then, 'Now don't say no before you've thought about it! Oh do, *do* say that you'd like me! You know I ride very well, and though I'm not as lovely as Polly, I am very pretty, and I look elegant on a horse. And I'm a lady, and we get on awfully well together, don't we? What do you think, Africa? Polly, what do you think?'

Africa said, 'I think you would be perfect for the position — no, don't fall on my neck! You'd be perfect, but your mother would never agree in a thousand, thousand years, so there's no use in even thinking about it.'

'But she would. Listen, she would! She wants me to get married but she knows I don't want to, and she's the last person in the world to be stuffy. And Papa would never make me do anything I don't want to do. It would be perfectly respectable, and you could even tell them that I'd meet lots more eligible young men that way than by going to balls, which is true, isn't it? And I'd be kept out of mischief, and I'd do exactly what you tell me to. And with Peter there, and you

227

being a married woman — and Tom, too, who's really almost like a brother — there'd be plenty of chaperonage. If *you* asked her,' she finished breathlessly, 'I'm sure she'd say yes.'

'I'm sure she'd say no,' Africa laughed. 'You really are an absurd child.'

'No I'm not,' Thalia said irrepressibly. 'And I'm not such a child, either. I'm twenty years old, you know — almost on the shelf. The point is, would you like me to come and be your instructress?'

'Yes, I would,' Africa said, staring at her, half laughing, half baffled, 'but that isn't the point at all.'

'Well just *ask*, wouldn't you, dear Africa?' Thalia wheedled. 'Just ask Mama and Papa and see what they say. If you're sure they'll say "no" there's no harm done, is there?'

'The harm would be that they'd think I was mad.'

'They probably think that anyway. Oh please, won't you?'

'Very well. If you really think you want to.'

'I want it more than anything in the world,' Thalia said solemnly. 'I don't ever want to get married. I want to be a woman of business.'

'What have you got yourself into, sister?' Polly said, laughing.

'I don't know,' Africa replied. 'I shall just have to hope for another Mr Paston to come along and take her off my hands.'

228

CHAPTER TWELVE

The usual clot of traffic which formed at the junction of Cross Street and Market Street had been thickened by a laden coal waggon which had got itself stuck half-way round the corner. The driver, now supported by a number of idlers and a wide range of oaths, was trying to back the team just far enough to free the rear wheel from the kerbstone behind which it was wedged, but the horses had taken fright at the crowds and the mass of vehicles all around them. With their heads up and their heels dug in, they were refusing to move in any direction.

The Hobsbawn barouche was one of the vehicles immobilised by the misadventure, but since it was a pleasant, sunny day, and they had happened to stop opposite a smart milliner's shop, Sophie didn't much mind. There was nothing she could do about it anyway, she thought philosophically, wondering idly whether the very high crown on that green silk bonnet would make her look taller, or have the opposite effect. She was keeping half an eye on Fanny, who was standing on the seat beside her and leaning over the folded hood of the carriage to stare at the traffic behind them. Sophie kept one hand on the hem of her skirt in case she should overbalance. No, she thought, such a very high crown would simply look ridiculous on her. She couldn't carry it off. Now the lemon *gros de Naples* was better, if it were in straw-colour: lemon would make her look too sallow . . .

'Hello, Sophie.'

The voice was so quiet that she thought she had imagined it. She looked around her. A tall, extremely elegantly-dressed woman was standing on the flagway beside the carriage. Could it have been her? She was wearing a heavy veil over her bonnet which completely obscured her face, so Sophie couldn't tell if it was she who had spoken. But as she stared the woman spoke again.

'Don't you know me?' Long hands in beautiful gloves of lavender kid rose to lift back the veil. Rosamund regarded her steadily, standing very straight as though presenting herself for inspection and approval. Sophie's heart went out to her — she looked so thin and pale — but she could think of nothing to say.

'You didn't reply to my last letter,' Rosamund said quietly. There was no reproach in her voice, but Sophie felt it keenly all the same.

'I — I meant to. Truly I did. But I couldn't think what to say.'

'And you refused my invitation to dine.'

'I'm sorry.'

'Are you?' Rosamund raised one eyebrow, and the ghost of a smile touched her mouth. 'Shall I ask you again?'

'No —' It was out before she could stop it. And yet she would have had to say it. 'Please don't. I would have to refuse. I'm sorry — truly I am —'

'Oh Sophie!' Now there was reproach, and it cut Sophie to the heart. 'Am I pariah, then? 'Am I so very wicked? I'm just your Cousin Rosamund you know, the same person that I always was.'

'But you're —' Sophie felt she was blundering again. Her cheeks were hot. She didn't want to have to have this conversation, but in fairness she could not refuse to answer. 'You're living with Lord Batchworth, and you're not — not married.'

'Living in sin.' Rosamund said flatly.

'It isn't right. I can't visit you on those terms,' Sophie said desperately. 'I'm sorry, but I *can't*.'

'You know that Marcus is refusing to divorce me?'

'I can't help it. It's still wrong,' Sophie said, and the pain of hurting Rosamund made her a little angry. 'Was it going on all those years, under my nose? Were you seeing him when you came to visit me here? If I'd known then — oh Rosamund, that was not fair!'

'No. I'm sorry too. But I can't change anything now. I wish

230

you would forgive me, but I see you won't, so I won't trouble you again.'

Fanny had turned round to see what was going on, and, still standing on the seat, was holding on to Sophie's shoulder now, and staring solemnly at the stranger. Rosamund looked at her now.

'And so that's Miss Fanny Hobsbawn. What a big girl she's growing.'

Sophie remembered her foolish, innocent plans for Fanny and Rosamund's daughter to become great friends. She thought of what Rosamund must be suffering, separated from her child as she was.

Rosamund began to turn away, reaching up for her veil, but then turned back just for a moment to ask quietly, 'Were they all well at Morland Place? You were there last month, weren't you?'

Sophie nodded. 'All well,' she managed to say.

Rosamund nodded too, let down her veil, and walked away. The slim, upright figure tugged at Sophie's heart and she wanted to call her back, but there was nothing she could say. She stared sightlessly at the display of elegant, useless hats, her throat aching with unshed tears.

Lord Greyshott felt rather as though he had been bearded in his den as he faced Africa across his business-room in Greyshott House. He had never come across a female quite like Miss Africa Haworth. She stood square on in front of him, her feet planted firmly a little apart, her hands clasped behind her back like a midshipman, and she met his gaze levelly in a way which, in any other female, would have seemed intolerably bold.

Yet there was nothing in the least mannish about her. Her face was not fashionably creamy, it was true, but her skin was firm and clear, her features fine, her mouth, he discovered with interest, distinctly pretty. Her dress was plain, but of fine kerseymere elegantly cut, her gloves and boots were those of a lady, and her bonnet was freshly trimmed with some extremely becoming ribbons.

Altogether in Lord Greyshott's opinion — and he was a man with as experienced and discriminating a palate for women as for wine — she was a female well worth kissing; and further, in his opinion, someone had been doing just that quite recently. But she had put a proposition to him which had all but floored him.

'I really don't know what to say to you,' he said at the end of a lengthy pause.

'Your first reaction must be to say no,' Africa suggested.

'Damned right it is — I beg your pardon. But the thought of my daughter *working*! If you was a man, my dear Miss Haworth, I'd thrash you for suggesting it. Yet I can see you're a sensible woman. You wouldn't put up an idea just to have it knocked down.'

'Thank you for your good opinion,' Africa smiled. He noted that when she smiled she had three dimples, one at either mouth corner and an extra one in her right cheek. 'If I may, I would like to tell you why I think you should say yes.'

'You may indeed — but won't you sit down?'

'Thank you, but I think better on my feet. I'm used to walking a quarterdeck to clear my head, you see, sir.'

'Walk away, then,' Greyshott said. He perched on the edge of his desk, folded his arms, and prepared to be entertained, if not convinced. Miss Haworth had a fine figure, and it displayed well when she moved.

'Well, sir, first of all, it's what Miss Hampton wants, and I don't need to tell that opposition makes her stubborn. Refuse her, and she will sulk and storm and mope. She may even turn her thwarted energies to less safe ways of expressing her rebellion.'

'True,' Greyshott acknowledged. 'But to agree for that reason would be to reward unfilial behaviour.'

'Yes, sir, if the object itself were culpable; but under my supervision she would be carefully chaperoned and usefully occupied. I should be very strict indeed with her, I assure you. Not only would she come to no harm, I should make her work very hard, and probably in a short time she would come to the conclusion that it wasn't what she wanted after all. She would then return to you chastened and dutiful, ready to do whatever you direct.'

Greyshott chuckled. 'You paint a delightful picture! Go on.'

'I understand that you want Miss Hampton to be married — and I agree that is the best provision for a gently-born female. But you have said, and I honour you for it, she shall not be forced to marry against her inclinations, and at the moment she is not inclined to marry my cousin Aylesbury.'

'You thrust home, Miss Haworth.'

'At the moment, indeed, she says she never wants to marry. But at my school she would meet — in the most unexceptionable way — a great many eligible young men of fashion, and if one of them did not take her fancy, they might at least make her appreciate Lord Aylesbury more. As I think you know, my sister is very soon to marry Mr Paston, whom she met in the same circumstances.'

'You might change the name, you know, to Miss Haworth's School of Matrimony!'

Africa grinned. 'Not yet, sir — not until I have a string of young ladies of my own to get off my hands! But in sum, my argument is that it cannot do Thalia any harm, and might do her much good. And since nothing else will satisfy her for the moment, it will save you a great deal of tiresome argument,' she added shrewdly.

'You read characters too, Miss Haworth?' Greyshott smiled, but then looked restive. 'All the same, my daughter an instructress? My daughter working for wages? It is not to be thought of. It would be a disgrace on the family.'

'I agree, sir —'

'You agree?'

Africa's smile was serene with the knowledge of having worked her way to this very point. 'Miss Hampton an employee would be unacceptable. But a partner in the business —a stockholder — that is something any gentlewoman might contemplate without disgrace.'

Greyshott laughed and slapped his knee. 'Damme, but you argue like a man! I like you for it, ma'am! I confess I like you! You want me to buy my daughter into your business — to present you with fresh capital. New horses, is it, ma'am? A new range of stables?'

'We are already in process of building a riding-house for indoor lessons, and I had thought of adding a tea-room,'

Africa said gravely. 'A great many young people come to watch their friends take their lessons, and mamas and even papas bring their children and stay to chat. A tea-room would add to their comfort and my profit. And think what opportunities for matrimony it would present!'

Greyshott was still laughing. 'If I were wearing a hat, I would take it off to you, Miss Haworth! But I still think it is a passing fad of Thalia's and she will not last more than a week under any sort of regular discipline.'

'If she does not, your problem is equally solved. You will have your daughter back, and an investment in a growing and profitable concern into the bargain.'

'You have persuaded me. I shall speak to Lady Greyshott this evening, and find out what she thinks about it.'

Rosamund and Jesmond met in the drawing-room before dinner. It was a pleasant ritual they had developed, to discuss what had happened to them during the day over a glass of sherry, to sort through the small change of their separate lives and share the amusing, the interesting, the annoying. But this evening Jes talked and Rosamund listened in silence.

Eventually he stopped in the middle of a story and said, 'What is it, my love? What's happened?'

Rosamund's face was carefully expressionless. 'I saw Sophie today. Her carriage was stopped by the traffic in Market Street.'

'Oh.' Jesmond studied her face. 'Did she see you?'

'I spoke to her.'

'Oh good! And did you ask —?'

'I think if I hadn't, she wouldn't have spoken to me. I think she would have pretended not to see me.' The mask slipped a little. 'She said she wouldn't come and visit me because we are living in sin.'

'Oh my dear!' For a silent moment he damned Sophie and all the respectable matrons of the world. He looked at the miserably bowed head of his love, and said, 'I'm sure it isn't her. I imagine old Hobsbawn's told her she mustn't see you. He is terribly proper, you know. Don't you remember I told you I had to egg him on to propose to Sophie, even though he loved her to distraction, because he thought it wouldn't be

234

right. He is so *very* nice, I'd swear it was him behind it, not Sophie at all.'

Rosamund stared into the amber depths of her glass, silent for a moment. Then she said, 'Why is Marcus doing this to us? To refuse to divorce me — it can only be spite. What difference could it make to him?'

'Would you feel better if we could be married?' She didn't answer. 'You know that in my heart you are my wife? That nothing and no-one will ever take you away from me? That I will be true to you until I die?'

'Oh Jes!' She struggled for control. 'Some people would accept us, if we were married,' she managed at last. 'We wouldn't be — such outcasts.'

She was losing the battle. The tears were beginning to seep over her eyelashes and down her pale cheeks. He couldn't bear it. He flung himself out of his chair and knelt before her, gathering her against him.

'My love, my own love! What does it matter? We don't care for them. We're together, and that's the important thing. After so long apart, we're together for ever.'

She drew a great shuddering breath, trying not to cry, though he could feel the heat of her tears on his neck. 'I love you, Jes,' she said; and it was a sad, lost cry.

'I love you too. Always, always.'

She had not come to it yet, he knew. He cradled her head tenderly, waiting. Finally she drew another gulping breath and said, 'The little girl was with her. Fanny. She looked at me so gravely —' A long pause. The tears were coming faster, scalding. Finally she cried, 'I want my baby! Oh Jes, I think about her all the time. All the time!'

No more struggle. She sobbed in his arms. Behind her the door opened, and over her shoulder he saw the butler appear to announce dinner and pause in dismay. A shake of the master's head, and the man retreated. Jes felt so helpless in the face of her grief, because there was nothing he could do about it. It had been there since she first came to him, and he brought her north to live under his protection. He sensed it even behind her laughter; when they walked together in the garden it poured into him through their linked hands; when she sat at the pianoforte, it seeped into her playing, so that

235

even happy songs took on a melancholy, minor-key sound. It slept beside them in their bed like a cold emptiness; and when he took her in his arms and loved her, he could feel it aching in her bones.

He had not wanted it to be like this. He had longed for her so many years, and dreamed of her coming to him, but always with joy, like a bird let loose from a cage winging its way gladly to freedom. He was filled sometimes with a murderous rage against Marcus; but more often it was against Hawker, who had interfered so fatally not once, but twice. Without his intervention, Rosamund might still have come to him when Kit died, leaving no hostage behind. And surely then Marcus would not have behaved so vindictively — for he had loved Rosamund, Jes believed, as much as he was able.

But there was nothing he could do about any of that, nothing but to hold his woman in his arms while she suffered, and to feel her pain. And now this, today — the last straw. To be shunned by Manchester Society was one thing, expectable in its way, and endurable; but for Ros to be shunned by gentle Sophie was quite another.

It was Jasper, he was sure of it. Well, perhaps there was something he could do about that. It would be little enough, but perhaps enough to begin the process of healing, so that they could begin to be happy together. The germ of an idea began to take root in his mind; a scheme to put Jasper in his debt and in his power. Rosamund's tears were lessening now, the storm passing over for the moment. He wouldn't say anything to her until it was done, in case of disappointment; but he thought he began to see how it might be accomplished.

James took Nicholas to school himself, partly because he was anxious about his son and heir, and partly because he had not been away from home since little Fanny was born. The gypsy in him, which had been too tired of recent years to raise its head, had suddenly sent a new surge through his blood. Perhaps it had been all the talk of Maurice Hampton's Grand Tour, together with Roland's and Thomas's reminiscences. At all events, he had suddenly felt the need for a wider horizon, and Héloïse, who felt his moods even if she didn't always understand them, urged the trip on him.

'You can see Nicky settled, and then go on to London for Africa's wedding. I should like to have gone myself, but I really cannot be away just now.'

'You need the change of scene far more than I do,' James said with a belated twinge of conscience. You're looking tired, Marmoset.'

'To say the truth, I keep thinking of poor Rosamund. I know she has done wrong, but Marcus's behaviour is very harsh. Perhaps,' she added tentatively, 'you might go to see him while you are in London.'

James looked at least part of his deep reluctance. 'I don't think that would do any good.'

'Perhaps not. But you are her uncle, and you have the right to worry about her. And I believe that everything ought to be tried.'

'Very well,' James said gloomily. 'I'll try to see him. But you ought to have a holiday from your cares too.'

'I am very well, my James,' Héloïse assured him serenely. 'I shall have my holiday when I go to Manchester for Sophie's new baby.'

'That is a very long time away,' James said severely. 'You've only just heard that she's pregnant again.'

'The time will pass soon enough. And May is a good month for me to go away from home. I can leave things very well in May.'

So it was decided. Héloïse had a long and serious talk with Nicholas the night before his departure, about the importance of remembering God in everything he did, in keeping up his regular observances, and in resisting temptation when other boys invited him to join in things he knew were wrong. 'If you are not sure, *mon petit coeur*, just ask yourself, "Should I be happy to tell Mama about this?" I never want my boy to be ashamed to tell me what he has done.'

'Yes, Mama,' Nicky said patiently. There was a world of excitement ahead of him, he was sure. The ushers would probably beat more — he was quite well aware that Father Moineau's hand was often stayed by his parents' anxiety over his health — but on the other hand there would be far more opportunities to escape detection at Eton than here, where everyone knew him and watched him all the time.

Héloïse smoothed a lock of his thin, light-brown hair back from his brow. 'And you must take care of yourself, Nicky. Remember always that you are not as strong as other boys, and that there will be no mother, or Sarah, or Matty to watch over you. Be sure not to study too long and make yourself tired.'

'I won't,' he vowed from the heart.

'And make sure you eat plenty, and change your shoes and stockings if they get wet. And write at once if you have need of anything, and we will send it, or send you money to buy it. You must not go without anything. Promise me that.'

'I promise, Mama,' he said sincerely, and bent his forehead meekly for her kiss. The allowance Papa had promised him had struck him as adequate, though not princely; but knowing he had *carte blanche* to ask for more at any time made all the difference. A boy with money in his pocket, as he already knew, was a boy with friends and influence. He meant to make his mark on Eton.

Later that night he took his private farewell of his brother, while they were alone together in the nursery preparing for bed.

'Well, you'll be able to lord it now for a few months,' he said disagreeably, watching Bendy fold his clothes carefully and lay them on the chest at the foot of his bed. 'You'll be king of the nursery. I suppose you'll wheedle the maids and try to make them love you best; try to make everyone forget me.'

Bendy looked up patiently. 'You know I wouldn't do that.'

'You couldn't anyway,' Nicky snapped. He reached out and tweaked Bendy's trousers out of his hand and threw them on the floor. 'Stop fussing about with your clothes and pay attention to me!' Bendy stood still and watched him, rather as a man watches a strange animal, and the dispassionate gaze irritated Nicholas more. 'Just remember that I am the eldest, and I am the heir. *Everything* will belong to me one day. If you want to be allowed to stay here afterwards, you'd better remember that.'

Bendy said nothing, only watched him calmly.

'I'm important, and you're nothing,' Nicky went on, desperate for a reaction. 'I shall find out everything you've done when I get back, and if I don't like it, you'll answer to me.' He shot out a hand and grasped Bendy's hair just above the ear and twisted. 'Are you listening to me?'

'Yes,' Bendy said, gritting his teeth. 'Let me go.' He wouldn't give Nicky the satisfaction of showing that it hurt.

Nicky let go of his hair, but grabbed his wrist instead with both hands and twisted the flesh to make it burn. Bendy gave an involuntary gasp, and Nicky was satisfied at last. 'That's to remember me by,' he said, letting him go. 'And don't forget — *I know where your foxes live.*'

Bendy turned away to hide the tears in his eyes, and picked up his trousers from the floor. After a moment he said quietly, 'I don't know why you are afraid. I would never try to take your place even if I could.'

'I'm not afraid,' Nicky said, yet his voice was naked.

'Morland Place is yours. Everybody knows that,' Bendy went on. There was no reply from behind him.

Africa and Peter Morpurgo were married in St Mark's church five weeks after Polly's wedding to George Paston, the date chosen so that the Pastons would be back from their honeymoon in time for it. Though it had been meant to be a quiet occasion, the church was filled to capacity, and many of the guests were people of fashion. Lord and Lady Theakston's friends were amongst them, and Lord Aylesbury's; Tom accounted for a wide assortment of influential people; all the pupils of the School of Equitation and their parents wished to be there; and there was a large naval contingent, friends of both bride and groom, including a great many sea officers who in more fortunate times might have been expected to be at sea and have missed the occasion.

James represented both Héloïse and Sophie at the wedding, and thoroughly enjoyed the lively mix of young people who danced afterwards at Lucy's house and made the occasion one of real celebration. He spoke to Morpurgo and found him sensible and likeable, and quickly became absorbed in a discussion with him of his and Africa's building plans for the school.

'And Greyshott is to invest in you, I understand?' James said. 'I rather wish I had been offered the opportunity. It

239

sounds as though you may make him a good return on his capital.'

'I hope so, sir,' Morpurgo said, 'though I think his lordship will be happy enough if we keep Thalia out of mischief for two months and return her to him with the desire for commerce worked out of her system.'

James laughed. 'I imagine Africa will have her hands full. But it seems to me that you must have difficulty in finding the right sort of horses for your purposes. You will have very special requirements, of course.'

'Yes, they must be docile enough to carry complete novices and the nervous, and yet be lively and handsome enough to satisfy elegance,' Morpurgo said.

'A matter both of careful breeding and careful schooling,' James said. 'You won't want very young horses, of course — too unpredictable. Yet older horses which come up for sale — especially blood horses — are likely to have bad habits; perhaps even hidden vices.'

'It *is* a difficulty,' Morpurgo acknowledged. 'Africa hopes to do some reschooling herself, but her time will necessarily be limited, and I haven't the skills.'

'I wonder if I might be able to be of use,' James said thoughtfully.

'You, sir?'

'Our own horses — those we breed ourselves, I mean — would probably be too expensive for you. We'd have to keep them too long,' he mused. 'We sell most of our racehorses at two and three years old, riding horses at about four; carriage horses a little later of course, at five or even six. To breed and school a horse for your purposes until it was five or six years old —'

'We could never afford it, sir,' Morpurgo said bluntly.

'No,' said James. 'But supposing I were to be able to buy nice-looking older horses with good conformation at a reasonable price, and school them for a few months —' The benefits of the scheme were occurring to him even as he spoke. 'I would have to travel all over the country. Private sales, breakdowns — Ireland too — that would be a fruitful source. There's many a gentleman in debt flees to Ireland with his stable.'

Morpurgo looked interested, but a little puzzled. 'Our needs would not amount to enough to warrant such extensive travels, sir.'

James smiled suddenly. 'No, of course not. But there must be hundreds of other establishments and even individuals whose requirements are similar to yours. And hundreds of good horses going to waste for want of a little schooling. And besides,' he added frankly, 'I should enjoy it very much. A new challenge with every horse!'

'It sounds like an exciting life,' Morpurgo said dubiously. He liked to know where he was with a horse.

'I'll speak to Africa about it later,' James said, coming back to the present reality of the wedding celebration and the fact that he was monopolising the groom's attention. 'I suppose I had better talk to Greyshott too,' he added with a chuckle, 'since he is a stockholder in your venture.'

While James was in London, Lord Batchworth paid a visit to Yorkshire, though not to Morland Place. His destination was Skelwith Lodge, the grand name given to the grand house the master builder had created for his wife and increasing family.

Skelwith had inherited from his father an ancient house in Stonegate within the city walls of York. It was still mentioned in all the best guidebooks as an outstanding example of fifteenth-century architecture, with a magnificent oriel window and a notable hammerbeam roof. But not caring to live amongst even the finest of stone mullions and linen-fold panels, as soon as he had married Skelwith had begun building a thoroughly modern house in its own pleasure-grounds.

The obvious choice for a coming man and his wife was the elegant and fashionable district of Clifton, which already accommodated such families as the Chubbs of Bootham Park and the Coweys of Beverley House. Skelwith Lodge was to be built to John's own design as an advertisement to his trade as well as a home, and it would not do to advertise in any but the best location.

As the carriage drew into the sweep in front of Skelwith Lodge, Batchworth stared up at the gleaming, stuccoed façade in wonder tinged with amusement. 'Lodge' was not a bit too grand for it. It might almost have attained to the title of *Hall*, for it sported such a profusion of balconies and bays and turrets and wrought iron, such gables, decorative brick-work, false parapets and crenellations, and above all such a battery of windows, that the word 'house' simply could not convey the power of its impact. Perhaps it would look better, Batchworth thought weakly, when the creeper had had time to grow up the walls and the rather scrawny laurels of the sweep had thickened out. As an advertisement, at least, it certainly illustrated every architectural flourish Skelwith might ever be asked for by a customer.

There was no doubt that Mathilde loved it, however, as was evident by the pride with which she received Lord Batch-worth in the morning-room. His importance as a visitor was proved by the fact that Skelwith himself arrived to greet him before he had exhausted the polite commonplaces, and thus saved him the trouble of having to ask for him.

It both amused and pained Jes that before Skelwith had been in the room five minutes he had managed to convey the news to him that Mathilde was increasing again. Jes expressed suitable congratulations.

'Thank you. We hope very much for a boy this time,' Mathilde said. The wistfulness was naked in her voice, and Batchworth guessed that she wanted a son for her husband perhaps more than he wanted one for himself. Skelwith was an affectionate father, and loved his four daughters with the tender passion of a man who had known what it was to have no-one to love.

'They're strong and healthy, my love, that's all that matters,' he had said to Mathilde. 'You wouldn't want to change our dear girls now they're here, would you?'

'You need a son to follow you in your business, dearest,' Mathilde retorted with pardonable anxiety. Well, after all, it was she who had to go through the pains and perils of childbirth, and she was already thirty-four years old. Suppose she were to go on having girls — where would it end? 'Lady Grey of Rawcliffe Manor — a near neighbour of ours, Lord Batchworth —'

'I have the honour of knowing Lady Grey,' Jes said with irony which escaped Mathilde.

'Then you will know that she had five girls and no son, and she has never known an easy moment in her mind.'

'But that estate is entailed, love,' Skelwith said gently.

'Yes, and when her Lord dies the title will go to his cousin, who can come and throw them all out into the street whenever it suits him. Of course,' Mathilde acknowledged, 'the cases are quite different; but if anything happened to John, and we had no son, who would run the business and find husbands for the girls?'

Skelwith intercepted this appeal with the ease of accustomedness. 'I shall arrange everything to suit whatever circumstances prevail, my love. You and the girls will not want, I assure you. And you really mustn't allow yourself to worry about it. It's bad for the baby. You don't want him to grow up with an anxious disposition, do you?'

The *him*, Jes thought, was a noble piece of tact. Before his wife could reply, Skelwith hurried on, 'But we have been unpardonably rude, Lord Batchworth. We haven't asked what brings you here, and though we're honoured by the visit, it cannot be simply for social reasons that you have come all the way from Manchester.'

Jes said what was polite. 'But the truth is,' he went on, 'that I have something in the line of business that I wish to discuss with you, Skelwith, if you can spare me the time.'

'If it's business, you had better come with me to my private room,' Skelwith said. 'You will excuse us, my darling, I know.'

Skelwith's private room was up in one of the towers, with a magnificent view over the surrounding countryside, and a number of conveniences which he was eager to show off. There was a speaking-tube through which he could communicate with the servants' hall below and, for instance, order refreshments to be sent up when he was working long hours; there was a closet with an ingenious series of traps and vents which could carry away waste without the least risk of lingering odours; there was a large library of books, especially works of reference, which were catalogued in such a way on a system of cards that Skelwith could put his hand to any volume he wanted within moments.

'And next year I am planning to have gas laid on to the

house, and gas lights in every room,' Skelwith concluded proudly. 'You may perhaps have heard that York's own Gas Company has recently been formed? We are not far behind London here, I can assure you.'

When they eventually got down to business, however, Jes found himself dealing with a very different man, sharp and shrewd, all nonsense abandoned.

'This building scheme that you and Mr Hobsbawn have devised between you cannot proceed because the Bishop will not let you have the land, and Hobsbawn will not build anywhere else, is that right?'

'In a nutshell,' said Skelwith. 'They are both stubborn men.'

'And your interest in the scheme is purely one of business?'

Skelwith looked uncomfortable. 'I am as charitable as the next man, my lord, but building is my business, and I have a wife and children to support.'

'Please, Mr Skelwith, I meant no disparagement, I assure you! It would be strange indeed if you were willing to put yourself out of pocket over something which is essentially another man's passion. I wish to understand clearly what the situation is, because I think there is something I can do to help all parties: you, Mr Hobsbawn, the mill hands — and myself.'

'A swathe of people to please,' Skelwith said with a wary smile. 'What is it you propose?'

'I have been to see the Bishop,' Jes said.

Skelwith's eyebrow climbed. 'The deuce you have,' he muttered, inappropriately.

'He is not such a bad fellow after all,' Jes went on. 'He is as reasonable as the next man when his interest is appealed to. Now you know, I assume, that Mr Olmondroyd applied pressure to him to make him withhold his consent to lease the land to you and Mr Hobsbawn? I won't go into what that pressure was; I will only say that I have been able to remove it, and that I am in the way of being able to supply a new pressure of my own to sway him in the other direction.'

'But what can it benefit you, sir?' Skelwith asked, frankly astonished.

Batchworth smiled. 'The thing is good of itself, you will

agree; and I have a strong personal reason for wishing to do Mr Hobsbawn a favour. Do I take it, then, that if I now go to him to tell him that the Bishop will lease him the land, you will be able to go ahead and build these damned houses he has set his heart on?'

'I'm afraid not. Hobsbawn has not yet managed to get together enough capital. Had the land been available, he would have continued with his efforts to interest investors in the scheme; now that you appear to have solved that problem, no doubt he will resume the attempt.'

Batchworth frowned. 'How far short of the needful are you?'

'At the last reckoning, Jasper had only secured a little more than half the capital needed. We could begin, but we could not finish; and frankly, sir, I'm not eager to begin unless I know we could finish.'

'This is not quite what I wanted to hear,' Jes said. 'Look here, Skelwith, I'll be frank with you. I want to be able to go to our friend and tell him that thanks to my efforts the scheme can go ahead at once.'

'Could you not perhaps —?' Skelwith paused suggestively.

'Not at the moment. My own capital is tied up in various ways, and it would be the deuce of a task to release it. Is there no way in which you could make the houses more cheaply?'

Skelwith smiled faintly. 'Oh yes, many ways.'

'What? But then, why —?'

'Jasper's "rational" design is a great deal more elaborate in my view than is at all necessary, especially considering the low rents at which he means to let them — and I wouldn't be at all surprised if that were not why so few masters want to invest in them. They'd think the hands would be spoilt, and infect others to demand houses as good.'

'And your sort of house — could the same number be built for the amount of capital to hand?'

'I think so. Perhaps. But Jasper will want his own design to be used.'

'Perhaps we can work out a compromise,' Jes said eagerly. 'Show me, if you will, the difference.'

The men pored over plans, and ideas fluttered about the room like disturbed bats.

'One of Jasper's problems is that he wants too many walls. Now if you build in terraces, like this, each household shares it walls with the next. The saving is immense. And if you build two terraces back to back, like *this* — there's only one wall to a house which isn't shared.'

'Yes, I see. Will Hobsbawn accept the idea, though?'

'Only if you can persuade him it's better than his.'

Later: 'Another way to economise is to make the walls thinner. Jasper wants them nine inches — one brick thick we call it — but it could be done with half brick thickness all through.'

'You'd save half the cost of the bricks.'

'Certainly.'

'Would he notice?'

'Not once they were up.'

And then: 'First-grade timber is deuced expensive, with the tax and the cost of transport so high.'

'Can't do anything about transport I suppose. Isn't there a cheaper timber?'

'Oh yes: third-grade is only half the price.'

'Would Hobsbawn notice the difference?'

'Not unless I told him.'

Later again: 'If we can cut down on some of the windows, it will help. The window tax is such a burden, it eats into profit.'

'With the houses built back to back, there'll only be windows on one side. And what about these privvies? You don't need a window in a privvy, do you?'

'Not at all. Better indeed not to have one. And you don't need so many privvies, either. One to twelve is too generous. Make it one to twenty and you can get another house in at the end, here. Two more rents, you see.'

At the end of two hours, John Skelwith straightened his back and said, 'With those modifications, it will be possible to build more than the number of houses Jasper wants for the money available.'

'Without compromising your profit?' Jes asked.

Skelwith smiled faintly. 'I promise you I would not cheat myself.' He looked at Jes curiously. 'Is it worth so much to you, this business? I would not have thought a man in your position needed gratitude from a man in Hobsbawn's.'

'He has something which I need very much,' Jes said gravely.

It took a long time to make Jasper understand what he had done, and what he proposed.

'Your scheme can go ahead,' Jesmond said again patiently. 'That is the nub and nexus of it. You can build your houses on that piece of land and see the mill hands properly sheltered.'

'But you say they will not be built to my design,' Jasper said dazedly. They were in a quiet corner of their club, but as it was a guest evening, even that was not particularly quiet.

'Not quite; but the differences make no real difference. In fact, Skelwith assures me they are an improvement: building the cottages back to back means that they will share each other's warmth. And it means, too, that more houses can be built in the space available. More of your hands will have a decent roof over their heads. No more cellars, Hobsbawn, think of that! No more cellars!'

'That is an object, I agree,' Jasper said.

'And it can begin at once. And building this way will be quicker.'

'Yes, yes I see,' said Jasper, who plainly didn't. 'But — forgive me, I'm quite bewildered — do I understand that you have somehow managed to persuade the Church to let me have the land after all?'

'Yes, I have, and it would be no use to ask me how, because that is a secret.'

'Olmondroyd —'

'Will not oppose you. I have seen to that. No man but has his price, Hobsbawn. You were not ruthless enough, that's all.' Jes was feeling light-headed — a combination of the atmosphere in the club and the thought of achieving his goal — or he would not have spoken so freely.

Jasper, however, was still struggling with another baffling question. 'But why have you done this? You've told me again and again that you didn't agree with my scheme. To do what you've done must have cost you a great deal of time and money —'

247

'A little of each, perhaps. Don't think of it.'

'I must think of it. Good God, how very, very kind! And still I must ask you — why?'

Jes leaned forward, coming happily to the point. 'I did it as a favour to you, Hobsbawn. I made possible the scheme closest to your heart in the hope of softening that heart. There is something I hope you will do for me in return.'

'I, do for you? I can't imagine what it can be — but if I can perform it, I will.'

'Rosamund is grieved because you will not allow Sophie to see her. It is breaking her heart, and what hurts her, hurts me. I beg you, in return for this favour, to do something which is equally important to me. Accept Rosamund, at least in private. Visit us, and let us visit you.'

Jes had expected chagrin, remorse, instant capitulation; but Jasper only looked grave, and began to shake his head. Jes stared in amazement and foreboding. Stiff Hobsbawn might be, but surely he was a good fellow underneath, not one deliberately to make another unhappy?

'My dear Batchworth,' Jasper said, speaking in such a low voice that Jes had to lean towards him to hear the words, 'you are quite mistaken. I have not forbidden Sophie to see her cousin. I would not do so. Do you think I would willingly deprive her of anything she valued? Indeed, I don't care if you live in sin with one woman or fifty; and I have the greatest pity for Rosamund in her plight, even though I suppose to some extent she brought it on herself. But if we all got what we deserved in this world, there would be few of us who would escape calumny.'

'But — then what —?' Jes stammered, dumbfounded.

'It is Sophie herself,' Jasper said gravely. 'Her religious upbringing has given her a strong code of rules which she cannot ignore. She views the world differently from us. I see you look doubtful, but I assure you it is Sophie's embargo, not mine.'

'You could persuade her,' Jes said desperately.

'I could not; and I would not try.'

'But at least — and least you could speak to her. Put the view — since you believe that she is wrong —'

'I don't say she is wrong, only that I don't agree with her.

248

But she feels it very much, and I would not raise the matter with her at the moment. You will not know, of course, that she is with child again. I don't want her upset in her delicate condition, and to speak of it would upset her very much. I'm sorry, truly sorry, but I cannot repay your favour.'

Jes was stunned. He could think of nothing to say. Jasper watched him in silent sympathy while behind them the sound of conversation, laughter, and the clink of glasses swelled and billowed like the clouds of cigar smoke around their heads. He's adrift on a sea of other men's conviviality, Jasper thought, and remembered the times he had been likewise. It was Batchworth who had rescued him, and told him that Sophie loved him and would have him if only he asked. And how Batchworth loved Rosamund! But Jasper could not rescue him, not at Sophie's expense.

'Later perhaps,' he said at last, 'when the child is born, I could talk to her about it, try to put the opposite view.'

'When the child is born,' Jes said blankly.

'That's not much use now, I know,' Jasper said sadly. 'If it's any comfort, I think the separation hurts Sophie, too — very much.'

'No,' said Jes. 'I don't think that is any comfort.'

CHAPTER THIRTEEN

Jasper and Sophie travelled to Morland Place for the Christmas Season of 1823. Jasper had not been entirely sure that the travelling was a good idea, because of Sophie's condition, but she had been seized with a longing for home and Maman, and he would not deprive her of what she wanted. The weather had been dry and frosty so the roads were not too bad, and the massive old Hobsbawn travelling berlin had been recently overhauled, so he hoped for the best. They took four horses and travelled slowly with frequent stops, and arrived safely at Morland Place on the evening of the second day. Both Jasper and Héloïse insisted that Sophie go straight to bed, and she rose the next day with no apparent ill effects.

The entire household was thrilled to have Fanny with them, and for the first few days she trotted everywhere, meeting flattery and sweetmeats wherever she went, chattering engagingly and winning hearts. Monsieur Barnard, having thoroughly disliked her namesake aunt, greeted her with suspicion, but soon discovered that she favoured her grandmother in looks, and thereafter became her willing slave. The only thing that disconcerted him was that she did not seem to understand French, which he had come to expect from all children.

'You do not teach it to her, Mademoiselle Sophie?' he asked in his own tongue. Sophie shook her head apologetically. 'But how will she make herself understood?' he asked piteously.

'*Personne ne parle le français à Manchester*,' Sophie explained kindly. Barnard seemed to think this a grave mistake, and pronounced that Manchester must certainly be a place *hors de la civilisation* and urged Sophie by all means to come back to live at Morland Place. But no, said Sophie, Manchester was a place most agreeable, and besides it was her home now.

Miss Fanny would grow up a *demoiselle vraie anglaise*, Barnard prophesied gloomily, as though condemning her to an early grave.

Thereafter he sighed and grew moist-eyed at the sight of her, addressed her always in slow and clearly enunciated French, and kept a secret store of Naples biscuits in his apron pocket at all times in case of meeting her. For her part Fanny found him fascinating and decided to adopt him. She would often be found in the kitchen sitting on the edge of a table swinging her short legs and chattering to him while he worked. She soon learned a few essential words of French, such as *bonbon*, *gâteau*, and *oui merci*.

Mathilde and John were frequent visitors, Mathilde now growing large with child, and eager to talk pregnancies with Sophie. The little Skelwith girls, Mary, Harriet, Jemima and Lydia, were introduced to their cousin and sent away to play. At first Mary and Harriet were inclined to be superior on account of their seniority and tried to command Fanny as they commanded their younger sisters; but Fanny had not been Papa's little princess since birth for nothing. She soon put them firmly in their place, and her nursery maid Janet was able to report proudly to Sophie that Miss Fanny was the leader in all their plays and had her big cousins 'eating out of her hand, ma'am, meek as you please'.

Jasper and John were glad of the opportunity to discuss the progress of the building scheme — the ground was already being cleared, and the first bricks were expected to be laid by the end of January. The two men spent many hours going over and over the plans, for Jasper was not convinced that the alterations to his original design were for the better. But John was a skilled persuader, and in the end could always conclude the argument by asking whether Jasper would prefer sixty houses of this sort, or forty of his sort. Since Jasper suspected that the real question was whether he preferred sixty houses of this sort or no houses at all, he had no reply to that.

The season was not without its shadows. Sophie seemed not quite in spirits, and Héloïse could not be entirely happy because Nicholas was not there. He had written home proudly to say that his 'best friend' Winchmore — son of Lord Hazelmere — had invited him home for Christmas to the family seat near Wycombe, and begged to be allowed to go. Héloïse was unreasonably hurt that he should prefer the society of a friend to that of his own family, but since he had been sent to school to make friends, and since one could not possibly object to such a family as the Winchmores, she had to pretend to be glad about it.

Héloïse was also worried about James's new scheme for reschooling older horses. She couldn't quite put her finger on it, but there was something about it that alarmed her. She acknowledged that James had always been known as the Best Horseman in the Ridings and could ride anything he could throw his leg across, as the saying was; but strange horses were unpredictable, and surely at the age of fifty-six he ought not to be seeking out unnecessary risks? There was also the fact that he intended travelling about the country in search of these animals. She had a deep and unspoken fear that his old restlessness, which she had thought cured for ever, was about to break out in a new and perhaps virulent form.

But on Twelfth Night all other concerns were wiped from her mind. After dinner Sophie felt a little unwell and went to lie down. An hour later Héloïse went up to see her and found her sweating and terrified, in pain; and before the clock struck midnight, she had miscarried her child.

Jasper sat by the bed, holding Sophie's hand and wishing she would cry. A passion of tears would have been better than that pale little face set like stone, and the blank eyes staring at nothing. He knew he must go back to Manchester soon, and he didn't want to leave Sophie like this, even though she would be in the best of care.

'My dearest, try not to be too sad,' he said. 'The most important thing is that you're all right. And there'll be other children. As soon as you're completely well —'

Sophie turned her head on the pillow to look at him. Her eyes were as dark and unfathomable as a tarn. 'No,' she said.

'What do you mean, no?' Jasper was genuinely puzzled. 'I

know we'd waited a long time for this one, but the doctor said you were perfectly all right —'

'You don't understand,' she said tonelessly. 'It was Twelfth Night when it happened.'

'Twelfth Night?'

'The night of prophecy. What happens then tells you the future. I'll never have another baby now. If only I could have held on until after midnight —' She turned her head away again.

'Oh Sophie, darling,' Jasper protested, 'you don't believe that! Surely you don't believe that? It's all superstition and nonsense.'

But she was not to be convinced. He ascribed it to the state of her mind after the shock and bereavement of the miscarriage. When she was well again and out of bed, her mind would take on a more reasonable frame. He would not talk about it any more now.

'In any case,' he said, 'I don't care if we don't have another child. We have Fanny and I have you, which is all that really matters. If I had lost you, my dearest —' He shuddered and pressed her hand, and after a moment she responded with a brief pressure of her own. She felt sore and battered and lost, and just at the moment she could give nothing. She was glad to know that he was there beside her, but she didn't want to talk to him.

Two days later Jasper was gone — reluctantly but inevitably, and comforting himself, if any comfort it was, that she didn't really need him at the moment, and in fact hardly seemed to notice he was there.

'She will come back to you,' Héloïse assured him as she said goodbye to him. 'It has been a shock, and she is in a state almost like languor. Soon her body will repair itself, and then the mind will be well also. Do not be afraid, dear Jasper. She will love you again as before.'

Jasper was unable to speak, but his gratitude was in one burning look and a swift embrace. Héloïse felt deeply for him. She knew from old experience how much harder it was to see someone you loved suffering than to suffer yourself.

After he had gone, she had found Fanny close behind her,

253

her eyes fixed appealingly on her face.

'Gran'mère?' Fanny had begun by calling her Grand-mama, but under the influence of Barnard and Héloïse's own residual accent the word had mutated into something much closer to the French form. 'Gran'mère, has Papa gone away?'

'Only for a little while, *ma mie*. You will see him again soon.'

'When can I see Mama?' As Héloïse hesitated — for Sophie had not asked for Fanny yet — she saw the child's eyes fill with tears. 'Mama's going to die, isn't she?'

'No, little one, of course not!'

'She is, she is. The baby died and now Mama's going to die. Janet said I was to have a little brother but now he's dead. I don't want Mama to die!'

Héloïse took her hand firmly and turned towards the stairs. 'Mama's not going to die. We'll go to her now, and you can see for yourself.'

The reunion was a success. When they first entered Sophie's room, she did not look at them, and Fanny was suddenly shy, holding hard to Héloïse's hand without speaking. Héloïse called Sophie's name and she turned her head and saw Fanny. For a painful moment there was no reaction; and then she held out her arms urgently.

'Fanny darling!'

Fanny scampered across the room and scrambled up onto the bed to be hugged, and Héloïse saw with relief, as Sophie closed her eyes and pressed her cheek to her daughter's head, the first glimmer of a tear.

Later that day she took up Sophie's dinner tray herself, and sat with her while she ate, feeling by instinct that the time had come for Sophie to talk. Barnard had prepared a delightful little dinner for the invalid, his old favourite who was also mother to his new favourite: a mouthful or two of his special pink parsnip soup, a morsel of chicken in a piquant orange sauce to tempt the palate, a tender fillet of trout reposing in a ruffled bed of *purée*'d carrots, a delicate omelette flavoured with dried mushrooms and raisins, and an exquisite tartlet within whose crisp golden embrace lay the last of his hoarded bottled strawberries from last summer.

254

Héloïse watched sadly as Sophie ate the soup, toyed with the chicken, sighed at the fish and abandoned the rest. It would break Barnard's heart to have the tray returned in that condition. Small as her appetite was, Héloïse felt she would have to slip into the empty bedroom next door with it and eat at least some of everything before taking the tray back downstairs.

Setting it aside for the moment, she said, 'What has happened is very sad, my Sophie. But it is time to lay it aside and think about the future instead.'

Sophie sighed. 'It's the future that makes me sad, Maman. I so wanted to give Jasper a son, and now I don't think there will be any more babies.'

'There is no reason to think that,' Héloïse began, but Sophie cut her short.

'Look how long it was after Fanny, before I conceived again. And it was not,' with a blush, 'because we did not try. And then when I finally did, I could not even manage —' She drew her lip under her teeth to stop it trembling. 'I could not even give it life.'

'It is for God to give life, my Sophie. We are only his vessels.'

'Yes, Maman, I know. But don't you see —' She paused, searching for words, and then changed tack. 'Do you believe we are punished for our sins?'

'Not always,' Héloïse said cautiously. She didn't know where Sophie was heading, so it was hard to know the right answer. 'If we truly repent, we are taught that God forgives us —'

Sophie was not really listening. 'You see, I keep thinking about Rosamund. She must be so miserable, being separated from her child. I think how I would feel if I could not see Fanny any more. And even more now — now that I've lost —' A pause. 'She did wrong, it's true, but does she deserve so heavy a punishment? Lots of other women do what she did, without suffering so.'

'We cannot know what anyone else suffers. What is punishment for one is not punishment for another.'

'I was angry with her,' Sophie went on in a low voice. 'I felt she had deceived me, used me for her convenience. I felt she had let me down, and let herself down. When I remembered Brussels; and afterwards, the long talks we had at Scarborough; when I remembered poor Philip Tantony; and when I thought of how Marcus must have suffered for her . . .' She looked at her mother, half afraid, half appealing, her eyes bright with tears which were very close to the surface. 'I wouldn't talk to her, Maman. I refused to see her, and I didn't even answer her letters. I thought I had to, because she was living in sin with Lord Batchworth and it wasn't *right*. We aren't supposed to encourage sin, are we? But then I began to wonder whether it was only hurt pride on my part — and I do love her — and she must be so very, very *miserable* —' The bleak word wobbled alarmingly, and the tears began to spill over. 'And now God has punished me! He's made me lose a child so that I can feel what she feels —'

Héloïse, deeply distressed, took her daughter into her arms. 'No my Sophie, no! God doesn't do such things! A loving Father would not be so harsh.'

'But He did! He is!' Sophie wept.

'It isn't like that. You must believe God has His plans for us all, and it is not for us to know what they are. Sometimes bad things happen and we don't understand. But He will never punish us, as long as we do our best.'

'Then *why*?' A desperate question, which Héloïse had heard so many times from grieving women; which she in her time had cried out too, angrily, railing against fate.

'I can't tell you why, *mon âme*,' she said sadly. 'I am not in His confidence. But I believe things happen for the best, in the long run. Let it make you a better, more thoughtful person, that's all. Then you will know that the sorrow has not been wasted.'

After a while Sophie pushed herself away and reached for a handkerchief and began to mop up. Héloïse watched her with the familiar feeling of helplessness. When they are little, she thought, you can keep them away from the thorns and the sharp stones and the fire in the grate that looks so pretty and burns so badly. But when they grow up you can only offer them words, and watch them grieve all alone.

'Do you think,' Sophie said at last rather unevenly, 'that I should see Rosamund?'

256

'I can't advise you, *ma mie*,' Héloïse said helplessly.

'Please do, Maman! You *are* wiser than me.'

Héloïse smiled a little, but shook her head. 'Only older. I can't tell you what to do. You must follow your conscience.'

'But when it gives me conflicting commands, what then?' Sophie pressed her.

'Well, well, if you force me to advise,' Héloïse said reluctantly, 'I can only say it is not for us to judge each other — that is God's business. And when you are not sure what to do, do what comes with the most love.'

'You think I should see her, then,' Sophie concluded.

'I didn't say that,' Héloïse protested.

But Sophie smiled with a return of gladness, like the first ray of spring sunshine after a wet February, and leaned forward to kiss her mother's cheek gratefully. 'Oh yes, you did,' she said.

Sophie went alone to Batchworth House, and in a common hackney instead of in her own carriage. She didn't quite know why, except that it had to do with her fear that Rosamund would refuse to receive her. Sophie would not blame her if she did. She presented herself at the front door a penitent, veiled and extremely nervous.

The butler who opened the door to her was a very old man, and Sophie thought he must be some elderly family retainer of Lord Batchworth's whose loyalty was stronger than his pride.

'Is her ladyship at home?' Sophie asked.

The old man shuffled backwards to admit her to the hall. 'I will enquire, madam,' he said. 'Who shall I say is calling?'

Sophie hesitated. It might seem insultingly formal to offer a card. 'Please say that Mrs Hobsbawn asks to see her,' she said finally.

He went away, and Sophie raised her veil and glanced about her. There was a slight film of dust over the side table by the door — one day's accumulation, perhaps — and no flowers in the vases. It was quiet, too, as though there were no servants about. It felt like a house shut up because the family was away.

At last the butler returned. Sophie braced herself for

rejection, but he said, 'Will you step this way, madam?' and turning, led the way back up the stairs. He moved so slowly that it gave her ample time to feel her nervousness to the full and to wrestle with the silly desire to run away. At last he reached a door which he opened to announce, 'Mrs Hobsbawn, my lady,' and stepped aside to let Sophie through.

Rosamund was standing alone in the centre of the room, in the middle of an open space of carpet, which made it look as though she had left herself room for flight. She was most elegantly dressed in a gown of twilled blue poplin over a lace chemisette, her hair arranged and curled by Moss's expert hand. There was nothing in her appearance to suggest the experiences she had been through; only to Sophie she looked much older, and her face was pale and set and unsmiling.

So for what seemed like an eternity Sophie stood just inside the door, staring at her, wondering what to say, how to cross the gulf between them. At last it was Rosamund who broke the silence.

'So, have you come to upbraid me again?'

Sophie shook her head, the harsh words further sapping her self possession. 'I have no right,' she managed to say.

Rosamund made a small movement of her head, rather like a cat which does not wish to be touched, and looked away from Sophie. 'I'm sorry about your miscarriage,' she said stiffly, almost without moving her lips. 'Jes told me —'

Sophie's hands seemed to have reached out without her volition, and her voice followed them, breaking through the stupid reserve. 'Oh Ros, I'm so sorry! It was wrong of me to set myself up in judgement. When I think I may have added to your unhappiness — oh please, please forgive me!'

Rosamund made a strange sound which might have been a sob or the beginning of a laugh, and somehow they had crossed the space between them and their arms were round each other. They were both crying a little. After a while she heard Rosamund say, 'Poor Sophie. Poor Sophie.'

'I've missed you,' Sophie said. 'I needed my friend.'

'I've missed you too.'

'Do you forgive me?'

'There's nothing to forgive. I did wrong, and you had every right to censure.'

'No right at all,' Sophie contradicted. 'In your position I would probably have done the same.' She put herself back to arm's length to look into her cousin's face. 'But, oh Rosamund, your little girl!'

'I think about her all the time,' Rosamund said quietly. She put her arm round Sophie's waist and led her to a sofa, and they sat down together, their hands linked for comfort. 'I think it must be my punishment. You know I never cared for babies. I used to call them little brutes.'

Sophie nodded. 'I remember.'

'I never wanted a child — not anyone's. But when she was born — oh Sophie, she was so small and perfect! I thought babies were ugly, but she wasn't. From the first minute she was beautiful.'

'I know. I remember. When Fanny was born —'

'Yes. Fanny is lovely! It brought it home to me so sharply when I saw her with you in the carriage that day, that that's what I would miss — just being with her in the ordinary way. All the days of her life — watching her grow up, hearing her call me —' She bit her lip, unable to go on.

'But surely, *surely* Marcus will relent?' Sophie said desperately. 'He can't be so cruel as to keep you from her always?'

'I don't think he is rational any more,' Rosamund said. 'I think the — the accident turned his mind. I write to him again and again, my mother writes to him, Papa Danby even tries to see him, but he won't respond. He's shut himself up with my baby and Barbarina — and she hates me as much as he does, or perhaps more. She blames me for everything. You know that Lord Ballincrea wanted to marry her?'

'No, I didn't. How sad. He died, didn't he, a few weeks ago?'

'Yes, in January. But she had refused him long before. She said she couldn't leave Marcus alone once I had gone; so that made it my fault again.'

'But you didn't want to leave, did you?'

Rosamund shrugged. 'No. But it was all my fault, from beginning to end. The first mistake was in accepting Marcus though I knew he and I would never suit. I can't blame anyone else; though I still feel my punishment is too harsh. Oh, but my poor Sophie,' she went on quickly before Sophie could speak, 'you've suffered too! I can understand now how sad you must be to have lost your baby. But there will be others, won't there?'

'I don't think so,' Sophie said. 'No, don't protest. I've thought about it a great deal, and I've brought myself to accept it. I have Fanny, and I'm very grateful for her. If God should send me another, I shall be grateful, but if not, I shan't rail. I have only to think of *your* loss to know how lucky I am.'

Rosamund gave a thin, sad smile. 'If I am useful as an object lesson, I suppose it has not all been in vain.'

'But you are happy with Jes, aren't you?' Sophie said hopefully.

'We love each other very much,' Rosamund said. 'I ought to learn from you, my good Sophie, should I not, and be grateful for what I have.' She pressed her hands. 'We'll comfort each other, will we? Even if you have to visit me incognito?'

Sophie blushed to think of the wrong interpretation which might be put on her coming here veiled and in a plain hackney. 'We are friends,' she said stoutly. 'I will visit you openly as I would visit any friend. And you and Jes shall dine with us. Jasper will see it in the right light, I'm sure.'

Rosamund, who knew from Jes what Jasper's attitude was, only smiled. 'What a lion you can be, little Sophie! You and I against the world?'

'If need be,' Sophie said bravely.

In April Mathilde bore her fifth child, and it was a girl. Her disappointment was acute, but John, though he had hoped for a boy, had almost brought himself to expect another daughter, and was prepared to admit defeat.

'No more,' he said, holding his wife's hand, and looking down at the baby on his other arm with his usual sense of mystery that they could start out so very unprepossessing, and yet soon become such pretty and beguiling creatures. 'Five attempts is enough in all reason.'

'But we must —' Mathilde began the automatic protest.

John interrupted firmly. 'I don't want a son at the cost of exhausting you, and perhaps impairing your health. We have five lovely daughters, and we must be content.' Quite apart from the question of Mathilde's health, he thought, there was the business of the dowries which would one day have to be found for them all. Girls were a drain on a business, and if they went on trying, what was to say they would not get even more of them? Six girls — seven — ten? Better to stop now, while they had something to preserve.

'But what will happen to the business?' Mathilde protested, weary, but game.

'We shall have to marry them off to suitable young men who can take over from me one day. A son-in-law will do just as well as a son.'

Mathilde met his eyes. It wouldn't, she thought, and they both knew it, but there was no point in voicing the thought.

James was deliciously amused when he learned that the latest little Miss Skelwith was to be named Melpomone. He shared the joke with Lord Anstey when he called on them one day.

Héloïse did not laugh. 'But it must be a mistake. You must tell them, my James.'

'Not I!' James chuckled. 'I can see their reasoning as plain as writing. Mathilde thinks it's something to do with spring, or burgeoning nature — a natural confusion with the word "pomegranate", I suppose.'

'Perhaps they think Melpomone was a wood nymph or something of the sort,' Anstey said, trying not to smile too broadly.

'But James,' Héloïse said gravely, 'it will be unlucky for the poor baby to be named after the muse of tragedy! Think what a burden for a little girl.'

'It's a tremendous joke,' James said with enthusiasm. 'Melpomone Skelwith, Queen of Tragedy!'

'She'll probably run away and go on the stage when she's fifteen, and end up marrying a duke,' Anstey said.

'There you are then! I forbid you to spoil the fun, wife,' said James. 'Let them call their babies what they will.'

Lord Anstey had come to discuss with James the proposals which were being put forward for a new road to replace a section of the Great North Road. 'From York to Peterborough, running straight as a die, cutting out all those unnecessary meanderings.'

'The Romans would be proud of you,' James commented.

'The Romans would have done it centuries ago,' Anstey said. 'We've got Telford to agree to do the initial survey — he's beginning more or less straight away, so I should think we ought to be able to get a Bill before Parliament some time in 1826.'

'But what can you need such a road for?' Héloïse asked. 'The Great North Road is already famous for its fine travelling.'

'The long-term plan is to improve the journey time from London to Edinburgh. At the moment the best speed is forty-three and a half hours, and this new road —'

Héloïse laughed. 'Dear John, forty-three hours is less than two days! From the capital of England to the capital of Scotland in less than two days! What can anyone want better than that?'

'This new road,' Anstey persevered, 'would take twenty miles off the distance and two hours off the journey.'

'Are our lives so frantic that two hours make so much difference?' Héloïse asked. 'And what would your traveller do with the time he saved? Build a cathedral, perhaps, or compose a symphony?'

Anstey shook his head. 'But two hours is only the beginning, my dear Héloïse,' he said. 'We mean to carry the improvements to the northern part of the road too, between York and Edinburgh, which is still very bad. Eventually the journey time could be brought down to thirty hours — the saving of more than half a day. Now that is significant, I think you will agree.'

'No,' said Héloïse defiantly but smilingly. 'What can it benefit men to rush about the country like that? Better for everyone to stay at home while they can.'

James felt there might be a message for him there, and looked the other way, whistling soundlessly.

'I understand your point of view,' Anstey said kindly, 'but I'm afraid it will not prevail. Everyone now believes we must have better and faster transport throughout the country if trade is to flourish. I think you will find that that will be the principal concern of the next decade or two. Indeed, it would have happened long ago if it hadn't been for the war. The war was a hiatus in the natural development of ideas. Before the war we had already begun our wonderful system of canals for transporting goods. If we hadn't spent twenty years fighting the French, we'd have built an equally fine system of roads by now for transporting people.'

'You'll never convince Héloïse,' James said, observing his wife's stubborn expression with amusement. 'I'm not so sure myself about the idea of a better road to Edinburgh. It would be vilely expensive — the Holyhead Road, excellent though it is, cost three quarters of a million pounds when all was said and done!'

'The expense is well justified,' Anstey said firmly.

'New roads for England is one thing,' James said. 'I agree with you we must have them. But why should we pay good English money to build a fine road for the Scots?'

Anstey laughed. 'It runs both ways, you know, James! England to Scotland and Scotland to England both.'

'Let them build their end of it, then,' James proclaimed with fine illogic.

'I'm sure they will,' said Anstey. 'Telford and McAdam are both Scotsmen, remember.'

James laughed. 'You can't better that for a Parthian shot! We had better change the subject.'

'I must be taking my leave in any case,' Anstey said. 'Oh — I almost forgot! I have a little snippet of news which I think will interest young Benedict.'

'Benedict?' Héloïse said in surprise.

'Yes, it's about tramroads — the Stockton to Darlington tramroad in particular. We saw some of its workings on our trip up north, and I thought he might like to know that the developing company has managed to secure a further Act of Parliament, which amongst other provisions authorises it to use "loco-motive or movable engines".'

'Do they really think it's feasible then?' James asked in surprise.

'Their chief engineer is George Stephenson, and he certainly thinks so. He's been experimenting with the idea for some years — without success so far, but he is a very innovative thinker. Who knows what will come of it?' Anstey chuckled. 'The clause about movable engines only narrowly escaped being struck out. Old Parfitt, who had to draft the actual wording, couldn't understand what it meant and concluded it must be nonsense!'

'So it is,' James said. 'Even if your Stephenson could make a locomotive engine that worked — which I doubt — horses are still just as fast and much more reliable, and fodder is cheaper than coal. But I'll pass the news on to Bendy all the same.'

'And to Father Moineau,' Héloïse said. 'I think he is even more interested in tramroads than Benedict.'

'Yes, it's true,' James said with a grin. 'Your trip to northern parts seems to have been his road to Damascus!'

Mr and Mrs Peter Morpurgo were entertaining at home in their pleasantly informal way, which attracted lively people from many interests. Conversation was varied. The fashionable young married group was discussing Caroline Lamb's latest series of blatant infidelities, which had resulted in her long-suffering husband's banishing her to the country, to Melbourne Hall. One lady of romantic tendency held that it was Lord Byron's death which had caused Caro's renewed outbreak; another that all the Lambs were insufferable and clannish, and any normal wife would have been driven mad by them. The gentlemen asserted that poor William Lamb's patience could not hold out much longer, and that he would be forced in the end to lock her up.

An older and more serious group was discussing the recent Select Committee report on the operation of the Poor Laws, which concluded that they caused more problems than they alleviated. Everyone was of the opinion that something must be done to relieve the agricultural poor, but no-one was able to suggest what.

Those of a commercial bent were discussing the improvements Huskisson — the Member for Liverpool — was bringing about now he was President of the Board of Trade, and speculating on which would be the next duties to be abolished. The taxes on beer and tallow were considered to be particularly unfair on the poor, since the rich man brewed his own beer and burned wax candles; salt, soap and tea were other essentials that ought to be relieved for the sake of the lower orders.

A naval group was supposing rather wistfully that the navy must do better once the Duke of Clarence was on the throne, and wondering rather uncharitably how the King managed to survive from year to year after such a life of debauchery.

Three unmarried young ladies were discussing hats and pretending not to notice four unmarried young gentlemen standing nearby who were discussing horses.

Tom Weston was telling Thalia Hampton about the new Chain Pier at Brighton which had just been opened, which boasted 1,100 feet of promenade furnished with a camera obscura, a sundial, two small cannon, a profusion of green benches and several booths serving mineral water. 'All for an entrance fee of tuppence. And what Brighton has, the other sea-side places will have too. I can guarantee that it will be all chain piers and promenades from now on, from Southend to Weymouth.'

'But what were you doing in Brighton?' Thalia asked, far more interested in him than in the place.

'I went down with Cleveley and Georgie Fleetwood to have a look at a horse.'

'You don't like horses,' Thalia objected.

'No, but I enjoy a change of scene as much as the next man,' Tom grinned.

'More, I should have thought,' Thalia said. 'Your Grand Tour has given you a taste for travel. Don't you ever mean to settle down?'

'On the contrary, I mean to get more restless as I get older. At the moment I prescribe small circles, but I shall have a larger pair of compasses one day, and then —' He shrugged expressively.

'But you might marry,' Thalia said casually.

Tom looked at her with a knowing amusement which she found both intriguing and annoying. 'I think not. I am only attracted to rich and titled women, and what rich and titled woman would have me?'

'I would,' Thalia said, nettled beyond prudence.

'I'm flattered, ma'am. But your Papa would have something to say about that.'

'I'm twenty-one. He can't stop me marrying whoever I want to.'

265

'He could cut off your allowance and refuse your dowry, Miss Hampton. That's as effective a way of stopping you as I can think of.'

Thalia sighed impatiently. 'But he wouldn't do that anyway. He simply longs for me to marry because he hopes it will make me give up the school.'

'And would it?'

'No, of course not. But you wouldn't mind that, would you? And you're Lord Theakston's adopted son, which makes you quite good enough for me. Papa would be simply delighted if you were to make me an offer. Oh Tom,' she added, abandoning all pride, 'won't you marry me? We'd be so happy together! I love you quite frightfully, and I'm sure you love me, or why would you spend so much time being nice to me?'

Whatever Tom felt — pleasure, dismay or amusement — it did not show in his face. 'My dear Cousin Thalia — if I may call you that — I don't deserve your good opinion, though I thank you for your flattering offer. But I'm afraid you have mistaken me. I shall never marry. My heart is already quite irrevocably given to another.'

'I don't believe you,' Thalia said, studying his face, puzzled. He seemed quite serious, and yet there was something odd about the look in his eye. 'Who is she? I've never seen you courting anyone.'

'You've seen me with her often enough. But she is a married lady.'

'Married? You don't mean you're —'

'Not at all,' Tom anticipated her. 'I've known her and loved her all my life, and I shall never love another. She is the source of everything good in my life. It is she who prescribes the radius of my circles, you see.'

Thalia frowned. 'I don't know what you mean. What is her name? You may trust me, you know — I can be discreet.'

'I doubt it,' Tom laughed. 'But it's no secret anyway. Her name is Lady Theakston.'

Thalia stared, not knowing whether to laugh or be annoyed. She had the feeling she was being roasted, but she didn't understand what was behind it. 'But she's your mother!' she protested at last. 'You're not serious.'

Tom said, 'I am quite serious.' His mocking smile was gone. 'Little cousin, let me give you some advice: marry my brother Roland. He will make you an excellent husband, and he won't mind about the school.'

Thalia tried not to look sulky. To be advised to marry elsewhere by the man one has chosen is humiliating. 'Roland doesn't want to marry me. He doesn't even love me.'

'Yes he does. He loves you to distraction; but he's shy, and rather proud. He won't show it because he thinks you don't love him, and he'd die rather than have an unwilling bride. You and he would deal excellently together, and I assure you that once you got to know him, you would love him very much.'

'I wouldn't. You can't say that.'

'I can, because I know him better than anyone else in the world, and I know you too.' He reached out and put a gentle finger under her chin, and lifted it slightly to make her meet his eyes. 'This is the best advice I can give you, Thalia, and the best advice anyone will ever give you: *marry Roland.*'

She stared into his eyes for a moment, felt lost and helpless and rather frightened; then snatched her head free and said crossly, covering up for herself, 'Well I can't marry him unless he asks me, can I? And he won't ask me, so your advice is nonsense!'

'He'll ask you,' said Tom. 'I promise you that.'

From Stanhope Place Tom walked across to St James's Street where, as he expected, he discovered his brother presiding over a game of faro.

'My brother, a gamester!' he cried in pretended shock. 'How has this come about? You will break my poor mother's heart!'

Roland turned and smiled at him. 'Oh, it's you! You are a clown, Tom! We're not playing high you know. It's the company I like more than the gambling.'

'As if you need to tell me that,' Tom said. 'May I take you away and have a private word with you?'

One of the other players, young Mr Bretherton, removed the cigar from his lips and scowled. 'Yes, yes, take him away by all means! Aylesbury has the luck of the devil. No-one else has a chance when he's at the table. Take him off somewhere, Weston, that's a good fellow.'

'And then come back yourself,' said Sir Harry Tooke more cordially, 'and we'll have a hand or two of whist.'

'You only say that because you know I'm the worst card player in the world,' Tom said genially.

'Of course,' Tooke agreed. 'I've lost enough tonight. If I don't win somethin' back, I shall have to sell the family silver.'

'Rough company you've got yourself into,' Tom said to Roland when he had ushered him out of earshot.

Roland grinned. 'Oh, they aren't so bad! They don't mean what they say, you know. They're the best of fellows really.'

'No, *you're* the best of fellows,' Tom said. 'All the rest of the world comes a long way second. That's why I want to see you happy.'

'I am happy,' Roland protested.

'Not entirely,' Tom said. They had found a quiet corner, and he turned to face him. 'You are still bothered too much by our mother.'

Roland looked embarrassed. 'I know you think I should stand up to her more —'

'I think nothing of the sort,' Tom countered quickly. 'I know I've said that sort of thing in the past, and it was very impertinent of me, besides being bad advice. Now I want to be even more impertinent, and give you some good advice. You must get married.'

Roland's expression changed. 'Now don't you begin on that song too!'

Tom caught his arm. 'Listen, dear brother. I was at Africa's house tonight, talking to Thalia —'

'Who is nutty on you, as everyone knows.'

'She's nothing of the sort. Do stop interrupting. She only pretends to be interested in me because she thinks you don't love her, and she's too proud to show she likes you without return.'

Roland was suspicious. 'You tell me she likes me?'

'My dear old fellow, she doesn't give two straws about me, I assure you. What she wants most in the world is to marry you, but her parents blundered over her feelings by being heavy-handed and issuing decrees — of course a lively, spirited girl like her is bound to rebel; and then you were so damned diffident, she got it into her head you were only going to marry her to please our mother.'

'Did she really think that? The poor little creature,' Roland said. 'No wonder she was so stiff and formal. *Of course* she couldn't marry on those terms — a creature so beautiful and clever and spirited and —'

'Yes, I have the catalogue already,' Tom interrupted hastily. 'Well, now that you know, what are you going to do?'

'What can I do?' Roland said helplessly. 'I must have ruined my chances now.'

'Has she married anyone else?'

'No, but —'

'Has she placed herself in such a position, virtually under Africa's guardianship, where you can obtain access to her on the most favourable terms for a private conversation?'

'Yes, but —'

'Then don't be such a fish! "What can I do?" indeed! Go and hang about the school and make a nuisance of yourself until she grants you an interview, and then make love to the girl. Tell her you adore her, and that she'll make you the happiest man in the world if she'll consent to be Lady Aylesbury. Tell her you love her so much you'll take her on any terms she cares to name, and if she won't have you you'll go and drown yourself.'

Roland's eyes were bright, staring at a private and obviously gratifying vision. 'Do you really think I could?'

'I really think you should. Do it, man! And I'll come and dance at your wedding.'

'I will then! I'll do it tomorrow. Oh Tom, you're so good to me. You've always been so good to me. I don't know how to thank you.'

Tom laid his own hand over Roland's, which was resting on his shoulder, and patted it. 'Thank me by being happy. Someone in the family's got to be.' He released himself. 'And now you can go back to your disreputable companions. I'll see you tomorrow, no doubt.'

Out in the street, Tom paused a moment, staring at nothing, a frown of thought pulling down his fine brows.

Then he sighed, shook himself, and turned in the direction of home. He walked lightly, like a cat; and like a cat he kept his counsel and walked alone.

woman m

CHAPTER FOURTEEN

Roland was some days gathering his courage for the task.
When he did finally present himself at the school, he found
Thalia in the manège overseeing the lesson of a very nervous
young woman. In the spectators' gallery the entire distaff side
of the pupil's family seemed to be gathered, along with a
number of her friends, who clasped their hands in anxiety and
gasped every time the horse moved, and then let out wild
cries of congratulation when the rider managed to stay in the
saddle.

Roland crept into a corner of the back of the gallery and
hoped not to be noticed. Thalia, he thought admiringly, was
doing wonderfully well not to be distracted by the audience,
and encouraged her pupil with patience and tact. When the
lesson was over and the trembling young woman had been
reclaimed by her nearest and dearest and the horse was being
led off by a groom, Roland presented himself to Thalia. She
greeted him pleasantly.

'Were you watching? I can't think why the Bryants keep
sending poor Caroline here. It's torture for her, and she'll
never be a rider.'

'I thought you were making progress,' Roland said. 'You
seem to me to be a born teacher.'

'Thank you. But there's nothing to be done with such poor
material. The whole thing is so silly: they wanted to marry her
to Freddie Banbury, and since he's horse-mad they persuaded her to pretend to like horses too, so as to engage his
interest.' She laughed. 'It worked so well he's not only
proposed, but he's talking of buying her a spirited little Arab
mare for a wedding gift! So now of course the poor girl has

271

to learn to ride, while it's as much as she can do to stay on. Really, people are such fools about marriage, don't you think? If she ends by breaking her neck, her family will be content so long as she dies Lady Banbury and not Miss Bryant.'

This was not encouraging. 'I suppose they're bound to try to do their best for her,' Roland said cautiously. 'Every young woman must want an establishment.'

Thalia eyed him curiously, and declined to argue the point. 'Did you come to see Peter? He's in the Park with three of Africa's young men. She's gone over to visit Polly. Isn't it good news about her baby? A boy first time, clever thing!'

'Yes, I saw Paston yesterday at Watier's. He was as pleased as Punch.'

'And now Africa's in the same way herself, did you know?'

'No I didn't. How splendid.'

Thalia made a face. 'It will interfere dreadfully with the business. There will be about six months when she won't be able to take lessons, so we'll have to find another instructress; and that won't be easy. Our precise requirements are not easy to fill.'

'I imagine not,' Roland said. 'There can't be many well-born ladies who would wish to be instructresses.'

Thalia looked at him sharply. 'Do I hear a note of disapproval, Cousin Roland? You think I demean myself?'

'Not at all! I didn't say so,' Roland said hastily.

'Mama thinks so, and Papa used to, though I think he's got used to it now. But your mama is on my side. At least, she said to me yesterday that she didn't blame me, and that when she was my age she was always wanting to *do* things, and not just sit in a parlour and simper.'

'Yes,' Roland said. 'But it was different for Mama.'

'How so?' Thalia asked sharply.

He took a deep breath. 'She was married; and a married woman has much more freedom. All the wild things Mama did, she did as Lady Aylesbury, and the world forgave her — on the whole.'

Thalia continued to stare at him, but did not reply. At last she said casually, 'You didn't answer my question: *did* you come to see Peter?'

'No, not Peter. I came to see you,' Roland said. The sound

272

of his own words made his heart beat rapidly, but he was launched now, and must ride the waves. 'I would like to speak to you privately for a moment, if I may.'

Thalia looked suddenly nervous. 'I have another lesson to take almost immediately.'

'I'll try to be brief,' Roland said.

'Oh, can't it wait for another time?'

'No, I must speak to you now.' Roland amazed himself by the firmness of his voice. 'Dear Thalia, I want to tell you how much I love you. I don't know whether I've managed to make that plain to you before.'

Thalia shook her head. Her cheeks were pink, her eyes cast down, her lips tightly compressed. For an instant Roland thought she was angry, before he realised, with dawning hope, that it was the reaction of shyness.

'I'm afraid I have been acting like an idiot, and I must ask you to forgive me. It was all my wretched nervousness. I've always been afraid of Mama, you see, and so when she wanted me to marry you — well, I think perhaps I didn't make it perfectly clear that I had been wanting that too since the first moment I saw you.'

'Oh Roland, please don't —'

'You must let me finish, now I've screwed up my courage,' he said with smiling self-mockery, 'for I may never manage it again. I love you very much, Thalia, and I want more than anything in the world to marry you. If you will only say yes, I will devote my life to making you happy; and you needn't think that I would be a stern, disapproving husband. I wouldn't want to stop you doing the things you like. I know you like teaching here at the school —'

'Oh, but I don't,' Thalia said, in such a low voice Roland thought he had misheard. She looked up. 'I thought I would, but mostly it's very dull, and having to come every day and not being able to do others things is such a nuisance. But Papa and everyone said I wouldn't like it, so you see I had to go on and not let them know.'

'Yes, I do see that. I'd feel just the same.'

'Would you? Roland, do you really love me?'

'More than anyone in the world.'

'More than your mother?'

273

'My mother?' He gave her a puzzled smile. 'What has my mother to do with it?'

'Oh — nothing. I don't know. I just thought . . .'

Roland regarded her thoughtfully. 'You mustn't think she would be always interfering. She isn't like that. She wants to see me married, but once I was married, she'd feel able to forget all about me and go back to her own interests. Oh Thalia, do say yes! As Lady Aylesbury you'd have all the freedom you could want, carriages, horses, a house in Town — everything.'

'But what about the School?'

'*What* about it?'

'Well, Papa bought me a share of it because he thought I wasn't going to get married — instead of a dowry, you see.'

'Don't worry about that. I don't care about a dowry.'

'But Papa might.'

'I'll speak to your papa. If he wants his capital returned, I'll buy your share for you. And you can be an owner of the school without having to teach in it, you know.'

'Thank you,' she said. She looked a little shamefaced. 'It would be making a great deal of trouble for you.'

'None at all! Nothing that I regard. Oh Thalia, does it mean that you will marry me? Please say yes!'

There was a moment of hesitation which almost unmanned him. She looked not *at* him, he thought, but rather *through* him, as though at some receding vision; and then she gave a faint, almost wistful smile.

'Yes,' she said, 'I will marry you.'

He lifted her hand to his lips and kissed it fervently. 'I'll make you happy, I swear it!'

'Yes,' she said. 'I think you will. But, Roland, it can't be at once. I can't leave Africa at a moment's notice, especially now she's increasing.'

Roland smiled broadly. 'My dear Thalia, if you think either of our sets of parents would allow us to marry at a moment's notice, you know very little about them! Our wedding will take months and months of preparation. Like it or not, it will be a very grand occasion.'

Thalia smiled too. 'A few weeks ago I should have thought

274

I would hate the idea of that; but now, I rather think I shall like it.'

It was Jasper's idea to have a ceremony of some sort to mark the completion of the rational housing. He had intended something modest to draw attention to the scheme, so as to thank the investors and to encourage further schemes of the sort. When he communicated the idea to James — who was a large investor — and to John Skelwith, it was not only received with enthusiasm but rapidly expanded into a Grand Official Opening Ceremony, and sprouted such side-shoots that it threatened to rival St Peter's Fair in excitement.

'How can we have an opening ceremony when there's nothing to open?' Jasper grumbled to Sophie. The need for the houses was so great that as each was finished a family moved into it, with the result that fifty of the sixty were now occupied.

'You could open the doors of the last ten houses,' Sophie suggested.

'Only by keeping them empty until the day, and I don't see the point of that. They are supposed to relieve suffering, not feed vanity.'

'Well, just one door then. Keep one house empty for the ceremony. Jasper dear, don't be so hard on your fellow men,' Sophie smiled. 'You must allow a *little* praise and self congratulation to those who do good, just to be sure they go on doing it.'

'Hmph!' Jasper plainly disagreed.

'And besides, it will be fun,' she coaxed. 'I'm sure the poor people will enjoy it too, and they have so little pleasure in their lives.'

'What pleasure is there in listening to speeches of self congratulation?' Jasper said, determined to be sour.

Sophie clasped her hands as a sudden idea came to her. 'I have it! We will give them a feast, there in the courts in front of their new houses! Yes, yes, I can see it all! We'll decorate the houses with flags and bunting, and set up trestles, and give them a party! The ladies from the Mission will help, I'm sure. And the poor people will dress in their best, and grand people will make speeches, and the band will play —'

'A band now, is it?'

'Of course we must have a band — and the new tenants will throw their hats in the air and cheer, and it will make them feel so much better!'

'The new tenants will be at work in the mills, my dear.'

'You must close the mills for the day,' Sophie said firmly.

Jasper began unwillingly to smile. 'That will give them something to cheer about — losing a day's wages.'

'Oh — yes, I hadn't thought,' Sophie faltered; and then brightened. 'But if we give them a feast, that will make it even. And just think how much interest it will raise in the whole idea! You want other mill masters to provide houses, don't you?'

'Not just mill masters — anyone will do. Bankers, builders, noblemen —'

'Then this will be your advertisement. They will see how you are esteemed for what you have done, and want to emulate you. But if there's no band and no flags and no speeches, they won't be nearly so eager.'

Jasper lifted her fingers to his lips and saluted them. 'You have a great deal of wisdom when it comes to human nature, haven't you, my wife?'

'So we will do it, then?' Sophie pressed.

'It will take a great deal of organising,' Jasper said unwillingly.

'Oh don't mind it, dearest! Rosamund and I will arrange everything, with Prudence and Agnes and some of the others. We'll form a committee, and raise subscriptions.'

'And who will you get to perform the actual ceremony? I suppose you will want someone to cut a ribbon or turn a golden key or something of the sort,' Jasper said ironically. 'I suppose it ought to be your papa, since much of the money came from him. Or perhaps it should simply be someone grand: the Lord Lieutenant of the County?'

Sophie was frowning in thought, but then her face cleared as she thought of the perfect notion for winning Jasper's approval. 'I have a better idea,' she said with a serene smile. 'Fanny shall do it. We will have Fanny to perform the opening ceremony.'

Once the principle had been accepted, Jasper wanted to

compound it by having the grand opening on Fanny's birthday, the fourth of March; but it had taken on a life of its own with the inclusion of more and more people on the organising committee, and it was decided unanimously that the weather was too uncertain in March, and that it would be a pity to see it spoiled by cold winds, rain or even snow. An outdoor ceremony needed warmth and sunshine: 'I hate the sight of an umbrella!' as one lady put it feelingly.

And so at last it took place on a day in the middle of May, 1825, and for once the gods smiled on human endeavour and sent them almost perfect weather. Jasper went down to the site early to see that all was in order, and although he arrived before eight o'clock, the courts were already seething with activity. Heroic efforts had been made to make them look pristine, as though all the houses were still unoccupied and not just the ceremonial end house. All were decorated with flags, and festoons of red, white and blue ribbon fastened with huge rosettes. The middens had been removed, the kennels and privvies cleared. Flowers and green boughs had been arranged here and there to give a fresher look, and even the windows had been washed to remove the accumulation of soot from the mills' chimneys.

Jasper had reluctantly agreed to close the mills for the day, and the air was a little clearer than it would otherwise have been, so the sun was shining down with unexpected power. Everything looked bright and cheerful. The tenants were busy setting up the trestles down the centre of the courts for the feast, and assembling a platform outside the ceremonial house for the speeches. It suddenly struck Jasper as being all rather silly, and he hastened away before his nerve gave out completely.

At home at Hobsbawn House no-one thought it in any way silly. The Skelwiths were staying there with their two eldest daughters, Mary and Harriet. The little girls were unusually subdued, plainly overcome with the realisation of how important Fanny was to be today, while they, who usually ruled the roast, would be as nothing. James was there, too, and had brought Benedict with him; Héloïse had sent her love, good wishes and regrets that she could not leave Morland Place at present.

277

The house party was joined for a late breakfast by Lord Batchworth and Rosamund, Prudence Pendlebury, and the Droylsdens. They were all going to travel to the ceremony together, and as Agnes said irrepressibly as they sat down at the crowded board, 'Today is a holiday, so we may as well start as we mean to go on.'

Jasper, never a great eater, lost his appetite entirely in the face of the great profusion on the table. Sophie and her cook had been in consultation for days. There was to be a dinner here tonight as well, and plainly Sophie didn't want anything to be lacking from the very beginning of the day. The centre of the table was dominated by a whole cold turkey, a vast ham wreathed with parsley, and a huge raised pie almost two feet across. Jasper surveyed them glumly. Of course they would reappear tonight as the sideboard dishes, but unless large inroads were made into them by their guests, he knew what he would be eating for the next week.

There was also a whole Stilton cheese and a pyramid of fruit, besides the hot dishes: buttered eggs, lamb cutlets, veal patties, rissoles, sausages, creamed sweetbreads, attlets of livers and oysters, and a dish of fried trout. Between these were placed the dishes of butter, the bowls of pickles, the baskets of bread and racks of toast, so it was not possible to see the table cloth at all.

Feeling rather faint, Jasper passed dishes back and forth, helped his near neighbours, and wondered as the conversational level rose how people could eat so much and talk so much all at the same time. He had a small slice of ham, a morsel of pie and some pickles on his plate to avert comment, but couldn't face eating them. He was toying with the idea of nibbling at a piece of bread when the footmen came in bearing two more covered dishes. Jasper met Sophie's eye down the length of the table and raised an astonished eyebrow. She smiled at him, but with faint apprehension, realising as she always did that he was not feeling quite one of the party. The two new offerings were presented to Jasper for his approval, and the covers whipped off. On the first dish were poached eggs, lying in a bed of hot spinach. Good God, but they looked revolting! he thought: like the eyes of drowned suicides staring up through a mat of seaweed. He tried to smile and wave them away as the second cover was lifted.

'Ah, beefsteak!' cried the indefatigable Percy Droylsden away on his left. He already had lamb cutlets, sausages and sweetbreads on his plate. 'I was afraid you might have forgotten it, and what's a breakfast without beefsteak? But I see you were cooking it fresh. I applaud you, Mrs Hobsbawn! Beefsteak should always be eaten quite fresh from the fire, while the juices are still running.'

'Hand Mr Droylsden the beefsteak,' Jasper said faintly to the footman, and on an inspiration added, 'and these eggs. You must try the poached eggs with your beefsteak, Droylsden! A delightful combination I assure you!'

Having weathered the egg crisis, Jasper turned his attention to the conversation nearest him. James was talking to Rosamund and Prudence Pendlebury about the Succession.

'It's obvious the King can't last much longer,' James was saying. 'He has abused his body for so long. It was touch and go on various occasions last winter. And York isn't much better — tortured with gout and dropsy, so your Aunt Lucy was telling me when I was in London last month.'

'But is it certain that the Duchess of Clarence can't bear another child, sir?' Prudence asked.

'A negative can never be a positive, Miss Pendlebury,' James said with a smile, 'but it looks unlikely. Certainly there's been no pregnancy since she miscarried back in 1822.'

'So it's to be the little Kent princess after all?' Prudence asked. 'How old is she now? Five?'

'Six, I think,' Rosamund said. 'They call her Victoria, don't they, Uncle? They've dropped the name Alexandrina, I understand.'

'That's right. And according to Theakston, someone or other referred to her in the House the other day as Heiress Presumptive without provoking any uproar, so it looks as though everyone's accepted the inevitable. I don't know how it will serve,' James added doubtfully.

Jasper spoke up. 'There's nothing wrong with a female heir. England did well enough under Elizabeth, after all.'

'Yes,' said James, still doubtfully. 'It depends rather how

she's brought up. I don't think anyone has much opinion of the Duchess's intellect, and the King hates the idea so much he won't notice the child. She isn't being brought up as a future queen should.'

'At least she has an establishment, now,' Jasper said. 'Didn't I read in the newspaper that the Government's given her a pension of six thousand pounds a year?'

'It's not what one would call a princely sum,' Rosamund said, 'but I suppose it ought to be enough for a little girl.' Her voice wavered on the last word. She didn't want to think about little girls. She changed the subject brightly. 'But what were you doing in London, Uncle James? You seem to be gadding about a good deal lately.'

'I was seeing how the first of my reschooled horses was settling in with your Cousin Africa. She's rather off her feet at the moment, of course, after having the twins and something of a hard time about it, I understand. Morpurgo's delighted with the boys, but Africa hinted to me she felt she'd done her duty in that respect, and it would be a long time before she went in for it again. Of course, we always used to have twins in our family,' James mused. 'They resurface every generation or so.'

The conversation having twisted itself treacherously round to babies again, Rosamund twisted it firmly back. 'What does my aunt feel about your travels? Surely you must be neglecting your duty to Morland Place? If she can't manage to be away, I wonder how you can.'

'But I am doing my duty,' James said, wide-eyed with innocence. 'Finding new and profitable investments, improving our fortunes. We can't sit still, you know, and hope that money will multiply in the dark like spiders. We have to go out —' a sweeping gesture of the hand, '— and tackle the world!'

Percy Droylsden looked up from his beefsteak, which had been occupying his whole attention until then. 'The world, Mr Morland? I admire your vision, sir. What do you think about South America? We are very interested indeed in the Latin states: newly independent, just ripe for investment and development. Brazil, Mexico — there are fortunes waiting to be made out there, sir, for the man with both capital and greatness of soul —'

'Pay no attention to him, Mr Morland,' Agnes broke in. 'He only talks like that because his papa won't let him speculate with the bank's money.'

'Speculate?' Percy said indignantly. 'It isn't speculation, I tell you, it's a solid certainty! Money in South America is as sure as — as —'

'As that three-legged horse you bet on last year at Newmarket,' his brother Harry interrupted.

Percy put on a dignified look. 'Horses I may mistake now and then, but I do understand investment, and I tell you, when I think of the fortunes waiting to be picked up in the Latin states, like windfall plums off the grass, why it makes me —'

'Quite light-headed,' Agnes finished for him sympathetically, and there was laughter. 'Don't you give him your capital, Mr Morland. If Percy's pa don't like it, it's not a goer.'

James laughed. 'I was thinking of something a little closer to home, where I can keep an eye on it. When I said the world, I really meant England.'

'A very natural confusion,' Lord Batchworth said sympathetically. 'Now if you really do have capital looking for a home, sir, I can thoroughly recommend a scheme close to home and close to my heart — the proposed tramroad between Liverpool and Manchester.' He looked down the table at Jasper. 'It's one of the few commercial subjects on which we agree, eh Hobsbawn?'

'There's no doubt a railway's needed,' Jasper said. 'Do you know we're bringing close on half a million bags of cotton up from Liverpool for the mills every year? Leaving aside all the other goods coming up, and finished products going down.'

'But you have the canal, haven't you?' James asked.

'We have three waterways, actually,' Batchworth said. 'There's the Mersey and Irwell Navigation, the Bridgwater Canal, and the Leigh branch of Leeds and Liverpool. But they can barely cope with the traffic as it is, and it's bound to increase. Already the delays are intolerable at certain times of the year.'

'But sir,' Benedict broke in with burning urgency, 'hasn't your Railway Bill just been thrown out of Parliament?'

Batchworth looked round at him and raised an eyebrow.

'Hullo! Have we a budding engineer at our board?'

'Bendy is tramway-mad,' said James. 'He and his tutor pore over the papers every day for any scrap of news about them. To hear the talk about reciprocal workings and malleable iron and T-sections, you'd think you'd strayed into a lunatic asylum instead of a schoolroom.'

Bendy flung his father a distracted glance, and then returned his gaze to Batchworth as to the horse's mouth. 'But sir, *why* was the bill discarded?' he asked urgently. 'It said in the newspaper that the survey was inaccurate. But it wasn't that, was it? It couldn't have been very bad, because it was Mr Stephenson who did it.'

'His great hero,' James explained.

'I'm afraid it was a bad survey,' Batchworth said. 'It was hurriedly done, and there were a lot of mistakes, though Stephenson's supposed to be the best man in the field. But that wasn't the real reason it was thrown out, all the same. It was the canal interest that killed it. We were up against some very influential men, and the prospectus — foolishly in my view — contained some fierce anti-canal polemic which set their backs up.'

'Not that they needed an excuse to resist,' Jasper said. 'They would have anyway. The canals are very profitable businesses. I should know, the transit costs I have to pay are huge! That's another reason we need a tramroad — not just for convenience, but for cheapness.'

'If we can establish a route which offers no delays, and cheap, safe transport of goods at a steady six miles per hour —' Batchworth began.

'But canal proprietors like the Marquess of Stafford won't care for that sort of competition. The profits from the Bridgwater Canal alone came to well over eighty thousand pounds last year,' said Droylsden.

James raised an eyebrow. 'If the canals are as profitable as that, perhaps I'd better invest in them instead.'

'No no,' Batchworth laughed. 'We'll present the Bill again, and find a way to square the good Marquess, and there'll be business enough and profits enough for all, I promise you. The future is with us — don't you agree, young engineer?' he added, looking at Bendy.

'Oh yes, sir! The tramways will be the thing,' he said fervently. 'And not just horse-working either, but with locomotive engines.'

'I don't know about that,' Jasper demurred. He looked at his plate, rather disconcerted to find that in his interest in the conversation he'd eaten the ham and the pie without noticing. 'Stationary engines are one thing, but no-one's ever managed to make a locomotive that worked properly.'

'Don't discourage the lad, Hobsbawn,' Batchworth said with a smile. 'I told you once before, didn't I, that you are not a visionary? But I can see that this young man is — and it's out of dreams that wonders appear.'

When the party arrived at Morland's Rents — the name which had been given to the three courts of new houses — the sun was shining and the band was playing 'See the Conquering Hero Comes'. The road was thronged with the carriages of the philanthropic rich, and the courts with the grateful poor. Great efforts had been made by the latter, as well as on their behalf, and Jasper, as he stepped down from the carriage, ran his eye over the nearest ranks and saw that they had all washed and were dressed in clothes which though old, sometimes frayed and often mended, were perfectly clean. Hair was tidily arranged, and some of the little girls were even wearing hair-ribbons, to their immense pride.

Jasper was as touched as he was surprised. He looked at Sophie, who smiled and returned the squeeze of his hand. 'Is this your doing?' he asked.

'Not just mine,' she disclaimed quickly. 'Everyone had a hand, and Prudence has worked hardest of all. The ladies at the mission got the clothes together and gave them out. Arranging the washing was the hardest part.'

Jasper could believe that; but there was no time for further talk. The crowds were parting before them, and he was being hailed as a hero as he led the way through. The houses might be called Morland's Rents, and John Skelwith might have built them; but the people who were to live in them knew whose was the real credit. 'Maister Hobsbawn' was cheered every inch of the way; and when he lifted Fanny up to carry her in the safety of his arm the cheers redoubled.

They reached the dais in front of the festooned house which was to be 'opened' and slowly the music and the cheering died away. The proceedings opened with speeches from a number of eminent people. Jasper began to feel a sense of unreality as he stood looking down over that sea of pinkish faces under respectfully bared heads, crammed into the narrow space between the houses. Half hidden in the middle of the listeners were the trestle tables with the food already laid out ready for the feast. Yet no-one so much as looked at it, let alone thought of touching it, though he knew all of them must be hungry. Another odd circumstance was that the trestles, for geographical reasons, had been set up over the kennel down the centre of the court. The kennel was — for probably the only time in its life — empty, and yet the fact of its proximity to the feast haunted him.

The speeches seemed very long to Jasper, but no-one fidgeted, and for all he knew everyone was listening attentively to every word. For himself, he had no idea what was being said. His attention wandered amongst the faces familiar and unfamiliar — to the ladies hats — to Mathilde looking enormously proud with a proprietorial glance now and then at her husband — to a pair of pigeons on the roof of one of the houses, warming their breasts on the slates — to a member of the band surreptitiously emptying the condensation out of his instrument — to a mill hand rolling his empty pipe slowly round and round in his fingers, his face fixed gravely on the speaker — to a dog at the edge of the crowd standing on three legs and delicately excavating the inside of one ear with the claws of a hind foot.

And then suddenly the moment had come: a change of pitch, eyes everywhere refocusing lower down, grave expressions slipping into the pleased, the amused or the sentimental. It was time for Fanny to 'open' the house. Sophie thrust her gently forward. She was wearing a white frock with a sash of red-white-and-blue ribbon, white lace mittens, and a chip bonnet decorated with white rosebuds, from which her long ringlets tumbled down behind.

She looked round at Jasper for reassurance, and his heart melted with love and something that was almost terror, because she was four years old, beautiful, and so very fragile.

284

She took the scissors from her grandfather with a gravity which was a mixture of infant self-possession and a kind of piety which came from knowing she was to do something inexplicably important and good. Her tiny hands were too small to make the scissors work: James had to put his hands over hers and work them for her. But it was done, the ribbon fluttered down, and hers was the honour and the blessing. A roar of approval rose up and Fanny turned her head in surprise. Jasper sought Sophie's eyes. She was smiling and crying at the same time. Beside her, Rosamund was too.

While the poor fell to feasting and the band to playing, and light refreshments were served to the gentry-guests, everyone with an interest — investors, potential investors, millmasters, master builders, philanthropists — wanted to look at the inside of the last empty house. They had to take it in turn, of course — it was too small for more than a few to go in at a time — and John Skelwith hovered nearby to be on hand to point out the salient points in whatever language was suitable for each individual. Different people wanted to find different virtues in the scheme: he meant to please them all.

Sophie and Rosamund went in alone, and stood inside the living-room — the only downstairs room — looking about them in doubtful silence. It had one door, one window, and a fireplace; plaster walls, an earthen floor; a staircase leading up steeply from the corner and bending round behind the chimney.

'It didn't look so small on paper,' Sophie said at last.

'It's so very dark,' said Rosamund.

'Yes,' said Sophie. She had seen the houses only once while they were being built, and then it was not possible to tell much about them, except that she had wondered a little that the walls were so thin. It was quiet now because the inhabitants were all out in the court feasting, but she wondered whether those walls would keep out any of the sounds of the people next door.

'I wonder if it is large enough,' she added at last.

John Skelwith came in behind them, seeming to fill the room, catching the last comment. 'Ten feet by fourteen,' he said. 'It's the usual dimension for a living-room.'

Rosamund stared round. 'Is it really ten by fourteen?' She didn't mean anything in particular by the comment, only that the space seemed so small for a whole family to live and cook and sit together.

But to her surprise Skelwith looked put out, and said, 'Well, in point of fact, we did pinch just a little from the width. It's actually ten by thirteen, but no-one is going to notice that, I assure you. And by taking a foot from each we were able to get an extra house in at the end of each row, which you'll allow is a great benefit.'

Rosamund looked at him carefully, wondering at his defensive tone. 'I should like to see upstairs if I may.'

'Of course, though there's nothing to see; just bedrooms,' he said.

Rosamund led the way with Sophie behind her. The stairs were narrow and steep, and opened at the top directly into the main bedroom. It was lit — if lit were the word — by a small window about fifteen inches by twelve with a fixed pane, not designed to open. There was no fireplace, but in one wall was a doorway without a door which led into the second bedroom, which had no window at all. The smaller room was ten feet by five, leaving the larger room ten feet by eight.

Rosamund backed out. 'Do they have to be so dark?' she asked Skelwith, who was watching her expressionlessly. 'Couldn't there have been a proper window in here — and a window of any sort in the small room?'

'I'm afraid windows cost money, ma'am,' Skelwith said. 'Besides, they let out the heat. It will be warmer in the winter without windows.'

'But must they live in the dark like mice?'

'You must remember these people are not like you and me, ma'am,' Skelwith said firmly. 'They are not used to niceties. Mrs Hobsbawn will tell you what they *are* used to.'

Sophie sighed. 'It's true, they will be very grateful for this.'

'You must ask yourself whether they would prefer a house like this which they can afford, or a larger house with fine windows which must stand empty because they could never pay the rent on it. And remember too,' he added, seeing Rosamund was still doubtful, 'that in foreign countries, the labouring poor are housed in tenements and sub-divisions of houses. Only in England does every poor family have a house entirely to itself, and that is something to pride ourselves on. I don't think you'll find any of the new tenants complaining, ma'am.'

'I'm sure they won't,' Rosamund said. She *was* sure they wouldn't; but that being the case, what was it that John Skelwith felt he needed to excuse himself for? It was an intriguing puzzle. Like a guilty dog, she thought, he wags his tail too much.

Jasper was taking Fanny back to the carriage, for the crowds were rather too inclined to want to pet her, and she was very small and only four years old. When he had lifted her in he stepped back, and noticed a family standing just by the entrance to the court, watching the scene within. They stood very close together, a man, a woman, and three small children. The children were barefoot and the woman wore only wooden shoes, but the man had boots — old and shabby, but well cared for. Their clothes, too, were threadbare and shabby, but there was an air about them of desperate decency. They looked at the scene of feasting before them — especially the children — with wistful eyes.

'Hullo there. Do you work for me?' Jasper asked.

The man turned to look at him, and snatched off his cap. 'No sir, I don't.' His accent was Irish, but he spoke well, like an artisan rather than a labourer. 'Would you be —' his eye wandered in search of help, and he saw the bright new sign on the end wall — 'would you be Master Morland?'

Jasper smiled. 'You must be new to these parts.'

'That I am sir. We've just come from Macclesfield.'

'That's a tidy walk. Well, I'm Master Hobsbawn, and those are my mills. They're closed today for all this.' He waved a hand round the scene. 'Looking for work?'

'That I am, sir. I'm a weaver, sir — O'Connor's my name.'

'Hand weaver?'

'Yes sir. But I can learn t'other sort.'

'I'm afraid I have all the weavers I need,' Jasper said. Weaving was so easy that anyone could learn it, which was why there was such an abundance of hand-loom men. The machines were rather more complex. But even as he said it he

287

saw the hope leave the woman's face, to be replaced by blank misery. The children kept their eyes on the ground, and in a flash of insight he knew it was because they could not bear to look at the food on the trestles which was not for them.

'Why don't you go and join in?' Jasper said. 'Have something to eat. There's plenty for all.'

The woman would have gone, but the children looked up at their father first for permission, and he stood firm. What it cost him Jasper couldn't imagine, but he said courteously, 'Thank you kindly, sir, but that's for your own people, as we can see. We must be getting on.'

Stubborn idiot, proud fool, Jasper thought exasperatedly; he had known weavers before, and their desperate clutching at gentility. They had always been the elite of the cotton workers, and they weren't going to descend to begging, even when they faced starvation. The man had actually begun to turn away. Jasper said, 'Wait a minute.'

They turned back. He couldn't bear the woman's face, the renewed hope in her eyes. 'I think after all I may have work for you. Come up and see me tomorrow at the mill.'

'Thank you, master,' the man said. The gratitude in his voice made it sound as though he were going to faint. Well, perhaps he was.

'And now that you are more or less an employee of mine, why don't you go and join the fun. You must be hungry after your long walk.'

The man smiled suddenly, and his face shed ten years. 'I won't deny that, sir.'

'God bless you, master,' the woman said fervently, and ushered her children towards the feast.

Batchworth lay in bed with Rosamund in his arms, listening to her thinking.

'I think you should go,' he said at last.

'How can I?'

'How? In my chaise, of course, with four post horses and every comfort that money can provide.'

'Don't tease, Jes. You know what I mean.'

'My darling, if your mother can invite you to Roland's wedding, you can accept. You don't suppose she will have issued the invitation without consulting the Greyshotts, do you?'

'That's exactly what I suppose. You know my mother. She cares nothing for anyone's opinion.'

'I think you're wrong. She doesn't care for it for herself, but she wouldn't deliberately spoil things for your brother. As for the Greyshotts — you can't think Helena would object to us on moral grounds; and Cedric was too intimately involved in everything to take up any sort of disapproving stance.

She sighed. 'You may be right —'

'I know I am.'

'But they aren't the only people who will be there. A Society wedding — St Margaret's — the Archbishop — members of the royal family. How can I face it all? And how can I bear it if they look away?

'There's no use denying there will be some who look away. But you will not care for their opinion.'

'Are you so sure of that?'

'Yes. You were never a coward, my love.'

'It isn't a matter of courage, Jes,' she said seriously. 'If I had never done wrong I could face the censure without caring, because I would know it was unjustified. But I *did* do wrong. I deserve to be shunned.'

This was painful. 'For loving me?'

'Not for loving you, but for giving in to my feelings.' A pause; and then, 'It's hard to remember now how it all came about. But when I was first married to Marcus — before I met you again — I was angry all the time. I thought I was angry with *him*, for not standing up to his mother, for not being the man I thought he should be. But really I was angry with myself for marrying him when I knew, really, that we weren't suited. Everything I did, I did in anger.'

'Everything?'

'Oh, not loving you. I couldn't have helped that, whatever the circumstances. I'd already made a start at Scarborough, you see, and when I met you again that time in York . . . But I should have resisted. I should not have given that love expression.'

Jes held her tighter, struggling against the analysis, for if she had done wrong, so must he have, and he did not want it to be so. 'Is it so bad? Thousands of people do it.'

'I can't answer for them, only for myself.'

'But *why* is it so bad?'

She sighed again, as though every word hurt her to utter. 'Because I made a promise. When I married Marcus I promised to "keep me only unto him", and I broke that promise.'

'But he —'

Her fingers touched his lips, stopping the words. 'It doesn't matter. It doesn't matter what he did or didn't do.'

'Doesn't it? A bargain must work both ways.'

'But the promise was not between me and Marcus,' she said. 'It was between me and God.'

There was nothing he could say to that. He held her for a long time and they both stared into the darkness, unspeaking. At last he said, 'I had thought you were happier lately. I hoped —'

'You weren't wrong,' she said. 'I have grown used to things. It's not that I don't mind them any more, but that they don't intrude so much. I do love you, and I've learned how to be happy to be with you.'

'Was that so hard?'

He heard the smile in her voice. 'No, my Jes. You are everything to me. If only we could have married in the beginning, I'd have been the happiest woman in the world.'

'Well, then.'

'It's just that Roland's wedding has brought things back to me. If we go, it will be the first time I have been in London since —' She stopped and began again, with difficulty. 'You've been there once or twice, you know what to expect. I don't know who I may meet, you see. Sophie told me — she had it from her mother, who had it from Lord Anstey — that Marcus goes out sometimes in a closed carriage. Is that true?'

'His condition has improved to the extent that he can get about. But he doesn't go into company. He has been seen being driven out, but no-one goes to the house. They live like hermits.'

'And — Charlotte?'

'No-one sees her at all.' He felt the tension in her body as

290

she waited for his answer. She was like a drawn bowstring. 'From the street the house looks as though it's shut up. They live at the back, apparently, where they're not overlooked.' He tried to think of something to comfort her. 'The garden is very large, isn't it? I expect she plays there.'

'I think of that sometimes,' she said slowly. 'I used to sit in that garden when I was carrying her. I loved it. I imagine her playing there and watching the birds I used to watch and sitting on the bench where I used to sit. And I tell myself that they both love her, and wouldn't want to hurt her.' Her voice seemed to grow fainter. 'But what will they tell her, Jes? How will they explain to her where I am?'

'They got rid of all the old servants,' he said. 'After you went, they replaced them all. So there will be no-one in the house who knew you. No-one to challenge whatever they choose to say.'

'You mean — they'll tell her I am dead?'

'It would be the easiest thing to do.'

There was a long silence. He tried to listen to her body, to judge how much it hurt her. But at last when she spoke, her voice seemed lighter. 'Perhaps that's best,' she said. 'If she thinks I'm dead, she'll never wonder about me, or want to see me and be grieved because she can't. Yes, it's better that way — better for her.'

It seemed to him desperately brave of her to look at it that way; the gladness in her voice touched him unbearably, and he couldn't speak for a while. At last he said, 'What about the wedding, then? Shall we go?'

'Yes,' she said. How ever much it hurts, she added inwardly. And then, 'I long to see them all again — Mother and Papa Danby and the boys.'

291

CHAPTER FIFTEEN

The Aylesbury wedding was on the twenty-fourth of June 1825, and Rosamund and Jes travelled down to London two days beforehand to stay at Upper Grosvenor Street with Lord and Lady Theakston. The boys were not there. Roland had rented a pretty house in Conduit Street for himself and his new bride, and Thomas was staying with him until the wedding.

It was a painful reunion. Rosamund thought her mother sadly aged in the last three years; Lucy thought Rosamund changed almost beyond recognition by her experiences. They embraced stiffly, awkward with the immediacy of their sympathy for each other.

Lucy felt as though she held her daughter's naked bones in her arms, and ached to offer some comfort, to ease the pain if only for a moment. 'You must come out with me in the Park tomorrow morning,' she said at last. 'You can have Hotspur if you like.'

'Thank you, Mama.' Rosamund knew what was really being offered, and was touched.

'Your aunt and uncle will be coming tomorrow with Benedict; and Sophie and Jasper with Fanny. Nicholas comes up from Eton. And we shall have guests for dinner tomorrow night.'

'Guests?' Rosamund was alarmed. One thing to decide to face society again, another thing actually to be presented with the necessity.

Lord Theakston anticipated her anxiety. 'Only family, m'dear. Lord and Lady Greyshott, and your cousins and their husbands.'

'Polly and Africa? I shall like to see them again,' Rosamund said brightly. Behind her she reached for and found Jes's hand. Polly and Africa happily married and with children now — the cousins she had grown up with, who had succeeded where she had failed.

The following morning she went down early to meet her mother for the promised ride in the Park — before anyone else was about, as the unspoken part of the suggestion ran. She was so anxious to be punctual she arrived in the hall even before her mother. It was not empty, however: Parslow was there, hat in hand, patient as a tree.

Rosamund faltered, and then ran on down the last half flight. Nothing moved but Parslow's eyes, but they rose to her face with a look both searching and reassuring.

'Well, Parslow?' She came to a halt in front of him, presenting herself like a child for inspection to hide the fear that he might even yet censure her.

'My lady,' he said. His voice was not quite uninflected. There was a warmth there which he had allowed to show only once or twice. It came to her then that he had arrived early in the hope of speaking to her alone.

'I have Hotspur outside for you,' he went on, as though she had asked. 'He's been going very well lately, for an old horse.'

'He's not old,' Rosamund protested.

'Rising eighteen,' Parslow reminded her. 'Her ladyship ought to be looking out for a new horse, as I've told her; but she doesn't like to think of parting with him. She is constant in her affections, if I might be permitted to say so.'

What he was saying was 'I am constant in my affections,' and Rosamund knew it. She wanted to touch his hand, but it was not possible, of course. Yet his love and concern were so tangible in the air between them that she said suddenly, 'Do you blame me? I did try, you know. I know the original fault was mine, but at the end I really did try.'

'Yes, I know,' he said. The hall was empty but for them. He seemed to come to a decision; she saw the very moment when he stepped out of his head groom's persona like a snake shrugging off a skin. 'I know the truth of it. I've watched over you since you were born. I would do anything I could to give you comfort.'

293

Rosamund grasped at the straw. Servants, she knew, had ways of knowing things, ways of communicating with each other. 'Can you find out how she is, how they treat her? My Lord Batchworth says she is never seen.'

'Its true. She is kept from the world; and the servants are forbidden to speak to anyone. But I will try.' His eyes flickered past her shoulder, and his mask was resumed so smoothly there seemed no transition.

'Ah, there you are, Rosamund,' Lucy said, coming down the stairs and pulling on her gloves. 'You haven't lost your habits of punctuality, I'm glad to see.'

It was still early enough for the Park to smell fresh, and for the promise of heat in the summer morning to seem pleasant. The horses were gay, and cantered along the dew-damp tan with their tails crooked like youngsters, snorting at each other and fly bucking. No-one about but grooms: Rosamund had no need to fear being stared at, but Lucy seemed ill at ease with her own thoughts, and talked almost at random, the nearest Rosamund had ever known her mother to come to *chattering*.

'It looks as though Mrs Fitzherbert has given in at last and means to let Minney Seymour marry George Dawson. His cousin Caroline Damer has settled all her estates on him, which makes him a suitable husband after all. If they do marry, Kangaroo Cooke stands to lose fifty guineas — he laid a bet with Alvanley years ago that they never would . . . Poor William Lamb has finally taken the plunge and separated from his wife. She's half mad, of course, and most of the time she's befuddled with brandy or laudanum or both. There's been loose talk of shutting her up in Bedlam, but it's all hum — I don't believe even that sour cat Emily Cowper would wish *that* fate on her . . . Young Maurice Hampton will be back in London in August from his Grand Tour. I suppose we must get used to calling him Maurice Ballincrea now, but it seems only yesterday . . .'

'Mama,' Rosamund broke through determinedly, 'tell me what people are saying. Will I be snubbed at the wedding? Ought I to go veiled and sit apart from the family?'

'Don't be silly,' Lucy said stiffly. Then, 'It won't be so bad. People get used to things. Good God, Lady Bouverie lived in

294

sin for twenty years with Lord Robert Spencer, and nobody shunned her! And it isn't as though you've run off with a footman. Batchworth is well liked and perfectly respectable.'

The echo of the last two words stopped her short. She looked at Rosamund nervously. 'What I mean is that there are worse cases and more recent cases; as scandal yours is *vieux jeux*. Some of the stiffer people will always cut you, of course; but it helps that Marcus doesn't go about, so no-one is required to choose between the two of you.' She sighed, and reached forward to turn a stray lock of Magnus's mane over to the right side. 'If only he would divorce you properly, so that you and Batchworth could marry. Remarried people are acceptable almost everywhere nowadays, even when the female was the guilty party. Look at Harry Uxbridge and Charlotte Wellesley, for instance. No-one points the finger at them now, though the elopement caused quite a stir in its time.'

When they got home after their ride and went in to breakfast, Rosamund expected to find Jes there, and was surprised to be told by a servant that he had gone out half an hour ago. But he had a large acquaintance in London, where the unequal rules of society meant that his protection of Rosamund had never caused him to be shunned. She supposed he had gone to look up a friend, and was only surprised that he had not told her beforehand that he meant to do so.

Even as she was thinking those things and helping herself to ham and eggs, Jes was standing at the great door of Chelmsford House and wondering what had ever brought him to suppose he might gain admittance. The clanging of the bell had long died away, and there was no sound from within. All the windows in the Pall Mall façade were obscured by blinds, and the slanting sun showed up the dirt on them. There was even a ragwort seedling which had taken root in a crack in the rendering under one of the steps. The house looked shut up and deserted, as though no-one had lived there for years.

He was about to turn away when a shuffling sound from behind the door was followed by the noise of the bolts being drawn, and the small door within the great door was opened.

A liveried footman peered out. Was it Jes's imagination, or did he blink in the sudden daylight like a disturbed owl?

'I wish to see Lord Chelmsford,' Jes said clearly and firmly, 'on urgent business.'

The man stared for a moment as though he had difficulty in understanding the words. 'His lordship don't never see nobody,' he said at last.

'He will see me,' said Jes, with more certainty by far than he felt. 'Have the kindness to send up my name, and say that I have urgent personal business with him.'

He gave the footman his card. The footman looked at it and shook his head doubtfully, and then began to withdraw, making as if to close the door on the petitioner. Jes interposed his body, fearing that if he went he might never come back. 'I will wait in the hall,' he said.

The hall was as dismal as the outside of the house, dark because of the drawn blinds and closed doors, echoing, musty-smelling. The footman went away, leaving Jes alone, and the silence of the house beyond the hall seemed absolute. He shivered, thinking most of all of the child, the little girl not yet three years old who was being brought up in this tomb-like prison; the little girl who must have in her face some look of Rosamund.

A clock somewhere in the distance struck the quarter. Jes waited. He heard the half and the three quarters. He wondered if the footman — a poor specimen, and presumably all that could be persuaded to work in these unnatural conditions — had simply wandered off and forgotten him. How long should he go on waiting here? Should he give up and leave? Should he seek out Marcus himself and risk the consequences? The hour struck, solemnly, and as the notes from the hidden clock died away a man appeared, coming down the great staircase; an old man in the garb of a gentleman's attendant.

He came up to Jes and looked at him searchingly. 'Lord Batchworth?'

'Yes.'

'I am Fadden, Lord Chelmsford's manservant.' He must be in his sixties, Jes thought, judging by the white hair, the bent shoulders and chalky, veined hands. Could Marcus get no younger, more able man to attend him? 'His lordship will see you.' The slight emphasis on the word 'will' showed the servant's own surprise at the decision. 'But I must ask you, sir, if you please, not to agitate his lordship. He is not accustomed to company and his health is uncertain.'

Jes stared at this manner of address. 'Are you his man-servant or his physician?' he asked sharply.

Fadden was unperturbed. 'Both, sir, in a manner of speaking. I was a surgeon in the army during the late wars. When his lordship has bad days, he is sometimes glad of my skills. Will you follow me, please?'

He led the way up the stairs, and Jes followed, feeling bemused. 'Is it one of his bad days today?'

'No, sir. Otherwise I venture to suggest you would not have been seen.'

On the first floor the man turned away from the staircase and led the way past the great staterooms, turning into a narrower corridor, and then through a pass door into another yet more narrow. They passed anonymous doors and obscure, uncarpeted staircases. Jes realised they had strayed into the back-stairs area of the house, the internal labyrinth of accesses from the servants' quarters to the public rooms which no master ever saw. He began to feel nervous. Was it possible he was being lured into an ambush? He thought of revenge, imagined the sudden scuffle, the blow on the head, the inert shape muffled in sacking removed from the house under cover of darkness. Would he disappear, never to be seen again?

Fadden led the way up some stairs, and then through another pass door, and Jes was grateful to find himself once more amongst papered walls and carpeted floors, back on the family side of the barrier. Moreover this part of the house was lighter and brighter, the window blinds were raised, and there was a smell and feeling of habitation. Through one of the windows Jes glimpsed the unkempt garden below. Marcus lived at the back of the house, as he had already been told. Fadden had simply led him there by a short cut.

'His lordship will see you in here, sir,' Fadden said abruptly, breaking a long silence, and opening the door by which he had just halted. Jes waited to be announced, but Fadden seemed to mean to wait outside, and Jes had no alternative but to walk past him alone into the room. He heard the door shut a behind him, and at the same moment he registered that the room was empty except for one seated figure in a chair by the fire. Though it was June, the fire was lit, and the chair was drawn up close to it. Jes walked towards it; the figure turned its head, and then rose slowly and with apparent difficulty to its feet.

'Well, Farraline? I should not have seen you, except that a certain curiosity moved me. I suppose I should call you Batchworth now, but old habits die hard. It was *Farraline* debauched my wife, and so I shall always think of you?'

Jes tried not to stare, but it was hard to recognise Marcus. His hair was quite white, his face lined like an old man's, and though he had stood up, he did not stand erect, but half crouched, holding onto the chair for support. He wore a kind of dressing-gown of dark red velvet, and on his head a strange, oriental-looking velvet cap embroidered with beads and gold thread.

'Chelmsford?'

Marcus's face drew into a bitter sneer. 'Yes, it is me. Hard to believe isn't it, that you and I are much the same age?'

'I haven't seen you since — since before — I didn't know —'

'How should you? Well, sit down if you want. I must sit, at all events. You may do as you please.'

'Your man said that this was not one of your bad days,' Jes said hopefully. 'I don't wish to upset you or tax you too much, but I do need to talk to you.'

Marcus stared into the fire. 'You and I can have nothing to discuss. You should be dead. If I had called you out instead of Hawker you would be dead. I will have no conversation with dead men.'

Jes fought with a feeling of hopelessness. 'Then why did you see me?'

Marcus turned back to look at him again. 'Curiosity. I wanted to know what it's like for you, living with another man's wife. Are you happy together? Do you sit by the fire in the evenings and laugh over what's happened? Do you laugh about me?'

'You can't believe that,' Jes said firmly. 'Rosamund has

298

been — and is — very unhappy. What happened was not her choice. She grieves dreadfully —'

'Good! Let her suffer. I hope she makes you suffer too. I hope you never know a happy moment, either of you.'

Jes stared at the stranger's face before him. 'How can you say that? You used to love her —'

Marcus interrupted. 'I used to be a man!' There was a silence, in which nothing was heard but the unimportant crackling of the fire and the distant soft heartfall of a clock. Then in a different voice Marcus said, 'Look at me! I can get about now — walk from my bed to my chair. Walk downstairs if I take enough time about it. Sit in a carriage while they drive me round the Park. I shall never ride a horse again. Fadden says I may one day walk without a stick. That's my life, Farraline. Don't you envy me?'

'I pity you from my heart,' Jes said quietly. 'And so does Rosamund. She would never have left you, you know. It was you who cast her out.'

'I didn't want her near me,' Marcus spat. 'I never want to see her again.'

'Then why not divorce her?'

Marcus's expression changed again. He looked cunning. 'Ah, that's what you've come about, is it? I thought it might be. Well, you can save your breath. I won't do it.'

'But why not? It can all be done without trouble to you.'

'She's my wife, that's why, and no-one else shall have her.'

'But you've just said you don't want her. You won't let her live with you —'

'She shall never set foot in this house! Do you think I'm a fool? I know what's behind this. She wants to come back here and steal my child — all I have left now. My only joy — my life! She shan't have her!'

Jes had realised some exchanges ago that he was not dealing with a rational person. So he said casually, as though he were not interested in the matter at all, 'It seems to me the best way to keep her away is to divorce her. Then she'll have no rights at all.'

'No rights — that's true.' Marcus said dazedly. 'But she may marry again. I've seen divorce bills go through Parliament. In the Lords we add a clause forbidding the guilty female to marry again, but the Commons always strike it out. If I divorce her, she may marry someone else.'

'Well, what do you care for that? She'll probably make him unhappy, and herself too. They'll be as miserable as you could wish.'

Marcus stared at him, looking first bewildered, and then angry. 'You don't have to humour me! I know who you are! I'm not mad, or stupid, or whatever it is you think! Do you think because I've been wounded *here*,' with a stabbing gesture towards the groin, 'that my mind has gone as well? God damn you, Farraline, with your pity! You want me to divorce Rosamund so that you can marry her.'

'Yes,' said Jes, abandoning all hope. 'Why not? You don't want her, and I do. I think I can make her happy. You used to love her, Marcus. You used to want her to be happy. What happened to you was not her fault — it was Hawker's, and you killed him. Your revenge is complete. Won't you in pity's name let her go now, and let her have what crumbs of happiness she can with me?'

'I used to love her,' Marcus repeated slowly. He stared at Jes, but unseeingly, his eyes fixed on some vision beyond. 'I do love her still. And Charlotte — Charlotte is the image of her. She is all I have left now. Charlotte is my only joy.' He stopped, and his eyes slowly refocused on Jes. 'Divorce her?' he said musingly. 'An expensive business. She'll expect a life annuity, I suppose?'

By the terms of a divorce bill the husband retained the wife's dowry and she also forfeited her pin-money and widow's jointure, so it was customary for an annuity to be settled on her by the divorcing husband. Since the husband was usually eager to be rid of his encumbrance and marry again, it was generally thought not too high a price to pay. But in this case — 'She would not ask it,' said Jes, 'and neither would I.'

'You're able to support her, I suppose,' said Marcus. 'But would you take her without a dowry?'

'I would. I have. I love her — I only want her happiness. If you will allow it, I will pay for the divorce bill, too.'

'I don't need your money.' Quite suddenly Marcus seemed to tire of it. 'Very well, she shall have the divorce. You may leave it with me. And now I wish you will go.'

Jes stood up automatically, wondering what it was that had changed Marcus's mind, wishing there were something he could do for Marcus, to make his life more tolerable. But there was one more thing he had to say, though it might be dangerous.

'And the child? Will you allow her to see the child occasionally?'

'No,' said Marcus flatly. 'She shall never see the child again. Never. Now get out.'

Jes went; but at the door he paused and turned, and said quietly, 'Marcus, we used to be friends. If there is ever anything I can do for you —'

'Get out,' Marcus said stonily.

Jes had to wait until they went up to dress for dinner for the privacy to tell Rosamund about his meeting with Marcus. She listened in white and suffering silence to what he had to say, and at the end what she asked first was, 'Did you see Charlotte?'

'No, nor Bab. Only Marcus and the two servants.'

Rosamund put her head in her hands. 'Why did he change his mind? What did you say?'

'I don't know. I've tried to puzzle it out myself, but I just don't know. Perhaps he remembered how he used to love you, and just relented.'

'But can we trust him? He might change his mind again.'

'He might. We won't know until it happens.'

She looked up. 'And if he does divorce me, will you still want to marry me? A ruined woman, with no portion?'

'I would want you naked and barefoot, even if I had to rescue you from the scaffold. I don't care about any of it, Rosamund. I love you, that's all.'

She gave him a thin, bleak sort of smile. 'I will try to be a good wife to you,' she said. 'I will try to give you a son.'

'I don't care,' he said deliberately, 'about anything but you.'

'Then you should.'

She stood up and put herself into his arms, and he held her quietly, one hand cradling her head. After a while he felt her smile. and put her back gently to look at her.

'What is it?' he asked.

'Oh, I was just thinking what a long, long way it is from Scarborough,' she said. He saw she had braced herself up, with that soldier's ability to put past defeat behind in the interest of the next battle. 'Now we must strike exactly the right note of sober happiness for the rest of our visit. Too sober would spoil the wedding, and too happy would outrage those who would expect us to be ashamed of ourselves. Thank God we shall be at home! To hear someone's butler announcing us as Lord Batchworth and Lady Chelmsford would quite undo me!'

It was a brave effort. 'You don't need to pretend with me,' Jes said gently.

'I know,' she said seriously, meeting his eyes. 'But you must let me.'

December 1825 brought a financial crisis which threatened the most grave repercussions. Speculation in the newly recognised states of South America had proliferated not wisely, but only too well, resulting in a 'bubble', which burst suddenly just before Christmas. Unlike some previous bubbles, it affected every part of the country, for the speculation had been funded largely on the notes of small country banks. Sixty of them, together with six London banks, failed; everyone seemed to know someone who had been touched by the tragedy.

In Manchester, Lord Batchworth called in at Hobsbawn House one morning looking for Jasper.

'He has gone to the mill, to be sure,' Sophie said.

'I called there, but they said he'd left. I thought perhaps he had come home.'

'No, I am not expecting him,' Sophie said, beginning to be alarmed.

'What is it? Has something happened? You look quite wild.'

Jes told her about the financial crisis. 'I am all right, thank God,' he said. 'Fortunately my money was tied up in too many other things to allow me to speculate in South America, even had I thought it a good idea. But I wanted to be sure you had nothing invested there.'

302

'I cannot say. Jasper has control of everything, of course. He has never mentioned South America to me — though I remember Percy Droylsden recommending it, now I come to think of it.' Her eyes were wide. 'He tried — one Sunday when they were here to dinner — to make Jasper invest. I thought he had refused. Do you think he was persuaded, then?'

'Knowing what I know of your husband,' Jes said soothingly, 'I doubt it. He is caution personified. It was just the most tenuous of anxieties on my part. I'm sure everything is all right.'

Sophie continued to look doubtful. 'But then, where is Jasper? He ought to be at the mill.'

'If he has heard the news, he's probably gone to the club to find out more. That's where I'll go now.'

'When you find him, please ask him to come home,' Sophie said.

'I will. But I'm sure there's nothing to worry about,' said Jes, taking his leave. He had decided not to tell her the rest of what he had heard that morning. Leave it to Jasper to break the news that Droylsden's Bank had failed, and the Droylsdens were ruined.

Jasper had gone to the club, to look at the papers and gather any fresh local news that might have emerged. He discovered Whetlore, his man of business, in possession both of the *Times* and the best armchair in front of the fire, and stopped for a few words with him.

'By the way.' Whetlore said in his usual tones of cheerful relish, 'have you heard that your old rival Olmondroyd is gone under at last?'

'Gone under?'

'Holed and sunk,' Whetlore grinned. I was talking to George Spicer only an hour since: it seems Olmondroyd's new building work was largely financed by Droylsden's Bank, and the creditors have called in the loans. What with his previous debts, the poor fellow hasn't a feather to fly with. Spicer was as blue as megrim too — his last account hasn't been settled yet, and from all I hear it was a big 'un!'

'You needn't sound so happy about it,' Jasper said, feeling

Whetlore at least ought not to be rejoicing in a fellow attorney's discomfort.

'Oh, it don't trouble me,' Whetlore said. 'I never cared for Spicer's methods, and he and Olmondroyd were as thick as thieves over a number of shady pieces of business. I should have thought you'd be glad, though, Mr Hobsbawn: you had no cause to love Olmondroyd.'

'I didn't hate him either,' Jasper said shortly. 'And I don't wish any man ill.' He was about to turn away, when curiosity impelled him to ask, 'Is he really completely ruined? Surely he will have something left?'

'Not a farthing. Even when his business assets have been sold, I understand there will be debts still uncovered. Spicer hinted that the Sheriff is already casting speculative eyes over the house and its contents. When all's been accounted for, I think Manchester will be bidding farewell to Mr O. He'll have to take to the road, I fear.'

It was a curious coincidence that as Jasper left the club half an hour later he should reach the door to the street just as Olmondroyd himself came in. Jasper stopped short, coming face to face with the man about whom he had been thinking and talking. He had no wish to stare at him but was unable, in the circumstances, to look anywhere else without appearing to be avoiding his eye. Olmondroyd looked no different from usual, except perhaps that he was a little sleepless about the eyes — but then many a Manchester manufacturer had that look these days.

Jasper would have nodded to him and passed on, but Olmondroyd stepped into his path, a set look coming over his face which Jasper took to be the first sign of a brewing storm.

'Good-day, Mr Olmondroyd,' he said, trying to sound calm and casual. Olmondroyd did not move or speak. 'Will you let me pass, sir?'

Still Olmondroyd stared. 'So, it's thee, is it, Jasper Hobsbawn?' he growled at last. 'Why is it I can never set foot anywhere in Manchester without rubbing my nose in thy spoor?'

'I have the right to be here. I'm a member of this club —' Jasper began.

'Oh, Ay'm a member of this clahb,' Olmondroyd

mimicked viciously. 'Tha jumped up little prentice! Thy mother's tongue's not good enough for thee now, then? I remember when tha was nothing more than a grubby snot-nose piecener, and tha dares now to talk to me about rights and clubs, and looking down thy nose at me as if tha were Joseph Hobsbawn himself, instead of his pauper bloody errand boy!'

'I assure you, sir —'

'Nay, *I* assure *thee*! I know what's in thy mind! Tha's heard all about me no doubt, from those gossiping leeches in there.' A jerk of the head towards the interior of the club.

'I heard that you have financial troubles, yes, but —'

'Troubles I've got, but I'm not finished yet, whatever tha's heard! I may be down, but I'll rise again, and when I do, by God I'll make a few folk in this town sit up and take notice!'

'I hope you do.' Jasper said quietly. 'I have never born you any ill will, sir, and I'm truly sorry for your present misfortune.'

A hint of puzzlement came into Olmondroyd's stare, but he snapped automatically, 'I don't want thy pity — *boy*! I've forgotten more about this business than tha'll ever learn. Aye, and everything I had and lost I earned by my own labours, not by creeping in under the master's table like a sneaking dog, and marrying the master's daughter!'

Jasper paled. 'You may say what you like about me, but you had better not speak lightly of Mrs Hobsbawn, or I shall be forced to knock you down,' he said in a low, angry voice.

Olmondroyd seemed to realise he had gone too far. His eyes shifted away from Jasper's for an instant, and seeing his surroundings he seemed to take new thought. After a brief pause he said more quietly. 'Aye well. Well. I'm not a patient man, Hobsbawn, you know that, and I've sorrows beyond bearing.'

'You will be forced to sell your mill, I understand. It is a great pity,' Jasper said gently.

Olmondroyd eyed him speculatively. 'I suppose you think you'll buy it?' Jasper said nothing, and it seemed to enrage him again. 'Think all tha likes,' he snarled. 'It's as near as tha'll ever get to being master of Olmondroyd's Mill — I'll see to that! I've got influence, and I've got friends, which is more

305

than tha can say — snatch-mutton!' And with that he thrust Jasper roughly aside and strode on into the club.

Jasper, suddenly aware of the doorman's open-mouthed interest in the whole scene, cursed inwardly and took his departure. It would be all through the club by dinner time that he and Olmondroyd had had words — and probably that Olmondroyd had had the best of it. *Snatch-mutton!* That was a joke too good for any servant to keep to himself, of course. He thought uncomfortably how easily the epithet might come to haunt him in the future.

Tramping homewards through the darkening streets to the comfort of Sophie's sympathetic arms, he decided not to tell her about his meeting with Olmondroyd. No reason to upset her with it. By God though he added wryly to himself, the old man stings like a dead wasp!

'So many people ruined,' Sophie mourned that evening as she and Jasper sat down to supper.

'We're all right,' he told her again, to comfort her. 'That's the main thing.'

'Yes, and I'm grateful that you were too sensible to speculate; but I can't feel much gladness when our friends are involved. What will happen to them all? Percy and Agnes, and poor Henry. And what will happen to Prudence? She is dependent on Percy. Her mother won't take her back.'

'I'm afraid the Pendleburys are done up too,' Jasper said. 'I heard at the club that Fred Pendlebury invested heavily, against his mother's wishes.'

Sophie put her hands to her face. 'It's all so dreadful! And the Worsleys too, you said — poor Mrs Worsley's widow's jointure, and her younger son a gamester into the bargain. Well, I suppose it was he who urged it. But Jasper,' she went on, self-interest overcoming compassion at last, 'we are all right, aren't we? Really all right?'

'I didn't speculate in South America; and thanks to my cousin's great foresight, the mills are our own, and not built on borrowed money. We are in the best position of anyone in Manchester to ride out storms of this sort. We are safe, my Sophie.'

Her relief was short-lived. 'Oh, but the poor Droylsdens!

306

And just before Christmas too. Jasper, do you think they would come and stay with us, just for a few weeks, until things are sorted out?'

'You could ask them, but I don't suppose they'd come. At least, Prudence might, and perhaps Harry, but Percy and Droylsden *père* will be too busy and too worried — and too ashamed as well, I should think.'

News came from York that Dykes' Bank was another which had failed. To Jasper's anxious question Sophie answered, 'No, with Swann's in Coney Street, thank God! But the Dykeses were friends of Papa's. He will be very upset for them.'

Like the ripples from a pebble dropped in a pond, the repercussions spread outwards. In London, bankers were called out of church on Sunday morning by demands for gold by country customers who held their notes, and had seen country banks close their doors. Town customers, noting the alarm, demanded the redemption of their notes too, and the run on gold began in earnest.

Lucy met the crisis with stoicism. 'Martins have always looked after my money perfectly well, and I see no reason not to trust them now. I can't go and collect bags of gold and keep them in the house. It's ridiculous.'

'I wish everyone were as trusting as you, my love,' Theakston said, turning the pages of the newspaper gloomily. 'This run is going to be the deuce. I can't think how many people will be ruined.'

'They'll all have to go to France. Waldegrave says that Boulogne is so full of English bankrupts, the local people have renamed the town gaol the *Hotel d'Angleterre*.' Her husband didn't respond, and she looked up at him with faint apprehension. 'What is it, Danby? Are we in danger? Surely Martins wouldn't have given my money to someone in South America without asking me? And I don't know anyone in Mexico or Brazil or wherever it is.'

He put his newspaper aside and looked at her gravely. 'It isn't like that,' he said. 'When you give your money to Martins to look after, they don't put it in a little box in the vault with your name on it.'

'Don't they?' Lucy asked quite genuinely. 'It always seems

307

to be there when I send for some.'

'They keep a little on hand for such requests,' Danby said, simplifying as he went along, 'but most of it they lend to other people and charge those other people interest for doing so. That's how they make a living.'

'Yes, I see,' she said doubtfully.

'But if all the people who have lent money to the banks decide to ask for it back at the same time, the banks will have to get it back from the people *they* have lent it to. And a great deal has been lent to industrialists to build new factories and buy new machinery and so on. They won't have the ready gold to pay back, so they'll have to sell everything. Factories will close, men will be laid off, stocks of goods and machinery sold off cheaply — the masters will be ruined, and all the people who depend upon them for a living will be ruined too.'

Lucy looked alarmed. 'But where will it end? If people like me discover that the money isn't there —'

'Precisely. But it never was there, you see. The business of banks runs on confidence. As long as everyone goes on believing, it's all right. But if they once start to doubt — it's like pulling at a thread and unravelling the whole garment.'

Lucy stared at him in dismay. 'But that's dreadful. I spoke about Boulogne in jest, but it's just like that dreadful time after the war when everyone was being bankrupted — all our friends — and we didn't know why, and there was nothing to be done about it except see them off.'

'Poor George going to Calais,' Danby agreed, remembering. 'But at least he brought it on himself with his own extravagance.'

'That's no comfort,' Lucy said, and drew a deep sigh. 'Sometimes I think nothing's ever really been right since the war.'

Upon which Lord Theakston thought it right to cross the room to her and offer her the silent comfort of his closer proximity.

Despite the cold and gusty March rain, Lord Batchworth had walked up from the mill to call on the Hobsbawns. Motherly Sophie had installed him in the chair nearest the fire, deplored the wetness of his trouser-bottoms, enquired tenderly about his stockings, and had only narrowly been persuaded by Jasper that their guest would prefer a glass of sherry to one of hot negus.

Jes had come to tell Jasper that Olmondroyd's new mill was at last formally up for sale. 'I met Whitworth, the magistrate, at the corner of the Liverpool Road. He'd just been to take a look at it.'

'Is he thinking of buying it?' Jasper asked. 'I suppose he must be one of the few mill masters to be in a position to do so. His interest in the canals must bring him a handsome income.'

'I suppose so,' Batchworth said. 'I thought you would be anxious to buy yourself, Olmondroyd's being so nicely adjacent to Hobsbawn's.'

'I should have bought him out gladly, but as things are —' He shrugged.

'But I don't understand why things are so bad,' Sophie said. 'When the financial crisis came last December, you said that it wouldn't affect us because we didn't have any loans for the banks to call in.'

'That's true, and we're better off than many,' Jasper said patiently. 'But the slump affects everybody. I hadn't properly appreciated at the time how much trade would fall off.'

'I don't suppose any of us did,' Batchworth said. 'You see,' he explained to Sophie, 'those masters who had to repay their loans were forced to sell everything they had, all at once, and for whatever price they could get. The market has been flooded with their stock, and nobody is going to buy our goods at full price when they can get all they want at bankrupt sales for next to nothing.'

'Everyone has a warehouse full of unsaleable goods,' Jasper said. 'We're all suffering. My mills are already on short-time working, and I shall have to lay off hands pretty soon.'

'I've laid off already,' Jes said. 'And you won't delay if you have any sense.'

'I'll delay as long as possible,' Jasper said. 'But I've stopped night-working, and on the whole I'm not sorry. I begin to think night-working is too hard on the hands, besides being unnatural. I wish you will not think of starting it when this crisis is over.'

309

Jes laughed. 'Now don't begin that argument all over again! You know that you and I will never agree about workers' conditions.'

'I thought it was only the need for legislation we disagreed about,' Jasper said. 'You surely can't believe that the hours and conditions of the children are satisfactory?'

'The factory children work no harder and in no worse conditions than the children of farm labourers. At least they're not working out in the cold and the rain. And you know perfectly well, in any case, that it isn't the work itself that the hands object to, but the regularity of it, and there's nothing anyone can do about that. They will simply have to adjust to it.'

'The regularity, yes — but what about the hours? Thirteen and fourteen hours a day — longer at brisk time. It leaves them no leisure —'

'Leisure?' Jes interrupted. 'Come now, you are not serious! What would they want leisure for? What could they do with it? Leisure is only a curse to them. Have you ever known a hand refuse extra work when it was offered? Are they not complaining now because we have gone onto short-time working?'

'Only because their wages have gone down,' Jasper said patiently. 'And that's why we need legislation. I'm not the only mill master who wants to shorten hours without reducing wages, but we can't do it unless everyone does it, or we'd be undercut, and that would be the end of us.'

'Well you'll never get me to agree with legislation,' Batchworth said. 'It's not the Government's business. Once let them start interfering in our lives, and there'll be no end to it. They'll be legislating on everything from the cradle to the grave, and our souls won't be our own any more.'

Sophie said to him, 'You pretend to be indifferent, but I've seen the subscription list for the relief of the handloom weavers, and your name was on it, with a very generous amount. You have as soft a heart as the next man, really.'

Jes grinned. 'Rosamund would never have spoken to me again if I hadn't given something! But that's straightforward charity, nothing to do with business. Certainly nothing to do with legislation.'

'Even I've had to cut down the work given out to my handloom weavers,' Jasper admitted reluctantly. 'With the machines one can cut costs and reduce prices, but that's not possible with the hand men. Their plight is pitiable, but what can one do?'

'Only what you are doing — lay them off and get up a subscription for them,' Jes said. 'There are too many of them, and things can only get worse. The machines do their work better, and they must find another trade or die.'

'But every weaver wants his son to be a weaver too,' Sophie said. 'I've spoken to some of them, and they're too proud to change trades.'

'Proud — or stupid,' said Jes. 'And what will your legislation do for them, Hobsbawn?'

'Nothing, I admit it. I suppose to be consistent with my views I ought to close down my weaving shed and abandon steam looms altogether, but of course I don't. It would seem a piece of folly to do so.'

'Quite right! There's hope for you yet,' Batchworth said. 'Progress is bound to create some victims, but that's no reason to abandon progress. March on, I say — and get up a subscription for those who get left behind.'

'Like the Droylsdens,' Sophie said. 'I can't think what's going to happen to them now that their bank has failed. Poor Agnes was in tears when she came to tell me. What can one do to help them?'

'The Government has addressed the matter of the failures,' Jes said. 'The old country banks were just too small to cope with a run, so the Bank of England's monopoly has been loosened to allow joint stock banks to be formed in future. It will mean a much more secure financial base, and make it easier for businessmen and investors to get together. That's to everyone's benefit.'

'But it doesn't help people like the Droylsdens, I'm afraid,' Jasper said.

'Couldn't they start up a new — what did you call it?' Sophie asked hopefully.

'Joint stock bank? Henry could, since he wasn't involved in the old company. But not the father or Percy, now they've been bankrupted.'

'Oh dear, it's all so upsetting,' Sophie said, her brow buckled with anxiety. 'Poor Prudence was talking last week about becoming a governess. I see that she must do something, but it does seem a dreadful waste of her abilities. And when I remember Miss Rosedale's stories about employers and how horrid they can be to governesses, I'm sure Prudence will hate it.'

'Now there I think I may have some good news for you,' Jes said. 'This is not certain, of course, and so I tell you in confidence — but while I was talking to Whitworth he happened to mention that he was playing whist in the club last night with Dr Hastings. He said Hastings was very gay, and hinted that he hoped soon to be announcing his engagement to be married.'

'Dr Hastings is to marry Prudence?' Sophie cried excitedly.

Jes made calming gestures. 'Whitworth said Hastings mentioned no name, but apparently said that the lady would not only make him a comfortable wife but would be able to help him in his work amongst the poor —'

'Then he must mean Prudence!'

'— and Whitworth told me that earlier in the day when he was driving along Deansgate he saw Hastings and Miss Pendlebury just turning into Simon Street, and that they appeared to be walking arm in arm.'

Sophie jumped up, clasping her hands. 'It is Prudence! Dr Hastings is to marry Prudence and she won't have to go and be a governess! And they will exactly suit each other. It is the best news in the world! Oh I'm so glad I could kiss you!'

'Really, Sophie,' Jasper murmured restrainingly, but he smiled too. 'I must say it's very good news if it is true. You are a very satisfactory gossip, Batchworth!'

'Rosamund says it's my greatest accomplishment,' Jes said modestly.

'How is she?' Sophie asked eagerly. 'Has she got over her cold yet? Will she be coming to see us soon?'

'She's improving. She's reached the tiresome stage now, which means it's all but over, so I dare say she will be out and about in the next few days.'

'And is there any news about —?' Sophie hesitated over the word.

'The divorce? You needn't be so delicate — I can bear the mention of it,' Jes smiled. 'Things are going along satisfactorily. It was always bound to be a slow business, you know.'

'I'm surprised it has happened at all,' Sophie said. 'I quite thought Marcus would change his mind — or simply not go on with it. It must be a great effort for him to be bothered with anything of that sort in his state of health.'

'When do you hope to have your Act passed?' Jasper asked.

'I don't think there's any chance of getting it through before the recess,' Batchworth said, 'but we hope it will go through early next session. You know my friend Huskisson's in the Cabinet, and he owes me a favour or two. He will put pressure on those in high places — Robinson at the Exchequer is a great friend of his. And the Theakstons have many friends, of course. Lady Theakston is anxious to have it all settled quickly, and she's an intimate of both Mulgrave and Melville from her navy days, to say nothing of Wellington.'

'What it is to have influence!' Jasper remarked.

'Interest is the most important thing in life,' Batchworth said. 'Just take, for instance, the Liverpool and Manchester railway. You know that the Bill failed in Parliament last year because of hostility from the canal interest?'

'Yes, I remember,' said Jasper. 'I said then, and I still say, that I can't see how you will ever square the likes of Stafford.'

'So I thought too,' Jes said with a grin, 'but we've done it! Not only squared the old man, but persuaded him to invest a hundred thousand pounds, all the extra capital we needed! Now it's all on the go: the Bill should go through this session.'

Jasper was astonished. 'But how did you do it? I wonder you even managed to get him to listen.'

'It was Huskisson,' Batchworth said. 'He's in favour of the railway because so many of his constituents in Liverpool have commercial interests, and it just so happens that when Stafford was British Ambassador in Paris during the Revolution, Huskisson was his secretary. He remembered him favourably, and so we were able to arrange a meeting between them. And of course, Huskisson has such a clear head and is such a genius with figures, he was able to show the Marquess quite clearly that far from ruining the canals, the railway would benefit them, and make profit into the bargain. He was so convincing, before he left the Marquess was almost pressing money on him. That man is worth his weight in gold!'

'So you really think this railway will be built?'

'Certain of it. Nothing stands in our way now. In four or five years' time, Hobsbawn, you will be able to send your finished goods down to Liverpool safely, cheaply, and quickly — at half the cost of the canal, and twice the speed.'

'Twice the speed?'

'With stationary engines and horse-working, at between five and eight miles an hour,' Batchworth said. 'The canal boats may travel at around five miles an hour, but when you allow for all the time lost at locks and tunnels the average over the journey is much less than that. I'm talking about a *constant* five miles an hour —'

At that moment the door opened, and the much-frilled cap and scrubbed, wholesome face of Janet, the nursery-maid, appeared round it.

'Oh! I beg your pardon, madam, sir,' she said. 'I did knock, but I'm afraid you didn't hear me.'

'Yes, Janet, what is it?' Sophie said sternly, knowing the answer perfectly well.

'I thought perhaps you'd like to see Miss Fanny in her new apron, before I took it off. I didn't realise you had guests, madam,' said Janet. She opened the door a little more, to reveal Fanny standing beside her.

Sophie sighed. Janet was always doing this. Fanny was dressed in a formal frock of pink muslin, her fair curls carefully brushed and decorated with a beguiling pink ribbon, her rosy, healthy face shining with recent washing and wreathed in welcoming smiles. As soon as she knew there was a visitor, Janet had obviously washed, brushed and changed her, and brought her down with this flimsiest of excuses. The fact was that Janet thought Fanny Hobsbawn the most remarkable and beautiful child ever born, and was convinced that everyone who came to the house must be pining for the chance to admire her.

Sophie knew she ought to be more strict with Janet, but she hadn't the heart to scold such unswerving devotion; and besides, she secretly agreed with her. Fanny was a prodigy, and as beautiful as an angel.

'Now, Janet, really,' Jasper began, seeing his wife hesitate; but Lord Batchworth interrupted him.

'Oh, please don't send her away on my account. I should love to make her better acquaintance, if she will let me.'

'Only too readily, I'm afraid,' Jasper said. 'All right, Janet, Miss Fanny may come in.'

As soon as permission was secured, Fanny, with a fine instinct for self preservation, went straight to her father with smiles and kisses, and then, standing between his knees with the air of a conqueror, she looked across at Lord Batchworth and shyly lowered the fans of her eyelashes to brush her rose-petal cheeks. Jes watched sardonically, perfectly well aware, after a lifetime of practice, when he was being flirted with.

'Shall I play you my new piece, Papa?' she asked sweetly, for Batchworth's benefit. 'Or shall I sing for you?'

'Not now, love,' Jasper said reluctantly, evidently so utterly enslaved by the tiny temptress that it gave him pain to refuse her anything. 'We have a visitor. Do you remember Lord Batchworth?'

Fanny raised the eyelashes just enough to flutter them at Jes. 'Yes, I *think* so,' she said with charming hesitation. 'Is he Cousin Wosamund's fwiend?'

'Delicately put,' Jes commented *sub voce*; and to Fanny, 'Yes, that's right, I am. Will you shake hands?'

Fanny came to him promptly, shook hands with gravity, then wound herself round the leg and arm of his chair, turning her face up to his and surveying him thoroughly. It seemed she liked what she saw. 'I was named after my aunt,' she vouchsafed suddenly, as though bestowing an important gift on him. 'She died before I was born, but Papa says I am like her, just a bit.'

'In looks only,' Jasper said quickly. 'Fanny is going to be clever and beautiful like her aunt, but she will have a luckier temper I hope — and a much longer and happier life.'

'Papa says that Aunt Fanny died of *p'vers'ty*,' Fanny said seriously. 'I asked Janet but she doesn't know how you catch it. Do you?'

Jes suppressed a smile. 'You must be a good girl, and always

315

do as your mother and father tell you, and they will make sure no harm comes to you.'

'Didn't Aunt Fanny have a mother and father?' Fanny asked, putting her finger unerringly on the weakness.

Jasper laughed. 'Don't, I warn you, get into debate with this infant Socrates! Janet, you had better take Miss Fanny back to the nursery now.'

Fanny drooped visibly with disappointment at the dismissal. Jes said quickly, 'I'm very glad to have made your acquaintance, Miss Fanny Hobsbawn. And one day soon I shall come and visit you again, and perhaps Mama will let me take you out for a drive in my carriage.' He glanced across at Sophie, who smiled and nodded. 'Would you like that?'

Fanny brightened. 'Yes please,' she said firmly. 'Will it be tomowwow?'

'No, not tomorrow, but soon.'

'What does soon mean?' she persisted.

'When the weather is better. I shan't forget, I promise. And Cousin Rosamund shall come too.'

Fanny considered this for a moment, and then said judiciously, 'I'd *wather* go with just you.'

Jasper laughed. 'Did I say infant Socrates? I meant infant Delilah!'

'What's a lilah?' Fanny asked with interest, glad still to be the centre of attention.

'A lady who rides alone in a gentleman's carriage,' Jes answered seriously. 'And I have to tell you, Miss Hobsbawn, that it's considered very fast and not at all the thing. Nice gentlemen don't care for fast ladies.'

'Don't you like fast ladies?' Fanny asked cautiously.

'Not at all.'

'Then I shan't be one,' she decided.

'I should think not, Miss Fanny,' Janet said, scandalised by the turn the conversation had taken. 'Come along now, if you please.'

Fanny allowed herself to be gathered up and urged towards the door; pausing there only to execute a polished curtsey and pronounce sweetly to the company in general, '*Good*bye, evwyone!' Then she disappeared, followed by her doting attendant.

Jasper and Jes met each other's eyes and burst out laughing. Sophie looked faintly puzzled.

'I don't know what you think is funny. It's naughty of Janet to bring her in so, but I didn't think she was bothering you.'

'I think she's delightful,' Jes said, 'but I have the feeling that only one or two meetings would have me as much round her thumb as her poor Papa! Tell me, does she always have difficulty with the letter "r"?'

'No,' Sophie said, disconcerted. 'It seems to come and go. Strangely enough she can always say it properly when she's alone with me or with Janet. Perhaps it's the excitement of being in company which affects her.'

'I'm sure that's what it is,' Jes said kindly.

CHAPTER SIXTEEN

Eastfield Farm was the last to get in its hay-harvest that summer of 1826, and the atmosphere was probably the more festive on that account. Benedict threw himself into it with a will, working up on top of one of the waggons alongside Philip Pike, the farmer's youngest son, catching the stooks as they were thrown up and stacking them.

It was a hot and prickly job, and there was no relief from the heat of the sun, which on that last day blazed down from a sky of purest blue. After an hour or two Mr Pike himself, a man of few words, silently took off his broad-brimmed hat and passed it up to the young master, and Benedict, having regard to the tenderness of his ears and the back of his neck, accepted it gratefully. It was a relief; but still maddening wisps of hay got themselves down his shirt and into his ears, and the hay dust got in his eyes and up his nose, and his hands grew sore from handling the hay which looked so soft, but felt so harsh. Benedict would not give less or complain more than Philip, who was a year younger than him; so the two boys worked steadily until the farmhouse bell rang at noon, and Mr Pike called a halt for dinner.

Benedict slid gratefully down from the waggon in Philip's wake, and trudged across the field to the shade of the high hedge where the men were gathering. The shade was as delicious as cold water, and the fringe of green grass that grew along it felt like silk.

Mr Pike, lighting his pipe against the harvest flies, spoke in the intervals of sucking the flame onto the tobacco. 'Now then — Master Benett — tha's done — a man's work today. Tha can tak thy dinner — wi' a clear conscience.'

There was a chorus of agreement from the other men. 'Coom and sit down then, master. Coom and rest thee.'

Bendy went, blushing with pleasure, and sat as they sat, on the grass in the shade, clasping his bare forearms around his knees. The Old Man — one of Pike's hands who was never known by any other title — came back from seeing to the horses and nodded to him, smiling toothlessly.

'Ah remember when thy father were th' same age, yoong master. He'd follow the harvest joost th' same way, alus in the thick of it.' The women from the house were bringing out the food, and jugs of cold buttermilk and October ale. Mrs Pike approached Bendy with the buttermilk, but the Old Man stopped her. 'Nay, missus, th' lad's doon a man's work — let him have a man's sup. Fetch him some ale.'

'Hold they peace, Old Man!' Mrs Pike said. 'Master Benedict'll be used to milk at home. He shall have what he likes.'

'Well, ma'am,' Bendy said tentatively, 'if you don't much mind, I'd prefer the ale. I've never really cared for buttermilk.'

The old man cackled shrilly. 'He s'l have what he likes! Course he shall! Send over that lass, missus — he prefers what she's got!'

'That lass' was Annie, an orphan whom the Pikes had taken in from the workhouse when she was eight to be a kitchenmaid, and who had been with them ever since, working at whatever task was set her. She scrubbed floors and washed dishes, fed the chickens, milked the cows, dug the potato patch, and was generally set to fetch and carry for any member of the family who happened to catch sight of her. She came over now in response to Mrs Pike's curt command, carrying the heavy ale pitcher, and as Bendy held up the pewter mug Mrs Pike had given him, she bent over him to pour.

He had known her all his life, and been aware of her only as a shadowy figure in the background, someone who was there but nothing to do with him, merely a landmark, like a tree or a gate. Now, suddenly, as she stooped over him, cutting out the sun for a moment, she stepped out of the background, and he looked up at her with a sense of discovery.

319

She was two years older than him, but looked fully eighteen or nineteen: a well-developed, plump girl with a broad, puggily pretty face. Her hair was light brown and wispy, always falling down from the knot in which she wore it under her cap; her eyes light blue and wide, set too far apart, which gave her a stupid look. The eyes were concentrating now on the stream of ale, and were half shaded by her eyelashes. The sunlight was diffused into a nimbus through the edges of her hair. Bendy noticed a sheen of moisture on her upper lip and the upper slopes of her breasts, which were straining the buttons of her bodice. Her forearms were bare, and the hair on them was thick and fine and golden. She smelled like a hot hayfield, and Bendy felt a strong stirring towards her.

'Thank you, Annie,' he said. She didn't look at him, but the fans of her eyelashes flickered, and the corners of her mouth turned up in an embarrassed but not displeased smile before she moved on to the next man.

Bendy watched her go, until he was distracted by Philip, seated beside him, who had broken a chunk from the wheel of harvest bread and passed the rest on to him. Bendy broke off his own piece and passed the wheel along, made aware of how hungry he was. Other food was passed around — cheese from the dairy, firm and creamy-textured, cold bacon in thick slices of marbled pink and white, wedges of Mrs Pike's own pork pie, hard boiled eggs, and freshly-pulled onions, crisp and juicy, and so sweet that the men could — and did — eat them like apples.

Bendy was in a fair way to tackling everything, ate with good appetite, drank deeply of the good ale, and joined in the conversation and good-natured chaffing of his fellow harvest-ers; but all the time, out of the corner of his eye, he was aware of Annie. He watched her moving about, serving and pouring, watched the curve of her cheek and her ridiculous snub nose, the soft weight of her breasts and the mysterious shadow that appeared between them when she bent forward to pour, the slow swing of her hips as she stepped through the grass. He ate and talked, but part of his mind was elsewhere, wondering, wondering. . .

The long day drew to a close: the blue shadows under the

trees had turned to indigo, the brassiness had faded from the sky, and the swifts were racing and shrieking high up in its cloudless, colourless depths. A clean, grassy smell of the cooling earth dispersed the smell of horses and sweat and bruised hay; and the last of the harvest was in. Benedict slithered down for the last time from the waggon top, and stood, hands on hips, surveying the bare field with a sense of achievement.

'Now then, Master Benett, I'm right grateful to thee for all thy good work,' Mr Pike said. He offered his horny, calloused hand, and Benedict shook it, rather touched. Others gathered round.

'Tha's worked like a Trojan, master!'

'Tha's doon a man's job today, master!'

'Willta stay for the feast, then, master?'

Bendy looked down at himself. 'I'm not fit for company.'

Mrs Pike, passing at that moment with a tray of mugs, paused to say, 'You'll stay, Master Benedict, I hope? There'll be no finery tonight. All the men are mucky. They clean theirselves in the yard under the pump, but I'll provide thee with a kettle of hot water and a private place to wash — that's only fitting.'

Benedict hesitated, more from diffidence than unwillingness, and the eldest Pike son, Ned, added anxiously, 'Now do stay, master! We eat out under the stars and 'ave singing and dancing, and Ma's hot pie an' peas. It's a rare do!'

'I'll see a message is sent to Morland Place, where you are,' Mrs Pike added. 'Your father always stayed to the feast, when he helped with the harvest.'

Surrounded by flatteringly eager faces, Benedict hastened to close with the offer.

When they reached the farmhouse, Mrs Pike ushered Benedict into a tiny apartment just off the kitchen. It was as small and spare as a monk's cell, containing a narrow bed covered with a grey blanket, a small chest, and a wooden chair. While he was still staring round him, Ned Pike came in carrying a folding washstand and basin, a small piece of soap on a dish, and a pair of brushes. He grinned shyly. 'Tha's no need for a razor, any road! Is there owt else tha needs? Lass'll be in directly wi' a towel an' hot watter.'

321

'Thank you, you're very kind,' Bendy said. Ned left him and he threw his jacket on the bed and began to take off his shirt, anxious now to be rid of the prickling strands of hay he had been holding captive all day. He pulled the shirt out from his waistband and had just thrust his hands up inside for the luxury of an abandoned scratch when the door opened again and Annie appeared, two hands occupied with a hot-water can, a clean towel hung over her arm.

Benedict jumped forward to help her, his heart suddenly thumping. 'Let me! That's too heavy for you.'

It seemed to confuse her. She blushed. 'Nay, master, I can manage. It's not fitting. Nay, I'm strong enough.' He desisted, and watched her in silence as she crossed the room and poured the hot water into the basin. Then she put the can down and turned to him, holding out the towel. 'Missus says it's a bit rough, but it's fresh from t'laundry.'

'I'm sure it is. Thank you, Annie.' He tried desperately to think of something to say to keep her there, but his wretched tongue failed him. Yet she lingered, as if she sensed he wanted to talk.

'Astow got everything?' she asked.

'Yes, thank you. It's kind of Mrs Pike to let me have this room.'

She began to smile. 'It's ma room, is this.'

'Is it?' How small and bare and dark, he thought; and then he thought of her sleeping in this bed, where his jacket now lay; thought of her taking off her clothes here, standing where he was standing. He thought of her body, and his own felt hot and jumpy. 'Then it's kind of *you*.'

'Nay, ah don't mind.' She met his eyes, and a surge of excitement went through him. She said shyly, 'Ah like to think of thee using it.'

Bendy had no idea what he was going to say next. He didn't even know what he wanted to say. 'Are you coming to the feast?' he heard himself ask.

'Ah'll be helpin' t'missus serve th' men,' she said.

'Will you — will you —?'

She seemed to want to help him along. 'Missus said ah was to make sure tha wanted for nothing. Serve Master Morland first, she said. Whatever 'e wants, see 'e gets it.'

322

Benedict had nothing to say. He thought his face must be scarlet, and could only hope Annie would attribute it to the effect of the long day in the sun.

The feast was at its height. The trestles had been laid out in the yard, lanterns had been lit, food and ale had been carried round, and the men had taken the edge off their day-long appetite. The Old Man had got out his fiddle, Ned Pike his flute, another of the men his bagpipe, and cheerful songs had been roared to the eaves and sent the roosting pigeons fluttering startled out into the night. Now there was dancing, and those who preferred to watch rather than perform were thumping the rhythm out on the table-tops with their fists.

Bendy had eaten, drunk, sung and danced. Now, as other men had done before him, he rose from the table with a muttered excuse and wandered off round the side of one of the barns, looking for a peaceful spot to relieve himself. He chose the barn wall, and stood gazing up into the dark, seeing the flitting shapes of bats fluttering to and fro like torn bits of sky blowing about.

When he had done, he turned to go back to the feast, and saw that he was not alone. Annie was standing in the doorway of the barn watching him. He didn't know how long she had been there. She was so still she might have been there all along, and the thought made him go hot and cold. Then he wondered what she was doing there at all, and the probable answer made him go hot and stay hot.

He walked towards her, trying to think what to say; but when he reached her, he discovered words were as unimportant as impossible. He put his hands on her shoulders; her face, patched with light and shadow, lifted to him, and instinct took over. He kissed her, felt her willing response, kissed her again wildly. His blood seemed to be rushing about his body uncontrolled; his head felt full to bursting. She backed and he went with her, glad of the privacy and darkness of the barn. It was full of hay, and the smell was part of the long day and the new sensations he had discovered; the smell was her. He put his hands on her breasts, and felt flesh, and suddenly wanted to plunge himself into them, to roll his face about in her flesh, to rifle her.

'Oh Annie,' he said, half sigh, half moan. They went down — he didn't know by whose volition — and were lying in the hay now, and everywhere his hands went they found yielding and flesh. He pressed his face between her magnificent breasts, slid his hands between her thighs. His body was hard and hot like fever, craving relief, and when she checked him, he thought he would die.

'Oh Annie, let me! Let me!'

'Nay master! What'll 'appen to me if I get in trouble?'

He hardly understood the words. He felt he must have her, would give her anything, promise her the world if only she would let him. 'I'll take care of you, I promise,' he said wildly. I won't let anything happen to you. *Please* Annie —!'

It seemed, miraculously, to have been enough. Now there was yielding again. He fumbled with his buttons, with himself, with her, and there was her hand to help him, cool and hard and kindly. He registered a moment's surprise along with the gratitude, and then everything seemed to happen at once, like being blown up by a mortar shell.

Afterwards, when he was able to breathe and think again, it was the gratitude which remained. He felt enormously tender towards her. He kissed her again, and she sighed in the darkness — not a sad sigh, but perhaps tinged with anxiety. Now with the slowing of his blood he understood what she had been worried about before, must still be worried about.

'Don't worry,' he said. 'If anything happens, I'll take care of you.'

'Aye,' she said, though perhaps still a little doubtfully. 'Thank you, master!'

She was older than him, but he was the one who had to offer protection. It made him feel strong and manly. 'You mustn't call me "master" — not when we're alone like this, anyway.'

'What s'l I call thee, then?'

'My name's Benedict; but my friends call me Bendy.'

She chuckled. 'Nay, there's nowt Bendy about *thee*, young master!' He didn't understand the joke, and laughed a little tentatively. She said, 'Tha'd best get back, or they'll be looking for thee.'

'I suppose so.' He stood up and straightened his clothing.

His body seemed to be singing and quivering with delightful new sensations — all her doing, dear, lovely, kind Annie. 'Can I —' he said hesitantly. 'Can I come and see you again. Privately, I mean?'

There was a silence; then her voice out of the darkness. 'If tha wants master. If tha wants — Bendy.'

The summer found James once more on his travels, and he turned up one day in July at Upper Grosvenor Street to find his sister and brother-in-law for once unengaged, and preparing to dine with only Thomas for company.

'You have only just caught us,' Lucy said. 'Thomas leaves tomorrow for Northumberland with young Maurice Ballincrea.'

'You will have to stop calling him Young Maurice sooner or later, Mama,' Tom said.

'When he shows himself ready for responsibility, perhaps,' Lucy retorted. 'Do you know, James, that boy has been back in England almost a year, without once going to visit his seat. Helena tells me the steward sends letters every week begging for instructions about the estate, and all Maurice tells him is to "do as he thinks fit and not bother him". I don't know what's wrong with the boy.'

'Yes you do, Mama,' Tom said with a grin. 'He's having much too good a time in London to want to go away. And after two years abroad with Lord Ashley, I can hardly blame him.'

'There's nothing wrong with Ashley,' Lucy said firmly. 'I've met him, and he's perfectly polite and pleasant. A little serious perhaps —'

'Everyone but you thinks him quite mad, Mama. He has such embarrassing religious enthusiasms.'

'— but that's hardly surprising when one looks at his parents,' Lucy finished firmly. 'Shaftesbury is *very* strange, and I cannot bear Lady Shaftesbury at any price. Poor William Lamb says she once told him she heartily disliked all her children. It didn't surprise me in the least.'

'At all events,' Tom said to James, remembering where they had begun, 'Maurice agreed to go north and do his duty on condition I went with him to advise him, and stayed on for the shooting, which I believe is very good up there.'

325

'So I understand,' James said, amused.

'And Danby and I are off to France next week,' Lucy said. 'We shall call in on poor George Brummell in Calais, and then meet Roland and Thalia in Paris and bring them home with us. I must say, it is the longest honeymoon I ever heard of. How the young people love to travel these days! Of course we never had the chance. I was only eleven when the French Revolution began. It still seems strange to me to be able to talk of going to France, just like that.'

'The war's been over more than ten years, my love,' Theakston pointed out gently.

'Yes, I know, but I can't seem to get used to it. I'm sure everything was much more fun when we were at war.'

The others laughed. 'Shame on you, Mama!' said Tom.

'I can't help it. It's true,' said Lucy. 'But what are you doing here, James? You haven't told us yet.'

'I've heard of some fine horses being sold at bargain prices, so I'm going to have a look at them.'

'What's this, another breakdown sale?' Theakston asked.

'In a way,' James said. 'It's the Earl of Southport's stable — you know of course that he died recently? Well, it seems that he had heavy debts, some of them to do with the South American bubble last year, and in any case I understand the new earl is not a great horseman. So the entire stable is to be sold off — racehorses, hunters, hacks and all.'

'And you're after a bargain?' Theakston said.

'I'm surprised at you, Jamie,' Lucy said severely. 'Surely you've heard the old adage that there's no such thing as a bargain horse. You get what you pay for.'

'And surely you've heard of the old adage about not looking gift horses in the mouth?' James retorted. 'The market is so glutted at the moment that I expect the prices to be very low.'

'I can't see what that has to do with anything. A good horse deserves a good price,' Lucy said magnificently.

'You must realise that the way you and I buy horses is quite different. You do it for pleasure, but I do it for business. You probably never even ask the price —'

'She doesn't,' Lord Theakston agreed. 'Too vulgar.'

'Quite so. Whereas I must haggle —'

'Like a horse-broker,' Lucy said scornfully.

'I am a horse-broker,' James pointed out.

'You never used to be. You were a gentleman.'

'But I always sold horses.'

'Sold them, yes, but didn't buy them, except for breeding. Selling the horses you breed yourself is *quite* a different matter.'

Theakston grew tired of the argument and cut into it. 'We were thinking of going to the sale ourselves — weren't we, my love?'

James said, 'Ha!', and Lucy looked at her husband reproachfully.

'Parslow's been trying to persuade me for ages to buy myself a new horse, or even two,' she said. 'He says Hotspur and Magnus are getting old, and that I ought to be bringing on some youngsters if I'm not to find myself with nothing to hunt in a year or two.'

'He's right,' Theakston said. 'You know he is.'

'Parslow's always right about everything,' Tom said. 'That's a rule in this house.'

'Don't be impudent,' Lucy told him. 'Parslow says that Lord Southport had a lot of fine young horses — very keen on bringing them on himself.'

'Why don't we go together, then?' James said. 'It will be much more pleasant.

'Provided you try to behave yourself like a gentleman and not like a horse-broker,' Lucy said firmly.

Nicholas arrived home at Morland Place with a mixture of feelings. He was sorry that his time at Eton was over, and he was sorry to part from his friends, particularly Winchmore, who was going up to Oxford in the autumn, and Billy Penshurst, second son of the Earl of Tonbridge, who was starting out on his Grand Tour almost at once.

On the other hand, it was good to be going home to a place where the servants worshipped him and the tenants pulled their forelocks to him, where his slightest wish was law, and everyone knew that one day he would hold all their fortunes in his hand. At Eton he had been a small fish in a large pond; at Morland Place he was the Young Master, and only his mother and father stood between him and absolute power. In such matters he agreed absolutely with Milton's Satan, that it was better to rule in hell than serve in heaven.

He was not pleased when he arrived home to find the undercurrent of an atmosphere he did not understand, and which distracted his mother from giving him the undivided attention he felt was his due. He could not quite put his finger on it, and had to wait until he could get his brother alone to find out what it was.

The opportunity came when they retired to dress for dinner. Nicholas was no longer to sleep in the nursery with Bendy. Now he was eighteen, he had been formally and ceremoniously installed in the North Bedroom, as befitted his status as heir to the estate. He was there now, standing by the fireplace and looking round with approval at the little touches of luxury he had not been accustomed to before: the armchair by the fire, the writing-desk, the decanter and glass on the table. He had not yet told his mother that he had been accustomed to smoke cigarillos at Eton. He was wondering how it would go down when he broke it to her, and whether the revelation would result in a box of them being placed beside the decanter for his manly comfort.

For the moment he would have to make do with taking snuff: he didn't really like the stuff, but he had developed an elegant and impressive routine around the action of taking it, which he felt gave him a great air of *homme du monde*. And he was starting a collection of snuff-boxes which he was determined would eventually make him talked-of throughout England. He took out his latest and proudest addition, and was examining it with pleasure when Bendy, on his way to the nursery, paused at the open door to look in at him.

'Hullo! What have you got there?'

Nicholas looked up, never displeased to have an audience. 'Oh, a trifle I picked up. Rather amusing actually. Here, have a look.'

Bendy crossed the room and took it from him. 'Oh, it's —' he began enthusiastically, and then stopped. It was an oblong box of fine filagree work, gold, with a small, very dark ruby at each corner. On the lid, and on each of the four sides, was a porcelain panel delicately painted in pastels. It was when he saw the

328

subject of the illustrations that Benedict stopped half-way through his exclamation of delight.

The painting on the lid depicted a plump Roman matron with her hair bound in a filet, dressed in transparent draperies, and bearing a long, thin ferrule. This she was applying with obvious energy to the backside of a naked child. The child was bawling, but the matron's expression was gleeful.

Puzzled, Bendy turned the box around, hoping to find on the side panels some clue as to the meaning. Perhaps it was the culmination of a story in episodes, he thought. But each of the panels depicted a similar scene: a Roman in a toga beating two naked young women, a naked woman whipping a naked man, a man beating a naked black slave, and a man and woman either side of a child, each bearing a bunch of birch twigs.

'Charming, isn't it?' Nicholas said as Bendy looked up at him at last. 'Exquisite work.'

Benedict handed it back rather hastily. 'Where did you get it?'

'Oh, I had it from a man at Eton, whose brother had been on a Grand Tour and brought it back from Florence. The Italians do this sort of thing much better than the French. I paid a pretty penny for it, I can tell you!'

'But — those pictures,' Bendy said doubtfully. 'Do you *like* 'em? I mean — they're all —'

Nicholas put on a superior air. 'Oh Lord, I'd forgotten how out of touch you people in the country are! I suppose you think thrashing's horrid, or something clownish like that.'

'You didn't think much of it when Father Moineau did it to you,' Benedict said shortly.

Nicholas blushed. 'I was too young to see the benefit then. Of course, I wouldn't expect a child like you to understand. You need elegance of mind to appreciate subtle pleasures. Besides,' he added hastily, 'everyone needs a thrashing now and then. It's good for you.' He slipped the box into his pocket, cleared his throat, and looked around him to avoid Benedict's steady, frowning gaze. 'What do you think of my room? Something like, eh?'

'It's very comfortable,' Bendy agreed. 'But won't you mind sleeping here.'

Nicholas stared. 'Mind? Why on earth should I mind?'

'Because of Uncle Ned. I mean, he died here. It would give me nightmares.'

Nicholas looked contemptuous. 'Everything gives you nightmares. I don't have 'em. Besides, Uncle didn't die *in* here. He died out of here, if you want to be particular about it.' That struck even him as being close to tasteless, so he went on firmly, 'Anyway, I don't believe in ghosts.'

'You used to,' Bendy pointed out. 'I remember when you and Harry stayed awake all night once, hoping to see the White Lady. And what about that time —'

'Childish nonsense.' How irritating younger brothers could be! 'Naturally I've grown out of that sort of thing,' he said loftily. 'I should have hoped you would too.'

Bendy didn't answer. A lifetime of being Nicky's brother had taught him never to volunteer any information that might be used against him. 'What was school like?'

'Not bad. The food was horrid, but there were some awfully decent fellows there.' He waved a dismissive hand. He had more important matters to discuss. 'Why is my mother angry with my father?' he demanded.

Bendy hesitated. 'She's not angry. Upset, perhaps.'

'What is she upset about?'

Bendy hesitated, but there seemed no reason not to tell. Nicky would find out eventually anyway. 'Papa's bought some horses.' He leaned against the door jamb and stared thoughtfully at the floor. 'There was a sale a few weeks ago — Lord Southport's estate — and Papa went to it. He bought six of Southport's youngsters to reschool — they've been run off for six months, ever since his lordship died.'

Nicholas shrugged. 'What's wrong with that?'

'Only that Papa says he means to school them all himself from scratch, and Mama thinks it's dangerous.'

'Papa's the best horseman in the Ridings — everyone says so.'

Bendy looked away. 'You asked me why Mama's upset. I told you,' he said indifferently. 'That's all.'

Nicholas eyed him cannily. He knew his Bendy. 'It's not,' he said. Bendy shrugged and began to move away. Nicholas shot out a hand and caught him by one ear. 'Tell me,' he suggested, twisting.

330

'Nothing to tell,' Bendy said, testing the grip.

Nicky caught his wrist too, and bent it up behind him. 'I'll "burn you".'

'Let me go. I'll tell you. It isn't a secret,' Bendy said, as Nicky twisted a little more. 'Mama's worried because Papa's not a young man any more. These youngsters are practically wild and hot as Hades, and Papa won't even let the rough rider take the edge off them.'

'Is that all?' Nicky released him.

Bendy backed away a little, rubbing his wrist surreptitiously. His ear felt swollen and hot, and he imagined how red it must look. 'I wouldn't talk about it, if I were you. Papa don't like it suggested that he can't manage a horse. It would only make him more reckless. And Mama worries about him, but she doesn't like to offend him.'

'Oh, I won't mention it,' Nicky said thoughtfully. He felt elated. He couldn't quite think how the information would benefit him, but he was sure he'd find a use for it some time or other: information of any sort was like coin of the realm to the man who knew what to do with it. Besides, it was always pleasant to find out something which might otherwise have been kept from him. And doubly pleasant to see Bendy trying not to cry.

In late October Rosamund and Jes went out to Grasscroft for a few days — Jes to see to some estate business, and Rosamund to enjoy some gallops over the stubble in the golden days of the season known as St Martin's Little Summer. Grasscroft was a pretty house, largely rebuilt in the middle of the previous century in the Palladian manner; but Rosamund did not feel at ease there. Despite the fact that the Dowager Lady Batchworth had long departed to live in France, Rosamund felt her spirit round every corner, watching her with disapproval. It was Marcus's mother all over again, she thought, and escaped out of doors as much as possible. She envied John Skelwith's wife: for all Jes had told her about the absurdities of the house at Clifton, at least it was Mathilde's own. No previous Mrs Skelwith had lived there and left her mark.

But as long as she could be out of doors all day, Rosamund

was happy enough; and the new horse Jes had bought her for her birthday in September (her twenty-ninth, she thought with amazement) was a delight. She rode Cedar up onto the moors every day and galloped until they were both tired, and came home glowing and hungry and with her mind emptied of everything but the wind and the sky, the rolling vistas of golden bracken and rose-purple heather, and the smudged indigo shadows of the distant hills.

A letter followed her there from Manchester one day, and was waiting for her when she came in from the stable yard. Jes, coming in later, found her standing by the fire, still in her habit, reading it through for the third time. Her face seemed to have become all planes and angles, he thought; though perhaps that was the effect of the leaping flames, throwing shadows upward and across her.

'What is it, my love?' he asked quietly.

She looked up. 'Just another letter from Parslow. My faithful correspondent.'

'Has he anything to tell you?'

'He still hasn't been able to catch sight of her, but the gardener tells him she goes out with her aunt whenever it's fine. She played with a ball the other day, throwing it to her aunt and catching it. The gardener heard her laughing once. And he heard from one of the maids that Barbarina has ordered a length of cherry-coloured velvet to make her a new winter dress.' Her eyes looked unnaturally bright. 'With a lace collar,' she finished.

It was so pitifully little. She fed her longing on such scraps, as he knew, and half of him wished Parslow at the devil for keeping the flame alive, while the rest of him knew that for her it was better than nothing, better than forgetting. As he watched her now she folded the letter and slipped it into her pocket. She turned her back on him and stooped to pick up the poker and jab it into a glowing log, sending a fountain of golden sparks up the chimney. He knew she didn't want him to touch her, but he couldn't bear not to.

'Here, let me,' he said painfully. 'You're ruining the fire.' He closed his hand over hers holding the poker, and felt her resistance.

'Leave me alone,' she said, without emphasis.

'Darling, please,' he said. She looked at him, turning her head just slightly, and he saw the reflection of firelight in the single tear she had allowed to escape.

'There's nothing anyone can do,' she said.

He took the poker from her, restored it to its place, and turned her to face him, taking her hands in his. She was a tall woman, but he was taller, just the right height to be cried on. That was his privilege.

'*I* have some news,' he said. 'I had a letter today, too.'

She made an interrogative sound, trying to be interested for his sake. He smiled at her effort. 'News for both of us, my love. A letter from London.'

She understood now. Her eyes widened. 'Jes —!'

He nodded. 'The Act is gone through, my darling. Your marriage to Marcus has been dissolved. You are a free woman — free to marry again, if you will.' She could not speak yet, and he took advantage of her silence. 'So before you have the chance to savour your freedom, and perhaps find out how many charming and eligible men there are in the world, I want to make sure of you.' He lifted her hand to his lips and kissed it. 'Lady Rosamund Chetwyn, I love you with all my heart and soul. Will you do my the supreme honour of accepting my hand in marriage?'

'Oh Jes,' she said, and burst into tears.

He held her against him, and for once being cried on didn't hurt him. He felt there was healing in it. 'All very well, my love, but I should like an answer. Did you say "Oh Jes" or "Oh yes"? Will you consent to be the next Countess of Batchworth, or must I go and hang myself with one of my own neckties?' She made an incoherent sound, and nudged against his neck, and he smiled over her shoulder at the ormolu clock on the chimneypiece. 'In default of a more graceful speech, I'll take that as acceptance.'

'I love you, Jes,' she said after a while.

'I love you too,' he said. She disentangled herself from him, and he put his handkerchief into her fingers. 'I always keep a spare one about me when I'm expecting to see you.'

'Oh Jes,' she said again, but in self-reproach this time. 'I do seem to cry an awful lot, don't I?'

'All my coats have moss growing on the left shoulder,' he said. 'But I don't mind.'

'I think things will be better now,' she said. 'Do you really want to marry me?'

'What sort of question is that?'

'I think perhaps I shall be able to feel more at home once we're married. This house, for instance — it always seems to me like your mother's.'

'You shall have as much money as you like to do it up in the first style. Change everything — drapes, carpets, wallpaper, everything. Make your mark.'

'Is that foolish?' she said shyly.

'Not at all. I understand and approve entirely. But save a little enthusiasm for Batchworth House. We shall probably be spending more time there than here, and it has never had a female's care lavished on it.'

'When shall we be married?'

'As soon as you like. As soon as you've thought where and how you'd like to do it, and who you'd like to invite. And where you want to go for a honeymoon.'

'A honeymoon?'

'Why so surprised? It is customary.'

'I feel too old for the word to be appropriate,' she said awkwardly. 'It sounds so young and — and bridal.'

'So are you, to me — my lovely bride. I want you to have everything. This shall be as if it's your first wedding, your only wedding. Everything begins here. The past is wiped out.'

Perhaps that was not the right thing to say. She had been listening to him with a faint smile, like someone being sung to delightfully but in a foreign language. Now the smile faded.

'What is it?' he asked anxiously. 'Don't be sad. Please don't be sad — not right this minute.'

'No — I was just thinking. I want to give you things too,' she said. 'I have done nothing but take from you from the beginning. I wish I could give you something.'

He took her back into his arms. 'Don't you know that you do?' he said tenderly. 'You are my life, my joy. And now you are to be my wife as well. What more could I possibly ask?'

334

She looked up at him seriously, seeming almost childlike in her sudden gravity. 'I should like to give you a child,' she said in a small voice. 'Do you think that I could?'

The question tore at his heart, and he fought not to show it. He thought of the pregnancies she had deliberately ended, the children she had refused to bear — some perhaps his own. He thought of her struggle to bear Marcus's child, and how she had had to tear that child from her heart. How could she ask him such a question? How could he answer it? But he saw — because he knew her and loved her absolutely — that it was neither naive nor foolish nor thoughtless nor even hopeful. She had sought for something to offer him, something as valuable in her terms as she perceived his offer to her. And nothing less than life would do. He already had her life; all she could do was to hope to offer him another as well, perhaps more valuable.

'I love *you*,' he said at last; and after a moment she nodded, understanding.

BOOK THREE

Future Echoes

Years, many parti-coloured years,
Some have crept on, and some have flown
Since first before me fell those tears
I never could see fall alone.

Years, not so many, are to come,
Years not so varied, when from you
One more will fall: when carried home,
I see it not, nor hear *Adieu*.

Walter Savage Landor: *Years*

CHAPTER SEVENTEEN

In January 1827 the Duke of York died. He had been ailing all winter with gout and dropsy, so his death was not entirely unexpected, but it had repercussions all the same. A number of lively young men lost a great deal of money on outstanding bets that York would outlive his elder brother and come to the throne. On the positive side, the Duke of Clarence, always hard pressed on account of his large family of greedy and ambitious bastards, was now heir apparent and he and his duchess were given an increase to their pensions out of the sum which had been allocated to York's use.

Lord Theakston strolled into his wife's sitting-room one day to bring the further news that the late Duke's famous cook, Ude, had taken up the position of chef at the new gambling club, Crockford's, which had been established in St James's Street opposite White's.

'Good news for them — it's bound to increase their membership. A club stands or falls by its kitchens,' Theakston remarked.

'Have you ever been there — to Crockford's?' Lucy asked absently. She had a letter open before her, and was only half attending.

'Only once — not my style really.' Theakston remembered, and smiled to himself. 'Got up like the drop-cloth in a pantomime! All gilding and mirrors and ostentation. The most preposterous great lamp on the staircase — half expected a genie to spring out of it in a puff of smoke!'

'Hmm,' said Lucy.

Theakston cocked his head. 'Somethin' troubling you, my love?'

'Oh — no, not really. This letter from George.'

'Ah, that!'

'It occurs to me that he might really be in trouble this time,' Lucy said, looking up. 'After all, everyone knew that York was his patron, and his credit must have depended a great deal on the idea that there was a good chance of York's succeeding to the throne. But now he's dead —'

'You think the good burghers of Calais may be pressing for their bills?'

'Well, there's all this stuff about sleeping on straw and eating bran bread —'

'One of George's favourite lines when he's pleadin' poverty,' Theakston reminded her. 'Doin' his own laundry is another. Not meant to take it literally.'

'Yes, but it makes me wonder all the same. And look here, he says Lady Waldegrave invited him to stay with them in Brussels, but he had to refuse because he couldn't afford to travel post and he can't bring himself to enter a stage coach. Would he really have refused if things weren't desperate?'

'Wouldn't be surprised if one or two creditors weren't making a nuisance of themselves,' Theakston said mildly. He did not tell her that he had received a separate note from Brummell, addressed care of his club, begging him for the immediate advance of fifty pounds to carry him over a difficult scrape. 'Send him something if you like,' he suggested. 'Pair of gloves, necktie or two, that sort of thing.' Lucy's attitude to her old friend fluctuated depending on her mood, but she was usually happy to send him gifts, if not outright money.

'I wish there were something positive we could do — this consulate business — but Canning won't put it to Prinny for fear of annoying him, and now York's dead . . . ' She sighed. 'So many of our old friends seem to be bowing out — the Duchess of Rutland last year, Mrs Bouverie, Castlereagh, poor Ballincrea —'

That was what it was about then. He sat down beside her and took one of her hands to pat it comfortingly. 'Have to expect it. Part of growing old,' he said.

'Well, I don't like it,' she declared, as if that were all it took.'

'Compensation, though,' he said encouragingly. 'One doesn't *mind* things so much. Would you want to be young again?'

Lucy looked startled. His question impelled her to look behind her down the vista of years, and the effect was rather like vertigo. She seemed to have travelled so far and so fast, as though in a speeding post-chaise, with the scenery whipping past the windows almost in a blur, leaving mileposts and people equally behind.

'Good lord! I really can't remember what it was like.'

Theakston leaned over and kissed her softly on her surprised lips. 'Stay here with me, then,' he suggested beguilingly. 'I mean to grow old disgracefully.'

They were disturbed before the interesting moment could develop fully. Lucy straightened abruptly, and proved herself still capable of blushing as the door opened and Roland came in.

He had become rather a dandy in his own way since his marriage, and everything about his appearance spoke the man of means and fashion. His hair was curled and pomaded, the points of his collar touched his cheeks, his coat sported the essential gathered shoulders and rolled collar, and the Hussar point of his striped waistcoat could just be seen between the tight waist of his coat and the immaculate primrose of his close-fitting pantaloons.

Lord Theakston took it all in with a practised eye, and, not in the least put out, greeted his stepson affably. 'Ah, Aylesbury, my dear boy. Were we expecting you?'

'Oh, I beg your pardon sir, Mama — I wouldn't trouble poor old Hicks to come all the way upstairs just to announce me. I hope you don't mind?'

'Not at all,' Theakston answered quickly for Lucy. 'New waistcoat?'

'Never mind about his waistcoats!' Lucy said sharply. What do you want, Roland?'

'I wondered if my wife was here,' he said awkwardly. He

was twenty-seven years old, but his mother still made him feel seventeen and inept.

'No. Why should she be?'

'Oh, no reason. I must have got it wrong,' Roland said hastily. 'I thought she said she was going to call in on you on her way back from the mantuamaker, but she must have meant her own mama.'

Theakston rescued him. 'If she was going to her mantuamaker, depend upon it she's still there. There's so much trimming and gathering on women's gowns nowadays, so many frills and furbelows, it takes 'em ten times as long in the choosing and fitting.'

Roland brightened. 'Yes, you're probably right, sir. I didn't think to call there first.'

'Good God, I should hope not! Never come between a woman and her mantuamaker! She'll turn up when she's ready.' He stood up. 'I was just going to walk down to my club — care to come with me? They've just turned up ten dozen of old sherry that someone brought in during the war and forgot to put on the cellar books. Found it hidden away in a corner. I'm eager to taste it.'

'Oh — well, yes — that is, if Mama don't mind —'

'My dear boy, *I* don't want you,' Lucy said. 'I'm going out myself in a moment.'

'Then, thank you sir, I will,' Roland said. 'I suppose if Thalia should call here after all —'

'Hicks will tell her where you are. Good heavens child, you'll meet her at home anyway,' said Lucy impatiently.

'Yes, of course I will,' Roland said meekly.

Thomas was alone in the cosy parlour of the Morpurgos' house, lounging in an armchair reading the newspaper, when the door opened and Thalia looked in. Her face brightened at the sight of him.

'Oh, there you are!' She came in and closed the door. 'No, don't get up. You look so comfortable.'

'I wasn't going to,' Thomas drawled. He turned a page and looked at her from under his eyelids. She was dressed with great care and in the latest of fashions, and she looked

342

meltingly pretty; the sight of her filled him with despair.

'How horrid you are!' she said gaily, drawing off her gloves and throwing them, with her reticule, onto a chair. 'You might come and help me with my bonnet. My fingers are so cold I can't manage the strings.'

'Why do you want to take it off? You aren't staying.'

'Yes I am. Don't be so disagreeable!'

He lowered his paper. 'Africa and Peter are both out — which by the way is why I came up here, for a little peace and quiet. You can't possibly remain here all alone with me, my dear Lady Aylesbury. It wouldn't do at all.'

Thalia raised her eyebrows. 'But you're my brother-in-law. What could be wrong with that? It isn't as though I were an unmarried girl, my dear Mr Weston. I'm a respectable matron now.'

Tom sighed, laying the paper aside. 'Matron perhaps,' he said, standing up, 'but respectable is another matter.' He crossed the room to her, looked down for a moment into her shining, teasing face, and then put his arms round her and kissed her long and thoroughly. He felt her first movement of shock, followed by a yielding pleasure. When he released her at last she swayed a moment before she regained her balance; her eyes opened with a drowned look, her cheeks were bright. 'There, is that what you came for?'

'Why — I — I —' she stammered, taken by surprise. Nothing of the sort!' she rallied herself at last. 'I simply came here —'

'You simply came here to try to torment me into kissing you, exactly as I have done,' he said. 'And as I mean to do again.'

He suited his actions to his words. This time her arms crept round him too, and she responded with a growing interest which left them both breathless.

'There, you minx,' he said at last. 'I hope you got what you bargained for.'

'I don't know what you mean,' she said faintly.

'Yes, you do,' he said roughly. The look in her eyes he found most disturbing. 'You've been flirting with me for weeks, and following me around trying to trap me in a private

343

place. Now you've managed it, but I must warn you it's a dangerous game. I am not a saint. I'm just an ordinary man, and like all men I can be dangerous.'

'You would never harm me,' she said with magnificent self confidence.

He shook his head, still unable to keep his eyes from her face. Her expression was promising all sorts of things she probably only half meant, but they were playing havoc with his blood. 'What I would like to do to you this moment would harm all of us — Roland included. God damn it, Thalia, you're married to my brother! Isn't that enough for you?'

She flushed and bit her lip, unable to answer.

'You depend on my keeping control, even while you do everything you can to undermine it. It isn't fair.'

'I only wanted —'

'Well it's not all I want,' he growled. 'But I've got just about enough sense to see where it would lead us. I love my brother, and I'm not going to play him false.'

Her eyes were filling with tears. He felt sorry for her, even while he wanted to shake her. The shame of refusal is hard to bear when you are so very young and pretty. 'I think you're being quite horrid to me,' she said.

'I'm not,' he said, and then again, but gently, 'I'm not. God, you're so pretty and so kissable it would be the easiest thing in the world to follow my instincts. But it isn't really what you want. You have the best man, Thalia. Roland is worth ten of me.'

'He isn't. You're —'

'You married him.'

'You told me to.'

'For God's sake —!'

'I love you.' She looked a little aghast as she heard herself say it, but then her expression resolved into defiance. He could almost hear her thinking, 'There, I've said it!'

He turned away from her. 'No you don't. You're just feeling too safe, longing for adventure. It's a dare to you — daring yourself to do something dangerous.' She didn't answer. 'I told you before I don't love you.'

'You kissed me,' she said with inexorable logic.

344

He turned back and met her eyes, and she shrank from the hardness in them. 'That was nothing to do with love.'

She held his gaze for a brave moment or two, and then turned away, fumbling rather blindly for her gloves. 'I'd better go,' she said. 'I shan't trouble you again. Perhaps you'd have the kindness to open the door for me?'

When she was gone he sat down rather suddenly, staring blindly at the fire. His hands were shaking, and after a moment he put them over his face and rubbed it slowly until the shaking stopped. I shan't trouble you again, she had said. But she would, as he knew very well, even if she didn't. 'I shall have to go away,' he said aloud. But then, he'd always known it would come to that one day. He didn't belong: he had been an exile since the day he was born.

Once he was home for good, and had horses of his own, Nicholas said with some justice that he must have a groom of his own too, to take care of them and attend him when he went out riding. James agreed, and proposed that there were several possible candidates up at Twelvetrees, promising young lads versed in the ways of the family, known and trusted from their childhood. To work for the Morland family, especially with the horses, was deemed an honour, and competition for jobs was fierce. Parents liked to get their boys taken on as young as possible.

None of them would do for Nicky, however. James was as dismayed as his head man when Nicholas announced in January that he had found a groom himself. The man, Ferrars, was practically a foreigner, for though he had been born in Wetherby he had been working 'down south' for some years and probably, the head man confided to James, learned bad foreign habits down there. Not only that, but he was an extremely disagreeable man to look at — small and weaselly, with prematurely thinning ginger hair, bad teeth, and a face covered so indiscriminately with freckles, blackheads and blemishes that it was hard to tell them apart. His manner was obsequious, his eyes were never quite still, and James felt he smiled too much — altogether too much for a man with green teeth.

345

'I don't know how you can want a man like that about you,' James said fastidiously.

Nicholas was unrepentant. 'But I like him, Papa, and I don't like any of the boys from Twelvetrees. *Mayn't* I have someone I like? I thought as Morland Place would be mine one day —'

'Oh, yes, yes, of course, if you really want him,' James said, as much puzzled as disappointed. 'Provided he does his work properly. You must take him on a month's trial to begin with.'

James pinned his hopes on the man's failing to meet Twelvetrees' high standards. But Ferrars proved disappointingly efficient. Hastings, the head man, and Cooper, the rough rider — who had worked together for so long they hardly needed to speak to each other any more — watched the new man like a hawk, and slipped in after he had left the stables to look his horses over for any speck of dirt or sign of neglect, but they found nothing. At the end of the month they reported glumly to James that they could find no fault with his work, and James had no alternative but to hire him.

After another two months, Hastings could still only report that he didn't trust the new man, without having any reason he could put his finger on. 'He never sits and talks with the rest of us when he has his leisure. Always off somewhere on his own,' Hastings complained. 'Cleans his tack when there's no-one else in the tack-room, too. No-one cleans tack alone if they can help it. It's not friendly.'

'Can't dismiss a man for not being friendly,' James said regretfully.

'No, master,' Hastings agreed sadly. 'And he and Master Nicholas are as thick as thieves.'

So one day early in April it was Ferrars who brought the horses up to the house for Master Nicholas. Nicky meant to ride into York to visit his tailor for a new spring coat.

'And there ought to be a parcel for me at the post office, sent up from London. I want you to call in for it while I'm at the tailor's,' Nicholas said as they rode out through the barbican.

'Very good, sir.'

346

Nicky turned to fix him with significant look. 'It's some books — Italian books — with lots of illustrations. Curious illustrations. If the parcel has arrived, I don't want anyone to know about it — anyone at home, that is.'

'Very good, sir,' Ferrars said with a different emphasis.

They turned onto the track and rode on in silence. They had only gone a few yards when Nicholas saw his brother coming home across the fields from the direction of Acomb Wood, at that easy dog-lope of his which ate up the distance. Nicholas turned his head away at once, so that Bendy shouldn't know he had seen him. He had noticed since he came home that Bendy quite often came back from that direction, when he had been off on one of his solitary rambles. Now what could be so fascinating that he went there all alone and secretly twice a week or more? Acomb Wood itself, perhaps, he mused. Maybe Bendy had found another fox? Or badgers even. No doubt there was some little secret animal the boy was visiting; and if Bendy had a secret, Nicholas wanted to know about it. He was master — or would be soon enough — and there were to be no secrets from *him* on his own estate!

Fortunately, owing to his own foresight, the means were at hand. 'I wonder where Master Benedict goes, when he goes off in that direction,' Nicholas said aloud. 'Do you suppose anyone knows, Ferrars?'

'No sir, I shouldn't think so,' Ferrars said neutrally.

'I wonder if anyone could find out,' Nicholas said musingly.

'Only if they was to follow him, sir; and no-one at Morland Place would have the impertinence to do that.'

'No, I suppose they wouldn't. Unless it were made worth their while.'

'Well, sir, that *might* be a different case,' Ferrars agreed.

'If, say, there were someone — a gentleman perhaps — who wanted to know where Master Benedict went, and a person were to find it out discreetly, without Master Benedict knowing — well, that gentleman might be very grateful to the person.'

'How grateful would you say that would be, sir?' Ferrars asked indifferently.

347

'A guinea, and a day off to spend it,' Nicholas said promptly. It was a lot, but knowledge of that sort was worth it to him. And besides, if he went short he could always get his mother to give him a guinea on some plea or other. His mother never denied him anything.

'That's fairish grateful, sir, I'd say,' Ferrars said judiciously, and they rode on in silence.

Two weeks later, Nicholas was up at Twelvetrees discussing with Ferrars and Hastings the arrangements for letting down the hunters for the summer. 'I want the shoes off them before you turn them out. Can't risk them kicking and blemishing each other,' Nicholas said. 'You'll have to keep them up another day or two, Hastings, until the smith comes.'

Hastings was piqued, and allowed it just to show. 'I can take the shoes off them myself, Mr Nicholas, or Cooper can. We've both done it a hundred times.'

'I'd rather the smith did it,' Nicholas said shortly. 'They're valuable horses.'

'Then Cooper can take them down to the smithy, sir, if your man's too busy to go,' Hastings said with delicate irony.

'And have them come back shoeless on that stony road? We'd have cracked hooves and a whole world of trouble,' Nicholas snapped. 'I'm not having my hunters risked that way. You keep them up and send for the smith. Those are my orders. Do you think my father begrudges the feed and the bedding?'

Hastings was too good a servant to say what he really thought. To keep Nicholas's hunters in the stables two days longer not only meant three stalls he could not use for other horses, but three lively horses which would have to be given walking exercise every day. And since Ferrars was out most of the time accompanying his master, it would be Hastings' lads who would have to give the exercise, keeping them from other tasks and making more work for everyone else.

'Just as you say, sir,' Hastings said at last, and breathing hard, he left them.

'Impudent man,' Nicholas muttered, and bent to run his hand over Nightingale's tendons again. 'Do you think these legs ought to be poulticed, Ferrars?'

'At Lord Somerville's we used to stand them in the stream,

348

sir, for half an hour three or four times a day. The cold running water brought the legs down a treat,' Ferrars said.

'That sounds just the thing! You'd better tell Hastings to arrange it. I shall need you with me today.'

'Very good sir.' As Nicky straightened up, Ferrars glanced quickly around to see that they were not overheard, and lowered his voice. 'About that other matter, sir.'

'What other matter?' Nicky asked vaguely.

'About where a certain person goes twice a week, all alone.'

'Ah, that!' Nicky had forgotten. He stared at Ferrars, his breath coming more quickly. 'You've found out?'

'There's a small hut on the edge of Low Moor, just in the fringes of Acomb Wood, on the far side of the wood from here.'

'I know it.'

'It's a sort of shippon really, but no-one uses it now. There's a couple of stooks of musty hay in there, and some broken traps left by the gamekeeper, that's all.'

'He keeps an animal there!' Nicholas said excitedly. 'I knew it! He was always mad for pets. What is it — a fox-cub? A lame deer?'

'No sir,' Ferrars said quietly. 'He goes there to meet someone.'

'Meet someone?' Nicholas frowned with bewilderment. 'Who on earth would he meet in an empty shed?'

'A girl from Eastfield Farm — maid-of-all-work called Annie. She was a pauper prentice from the workhouse. The Pikes took her in as a scullery maid some years ago.'

Nicholas frowned, pursuing memory. 'Yes, I think I remember some draggle-tail in a sacking apron. But what can he want to meet a child like that for?'

Ferrars smiled mirthlessly. 'Beg pardon, sir, but you've been away a few years, haven't you? It isn't a child he meets, not by any means.'

Nicholas's eyes widened. 'Good God! You don't mean —?' He calculated the years. 'But — but that's disgusting! Outrageous! Benedict's only —'

'Grown up, sir — both of them. I don't know what the girl

was like before, but she's come up a treat now.' His hands sketched vague but comprehensible shapes in the air. 'Plump as a spring chicken, and as tender, I'd guess, sir.'

'Is she now?' Nicholas mused. So his little brother was keeping a secret animal, all right — but it wasn't the way Nicky had expected. Well well! He grinned to himself. That was bound to prove a useful piece of information. His first impulse was to tell his father, or to threaten to tell his father, so as to see Bendy squirm. But on second thoughts, it might be more fun to have her himself, take her away from Bendy and get at him that way. A pauper slut wouldn't be difficult to seduce, especially since he had money and Bendy had none. In fact, he couldn't think how his brother had been securing her services until now. Unless, of course, he thought with a sudden coldness, Ferrars was mistaken.

He narrowed his eyes. 'Are you sure about this? How do you know what he gets up to in that hut?'

'Followed him, sir; and watched them through the window,' Ferrars said, and a mossy smile slipped past his thin lips at the memory. 'Saw everything.' He coughed slightly. 'You did say a guinea, sir?'

'Yes, yes, you shall have it,' Nicholas said absently. He was thinking hard. At last he said, 'I think I may have some other little tasks for you to do for me — private tasks, you understand. If you perform them to my satisfaction, you won't find me ungenerous.'

'I'm always happy to oblige you, sir,' Ferrars said meekly.

In February there had been another political shock: Lord Liverpool was discovered unconscious in his library, having suffered a paralytic stroke from which he was not expected to recover. He had been Prime Minister since 1812 — an astonishing fifteen years. He had often been derided as a man without abilities, and yet it was hard to think who else could have held together through peace and war so many cabinets of such varied composition.

Canning was the obvious choice as a successor, and the King wanted him in order to keep out the Whigs, but there were those of his own party who distrusted him. Wellington,

Eldon, Peel and some others thought him too liberal, and disagreed with his views on tariff reform and the Catholic Emancipation. They resigned; and after considerable bargaining four Whigs agreed to join the Cabinet to form an uneasy coalition government.

In spring a zoological garden was opened in Regent's Park, with dire warnings in the newspapers about the danger of wild beasts escaping and devouring the good citizens of Harley Street and Cavendish Square. More warnings were issued over the opening, as a result of Brougham's activities, of a new University in Gower Street which had no connections with the Church. Non-conformists and even atheists were to be allowed to study there, and there were to be no religious tests for its teachers either — to the outrage of many who believed that the separation of education from religion would bring about a new Sodom. Moreover, the 'Godless Institution' intended to abandon the exclusively classical curriculum of Oxford and Cambridge and introduce 'modern' and 'scientific' studies, on the basis of utility rather than hallowed precedent. The damage to men's minds, and to society as a whole, of such a proceeding was pointed out with palpitating horror to the readers of the more serious journals.

These terrors passed Lucy by, however, for she had much weightier matters to occupy her mind all that spring of 1827. Rosamund was to be married to Lord Batchworth; and since they wanted to be married quietly at home, while Rosamund particularly wanted to have her family about her, Lucy was to travel to Manchester for the first time in her life.

'It isn't Australia or China, Mama,' Tom said with amusement when he saw the scale of her preparations. 'Manchester's only about a hundred and eighty miles away — not even as far as York.'

'Never mind! York is a proper city with a cathedral and fine houses and *proper roads*! Manchester is just an overgrown village filled with factories and Irish peasants. Why, George Brummell gave up his commission in the Hussars rather than be posted there! There's simply no knowing what one will encounter. As to the journey — Batchworth assures me there are posting inns all the way, so I have to assume we will be able to get changes, but if we should find ourselves stranded, I want to be sure we have everything we may need with us.'

Even Docwra, Lucy's maid, who had come from Ireland herself a very long time ago, was gloomy. 'Far better Lady Rosamund should have come to London and got wed properly,' she grumbled to Parslow. 'Manchester's a rough sort of town, from all I've heard, and full of people from Sligo and such like uncivilised places. Sure, an' what would they want to be living there for anyway? Hasn't his lordship plenty o' money, and couldn't he buy my lady a nice house in London like any proper gentleman?'

Lucy, Danby and Thomas were to go; but it was not long before their party was increased by the addition of Roland and Thalia. Roland said that Rosamund was his sister, and of course he wanted to see her married; but Thomas had the uneasy suspicion that it was Thalia who had initiated the idea. Lucy was pleased all the same. 'Rosamund wants her family about her. I'm glad you want to come, Aylesbury, and that Thalia has no objection.'

When it came to planning the journey, Lucy was torn between the speed of a chaise-and-four and the stoutness of a travelling coach. Danby with an inward shudder, finally persuaded her that the less time they spent on the road the less chance there was for an accident to find them, so a chaise-and-four it was to be.

Thomas took over the task of secretary, and arranged everything. He not only wrote ahead for the accommodation — for they were to stay overnight at Leicester — but he also thought it prudent to order the horses well in advance. Though he did not share his mother's fears that the road would prove so primitive and unfrequented as to be quite without post houses, he did think that two nobleman's chaises travelling together and requiring eight horses each change might strain resources.

The servants, by dint of spending much longer on the road on each of the two days, were to manage with a single pair only. Thomas didn't envy them. Although Roland had generously offered to share his man with Thomas, Lucy could not contemplate travelling so far and for so long without Parslow as well as Docwra, and so with Thalia's woman and Lord Theakston's man they would still be crowded five to the carriage, to say nothing of the overnight luggage which had to go with them. The bulk of the luggage was sent on ahead by carrier so as to be there when they arrived.

The day came, and the departure was enough of a spectacle to draw quite a crowd of idlers. Two handsome carriages and eight fine horses, along with four post boys in their drab coats and black caps, would have been rewarding enough to draw spectators; but there was luggage to be carried out and strapped on, a large basket of provisions to invite speculation, and finally the ceremony of the servants lining up to say goodbye as the gentry folk came down the steps in all the glory of elegant travelling-clothes.

Where they were going and why was warmly canvassed amongst the onlookers, most of whom had never been more than two miles from the street where they were born; and even after the carriages had moved off — amid much ostentatious whip-cracking from the boys, who liked an audience as well as the next man — the crowd did not at once disperse. They stayed to watch the butler remove the knocker from the door and the footmen close the shutters on the lower windows, and to debate amongst themselves what it must be like to travel with no greater trouble to oneself than climbing into a waiting coach.

The party took their long stop at the Swan in Bedford, a handsome establishment on the river front beside the bridge, where a collation had been prepared for them in a private parlour. After Bedford Lucy began to feel that they were entering foreign territory as the names on the signposts became less familiar. Until then, the Great North Road, her touchstone of civilisation, had run more or less parallel with the Leicester road, but now they began to diverge, flinging apart more and more steeply and plunging Lucy into *terra incognita*. But the road was still excellent, with a fine surface, plenty of traffic about, and the toll keepers prompt at their gates in response to the peremptory summons of the horn.

'Quite as good as the Great North Road,' she confessed grudgingly.

'What a marvellous thing it is,' Theakston responded, 'to be rushing along at twelve miles an hour with hardly a bump to discommode us — changes ready and waiting — off again within minutes. One end of the country to the other in no more than a couple of days. In fact at this time of year, if we'd cared to set off at dawn and take no stops, we could have been in Manchester by sunset of the same day! What times these are for travellers!'

'And what a difference in our lifetimes,' Lucy said. 'Even ten years ago the turnpikes were not nearly so well-kept as this. Do you remember that stretch of the North road near Hatfield, Danby? Butter-maker's Row, you used to call it, it shook us up so much.'

'It's not so much the keeping as the method of laying the road that makes the difference,' Danby said. 'With the Macadam method, the road actually gets better as it's used.'

'Does it? How can that be?' Lucy said in surprise. 'I thought they just used a better sort of stone nowadays.'

'No, Mama,' Tom answered her with a smile. 'It's laid in a special way, with the stones end up. As the carriage wheels go over them, they grind the edges of the stones into dust, and the dust gets packed down into all the little gaps in between. So the surface gets harder and smoother all the time.'

'It's hard to believe, but I take your word for it. But why don't they lay all roads like that?' Lucy demanded.

'The expense, I suppose,' Danby said. 'Who would pay for it? Unless there's plenty of traffic, a turnpike wouldn't pay. And how many private landlords would be willing to build an expensive road for other people to use?'

They stopped for the night at The Bell in Leicester, and in spite of the ease and comfort of the journey, Lucy was glad to get out of the carriage in which she had been sitting for eight out of the last eleven hours. The servants had arrived not long before, and the rooms Tom had ordered were ready with hot water, wax candles, and fires in the grates — welcome even at this time of year after so long sitting still. In her room Lucy found Docwra laying out her evening gown and supervising two inn servants who were putting Lucy's own sheets on the bed. Docwra had spent twelve out of the last twelve hours sitting in a carriage, and she moved a little stiffly. Lucy reflected briefly how her bones must ache — she was not a young woman any more.

'Is your own room comfortable?' she asked. 'Are they taking care of you?'

'Yes, my lady, thank you,' Docwra answered. 'I'm in with Lady Aylesbury's woman, but it's a good, big bed.'

Lucy thought of Parslow, who hated sharing a room, never mind a bed. Would he have to share with Roland's man as well as Bird? She had known him before now choose to sleep with the horses in preference to such a fate. 'How will Parslow manage?' she asked.

Docwra waited until the inn maids had departed before turning to her mistress with a grin. 'He has a room to himself, my lady — hardly more than a cupboard, really, but private all the same, which is all he cares about. Mr Thomas arranged it, the way Parslow wouldn't have to find himself a haystack for the night,' she added with a grin. 'Mr Thomas knows everyone's little foibles, my lady.'

'So it seems,' Lucy said. She believed in taking good care of her servants, but even she would not have gone to so much trouble, coming of a generation when a little stoicism was considered no bad thing for master or man. 'Well, be sure they give you a good hot supper, and not just cold cuts.'

'Thank you, my lady. Mr Thomas ordered that for us too. There's a roast ham and pease pudding, I do know — for one of the maids mentioned — and what else besides we shall see. We shan't go hungry, my lady.'

'Mr Thomas seems to have thought of everything,' Lucy said with a small smile. 'I can't wait to find out what he's ordered for our dinner.'

The Bell was noted for its cooking. The party gathered, changed and refreshed, and with the good spirits which usually followed being released from a carriage, to an excellent dinner which featured amongst other dishes ducklings with green peas, roast carp with a sharp sauce, a fine dish of broccoli with eggs, and a steak pudding so meltingly

355

delicious it could be eaten with a fork alone. The inn's cellars provided a sound if not distinguished claret, and since Hicks had had the foresight to put in two bottles of his lordship's own brandy 'just in case', the meal promised to end as well as it began.

Lord Theakston kept Thalia amused with outrageously exaggerated tales of his life in the Hussars, and Thomas used all his skills to draw Roland out and create a conversation between him and their mother — never an easy thing to do, but well worth the effort — and the evening passed delightfully. Lucy retired to bed feeling that Danby was right, and that these were great times for travellers.

The next morning Thalia suggested that Thomas rode in the Aylesbury carriage, so as to give Lord and Lady Theakston more room to stretch their legs. Roland endorsed the request eagerly — Thalia had not been the best of conversationalists during yesterday's journey — so Tom was obliged to consent. The party took a nuncheon at Matlock, but did not stay long, since Thomas told them that the longest part of the journey was to come.

'I thought we must be almost there,' Lucy complained.

'It's not so far in miles,' Tom explained, 'but after Rowsley the road leaves the Derwent river and starts to climb. We have to go over the hills to get to Buxton, you see, so the travelling is bound to be slower.'

'What will the road be like?' Lucy asked. Here, she thought, must be where they parted with civilisation.

'Buxton is quite a noted beauty spot,' Thomas said. 'A great many people of fashion travel this way to view the scenery, so I think the road must be quite good. The post boys think well enough of it.'

'Nevertheless, I think you had better come in our carriage,' Lucy said, 'just in case anything happens.'

The scenery was magnificent, and despite the slower travelling there was not one of them but was glad of the opportunity to see the country. But they were all, if for different reasons, beginning to think about journey's end with fond anticipation by the time they caught their first glimpse of Manchester in the distance. They mounted a hill

356

top, and saw before them a fine open champion, watered by the River Irwell, and dotted with good-looking houses with parks and pleasure gardens. Beyond was the town itself, a close-packed huddle of buildings which seemed to crouch under a thick pall of black smoke.

'Good God!' Lucy exclaimed, 'What is it? Is there a fire?'

'No, Mama. That's the smoke from the factories,' Tom answered.

The tall chimneys reared up from amongst the lower roofs, dozens of them, hundreds perhaps, and each one spouting its column of smoke to attach it to the blanket above.

'How can people live like that?' Lucy wondered to herself. No-one answered. Country dwellers always complained about the smoke and dirt of London, but it was nothing like this. A silence almost of apprehension descended on them as the carriage took them closer.

'My parents went to visit a factory once,' Lucy remembered suddenly. 'It was in a valley by a river — a water-mill. I remember my mother saying that when the millhands finished work, they had a lovely green valley to come out into.'

Theakston roused himself. 'It's not all bad you know, my dear. Think of the employment provided, think of the goods created— cheaper clothing for thousands and hundreds of thousands. We ought to see that smoke as the sign of vitality and useful activity.'

'That's true,' Tom said. 'I expect the mill masters are glad to see it — and the mill hands too. It means everything is going on as it should.'

But still Lucy didn't like Manchester, and she didn't know why Lord Batchworth should choose to live there. The outskirts were pleasant enough, where the houses of the rich were situated, but the centre of the town was dark, grey, grim and ugly. There were hardly any private carriages, few distinguished public buildings, only one street of decent shops as far as she could see; and always to either side glimpses of vile, dark, filthy alleys and courts, cramped and mean. The people she saw, too, seemed pallid, undersized and sickly, not a handsome or well-looking person amongst

357

them. She was used to Yorkshire where the lower orders were prosperous, where even the poor were stout, hale and well-set-up in comparison with this, their children ill-shod and dirty but still rosy-faced. She was glad when they left the centre behind and passed once again into the greener outskirts of Cheetham. They were to spend a day or two at Batchworth House before travelling out to Grasscroft, where the wedding would take place.

Batchworth House was handsome enough, though rather over-decorated for Lucy's taste; but they were ushered into a large hall by decent-looking servants, and there could be no doubt as to the warmth of their greeting by Rosamund and Batchworth, who came down to receive them.

'What is this place I find you in?' Lucy said bemusedly as she kissed her daughter. 'I feel as if I've travelled past the mouth of hell itself to get here.'

'Ah, Manchester is a surprise when you see it for the first time,' Batchworth answered cheerfully. 'But it has its own charm, I assure you. And the smoke may be a nuisance, but it is very necessary. We look on it as a sign of prosperity. When the chimneys are smoking, all is well.'

'Just what I said,' Tom remarked. 'You see, Mama, how I understand the modern world?'

'I don't think I want to,' Lucy said.

'But you enjoyed the benefit of the fine roads all the way here,' he said persuasively.

'If the roads hadn't been good, I shouldn't have come at all,' Lucy pointed out.

'Well now you are here, Lady Theakston,' said Batchworth, 'you must see the inside of a mill, so that you know what it's all for! Do let me take you on a tour of one of my factories tomorrow. I'm sure it will amuse you.'

'Amaze me, perhaps you mean,' said Lucy.

'That too,' Batchworth promised.

CHAPTER EIGHTEEN

Almost despite herself, Lucy found the mill impressive. Only Lucy, Danby and Thomas went. The invitation was extended to all, but Thalia expressed refined horror at the idea of entering a factory, and Roland naturally chose to stay behind with her, though he would really have liked to see what a mill was like. When Thomas did not decline the invitation, Thalia half wanted to change her mind, but with his satirical eye on her, felt she could not. 'I'll show you the sights of Manchester instead,' Rosamund promised, and she had to be content with that.

'It's my third mill I want to show you,' Batchworth said in the carriage on the way to Ordsall. 'It used to be a spinning mill, but I've enlarged it and changed the plan to my own design, and I'm immensely proud of it. I believe it will be the pattern for the future. I call it my cotton factory because all the processes for making the cloth are carried out under the one roof.'

It was certainly an impressive building, built in the shape of a letter E without the central stroke. The long side was three hundred feet long, the wings each sixty feet; and the whole was seven stories high, brick-built under a slate roof. A little behind the right-hand wing was the mill chimney, a massive affair mounted on a small knoll.

'Allowing for the digging-out underneath the knoll,' Batchworth explained, 'it gives us a three-hundred-foot draw to the furnaces.'

'It's a large place,' Lord Theakston commented mildly as the carriage pulled up in the yard. 'Bigger than I supposed.'

359

'But when I tell you that in this one factory we do all the work that would formerly have occupied the entire population of a district of three or four villages — carding, roving, spinning, weaving —'

'Good God!' said Theakston, struck by the idea. 'You mean you employ thousands of people in there?'

'Only hundreds. You see, the most skilled hand weaver, working without interruption, accident or sickness — which of course is never the case — can produce at best two pieces a week. One piece is more usual. But a steam loom can produce three and a half pieces a week, week in week out; and mine are of the new design, so a boy or girl of fourteen — most of ours are girls as you'll see — can operate two looms quite easily. Seven pieces a week per operator, without variation in speed or quality. Consistency is a great factor.'

He led the way into the left-hand wing of the factory, where his office was.

'But is the work as good?' Lucy asked. Again, she had only her Yorkshire experience to inform her. It was the wisdom of the North Riding, where only woollen goods were produced, that no steam loom could ever replace the hand weaver. In the West Riding steam looms were making rapid progress with worsted weaving, but even there much more was still woven by hand than by machine, and the machine was seen as an adjunct, not something that could ever take over completely.

'Oh, it's much better,' Batchworth said. 'You see, a hand weaver can't produce a piece of uniform evenness. A weaker or stronger blow with the lathe alters the thickness of the cloth. As his arm grows tired, his blows will be weaker; then he stops for the night and begins again the next morning with a stronger blow than when he left off. But the machine gives an exact and steady blow, precisely the same every time from the beginning to the end of the cloth, and the result is very fine and perfectly uniform cloth. It is simply not possible for a hand weaver to produce that quality. Come, I'll show you.'

In his office he brought out sample lengths of cloth, one hand-woven, the other machine-woven. The difference was remarkable. Lucy and Danby, each in their own way a connoisseur of cloth, were instantly converted.

'There is no comparison,' Lucy agreed. 'I can't think why anyone uses hand weavers at all.'

'They won't for much longer. Already the hand weavers are finding it difficult to get work, and as the design of the machinery improves and the machines themselves become cheaper to make, the process will accelerate. The cost of installing the steam looms, together with the uncertainty of the market, has inhibited mill masters in the past. But that's changing now. At the end of the war there were only about two thousand power looms in the whole country; today there must be twenty thousand. And in ten years' time I would wager there'll be a hundred thousand.'

'And no hand weavers?' Tom asked.

'Not for cotton.' He smiled suddenly. 'Of course, Jasper Hobsbawn will tell you a different tale. He is convinced there must be room in the business for both sorts, and he employs as many hand weavers as he can out of pure sentiment. I'm afraid your niece, ma'am, drives him on.'

'Sophie?'

'Mrs Hobsbawn's heart is so tender she would sooner ruin herself and her husband than see an out-of-work weaver starve.'

'What would you do with them, sir?' Tom asked.

Batchworth shrugged. 'I'm sorry for them, of course, and I give my tithe to the charity for their relief, but it would be a nonsense for me to give them work which can better be done by the machines. In the end, that would benefit no-one — my business would fail and all my hands would be out of work. No, the hand weavers must learn other work, or they must starve. It can't be helped.'

'History is pitiless to the loser,' Theakston said gravely.

'Quite right too,' Lucy said vigorously, with all the certainty of one of history's winners. Her husband looked at her with an inward smile. He remembered how she had run away to sea at the age of fourteen; how she had organised a hospital in Brussels after the battle of Waterloo. Lucy would always have survived, whatever the circumstances.

'While we are here in my office,' Batchworth said, 'perhaps I can show you the plans of the factory. I think you'll

361

understand it better if you see the drawings first. I designed it myself — with the help of engineers of course — and I believe it to be a model of economy and efficiency.'

He laid out the plans on his table, and they gathered round him while he traced the areas with his forefinger.

'You saw the chimney, of course, and that connects by underground flues to the boilers, which are housed *here*, next to the engines. Two eighty-horse-power steam engines — they take up four stories of the far wing.

'Now the main building — the looms must have a stable base, so those are housed on the ground floor, here. Weaving needs a warm, humid atmosphere, so we pump hot water from the boilers in pipes continuously round the perimeter of each shed...

'You see in this factory we spin both the warp and the weft yarns ourselves. The warp is spun by throstle frames on the first and second floors, the weft by mules on the fourth and fifth floors. Between them, on the third floor, are the preparation rooms. We have carding engines here, then drawing machines, then the roving machines at the end which turn the drawn fibres into fine cords, called rovings. From there the rovings can be taken either upstairs to the mules or downstairs to the throstles.'

'Sensible arrangement,' Theakston commented.

'Thank you. It was my own thought,' said Batchworth, pleased. 'For the rest, the upper floors hold various dressing-rooms, and this wing, as you see, houses the offices, the counting-house, and the storerooms. So, now, perhaps you'd like to see the machines themselves?'

The first, most immediate impression inside the factory was of the terrible din of the machines, a demented, deafening whirring and clicking punctuated by a regular thumping sound like the beat of a giant heart. It was hard to bear, harder even than the pungent smells of oil and cotton and dirty bodies; or the peculiar airlessness which made it so hard to breathe, which was a combination of heat, lack of ventilation, and the cotton dust with which every breath was laden. Lucy, perhaps inured by her experiences in ships and hospitals, soon managed to shut these inconvenient sensa-

362

tions out from her consciousness, and became wholly engrossed by the machines which Batchworth presented and explained to her as though they were favourite children. Her husband did his best, and was able to evince a certain amount of interest, though he was concentrating much more on not touching anything, and counting the moments until he could leave the place.

Tom found more interest in studying the operators. Few were men, and of those none seemed to be older than twenty-two or -three; they were thin and pallid, and had about them a crooked or unfinished look, as though they had been badly moulded at some malleable stage of their creation. Tom wondered if there were no older men because none lived to a greater age: perhaps something fundamental unfitted men for factory work. It did not seem an impossible hypothesis.

The women were better, cleaner and more respectably dressed, and seeming fitter and more alert. The younger ones were mostly loom operators, the older ones spinners; and they had energy and interest enough to glance up from their work as the visitors went by, and, in some cases, to follow Tom slyly with their eyes. But the majority of the workers were children. They were small and sickly-looking, bare-footed, extremely dirty and ill-dressed. Some of them had deformities, missing fingers and toes, scars of old injuries; all of them looked undernourished, and many appeared to be no older than seven, though Tom supposed it might be hard to tell their true age. They scrambled about under the machines like little pallid trolls, and yet nimbly enough, and with extraordinary confidence. Tom felt he would not have cared to go so near those flying levers and wheels.

When the party had finished with the machines and passed out onto the comparative quiet of the staircase again, Tom asked Batchworth, 'Do you have many accidents with the machines? They look so quick and so dangerous, and with all those children running about —'

'No, very few really,' Batchworth said. 'The modern machines are much safer than the older types, and the dangerous ones are boxed in and only skilled hands allowed near them. Accidents are so very expensive, we can't afford to take chances. The engineers' bills are far greater than the surgeons', I can promise you! Of course, there will always be some hands who are careless or stupid, but we haven't had a serious accident here in two years.'

'But the children — I couldn't help noticing that many of them had scars and missing fingers —'

'Yes, I'm afraid that's true,' Batchworth said. 'The conditions they live in are so bad, and their parents so little able to watch over them, that they're always hurting themselves. Gangrene and other infections account for a great many amputations; and some of the children have fingers and toes bitten off by rats when they're still babies.'

'Good God, how disgusting,' Lucy cried.

'The old tenements and the cellars are the worst places, where the poorest of the Irish live. Often the men are too debilitated to work even at the simplest tasks, and the children go out to work to keep the whole family. I won't take children on without at least one of their parents to oversee them, but some of the mill masters do, because they work so cheaply — a false economy in my view. But the worst of it is there are so many Irish coming in, there are simply not houses enough in Manchester, and the competition for the poorest lodging means that even some of the factory hands are badly accommodated.'

'Isn't Mr Hobsbawn doing something about that?' Lucy asked. 'Héloïse told me he had a scheme for building houses for his mill hands.'

'Oh yes,' said Batchworth, leading the way out. 'John Skelwith built sixty houses for his factory hands, and very much needed they were too; but it's the merest drop in the ocean. Other undertakers have seized on the idea since then, and Skelwith is very busy at the moment, competing with our native builders to provide the maximum number of houses for the smallest possible outlay. I'll take you past one of his schemes on the way home, if you like.'

'I should be interested to see what's he's up to,' Lucy said.

'But for every house they build, three more families appear. And it isn't just the Irish — country labourers who can't get work through sickness or ineptitude come into town looking for lighter jobs; and unemployed weavers; and petty criminals who think they can escape notice here.'

'It's the same in all cities,' Lucy pointed out.

'I suppose that's true, ma'am. It's just that with us it's all happening so quickly.'

James and Héloïse arrived the next day, with Benedict. Lucy greeted them affectionately and surveyed them with interest. She thought James was looking extremely well: apart from his grey hair, he looked much younger than his years. On the other hand she thought Héloïse — who was only a year older than Lucy — was looking ill. She had always been small and thin, but now she seemed no more than skin and bone. Her face was lined and her eyes lacklustre. She looked, Lucy thought disapprovingly, like a little old woman.

'I can see you must have been doing things you shouldn't, Jamie,' Lucy said when he had given her a hearty kiss. 'You always thrived on wrong-doing. What has this brother of mine been up to, Héloïse?'

A quick glance passed between them, but Héloïse said only, 'Nothing, nothing. It is good to see you, dear Lucy! You have not changed in the least.'

'I've been getting about the country, that's all,' James answered the question his wife had avoided. 'A change of scene does everyone good. I try to persuade Héloïse to come with me, but she prefers to stay at home.'

'Someone must take care of things,' Héloïse said.

'That's what Nicholas is for, my love. Leave him in charge, let him try his wings. He can't learn too early. You wouldn't believe how hard I had to work to persuade her even to come this far and for a few days,' he added to Lucy.

'Nicholas is too young,' Héloïse said. 'Morland Place is my responsibility.'

'Father Moineau will keep him right,' James said carelessly. 'That's why we brought Benedict, so as to leave him free to keep an eye on Nicky. You need a rest as much as anyone, Marmoset — and I mean to see you have one.'

'Father Moineau cannot take care of the house,' Héloïse pointed out.

'Mrs Thomson is quite capable of taking care of things for

a few days,' James said. 'And if there's anything she doesn't understand, she can always send word to Mathilde, and she can send Miss Rosedale over.'

'Miss Rosedale has five little girls to take care of,' Héloïse said, and then with the air of one changing the subject, turned to Lucy to say, 'Did I mention in my last letter that Mathilde is with child again?'

'No, you didn't,' Lucy said, trying for her sake to be interested. 'I thought they didn't mean to have any more.'

'They didn't. I think it came as a surprise to them both. But Mathilde is delighted — she's sure it will be a boy this time, and she so wants to give John a son.'

'And is John pleased?'

'To tell the truth, I think he is not. He is convinced it will be another girl, which will mean another dowry to find one day. But when it comes, he will love it. Babies bring their own love with them.'

'Hmph,' said Lucy, who had always thought babies quite unnecessarily lacking in charm. 'John seems to be doing well for himself, if what Batchworth tells me is true. His housing schemes are everywhere in Manchester. Tell me, what on earth made you invest in one?'

'It was James who decided on it, not me,' Héloïse said mildly.

'But the money is yours, after all,' Lucy said, with no thought for masculine pride.

James, who had been talking to Rosamund and Jes, caught the drift and turned back to say, 'What does anyone invest in anything for? Profit, to be sure.'

'But how will there be profit from houses built for the poor?' Lucy asked.

'They'll pay rent, of course. The mill hands are not indigents, you know. They're the elite of the lower orders.'

'That's true,' Batchworth said. 'When we're on full-time working, they earn good wages.'

'But as we drove through Manchester, I saw people of the lowest condition down every side street — practically beggars in rags. Don't tell me you can make a profit out of them!'

'What you saw was not factory operatives,' Batchworth

said. 'I did tell you, Lady Theakston, that we get hundreds of labourers and petty criminals flooding into Manchester in the hope of work, most of them unfit for any but the most menial tasks. Factory work is too skilled for them, and when they can't get jobs digging or hauling or unloading waggons, they starve, or turn to begging or stealing. They give a bad name to factories in general because visitors think all people in these parts are mill hands.'

Lucy did not look convinced, but Rosamund asked her, 'What did you think of the new housing, Mother? Jes took you to see the building at St Loy Street, didn't he?'

'I don't quite know what I'm supposed to think of it. They seem to be fitting a great many houses into a small space, but I suppose that's all to the good, isn't it?'

'Sophie's worried because the St Loy scheme crowds them even closer than Morland's Rents. It was John Skelwith suggested making the rooms smaller — nine feet by twelve instead of ten by fourteen — so that they can get another two houses to the row.'

'Is that wrong?' James asked, perhaps a little defensively.

Rosamund frowned. 'I don't know. The houses are already so cramped, back-to-back with no gardens, facing each other across the narrowest possible court, no paving, no water, only one privy to twenty houses —'

'Better that than no house at all,' James said quickly.

'Better that than the tenements and the cellars,' Jes agreed. 'Anyway, we mustn't be having this conversation when Sophie and Jasper arrive, or we'll talk of nothing else the whole week.'

'What would you like to talk about — politics?' Lucy enquired ironically.

James grinned. 'I don't think so. Batchworth's views on the Corn Laws are bound to be in direct antipathy to mine. Your friend Huskisson is out to ruin us with his sliding scale! Even in bad years we can't seem to get the price of wheat up to eighty shillings. We need more protection, not less.'

'But even at the rate it is, it's still too high to feed the people at a reasonable price,' Jes responded instantly. 'The protection does no good to anyone. You farmers are growing corn on land

367

that was never meant for it, that's what's wrong. It costs you too much to grow, so of course you don't get a decent return when you sell. You should be turning that marginal land over to sheep, or vegetables, or poultry. That way —'

'Oh stop!' Rosamund cried, putting her hands over her ears. 'The next step from here is always parliamentary reform, and I can't bear that argument again! I think we should go in and take a nuncheon, and try to talk in a civilised way about my plans for redecorating.'

Batchworth grinned. 'What, wallpapers and drapes and carpets? Is that what you call civilised?'

She slipped a hand through his arm. 'If you're *very* good, I'll let you tell them about the conservatory you want to build on the back of the house.'

'Ah, that's different.' Jes put on the parody of a meek face. 'I'll be good, Mama!'

'They seem happy, don't you think?' Lucy asked Héloïse. They were sitting side by side on a sofa in the vast drawing-room, while the rest of the company was occupied in various ways about the room. Sophie and Jasper had arrived with Fanny in time for dinner, and they were all to travel to Grasscroft together tomorrow. At the moment Sophie was turning for Rosamund, who was playing the piano while Thalia sang. Jes and Jasper were standing nearby deep in a conversation about canals to which Benedict and Roland were listening with interest. James and Lord Theakston were having a discussion about horses to which Thomas was pretending to listen with interest.

Héloïse looked up from her needlework. 'Sophie and Jasper? Yes, I think it has proved a very happy marriage. James and I were doubtful when he asked for her. I suppose no parent ever thinks any man is good enough for their daughter, and Jasper had no fortune. But it was him she wanted — and it seems as though she chose wisely. Certainly he is devoted to her.'

Lucy smiled. 'I agree with all that, but actually it was Rosamund and Lord Batchworth I meant.'

Héloïse laughed ruefully. 'A mother's selfishness. I am

sorry.' She looked again at the group on the other side of the room, and saw Batchworth glance, not for the first time, at Rosamund, just at the same moment as she looked up from the music and sought his eye. The light from the candles burnished her red-gold crown of curls; her head bent like a flower on the long stem of her elegant white neck.

Suddenly Héloïse was transported back to Brussels, to the musical party she and Lucy had given as part of the coming-out celebrations for Sophie and Rosamund. Rosamund had sat just so, playing the piano while Philip Tantony sang, and they had looked at each other in much the same way. How long ago that had been! Then Rosamund had been an untried girl, full of fire and impulsive dreams. Now she was a mature woman, almost thirty years old, a divorcée, and the mother of a child she would never see again.

'If we had only known how things would be,' Héloïse murmured.

Lucy knew exactly what she meant. 'A very good job we did not,' she said firmly. 'But doesn't Batchworth remind you just a little of Tantony? Oh, not in his looks, but in his manner. There's a gentleness about him and yet he's not at all weak. I can't help thinking that he is just the man to make her happy.'

'Rosamund thinks so,' Héloïse agreed. She did not see much resemblance between Batchworth and Tantony. In an odd sort of way, she thought the Earl much more like Lord Theakston, and she almost said so, but then glanced at Lucy and changed her mind.

'If only she could have met him first,' Lucy sighed. 'But he was with his regiment in America when we went to Brussels; and when he got back he went straight to Paris, so we missed him again. It's such a waste.'

'God arranges these things for his own ends,' Héloïse said after a moment.

Lucy looked at her sharply. 'That's all very well, but what about Charlotte? You have your granddaughter.'

'Oh Lucy,' Héloïse said, looking at her with helpless sympathy. 'No-one ever promised that life would be easy.'

Lucy smiled a little stiffly. 'Yours and mine haven't been —

yours particularly.' Héloïse shrugged a little, but Lucy went on quietly, 'Won't you tell me what's the matter? I'm not a noticing person, but I can't help seeing you're not happy. Is it James again?' Héloïse's eyes sought her husband automatically, and Lucy saw how much, after all these years, she still loved him. 'What is it, Héloïse? Tell me.'

Héloïse yielded. 'I'm afraid for him. He has taken up horse-breaking, and he's too old for it. He's sixty, Lucy, only think! Men of sixty sit by the fire and dream. They don't rush about the country buying up bad young horses to break their bones for them.'

Lucy was trying to understand, but since she had ridden before she could walk, she could not view horses with any alarm. 'James is the best rider I know,' she said. 'And we've both fallen off a hundred times without hurting ourselves. Riding isn't really dangerous. If you rode more yourself, you'd understand that. You mustn't worry about it. James knows exactly what he can do in the saddle.'

Héloïse looked at her helplessly. How could she explain the change which had come over James, the restless strain she sensed in him which was driving him to do things beyond reason? He was like a condemned man trying to spend all his money before it was too late. What had begun as a mild extra interest — sparked off by Africa's need — had become an obsession.

'He has changed, Lucy,' she said at last. 'I don't know if I can make you understand; but in the years after Edward died, he was so happy, running the estate and being proud of it, content every evening with what he had done that day. A man sure in his own place. Now he's never still, never content. He no sooner sits down than he is up again. All this travel — it tires him, yet he seems always to be planning another journey. And for what? We don't need another kind of business. His duties about the estate are neglected when he goes away. What good to make money from selling reschooled horses, when our own go unschooled for want of his being at home?'

'James always was a restless sort of creature, never settling to one thing for long. Our mother was in despair over him. It's just the way he is.'

370

'But he wasn't. For a long time he wasn't. Now he has changed — and I don't know why.'

Lucy was out of her depth. She laid a comforting hand on Héloïse's arm, and said, 'I expect he'll get over it. I shouldn't worry if I were you. He's looking extremely well, and that's everything, isn't it? If his new interest were too much for him, he wouldn't be looking so bonny.'

Héloïse smiled faintly, knowing there was no point in discussing it further. 'I expect you're right,' she said.

'Of course I am. You always did worry too much, didn't you?'

'Yes. But that's just the way *I* am.'

Early the next morning — her wedding day — Rosamund slipped down to the stables alone. None of the guests was up, but in the stables the morning activity had begun. The horses had been watered and fed, and now the boys were mucking out while the men began the grooming.

As she expected, she found Parslow there. Lucy had brought no horses with her for him to take care of, and idleness was intolerable to him. By some alchemy he had persuaded Jes's head groom, a jealous tyrant by the name of Padworth, to allow him to groom one of the horses, which he had on pillar reins out in the yard. He straightened up as Rosamund came towards him, and the horse whickered softly in greeting.

'What do you think of him?' she asked, slipping a titbit under the enquiring muzzle. The horse was Wayfarer, a good-looking bay which Jes used as a road horse. He was broken to side-saddle too, and Rosamund had ridden him on occasion, which was why he had been allocated to Lucy's use while she was here. 'Lord Batchworth has good judgement in horses, don't you think?'

Parslow ran a firm hand over the bay's crest and neck. 'He's a good sort,' he allowed. 'Nice eye, plenty of bone, pleasant to handle. Every stable needs one or two like him.'

'Praised with faint damns,' Rosamund said with a smile. 'You don't think much of him.'

'On the contrary, my lady, I like him very much. A good,

honest horse can't but be valued. He isn't what your ladyship's mother would buy for her own pleasure, but she'll find pleasure riding him all the same.' He met Rosamund's eye with a glint of mischief. 'Your ladyship's chestnut, now, is another matter.'

'Cedar? You like her?' Rosamund asked eagerly.

'Too light in the legs,' he answered promptly. 'A park horse, my lady. I hope you don't take her out on the moors?'

After a startled moment, Rosamund laughed. 'You're roasting me! She's as surefooted as a cat. Like the Duke, she believes in going lightly over heavy ground. She's not one of your plodders — an airborne spirit is my Cedar.'

'Then she suits you, my lady, and I'll say no more,' said Parslow. He turned to Wayfarer again and resumed his brushing. The horse sighed with pleasure and shifted its weight from one foot to the other, leaning into the delicious, penetrating strokes.

After a moment, Rosamund said quietly, 'Have you any news for me?'

Parslow didn't interrupt his rhythm. He spoke in a low but perfectly audible voice, without looking at Rosamund. 'I still have not seen her, my lady. But I have a new source of information — Lord Chelmsford's coachman. Living in the mews, he is more accessible than the house servants. I've found out which tavern he likes to visit of an evening, and he has proved — amenable.'

'To bribery?' Rosamund was slightly shocked. Somehow she had expected all horsemen to be absolutely honest.

'To flattery, my lady,' Parslow corrected.'In London, being in her ladyship's service has bestowed on me a certain reputation. Dickson proved not insensible of the honour of being noticed by me. To be seen drinking a pint of old ale in my company makes him quite talkative.'

Rosamund smiled faintly. 'And what has he told you?'

'His lordship's condition is still improving. He's able to get about quite easily now. There's even speculation amongst the servants that he might think of remarrying one day.'

'Is that true?'

'True that there's speculation. What his lordship's intentions are must be beyond my discovery.'

'Yes,' Rosamund allowed. 'Go on.'

'It seems that they think him a widower, my lady – his wife killed in the accident which crippled him. So far Dickson has not discovered any differently, and he is the only servant, apart from the gardener, who has contact with the outside world. I imagine care is taken to ensure the secret is kept from them.'

'And what of — my child?'

'Dickson has taken his lordship and Lady Charlotte out together in the coach on several occasions recently. They drive about the streets and the Park, but they do not stop or visit any house, and never speak to anyone. Sometimes they drive out to Richmond Park, and when they reach some secluded place, his lordship and Lady Charlotte get down for a walk. They never stop if anyone else is about. For the rest, it seems she is confined to the house and garden, in the company of his lordship or Lady Barbarina. But the gardener told me that he had it from the kitchen maid that outside tutors come in four times a week now to give lessons.'

'What lessons?' Rosamund asked. Her hands were clasped tightly together, her attention painfully strained, as though she might draw more information out of Parslow's words than they held, if only she tried hard enough.

'Music, dancing, French and drawing, my lady. It seems to be a matter of surprise amongst the servants that the tutors come from so far afield. The music and dancing master comes from St Albans, the French tutor from Clerkenwell, and the drawing master from Hammersmith.'

'Far apart from each other,' Rosamund commented dully, 'and far enough away not to have heard anything about the family.'

'So it seems, my lady,' Parslow said, turning his head to look at her with sympathy. 'No doubt they were very carefully chosen to know nothing of Lady Charlotte's history.'

Rosamund's lip trembled, and she caught it between her teeth, staring sightlessly at the cobbles. After a moment she said, 'He is mad, isn't he?' Parslow didn't answer. 'To bring up a child so —'

'She seems,' he said carefully, 'to be happy. Both my informants speak of her laughter and liveliness.' He hesitated before venturing an intimacy. 'The human child is very adaptable. If she has known no other way of life, it will not seem strange to her.'

Rosamund looked up then. 'She knew *me*. For a little while only, and she won't remember it; but the knowledge is there somewhere, in her blood and her bones.'

When they retired to dress for the wedding later that morning, Jes went with her to the door of her room, and caught up her hand.

'Do you want to tell me about it?'

'About what?' Rosamund was startled.

'What you have been brooding about since breakfast. Come, love, you don't think you can hide your feelings from me?'

She looked at him for a moment, and then nodded slightly and led him into her room. Moss was through in the dressing-room laying out the gown; they could hear her moving about, but if they spoke softly she would not hear them.

'I went down to talk to Parslow this morning,' Rosamund said.

'Yes, I thought you had.'

She told him what Parslow had said. 'Jes, what if he does marry again? What will that mean for Charlotte? She'll have a stepmother —'

'Not all stepmothers are wicked, love.'

'If there were more children, boys, she'd be disinherited.'

'You surely can't mind that? What does it matter if —'

'No, what I meant was — I wondered if, in that case, he would let me have her back.'

Jes looked into her eyes, and flinched from the agony of hope there. Was it better she should live with delusion, or face the truth? He wished he were wise enough to know for sure: he was terrified of hurting her further. But no, some wordless core of him knew it was better to live in this world than to escape into fantasy. 'Darling,' he began, and he saw the light go out.

'No,' she said. 'No, I suppose not.'

He forced himself to continue. 'To begin with, I have serious doubts that there could be children. When I saw him last he could barely walk. Whatever improvement Parslow has been told about, I don't think there could be children.'

She shuddered. 'I would never have wished that on him. Oh God, Jes —'

'I know. I know.' He pressed her hand, and felt her take hold of herself. 'I don't believe he would even marry again, unless it were for companionship — and he doesn't seem to relish company. No, it's just servants' talk. I should think no more about it, if I were you.'

She managed a watery smile. 'I have tried.'

'I know you have. You are very brave.'

'And this is our wedding day. We must be happy.'

'Must be?'

No smile now, but the look in her eyes was enough. 'I love you, Jes.' She hesitated, and went on, 'I don't want you to think that — that being with you is second best, that it's only compensation for what I've lost. I do — delight in you, my dear.'

He lifted her hand to his lips, and then laid it against his cheek, and she stepped close and put her arm round him, for once as though she were the man.

Everyone was gathered in the hall at twenty before eleven, and Rosamund and her Jes came down the stairs arm in arm. There was no sign of sadness in the bride's face: she was calm and happy, her eyes bright and soft, her step steady. For a moment everyone gathered round, offering their gladness and affection, and then the whole party walked off, out into the sunshine and through the park to the church which stood just outside the gate. The rector and the clerk were waiting there; the simple service was spoken. Lord and Lady Batchworth smiled at each other, turned to receive the congratulations of those who loved them best; and then the party left the church and walked back to the house again.

A very festive nuncheon was laid out ready for them, a great many bottles of champagne were opened, and the gathering grew comfortably merry.

'Very different from her first wedding,' Lucy commented to Héloïse. 'Then it was the Abbey, a vast banquet and ball, Prinny and York popping in — all the fuss and feathers. This is different from any fashionable wedding I've ever been to. And yet, you know, I couldn't help thinking that in many ways it was the nicest. When we came out of the church into the sunshine, and the bells started ringing —'

'It reminded me of my wedding to James, at Morland Place,' Héloïse said. 'And your first wedding, Lucy, to Lord Aylesbury — do you remember? That was at Morland Place too.'

'You were my matron of honour,' Lucy said, her brow bent with the effort of memory. 'You had on a yellow gown, I think, and ribbons in your hair.'

'So I did. How clever of you to remember.'

'Chetwyn was all dressed up in blue and white satin, like a prince in a fairy-tale. I thought he looked so absurd in it! Edward was groomsman, and the three of us had to avoid each other's eyes, or we'd have burst out laughing. Lord, what a long time ago it all was!'

Héloïse looked across at Rosamund, standing with Jes and talking to James and Lord Theakston. She was laughing at something Theakston had said, and as she laughed, she put her hand on Jes's arm to make sure he was sharing the amusement with her.

'They are so well suited, it is a joy to see them together,' Héloïse said. 'I think it's the nicest wedding I was ever at.'

Lucy turned to look at her, and her expression was soft. 'Yes, I think so too. Quite the nicest.'

'If I were Rosamund, and I'd married the man of my choice at last, I should think it a great shame to be put off with such a dismal little nothing of a wedding,' Thalia said. 'Batchworth may be handsome, but handsome is as handsome does. Anyone would think he was ashamed of her. I can't bear a man to be paltry.'

'I'm sure he must have discussed it with Rosamund,' Roland said. 'He wouldn't have chosen a small, private wedding unless it were her choice too.'

'Oh, I don't know. You men are all alike. You'd all be tyrants if we let you,' she said with spirit.

Roland smiled. 'Even if you believe that, you can't think anyone would ever be able to subjugate my sister? And do I tyrannise you?'

Thalia looked him over judiciously. 'Well, no, I must say you are a very superior example of your sex. You treat me quite like a human being. And I will say you are never *mean*. I've never known you quibble about anything I've wanted, or try to give me anything but the best.'

'I love you, that's why,' Roland said, pleased with the way the conversation was going.

'No it's not,' Thalia said, surprising him. 'You'd be just as good and generous to me if you didn't care for me at all. It's the way you are, Roly, that's all.'

He didn't know whether this was a good or a bad observation, and while he was pondering it, she had continued on her own line of thought.

'Do they really mean to live here all the time? I can hardly believe it.'

'Well, no, I think they mean to live at Batchworth House. This is only their country seat.'

'Don't be tiresome, you know I didn't mean that. I meant up here, in the north. How can they be so dull? Or do you think it's another of Batchworth's economies, hoping to save the expense of a London house?'

'I don't know where you get the idea from that he's ungenerous. He adores Rosamund, and there's nothing he wouldn't do for her. Besides, he's vastly rich — a London house would be nothing to him.'

'Well, then!'

'I think it's Rosamund's choice. She still fights shy of going into company. She's quite sensitive, you know. I think she would rather stay here all the time, than go to London and risk being snubbed.'

'Then she's a great coward,' Thalia said boldly. 'I would always sooner do the something than the nothing. And she's a fool besides: the Countess of Batchworth, with a large

377

house and smart dinners, will never be snubbed. It's not as if Chelmsford goes about. I dare say everyone will have forgotten in a twelvemonth that she was ever anything *but* Lady Batchworth.'

'Perhaps in a twelvemonth she'll have changed her mind,' Roland said peaceably. 'Talking of changing minds, have you made up yours about August? Do we go with your brother to Northumberland, or would you prefer somewhere else?'

'I don't know. I can't decide,' Thalia said vaguely. Across the room Tom was talking to Sophie and making her laugh; Jasper was watching with the wistful air of the child who has not been invited to join the game. She knew just how he felt. 'Won't Northumberland be very dull?'

'Tom enjoyed it when he went with Maurice the year before last. Of course they were shooting, which I know you don't care for, but the country is very good for riding, and there were parties at all the big houses, so they didn't want for company and dancing.'

'I don't know,' she said again, hesitantly. How could he find so much to say to dull, plain Sophie? 'Will Tom be going this year?'

'Oh yes, I think so. And I believe there's some talk of my Cousin Nicholas from Morland Place going up with a party — Winchmore and Penshurst and so on.'

'Well, then, perhaps I will,' Thalia said generously. 'I know you want to, don't you?'

'Yes, but not unless you like it.'

'If you're happy, I will be,' she said with a sweet smile which made him feel flushed and happy. 'We'll go to Maurice's. I'm sure I can find something to do to amuse myself while you're all out shooting.'

CHAPTER NINETEEN

Benedict had been surprised when Nicholas insisted on
staying at home while everyone else went to Manchester for
the wedding. Since he came home, Nicky had shown himself
eager for any change, and particularly when it meant staying
in the house of some noble personage. The reason he gave
was even stranger.

'I know you're never satisfied that Morland Place is being
looked after when you're away, Mama, but I really want you
to go, and to enjoy yourself. If I am here to take care of things,
you'll be able to put all your worries aside. After all, Morland
Place will be mine one day, so who could have its interests
more at heart? And I know just how you and Papa like things
done. Besides,' he had added as the clinching argument, 'the
servants are all so well-trained, they know just what to do. It's
really only a matter of being on hand to reassure them.'

Benedict could see that his mother was touched by Nicky's
concern for her, and though she was still hesitant about
leaving the place in his care, it was more out of habit than
because she doubted his abilities. Nicholas, however, played
her hesitancy to his advantage. 'Of course, Mama, if you
don't trust me —' he began in wounded tones.

Héloïse hastened to reassure him. 'Of course I trust you,
my darling! Who better? And as you say, no-one could have
more interest in keeping everything in order.'

'You say that, Mama, but unless you agree to go to the
wedding — which I *know* you want to attend — I shall have
to conclude that you don't trust me after all.'

So there was nothing she could do but agree. Having won

379

his point, Nicholas pressed home the advantage by making her promise that they would stay two weeks at least. In this he had his father's support. 'You haven't had a proper rest for years. It would do you so much good to get away from Morland Place for a time, and there's no point in travelling all that way just for a few days. I think we ought to make it three weeks. Sophie and Jasper will want us to stay with them as well; and I want to have a look at the factories, and see how John's new building scheme is coming along. Three weeks might not be enough indeed. I think perhaps four would be better.'

Four proved harder to get past, and in the end they both had to settle for three weeks with a possible extension, if everything went well, and on condition that Nicholas wrote daily to report that all was well. Nicholas seemed pleased enough with the result.

Benedict, though puzzled as to why Nicky wanted to stay home, was pleased too. He was at a time of life when there can't be too much change and travel, and to be going to Manchester meant going closer to the Liverpool and Manchester railway, with the near certainty of finding out a great deal more about it than could be gleaned from the largely indifferent newspapers. Lord Batchworth, indeed, being one of the interested parties, was bound to be able to give him detailed information; and if they stayed long enough, there might even be the chance of being taken to view the workings.

His only regret was at the thought of not seeing Annie for all that time. But he told himself — and her — that it was only four weeks and that she would still be there when he came back, and after all the chance of possibly seeing a railway might only happen to a man once in his life. The things that he and Annie did together, while deliciously exciting at the time, were, he guessed, fairly universally available once one got to a sufficient age to have command of time and money.

So he went with anticipation; and on his farewell visit to Annie, gave her a scarf which he had bought from a pedlar with the last of his pocket-money. He reckoned he probably wouldn't need any money in Manchester; and if he did, well, perhaps Papa would advance him something on next month's. Annie was delighted with it, cried a little, called him generous and foolish, and said she would miss him terrible while he was away. She seemed to feel guilty that what she called 'the flowers' had come that day, which meant that she could not give Benedict everything he liked, but he kissed her and told her not to be silly, that he liked coming to see her anyway. They talked a while, and then he left her, trotting home on the now well-worn path through the woods, sensible of a relief that at least he would be going away without an unanswered question hanging over him. He and she had been 'careful', and up till now nothing had happened; but Bendy was aware that if their luck ran out, there would be terrible trouble to face at home.

They stayed just over four weeks in Manchester, and on their return it was a day or two before he could get away on his own. He passed Annie a message in the way they had devised between them: he sent the gamekeeper's youngest son with a white flower to be left on the top of the farmyard wall, which meant that he was waiting for her in the shippon. He knew the times of day when it was easiest for her to get away from the farm. The flower was sent, and he waited three hours, but she didn't come. Twice more he tried to make the assignation, twice more she failed him; and after the third disappointment, unable to bear the suspense of not knowing, he walked over to the farm in the gathering dusk to see for himself.

Everything appeared normal. The farmhouse hadn't burned down; the same people were coming and going about their usual tasks. He sidled along the wall, keeping out of sight, until he could get a view of the kitchen door. People went in and out; Mrs Pike appeared at the open door to empty a bowl of water; another maid, Beattie, threw out some scraps which the chickens scuttled for. The chickens would have to be shut up before dark, and that was Annie's job: he could catch her by the henhouse for a brief word, at least find out if she had seen his signals.

But five minutes later, it was Beattie who came out with the meal-can and rattled it with a spoon as she crossed the yard to bring the chickens running. Puzzled, Benedict crept round the wall towards the henhouse. He would have to ask Beattie where Annie was. Perhaps she was ill. He was worried about her.

He had just reached the gap where the wall had broken down and was stepping cautiously over it when a late chicken, in a panic at being left out, hurtled over it and shot between his legs squawking loudly. Benedict let out a yell of surprise and the dogs all began barking at once. Beattie looked round in alarm, and Benedict was making frantic signals of reassurance and supplication to her when a hand like a plank descended onto his shoulder from behind and almost stopped his heart.

'Now then, young feller, was does tha want, creepin' round folks' houses this time o' night?'

Benedict turned his head sharply, and he and Mr Pike regarded each other with almost equal surprise. 'Hi — I — ha—' Benedict gasped helplessly. He couldn't think of a single excuse or even reason for his presence.

Mr Pike gave him a plain look in which there gleamed a grain of cynical amusement. 'Now then, Master Bennet,' he said. 'It's thee, is it? Well, if tha's come to see Annie, tha's left it ower late. She's gone.'

'Gone?' Bendy gasped, too far out of his wits to deny that was his purpose.

'Aye, gone.' He regarded Bendy's face for a moment, like a pugilist allowing his floored opponent the opportunity to get up again. Bendy stayed down. 'Nay, lad,' Pike said a little more kindly, 'I knew all about thee an' her in yon shippon, did tha think it were secret? T'missus were shocked, but I told her to mind her knitting. A lad's got to find out one way or another, to ma mind, and I knew tha were man enough to stand by t'lass if it come to owt. But she's gone now, ungrateful hussy, an' tha might be best off wi'out her when all's said.'

It was the longest speech Bendy had ever heard from the farmer. He felt warmed by the sympathy it implied, but still he had questions to ask. She could not have found out she was pregnant and run away in a panic, so what had become of her?

'But — but where did she go? When did she leave?'

'Two days after thy last visit, master, not a day more, she upped and left. Packed her few bits in a bag. Told t'missus she 'ad means of betterin' herself. That's it an' all about it. Where she's gone I no more know than thee or t'devil. Now then.'

'Was she — well?' Bendy asked at last, trying to understand, working over the words in his mind like a potter with a very small and inferior bit of clay.

'Well? Aye, well enough for all I could see. She just went.' He thought for a minute, and then put his hand on Bendy's shoulder again and squeezed it in a gesture of comfort. 'Got ideas above her station, I shouldn't wonder. Tha's best off, Master Bennet. Don't fret over the likes of her.'

Which was all very well, Benedict thought as he walked home through the dew-smelling dark, but an unanswered question was bound to make one fret. Besides, he had made himself responsible for Annie, and he needed to know that she was all right. And besides again, it wasn't *like* her. He thought of how touched she had been with the scarf. She wouldn't just have gone without saying goodbye.

In August, only a few months after taking office, the ailing Canning died. Lucy was surprised at how much she minded. She had always felt equivocal about Canning, going along with the usual view that he was 'too clever', suspecting his liberal views on certain subjects, and yet, like Mrs Arbuthnot, falling victim to the charm and intelligence of the man whenever she met him.

His death removed the last great leader who could unite the parties, and the choice seemed clear between Lord Grey and the Whigs, or Wellington and the High Tories. The King, however, would not make such a choice. He wanted a Tory government, hating the Whigs as he had always done; but he would not forgive Wellington for having resigned in February. So he tried for a compromise, a Canningite cabinet without Canning, and approached Robinson to head the ministry. Robinson, who had been Chancellor of the Exchequer under Lord Liverpool, had been created Viscount Goderich under Canning's ministry and made Secretary for War.

'Goderich for the Lord's sake!' Lucy exclaimed when she heard. John Anstey, recalled to London by the crisis, had discovered she was still in Town and stepped up to see her. '"Goody" Goderich, as firm as a bulrush! How will he be able to hold together that hotch-potch?'

'I don't think he will,' Anstey said. 'It will all collapse sooner or later — sooner by my guess. He won't be able to command a majority in the Commons and that will be that.'

'Prinny chose him *because* he's a flexible man,' said Theakston. 'He hopes to be able to dominate him.'

'The King's making John Herries Chancellor of the Exchequer doesn't help,' Anstey said. 'Everyone suspects him of selling official information to the Rothschilds during the war.'

'He didn't,' said Lucy firmly. 'I knew the Rothschilds very well. They had their own sources of information, usually better than the Government's. They'd have been more likely to sell information to Herries than vice versa.'

'But no member of either House has ever let the truth get in the way of a good prejudice,' Anstey said with a smile. 'Of course I understand that the King wants Herries because he thinks he'll be able to get more money out of him. The rebuilding of Buckingham House must be costing a fortune.'

'It is,' said Lucy. 'Alvanley says Prinny'll run out of money in a month or two, and that will be the end of it. Nash's ideas don't come cheaply.'

'Still, having Herries in the Cabinet isn't going to make things easy for Goderich,' Anstey concluded.

'He'll have some Whig support,' Theakston said. 'Althorp will probably vote with him at a pinch, and Russell.'

'I think Brougham will give him a chance, too,' Anstey said. 'And William Lamb will go with him for Huskisson's sake — they admire each other tremendously — and Palmerston for Lamb's sake.'

Lucy sighed. 'I don't know how it is these days, but in the olden days you always knew where you were. There were Whigs and there were Tories; now it's all groups and friends. There's Canningites, and Eldonites, and Greyites, and Wellingtonites. There's Whigs who act like Tories and Tories who seem more like Whigs. How do you manage to make sense of it, John?'

'I don't try to. I've been around a long time, my dear Lucy, and I've learnt the value of watching from a distance. But I'll tell you one thing: Canning was a great liberal, but the loss of him is going to give impetus to the liberal movement. He managed to keep out demands for Parliamentary Reform because the industrialists looked on him as sympathetic to their needs. Now he's gone, there'll be no-one to placate them. You'll find the demands will grow year by year until they're overwhelming.'

'I don't believe it,' Lucy said firmly. 'When it comes down to it, no-one can force Parliament to reform itself. It's they who have the final say, and they aren't likely to vote themselves out of power, are they?'

'That's true,' Theakston said, struck by his wife's cleverness. 'No-one can make them, after all.'

'We'll see,' said Anstey. 'Why are you still in London, by the by? I thought you'd have been in the country by now.'

'Look out of the window,' Lucy said shortly. Outside were grey skies and swathes of cold, gusty rain. 'It's no pleasure to anyone to be in the country in weather like this. I can't imagine why August is called summer.'

'Besides which,' Theakston said kindly, 'the children are gone up to Northumberland, and Wolvercote without Tom is as dull as London without Tom — ain't that so, my love? There's still time to go and join them, you know.'

She returned her husband's smile lovingly. 'A pretty fool that would make me, running after my own son like a green girl! Sometimes, Danby, I wonder what you think I have in my head by way of stuffing.'

Grey skies over Manchester were nothing unusual, but this August they were still noticeably greyer. The rain washed the soot out of the air and left it in dismal streaks down windows and walls; the streets were hazardous with splashed hems and clashing umbrellas. Sophie, sitting at the breakfast table opposite Jasper, had sighed once already on looking out of the

385

window. Now she sighed again, and this time drew his attention from the newspaper.

'What is it, my love?' He noticed the letter in her hand — one of the regular bulletins from Morland Place, he could tell by the bulk. Héloïse was a prolific correspondent, and only the pleasure Sophie got from the letters reconciled Jasper to the expense of them. But if the letters were going to make her unhappy, it was another matter. 'Not bad news, I hope?'

'Oh no, on the contrary. It's excellent news. Mathilde has had her baby, and she was right all along: it was a boy.' She looked down at the page. 'Born last Tuesday, small but very bonny, Maman says, and they're going to call it Joshua. Maman thought it should have been called James, but she says at least Joshua is better than John, because there are so many of them, and they'd have been bound to call him Jack anyway.'

'Well, well! So Skelwith has his heir after all?'

Sophie looked up quickly to catch his expression, hoping to discover how much he minded about it. She could read nothing from his face, which in itself struck her as ominous. 'It was lucky that he was at home, too,' she said. 'He's been so much in Manchester this past year he might easily have missed it all.'

'I can't think what you suppose he might have missed. The baby would still have been there when he got back.'

'Oh, but the excitement,' Sophie said anxiously, 'and being able to see the baby right away! Don't you remember when Fanny was born, and they brought her down and put her in your arms? You wouldn't have wanted to miss that moment, would you?'

'No; but whenever she was first put in my arms, it would have been miraculous. It wouldn't have mattered whether she was ten minutes old or twelve hours old, would it?'

'Yes it would! And besides, I wanted you to be there, to know you were in the house. And you wanted to be near me, too, didn't you?'

'Of course, love. Don't look so reproachful! We weren't talking about me, remember, but about Skelwith; and he's such a practised father, I dare say the magic has worn off by now. This one was his sixth, remember.'

'Yes, but his first son!' Sophie said it before she thought; and her own instant awareness of the words caused the silence which followed, which she interpreted as pain on Jasper's side. Oh Jasper, I'm so sorry!' she cried.

'Sorry? Whatever for?' he said with broad astonishment; but he knew, of course, and a moment later stopped pretending not to as he saw large glinting tears welling over Sophie's lower lashes. He flung his napkin aside and went round the table to her. 'Oh darling, Sophie, don't cry!'

'I should have given you a son! I wanted to give you a son, and I couldn't!' she cried, rather incoherently into Jasper's waistcoat as he clasped her awkwardly to him, he standing, she sitting. The sight of her bent head below him, in the frilled but matronly cap which always made her seem to him like a little girl playing house, filled him with almost unbearable tenderness. 'I've failed you!' she wept.

'No, no you haven't. I've failed you just as much,' he said.

'But it's my fault.'

'It could just as easily be mine,' he said.

He was rewarded, at least, by a check of surprise in the tears. Sophie, wifely creature, had never thought that perhaps the lack of pregnancies might be due to some deficiency in Jasper; but he had thought it — often and naggingly in the middle of wakeful nights, when she lay warm and sweet and perfect beside him, sleeping the sleep of the innocent.

'It doesn't matter, anyway,' he said firmly. 'We have Fanny, and Fanny is the most wonderful child who ever lived. Do you really think I would swap Fanny for any boy?'

She detached herself from his fob pocket and looked up at him with a touching mixture of hope and doubt. 'But I always wanted you to have a son *as well.*'

'Well I haven't, and I don't care,' he said. 'I love Fanny, and I love you, and I'm perfectly happy. Let other men have all the children they want. I have what I want. And —' as she was evidently about to refute his blithe statement — 'before you call me a liar, my precious love, just consider this: that every time you had a child, I would have had to risk losing you. I'd have spent months of agony and remorse wondering what I'd

387

done and how much I'd live to regret it. I honestly don't know how any man can be willing to put his wife through it a second time, having survived the first. No child would be worth losing you for, Sophie; so when I tell you that I am perfectly happy having you and Fanny and no more, please do me the justice to believe I am telling you the literal truth.'

'Oh — darling,' she said falteringly, her wet face turned up to him, and a look of such love and relief and gratitude shining in its transparency that he felt absurdly guilty for occasioning it when he was, in his own judgement, so patently unworthy of such devotion. It seemed necessary to sit down and be practical for a moment just then, so he pulled out his handkerchief and gave it to her, and while she was blowing her nose he went back to his place and buttered a piece of toast he had no intention of eating. When these activities were complete, he managed to look at her again, and seeing how pale her face was and how grey the skies outside, came to a conclusion.

'This August is so dismal, it's not surprising you are feeling rather blue. What you need is a change of scene. In fact, I think we all do. It's slack time now— why don't we go away somewhere for a little holiday, you, me and Fanny? How would you like to go to the seaside?'

Sophie hesitated. 'Oh, a holiday with you would be wonderful! But won't it be rather unpleasant by the sea in this weather?'

'We could go to Scarborough. It always rains less on the east coast.'

'Hmm, yes —'

He stopped teasing her. 'Or we could go and visit Morland Place, if you like. You could see your mama and papa and your brothers and Monsieur Barnard — and Mathilde's new baby.'

The sun was out now. 'Oh Jasper, really, could we? Wouldn't you mind?'

'Of course not. I should enjoy it very much myself. And that good Yorkshire air and Yorkshire food will put the colour back in your cheeks. You're looking rather peaked, you know.'

Sophie put her hands to her face. 'Am I? Oh, I'm sorry!'

Jasper grinned. 'Now don't start finding something else to blame yourself for.'

Despite the wet weather, the Theakstons eventually decided to leave Town and go down to Wolvercote for a few weeks. One of the agreeable things about the new Lady Aylesbury was that she seemed to have no jealousy of her mother-in-law, and was quite content to allow her the run of the place, whether she was in residence or not. It was lucky that it was so, since Wolvercote had no dower-house. Eviction would have meant that Lucy and Danby would have had to buy a new place of their own, and their finances would hardly have run to the sort of establishment Lucy preferred.

The Isis had flooded again, and ducks were paddling happily across Port Meadow. 'We shan't be taking our gallops in that direction, then,' Lucy commented, peering through the rain. The park was above the flood level, though, and the great chestnut trees simply looked handsome when they dripped with rain, each sheltering under its spreading canopy a small colony of deer or cattle. The chaise came round the curve of the white road, and there was the house, strange and heterogeneous collection of styles and buildings that it was, but familiar now, and therefore dear to Lucy. She had come here first on her honeymoon; two of her children had been born here, and all had been brought up in this house and park. Soon, she supposed, her grandchildren would begin to colonise the nursery — if Roland and Thalia would get on with doing their duty, that was. Her mind touched lightly on the thought of Charlotte and flinched away again.

'It doesn't look as though the rain means to hold up,' she said as they drew up before the steps. 'I think I'll ride this afternoon anyway. A little wetting never hurt anyone.'

'If water were harmful, sailors would die young,' Danby said pleasantly, quoting one of her own favourite sayings back at her.

A footman was coming down the steps to open the door, and Savage was waiting at the door with a deferential smile.

'Welcome, your ladyship. My lord. I trust you had a

389

comfortable journey? Mr Weston is here, my lady. He arrived yesterday.'

'Tom?' Lucy's face lit with gladness. 'What can he be doing here? Where is he now, Savage?'

'He took breakfast in his own apartment, my lady, but I believe he rang from the billiard room for coals half an hour ago.'

'I'll go and see him straight away. He can come riding with us this afternoon, Danby, isn't that splendid?'

'Splendid,' Theakston said. Lucy was divesting herself of her outer garments with the eagerness of a maiden on her way to meet a lover. He drew out his watch. 'Time for a little something, don't you think, m'dear?'

'Oh, yes, of course. Is the fire bright in the billiard room now?'

'Yes, my lady.'

'Then send along some wine and a nuncheon straight away, if you please.'

'Very good, my lady.'

Theakston followed Lucy along the passage to the billiard room, his leisurely pace having to lengthen to keep up with her rapid steps. It was his favourite room at Wolvercote, a long, low apartment at the back of the house with French windows leading onto the lower terrace. The table itself occupied one end, standing upon a floor of polished wood and surrounded by the clubbish accoutrements of leather chairs and convenient tables designed to accommodate humidor and decanter. The other end of the room was carpeted, and around the focal point of a large and handsome fireplace was gathered a comfortable collection of chairs and sofas, some bookcases of undemanding reading, and a low table which always bore the newspapers and a selection of such periodicals as would tempt a gentleman's taste.

It was a room in which to be at ease and talk of unimportant things; it was also the only room in the house that had ever allowed smoking. The door was open and a few yards off they heard the evocative click of two ivory balls kissing in the middle of a green field. They entered to see the fire blazing brightly to the left, the rain streaming down the windows straight ahead, and to the right Tom lining up a shot with a frown of concentration on his face.

'My dear boy!' Lucy cried. 'What are you doing here? I thought you were in Northumberland.'

He had evidently been lost in thought, for he started, and the spoon of the cue slipped and struck the ball, which rolled off uselessly in the wrong direction. He put the cue down carefully.

'Mother. I didn't know you were coming.' He stepped forward to kiss her. 'Sir. When did you arrive?'

'Only five minutes ago. Savage said you were in here. I've ordered a nuncheon here. I don't expect the other rooms will be warm yet.'

'I don't suppose so,' Tom said, following her towards the fire. 'It's strange how reluctant the servants are to light fires in August, whatever the weather. As though there were a rule about it, like oysters.'

'They have the cleaning out of them, I suppose, poor things,' Lucy said indifferently. 'Didn't you go to Northumberland after all?'

'Yes. I came back yesterday.'

'Alone?'

'The others are still there.'

Danby could see that Tom was reluctant to enter into the subject, but Lucy pressed, as she was bound to do, for information about her beloved. 'But why did you cut it short? You were to have stayed until the middle of September, weren't you? Wasn't the sport good?'

Tom smiled at her in his most beguiling way, handing her into an armchair and bending over her solicitously. 'Oh, I'm not such a great sportsman, you know, Mama. Slaughtering birds palls on me quite quickly, and I just took a fancy to come home. How is London? How's the crisis coming along? Shall we have Catholic Emancipation by Christmas, or will it all end in tears?'

Lucy, fresh from the gossip of Cabinet manoeuvres, was more than willing to be diverted, and quite forgot what she had begun to ask. Tom kept her talking; the nuncheon was brought in; and afterwards the horses were ordered and they went to their rooms to change for riding.

Lord Theakston was not quite so easily diverted, and the question mark Tom had intruded into his thoughts nagged at him gently all day. When he went down to the drawing-room before dinner, he found Tom there alone, sitting and staring into the fire. Theakston had entered quietly, and Tom was not aware of his presence; for a few moments he studied his adoptive son in silence.

Tom in the severe black and white of evening-dress was strikingly handsome. There was no noticeable fashion about him, as there was about Roland, but in the meticulousness of his dress he was more truly the dandy, more closely in the style of Brummell. He looked very like his father; Theakston had to search for any likeness to Lucy, and found it only in a faint and ghostly resemblance, not to be pinned down in any particular feature. Roland looked far more like his mother, and not a little like his maternal Uncle Edward; there was hardly any resemblance between the brothers, which of course had always been to the good.

Theakston had liked and admired Tom's father, and to begin with had loved Tom for both his parents' sake. But although before he adopted him as his heir, he had come to love the boy for his own sake too, he could not say he had ever understood him. The enigma of Tom's character was absolute. What he liked, or thought, or wished were as obscure now as they had been ten years ago. But Theakston, like many a man of few words, had strong instincts, and he knew that something had been troubling Tom for some time. Not only that, but he knew it was something Tom didn't want Lucy to know about.

Tom looked up, suddenly becoming aware of Theakston's presence. He stood up quickly, and his face appeared flushed —though that might only have been from the heat of the fire. 'Sir? I didn't hear you come in.'

'You were a long way away,' Danby agreed, taking the chair on the other side of the fire. 'Sit down, my boy.' Tom sat and looked at him enquiringly, a polite smile concealing everything. 'I think perhaps you ought to tell me about it. Your mother is still dressing. We have a quarter of an hour to ourselves.'

Tom was silent, as though debating whether or not to deny everything. But in spite of his precocious maturity, he was only twenty-three, and he loved and trusted his stepfather. 'You won't tell her?' he said at last.

'Not if you don't want me to.' Another silence. Tom clearly needed priming. 'Why did you come back from Northumberland?'

Tom drew a deep and shuddering sigh, and then everything came out in a rush. Danby listened in grave silence, his eyes never moving from Tom's face, his face revealing no surprise nor shock nor disapproval, only calm and sympathetic attention. At the end of the recital Tom paused a moment, and then concluded, 'I think I shall have to go away.'

'Away?'

'Right away. Abroad.' He bit his lip. 'I could join a regiment, if my father's money would run to a commission. I think I'm too old for the navy,' he added.

'By far,' Theakston said, not responding to the shaky joke. He was thinking. 'You've never struck me as a soldier.'

Tom made a face. 'I don't think I am. I think I should hate it of anything.'

'Then don't be a soldier,' Danby said simply.

'I must do something. If I stay in London, she'll go on pursuing me. I don't want Roly to find out. I don't want to hurt him.'

Danby looked at him thoughtfully. 'Can't you discourage her?'

Tom began to say no, and then met his stepfather's eyes, and realised that only the truth would do between them. 'If I had from the beginning. If I'd really meant it. But I was weak. I was attracted to her, and let her see it. And now of course —' He shrugged. 'After Northumberland, it's too late.'

'You don't mean to repeat it?'

'No, but — she'll come after me. I know her.' There was a silence, and Tom watched Theakston's face, hoping for a miracle, for the solution to the problem.

393

Danby thought a long time. The clock ticked on, and then gathered itself breathily to strike the three-quarters. The sound roused him. Lucy would be down soon. Decisions must be made.

'I don't want you to go abroad,' he said. 'Apart from my own wishes, it would be a blow to your mother. She can't bear to part with you.'

'I know. I don't want to leave her, but —' He left the sentence hanging hopefully.

'You ought to have a career,' Theakston said. 'Would you like a seat in Parliament?'

Tom brightened. 'Is is possible?'

Danby smiled. 'Whole point of our system, to get the right men in. That's why we don't want Reform. Never know who you might get then. Oh yes, I think between us we could get you a seat.'

Tom's frown returned. 'But that doesn't solve the problem of Thalia, sir.'

Danby leaned forward, placing his hands on his knees for emphasis. 'You've got to be determined not to repeat your folly. Really determined.'

'Yes, sir. I am.'

'Very well. Interest yourself in your career, keep busy, find a circle of friends that doesn't include her. Meanwhile I'll speak to her, make sure she leaves you alone.'

'Would you really, sir?'

'She'll listen to me, I think.'

Tom nodded. 'But I can't avoid them entirely. I wouldn't want to. Roland's my brother. How can I be in company with them — now?'

'You'll have to work that out for yourself, my boy. But I think I'll have a word with Roland too, while I'm doin' my good deeds. It's time he set to and got himself an heir. Once Thalia starts increasing, it'll occupy her mind wonderfully.' He stood up and walked across to the decanter. 'Spot of sherry?' He began to pour, watching the golden liquid glint as it rolled into the glass. 'This business — all deference to your attractiveness, old fellow, but I think it's just high spirits with her. I believe she's genuinely fond of Roland.'

'Yes,' said Tom, fixing his eyes, too, on the crystal. 'Yes, I'm sure she is.'

In January 1828, as Lord Anstey had anticipated, Goderich proved unequal to the task of holding together the disparate entities of the Cabinet. A quarrel had broken out between Huskisson and Herries over the Finance Committee. Huskisson wanted Althorp as chairman, and Herries declared he would not serve with him. Huskisson declared he would not serve without him. Unable to decide between them, Goderich — whom the King anathematised as a 'damned, snivelling, blubbering blockhead' — resigned his office in tears.

The coalition was doomed, for there was no-one left to lead it. No-one would serve under Brougham; Grey would not take office without the promise of Catholic Emancipation; William Lamb, though he had the necessary emollient qualities, was thought to be too young and inexperienced. The King had no alternative but to approach the Duke of Wellington and ask him to form a Tory ministry.

The old soldier had no particular enthusiasm for the office, but his sense of duty forced him to accept. The Whig members resigned, but by promising to exclude the Ultra Tories like Eldon, he managed to keep the former Canningites like Huskisson and Palmerston with him. Robert Peel came back in as Home Secretary, and Herries went to the Mint, where he would annoy fewer people, to allow Goulburn to become Chancellor of the Exchequer.

Still it was an uneasy sort of household, and there were doubts from the beginning that Wellington, who hadn't a tactful bone in his body, would be able to hold it together. He would never, it was said, be able keep his dogs from the throat of Huskisson, whom they despised as a vulgar upstart, but who was essential to keeping the Canningite vote.

Moreover, Wellington, Peel and Goulburn were viewed, rightly or wrongly, as intolerant and reactionary, and as such might be expected to inflame Whig passions in the Commons, rather than placate them.

'John Anstey may have been right,' Lucy commented

thoughtfully to her husband, 'that Canning's death will encourage the liberal movement.

Anstey was not to have the satisfaction of seeing himself proved right, however: he had died in December 1827, quietly at home, in his sleep. It was a great blow to Lucy: John Anstey had been there all her life, a steady influence and staunch friend, always ready to help, to advise, to serve. It was to him that she had turned so often at the crises in her life, and he had never failed to help, even though many of the things she had done must have startled him. Lucy cried when she heard the news of his death, and cried again at his memorial service, which she went north to attend in January, in spite of the season and the bad weather.

There she met, for the first time in years, Anstey's eldest son Jack, now, of course, Lord Anstey in his father's succession. Many years ago, Lucy had been able to be instrumental in promoting Jack's career at sea, through her friendship with Admiral Collingwood — the one time she had been able to do John Anstey a service in return for all his for her. Jack Anstey was now a captain, and a grown man of thirty-three, pleasant-faced and mild-tempered, but with that firmness of speech and character which came from commanding one of His Majesty's ships at sea.

He had been fortunate in gaining his promotion to post rank in 1816, just before the navy had begun to be cut back. Since then a mixture of luck, interest, and his own abilities had kept him almost constantly employed. The question before him now was, should he give up his career? On the surface of it, there seemed no immediate need. His brother Benjamin was ready trained and waiting to take over as superintendent of the family business; Alfred had taken his seat in the lower House last year, and so could represent the family in Parliament; and Harry was studying the law.

Jack's uncertainty was so great that he took the step of travelling down to London to consult with Lady Theakston, whom he regarded not only as patroness but as the fount of all wisdom — a judgement which made Lord Theakston stare.

'You see, ma'am, there's my mother she's been ailing for

396

years now, and although she won't say so directly, I know she wants me to stay at home. And there's my seat in the Upper House! I feel I owe it to my father not to neglect my duty there.'

'Quite right,' Lucy approved briskly. 'Then what is your trouble?'

'I should miss the sea,' Jack said frankly. 'And the life. But I think most of all I should miss the responsibility. I don't think I could bear to be idle. Ben looks after the business, and he knows all about it — I couldn't do better than him, even though there might be a role for me as figurehead. Of course, I'm head of the family now, and there's my mother and sisters to watch over, but — but I don't think that would be enough for me.'

'You have to think about providing an heir,' Lucy said bluntly.

Jack smiled. 'I don't think that's a matter of urgency. I've three brothers — though only one of 'em's married yet. But the thing is, you see, ma'am, I have been serving my King and my country since I was eight years old, and I need to be useful.'

Lucy nodded. 'I quite understand; and I don't think you need to worry about that. If you wish to stay in England and be useful, I can tell you that they have great need of you at the Admiralty. Captains with your experience at sea and your family and background are not easily come by. Leave it to me. I'll talk to Melville and the Duke. I'm sure they'll snatch you up at once.'

The matter was soon settled. A meeting was arranged between Wellington and Anstey, and the Duke liked him so much that he declared he would be wasted at the Admiralty, and that as soon as Jack had taken his seat, he would like him to lead a new Select Committee to review the operation of the Poor Laws.

In vain did Jack protest his complete ignorance of the Poor Laws and of the rural scene in general. In the Duke's view the experience of housing and victualling large numbers of men in confined spaces and on limited funds, as well as the understanding of human nature — particularly lower-deck

397

human nature — he must have gained over long years as a frigate-captain, made him the perfect candidate for the job.

Other matters were being settled advantageously at that time. The search for a Parliamentary seat for Thomas was resolved with unexpected ease by the sudden death of the elderly Member for Winchendon. Winchendon Manor belonged to the Aylesbury estate, and was in fact leased to a distant Cavendish cousin. The seat was therefore virtually in Roland's gift, and a very little trouble and expense was enough to secure the loyal electorate's votes. Carriages were laid on to take them to the poll, with a magnificent supper afterwards at the Manor, and a handshake for each from Lord Aylesbury himself; and thus Thomas Rivers Weston was duly returned as the Member for Winchendon of His Majesty's House of Commons in Parliament.

Lucy, in fact, opined that Roland needn't have bothered about the supper. 'They'd have done their duty without that,' she said, 'and it must have cost you several hundred pounds, with the hire of the coaches and the orchestra too.'

Roland was unrepentant. 'It doesn't do to be paltry. Treat them right this time, and they'll remember it the next. Besides, it was fun. I enjoyed it, and so did Thalia.'

Thereupon Lucy had no more to say, for she had already learned that where Roland was concerned, Thalia's happiness was paramount, and he could be quite forceful in securing it. For the moment, Lucy had no quarrel with that, for Thalia was at last doing her duty. In November she had announced formally that she was with child: the heir to the title and estate of the Earl of Aylesbury was due to make its appearance in June 1828. Roland was thrilled and delighted, predicted confidently that it would be a boy, and already referred to Thalia's increasing forward projection as 'Lord Calder'.

Thalia also seemed pleased, even complacent. Lucy had half expected her to resent the curtailment of her freedom, but she seemed happy making her plans and settling into a more domestic frame of life. She and Roland gave up the house in Conduit Street as unsuitable, and took instead a much more handsome establishment on Berkeley Square, which Roland said with satisfaction would do for them for a permanence. In her approaching motherhood she developed an intimacy with her cousin Polly Paston, who was expecting her third child at more or less the same time as Thalia's first. Despite their age difference, they got on very well, having similar tastes in most things, and under Polly's influence, Thalia's interests began to widen and her information to improve.

The cousins soon formed a circle with Lady Mary Hope — Thalia's old friend Mary Penshurst who had married Sir Henry Hope — who was also increasing; and another Mary, Viscountess Petersfield, who as Lady Mary Fleetwood had been a *débutante* at the same time as Polly.

This quiet and matronly circle replaced to a large extent the more dashing friends she and Roland had shared, and Tom found, to his relief, that he had no difficulty in avoiding coming into contact with her. He saw Roland at their clubs, and dined alone with him often to discuss Parliamentary business, so their friendship and closeness was not broken. When he dined with Roland and Thalia together, it was usually *en famille* with the Theakstons or Greyshotts or both, which was safe and unembarrassing.

His mother, it was evident, had never suspected his trouble, for which he was both glad, and grateful to his stepfather. The subject had never been raised again between Thomas and Lord Theakston. Whether Theakston had carried out his intent of talking to Thalia and, separately, to Roland, he had no way of knowing. He only knew that everything had turned out exactly as Lord Theakston had planned.

Only when Thalia's baby was born a month early, on the eighth of May, did Thomas sometimes catch Lord Theakston looking at him thoughtfully. Certainly the baby was big and healthy for one so premature, but Thalia seemed uncloudedly happy, and looked with affection on Roland when he took his son into his arms and paraded him round the room. The baby was christened at Wolvercote, amid great ceremony and an army of relatives who emerged from rustic manors all over the country to welcome William James Cavendish Manvers

Chetwyn, Viscount Calder, heir apparent to the earldom of Aylesbury, into the family.

Thomas, taking his turn at holding the precious bundle, and with his brother's affectionate arm across his shoulder, looked down into the amorphous features and comforted himself that whatever the truth of the matter, the small viscount would have exactly as much Chetwyn blood in him, whichever of them was the father.

CHAPTER TWENTY

May 1828 brought not only the birth of an heir to the Earl of Aylesbury — as Lucy said sadly to her husband, the first of her grandchildren that she was likely to keep — but a further Cabinet crisis.

'The trouble with the Duke is that he hasn't a how to be tactful,' Lucy complained, somewhat to Danby's surprise, since tact was a notion largely foreign to her nature too.

'He did his best, Mama,' said the Member for Winchendon, who was dining with them at Upper Grosvenor Street. 'He complained that the reason he was getting behind with business was that he was spending so much of his time "assuaging what gentlemen call their feelings".'

'He's a soldier, not a politician,' said Lord Theakston. 'He likes unquestioning obedience to orders. It don't suit him to "by your leave" and "if you please" fellows he thinks ought to be doin' their duty.'

Tom grinned. 'Oh, quite. But what *is* their duty? What if their conscience and the Duke bid 'em vote different ways?'

Theakston smiled at his son. 'Can't say. I'm a soldier too — never had to worry about conscience. Mind you, I never supposed politicians did either.'

'Needlessly cynical, sir,' Tom laughed. 'All the same, I think the Duke's done himself up this time.'

The crisis had its origins in the decision to abolish two particularly corrupt rotten boroughs, East Retford and Penryn. The Government proposal was that the seats should be

401

transferred to their neighbouring counties; but Huskisson and Palmerston suggested that here was an opportunity to enfranchise two rapidly-growing towns — Birmingham and Manchester, which had no representation at all. This idea was not acceptable to the High Tory wing of the cabinet, but at last a half-and-half compromise was thrashed out: East Retford was to go to the county, and Penryn was to be allocated to Manchester.

However, despite frantic effort on the part of Lord Batchworth, who called to his aid close friends such as his brother-in-law the Earl of Aylesbury, and the new Baron Anstey, to support the small Whig-commercial-reformist interest in the House of Lords, the noble lords refused by a large majority to countenance the creation of a Member for a place like Manchester.

As Lord Greyshott said to Lord Theakston in the ante-room, 'Once you start down that road, where does it end? Turn the House into a bear-garden. Mill masters and iron masters and greengrocers and God knows what! Reform this and change that — shan't know where we are. Have the Papists in here next! I didn't fight the French for twenty years to have the House crawling with idolaters!'

Lord Theakston forbore to remind Lord Greyshott that he had spent the twenty years of the war migrating safely and comfortably between his clubs and a few select country houses, and confined himself to agreeing sadly.

When the motion to transfer the Penryn seat to Manchester was defeated, Huskisson and Palmerston expressed their protest by voting against the Government on the transfer of the East Retford seat to the county. That evening Huskisson wrote to the Duke saying curtly that his seat on the Cabinet was at the Duke's disposal. To Huskisson's dismay, Wellington chose to regard that as a letter of resignation and informed the King straight away of the Member for Liverpool's decision.

'The trouble is, Huskisson hasn't any tact either,' Tom said. 'It was a very brusque letter — almost rude. And it's no use his saying afterwards to his friends that he never meant it to be taken literally, when he's too proud to ask the Duke's pardon.'

'Wellington wouldn't have given him his seat back if he'd begged on his knees,' said Lord Theakston wisely. 'He's never liked Huskisson, and he's glad to be rid of him.'

'Yes, but he'll take the rest of the Canningites with him,' said Tom. 'Palmerston and Lamb have already resigned.'

Lucy shrugged. 'The Duke never wanted 'em in the first place, if you ask me. You know how anti Catholic Emancipation he is.'

'True, Mama, but he'll find it a difficult job to govern the country with nothing but the High Tories to support him. And whatever you think of their politics, Huskisson and Palmerston are very able men the country can ill afford to lose. William Lamb was doing a good job in Ireland, too.'

'Poor William Lamb,' Lucy said — his name always seemed to couple itself with the epithet quite automatically. 'He needs office to keep his mind from his domestic troubles.'

'Sendin' him to Ireland was goin' rather too far, though,' Theakston commented solemnly. 'No good cuttin' off a man's head to cure him of a headache.'

'Well, he'd have been back soon enough anyway,' said Lucy. 'That drunken ruin of a father of his can't last much longer, and then he'll be taking his seat in the Lords as Lord Melbourn.'

'His sister thinks he'll be Prime Minister one day,' said her husband. 'Said so to Mrs Arbuthnot yesterday.'

Lucy was dismissive. 'She would say something like that! I can't bear Emily Cowper at any price,' she said impatiently; and then, 'Where did *you* see Mrs Arbuthnot?'

'Oh, just popped in as I was passin',' Theakston said airily, winking at Tom with the side of his face furthest from her. 'How's your cousin Polly these days, Tom? Seen anything of her? We haven't seen her for a week or two. Still well, is she? Must be getting near her time by now.'

Tom, always alert to his stepfather's interest, picked up his cue gracefully.

'I haven't seen her lately, but I spoke to Sir Henry in Watier's the other day . . .'

*

Father Moineau's indisposition with a cold coinciding with a hanging day in York had led Benedict to press for a holiday; and remembering how precious were the unexpected holidays of his own youth, the priest had yielded, and taken himself gratefully back to his own room.

Having been brought up with a tender conscience, Benedict went first to his mother to see whether she wanted any help with anything. He found her in the laundry-room mourning a damask table-cloth on which Nicholas had spilt his burgundy wine one evening last week.

'It is a great pity, but I do not think it will ever come out. If only he had told someone at once; but he had sent the servants to bed, so it was left there all night.'

'Can't it be bleached out?' Bendy asked sympathetically.

'Not entirely. It will still leave a mark.' She sighed. 'And it was a favourite of mine. Your grandmother gave it to me when I was first engaged to your papa. Do you see the little hares and the sprigs of heather all woven in with the *fleurs de lys* around the border. Ah well, it was very old,' she said, trying to be brisk, 'and one should not grieve for the things of this world. Where do you think of going, *mon chou*?'

'Into York, Mama, just to see the fun. Is there anything you want there?'

'Yes, my own, if it will not be a great trouble to you, you might take back my books to the library, and if they have the third volume, which I left behind last time, bring it to me. That is the Select Library in Blake Street, do you know it?'

'Yes, Mama. Anything else?'

'Oh no, I would not trouble you. It is some ribbon I wish to match, but I shall go in myself another day. It will be so crowded today — I wonder you should want to go.'

'That's the fun of it,' Bendy said with a grin.

Héloïse shook her head. '*Ca me dépasse!* You will be careful, my son?'

'*Bien sûr, ma mère,*' he replied in kind, and took himself off.

There was no point on such a day, he thought, in taking a horse into York, so he walked across the fields, passing into the city by Micklegate Bar, which looked so denuded and vulnerable now without its barbican. The Corporation, being prevented by law from pulling down the city walls without an Act of Parliament, contented themselves with knocking holes in them piecemeal in the name of 'improvement'.

Micklegate was filled with carts and carriages, all but stationary as they waited their turn to cross the river. Despite being twice as wide as the old Ouse bridge, the new one didn't seem to have eased the traffic problems at all. It was a toll bridge, and there always seemed to be an argument going on over whether, and how much, toll should be paid. Benedict, slipping easily through the crowds like a lean dog, reached the toll gate to find a country waggon holding everything up. It was loaded high with crates of chickens and eggs for the weekly market in Pavement, but there were also two sheep tethered amongst the boxes. The red-faced proprietor was arguing fiercely that they were pet sheep, not for sale, and that they should therefore be toll-free. The tollkeeper, equally red-faced, was calling him a liar and enquiring whether he thought him an idiot. A large clot of pedestrians had gathered interestedly in the hope that the farmer would answer in the affirmative.

Benedict crossed the bridge and cut through the back courts and lanes to Davygate so as to avoid St Sampson's Square, where there was another market going on, and thence into Blake Street. In the elegant hush of the Select Subscription Library he yielded up the two volumes of *Fordyce's Sermons*, learned to his secret relief that the third volume was not available but had been placed on order for Lady Morland, and went out again into the noisy street lighter by several pounds and feeling free and festive.

The hanging was on the other side of the city, on St George's Field, opposite the castle. A new 'drop' had been erected there some years before because of the disruption caused by the condemned having to walk through the streets to the old Tyburn, which had been on Toft Green. Benedict rather regretted the move, which meant there would be no more last-minute attempts at rescue, nor chances for the condemned to rave and harangue the crowd on their way to the scaffold, in the way his father had described from his own boyhood.

405

Still, the hangings remained very popular, and a huge and festive crowd always gathered on St George's Field to watch. Benedict liked the people and the pedlars and the pie-sellers, the balladeers who sold song-sheets about the crimes of the condemned, the ale-booths and taffy-stalls and hot-chestnut braziers, and the pickpockets and racketeers and the men with dancing dogs who hung about the fringes of the crowd. There would be four hanged today, out of the forty-two condemned at the last assizes — most sentences were commuted before execution day. Benedict never actually watched the drop, but there was no doubt there was a horribly thrilling moment when the whole crowd would gasp as one, and let the breath out in a communal moan.

He decided to cut through St Helen's Square and walk down Coney Street. There was a tobacco shop on the corner which fascinated him, because it had a dragon's head made out of metal secured to the wall beside the door, from whose nostrils leapt two flaming gas jets for the convenience of passing smokers. Also in Coney Street was the Black Swan Inn where there was always something amusing to look at, since twenty coaches a day pulled into and out of its yard. The George Inn opposite maintained a tremendous rivalry with it for the private trade, and sometimes ostlers or post boys would run out in the road and try to cajole chaises into the yard of one or the other. Benedict lived in hope of witnessing a full-scale battle developing in the middle of the street.

He was standing just outside the yard of the Black Swan, watching the departure of the slow stage for Malton, when the flicker of a familiar face caught his eye. He turned his head to look at a woman coming out of the lane on the opposite side of the street, and realised with a start that it was Annie. He hadn't seen her for more than a year, since that last farewell in the shippon when he had given her the scarf. He had wondered about her for months, and then gradually, knowing he would never know what had happened to her, had dismissed her from his mind. Now as he saw her, all his old affection and new curiosity rushed through him. He shoved himself off the wall and darted across the road,

dodging through the traffic to catch her before she disappeared in the crowds.

'Annie! Annie!'

She had gone twenty yards before he caught her up, and
she heard him over the noise of the street. She turned with a
start, and for a moment she looked frightened until she saw
who it was. Then she looked more than anything perplexed.
There was no welcoming smile for him, only a look of faint
apprehension.

'Annie,' he said, halting in front of her, 'it's me, Bendy.
Don't you know me?'

'Yes,' she said after a moment. 'Yes of course. I didn't —
I thought you were —' She stopped again, looking confused.
She was speaking differently, he noticed: her accent was less
marked, and she had said 'yes' instead of 'aye' and 'you'
instead of 'tha'. She really must have bettered herself, then,
he thought, remembering what Mr Pike had said she had told
him. Her clothes were certainly of better quality, and she was
wearing good shoes, a plain, decent bonnet and even gloves.
She looked, not like a lady of course, but at least like a
respectable tradesman's daughter.

'You look prosperous, Annie,' he said. 'You must be doing
well for yourself.'

'Aye — I mean yes, I am. Thank you. And how are you,
Master Morland?' she added with an obvious effort.

'Oh, I'm very well, thank you.' Now that Bendy had had a
chance to study her face, he didn't think she was looking so
well. All the bright colour he remembered had gone from her
cheeks, and she looked pale and, somehow, rather puffy. Her
eyes were dull, without their sparkle, and the lids looked shiny
and perhaps a little swollen, as though from a prolonged fit of
crying. She was still plump, but there was something nervous
or perhaps depressed about her.

'I wish you hadn't gone away without saying goodbye to
me, though,' he said gently. 'Why did you go away?'

She opened her mouth and closed it again, looking away
from him nervously down the street. Perhaps she had a jealous
keeper, he thought. Certainly she had a keeper of some sort: the
bonnet was not a cheap one, and showed a gentleman's taste.

'I don't mean you any harm, Annie,' Bendy said, still gently. 'I was worried about you when you disappeared. I only want to know you're all right now. If you don't want to be seen talking to me here, why don't you step across the road with me, to St Martin's churchyard. There's a bench there and we can sit down —'

She flinched, and said, 'No, no, I must go on! I'm sorry, Master Morland, but I must —! Oh, goodbye to you!' And with that she turned and hurried away from him, pushing through the crowds so blindly that she might have been in flight. He didn't try to pursue her. Puzzled, he turned and walked back the other way, seeing and hearing nothing of what he passed.

He didn't want to go to the hanging now. His festive day was spoiled. He thought he might just stop in at the York Tavern and have a quiet quart of ale, and then walk home. But the day's surprises were not over yet. As he passed the arch into the yard of the York Tavern, he looked in automatically, and saw Ferrars leading his brother's road-horse into one of the stables. He stopped and looked again, thinking his eyes had played tricks on him, but it was Checkmate all right, and he recognised Nicky's saddle and black sheepskin numnah too.

It was very odd. Bendy knew perfectly well that when Nicky rode into the city he always left his horse at the Bunch of Grapes in Grape Lane, just as his father had always done. Why should he suddenly change for a strange stable? And why hadn't he said he was coming into York? That morning at breakfast he had said he was riding out to Heslington to see a friend. It was very odd.

However, he told himself with a mental shake, it was plain that whatever Nicky was doing, he didn't want it to be known, and if Benedict remained where he was, Ferrars coming out of the stable would see him. What Ferrars knew, Nicky knew within the day, and Bendy knew to his cost what Nicky was like when annoyed. He hurried away, abandoning the York Tavern. There were three hundred hostelries in York, any one of which could accommodate him with his ale, and without his brother's groom.

★

The Autumn Horse Fair at York was one of the most important in the land, attracting buyers not only from the Ridings, but from all over the country, from London, from Ireland, and even from the Continent. James sold most of his racehorses during and just after the August race week, but the Michaelmas fair was his market-place for hacks, carriage horses, and hunters.

It was a hectic time, and with all the grooming, clipping, exercising and schooling that had to be done, in the two weeks before the sale there was work for everyone who had his full complement of limbs and eyes.

'It's at times like this that I really miss Edward,' James confided to Héloïse. 'He had such a sure hand with the young horses.'

'Doesn't Nicholas help?' Héloïse asked. 'I thought he'd been working really hard for you.'

'Oh yes, I couldn't do without him,' James said hastily, 'but the fact is there's work for him *and* Ned, if only I had him, and a dozen more besides. I'd take Polly back if I could!' He eyed his wife speculatively. 'What about you, Marmoset? Would you care to drive a pair of horses round the fields for me?'

Héloïse laughed. 'Not for a prayer! You had better stick with Nicky, my James.'

'He's a great help, of course, but I really need someone to help me with the young hunters. Nicky —' He hesitated. 'I don't know, quite. He's a little heavy-handed with them sometimes. Doesn't seem to distinguish between a horse being difficult, and one that's uncertain and nervous. He gave that young chestnut with the blaze a tremendous beating the other day because she wouldn't go through a gate, when really she was just frightened of it, and needed coaxing.'

'He's young himself,' Héloïse said peaceably. 'He'll learn.'

'Yes,' James said. 'But it doesn't help my problem now.'

Héloïse put down her needle, a sign of great emotion. 'If you did not have all these reschooled horses to deal with you would have time for everything else without driving yourself so.'

'Ah, but I'm going to sell a great many of those at the fair,

409

and make a large profit, so you'll see the point of it by and by.'

'I would be glad if I thought you would not at once buy more of them,' Héloïse said severely.

'Oh — I might, I suppose — if there are any bargains that strike my eye,' James said airily.

'But where will it end? At first it was just a few for Africa. Now it is dozens every year.'

'But the challenge, Marmoset! You don't understand. To see the quality in a horse, only masked and trammelled by bad schooling or ill-treatment, and to bring it out — I think sometimes it must be the way a sculptor feels when he looks at a block of stone and sees the statue inside.'

Héloïse sighed, but said no more. She had had the argument before so many times that she knew she could not win it.

Henry Anstey was visiting his old friends Nicholas and Benedict. On long vacation from Oxford, where he was reading law, he had spent part of the summer visiting the works of the Liverpool and Manchester railway. Since the tour of Northumberland and Durham when they were boys, he had been enormously enthusiastic about railways. This had caused a slight coolness between him and Nicky, who disliked to see his former lieutenant getting on so well with his little brother.

'I can't think why you wanted to waste so much time on it,' he said loftily. 'There's nothing new or interesting about tramways — certainly nothing *gentlemanly*.'

Harry was apologetic at first. 'Oh, but you see, Papa was so very keen, I feel I ought to see what can be done to fulfil his dream. You know he wanted us to have our own tramroad from the mine to the canal, eventually from the mine all the way to York —'

'Dream is right!' Nicholas sneered. 'It will never happen, and I'll tell you why: not a single landlord between Garforth and York would ever allow you to take it across their land. I know I wouldn't.'

'But a tramroad would be awfully good for your Papa's

410

business,' Harry said, rather hurt at the attitude. 'So many more horses would be needed, and in general trade it would mean —'

Benedict burst in at that point. 'Oh but Harry, if you're going to have a railway, it's such a waste not to go the whole way and try for a loco-motive engine! Horses are well enough, but they can't pull half the load.'

Harry turned to him with the relief of a stranger in a foreign land meeting someone who speaks his own language. 'Well, of course, it would really depend on whether anyone could invent a really *reliable* locomotive. They've all had their troubles so far —'

'But what about the *Royal George*? I read about her — she was built by Mr Hackworth for the Stockton to Darlington way, and she's been operating successfully for a year now. She has a *huge* boiler, and two vertical cylinders, so that —'

'Yes, but the layout is inconvenient, with the return flue and the firedoor in front. It means she has to push her coal tender before and pull the water tender behind. Besides, she's very slow, no faster than a canal boat. She does well enough as a colliery locomotive, but she'd never do for the Liverpool and Manchester, with the variety of goods they hope to handle. They need speed as well as strength and reliability.'

'Have they decided on the method of working yet?' Bendy asked. 'Oh, I wish I had been able to go with you, and see what you've seen! It must have been wonderful!'

'Some of the works are remarkable,' Harry agreed. 'Tunnels and cuttings and embankments such as you can't imagine! It's a marvel of engineering. But the committee still hasn't decided on the motive power, whether it should be stationary or locomotive engines. The trouble is that no-one has any experience of successful working by locomotive, whereas stationary engines and cable haulage have proved their worth over and over.'

'I thought your precious railways were to create a demand for horses?' Nicky said.

'Oh, well, here it would, perhaps, but they decided some time ago that for the Liverpool and Manchester, horses would not be able to cope with the volume of traffic.'

411

Bendy burst in again, waving the question of horses aside. 'Of course horses won't do! But neither will cable haulage — a single breakdown anywhere on the line brings all the traffic to a halt. I bet George Stephenson is against it!'

'Not entirely,' Harry said. 'You must remember that he has designed lots of successful cable-haulage lines. And the Liverpool and Manchester is to have a cable haulage system for the steep tunnel at Edge Hill up from the docks.'

'I don't say stationaries aren't useful in their place,' Bendy said generously, 'and where the incline is too great for a locomotive, obviously you must have them. But for the rest — oh *surely*, surely they won't make do with dull old cable haulage!'

'There's no use your getting in a passion,' Nicky said disagreeably. 'Whatever they decide on, they won't ask *your* opinion — and it's none of your business anyway.'

'Oh, but it's interesting, Nicky,' Harry said mildly. 'You must own —'

'I own nothing of the sort! And I think it's too bad of you to come here to see me and then spend your time encouraging my brother to behave like an outsider. No gentleman of refinement would talk about railways and steam locomotives and whatever else it was. I was going to ask you to come to my club with me, but on second thoughts I don't think I would find any pleasure in your company while you're in this state of mind.'

Before either of them could speak, he had stalked haughtily out of the room, leaving an embarrassed silence behind him.

'Oh dear,' said Harry at last. 'I didn't mean to offend. Does he really hate the railways so much?'

Bendy shook his head. 'There's no knowing what he minds,' he said simply. 'But never mind him now — tell me about the Liverpool and Manchester. They have malleable iron rails, don't they? Are they mounted on wood or stone?'

'Oh, some of each. You see . . .'

Amongst enthusiasts, no detail can ever be dull.

Nicholas escaped his father's eye with difficulty. So close to the horse fair, it was hard for a man to find the leisure to sit

412

down and think, he thought to himself bitterly as he poked his head cautiously out of doors. He managed to slip into the stables without being seen, but was forced to the indignity of tacking his own horse. Ferrars had been recruited to the tedious and dangerous task of schooling carriage horses to back between the shafts, stand still while they were hooked up, and walk forward slowly and gently to take up the strain. It was never possible to know beforehand how a horse would react when the wheels started to come after him, and he found he could not get away from them. Some resigned themselves quite quickly; some in those circumstances felt it best to refuse to move at all in any direction; others went wild with fear. The first and second sort accounted for the tedium of the task; the latter sort for the danger.

Nicholas tightened the girths and pulled down the stirrups while still in the stable, so that when he led Checkmate out into the yard, he had only to jump into the saddle and ride off. All the same, he was shouted after before he was through the barbican. He ignored the shouts, clattered across the draw-bridge, and put Checkmate into a hand canter down the track towards York.

The whole journey his thoughts were a grumbling accompaniment to the rhythm of Checkmate's hoof-beats. His father working him to death like some kind of servant or stablehand ... Harry Anstey coming to see him and then spending all his time talking to that little swine Bendy ... Father Moineau giving him a pi-jaw yesterday about drinking too much at dinner — as if it was any of *his* business ... Mama telling him he was extravagant when he ordered a dozen silk shirts from London instead of having some cack-handed local female make them up. He'd told her that he thought that was why she'd sent him to Eton, to acquire a gentleman's tastes, and instead of apologising she'd actually spoken quite sharply — to *him*! — and said being a gentleman didn't depend on paying twice as much as necessary for everything. He'd held his tongue pretty well at that point, everything considered, since he might well have asked her what it *did* depend on in that case. But she was his mother after all, though sometimes she didn't seem to remember what was due to him as heir — and forgot that he was delicate, too, and wasn't supposed to be upset. All the doctors said so. But none of them understood him. He was too good for the lot of them, that was the truth! Sometimes he felt he hated everybody — and that bloody little swine Bendy most of all, stealing his best friend away from him like that . . .

He passed the preparations for the horse fair, which was held just outside Micklegate Bar, and rode into the city, leaving his horse at the York Tavern. The ostler gave him a funny look, he thought — probably wondering why he didn't have a groom with him, like a proper gentleman. Well, that was Papa's fault, though he could hardly tell the ostler so, which made him cross again. He threw the man a shilling with a lofty air, hoping that would put him in his place, and went out into the street. Little Helen Yard was one of the courts between Davygate and Little Stonegate, and the apartment he had taken for Annie was on the upper floor of a house, with its own private stair. The ground floor was a workshop for a stained glass artist, so it was a quiet and respectable yard, and he could come and go without comment.

Since he hadn't told her he was coming, it was perhaps unreasonable of him to be annoyed that Annie was not there waiting for him, but annoyed he was all the same. He spent some time looking through her things to make sure she had not been buying anything she shouldn't, or accepting presents from other men. Then he sat down on a chair opposite the door to wait, and thought about how he had taken her from Bendy.

It hadn't been difficult. She'd refused just at first, and she'd cried when he told her that he'd tell her master what she'd been up to and get her sent to a house of correction. She'd cried again when she told him that Bendy was good to her and that he'd bought her a scarf, and that she'd sworn to be true to him. That was his cue to win her over.

'I'll give you more than a scarf,' he'd told her. 'I'll give you a silk dress, and a room of your own, and you can swear to be true to me instead.' And as the clinching argument, 'I shall be

414

Master of Morland Place one day. You have to do what I tell you.'

Since then, there had been one or two little outbursts of rebellion, but he knew how to deal with those, and on the whole she'd settled down quietly and gratefully to her new life. Gratefully, yes — after all, he was very good to her. He'd bought her new clothes, she had nice things to eat and a room of her own, he'd taught her to speak better, and had even started teaching her to read — though he got bored with that quite quickly, so the lessons were spasmodic. And all he wanted in return was for her to be there when he came to see her. He began to work himself up into a passion. It wasn't much to ask, was it? It wasn't as if he had time to visit her all that often, what with Papa treating him like an unpaid groom . . .

He heard her footsteps on the stair, and a moment later the door opened and she stepped in, carrying her market-basket on her arm. She was humming to herself, but the sound stopped as though cut off as she saw him, and the expression of dismay on her face was almost comical.

'Oh — oh — Nicky! I — didn't expect you.'

'So I see,' he said grimly. The colour was draining from her face, leaving it almost yellow. 'And where have you been then, my fine lady?'

'Only — only to the — to buy some things.' She could hardly speak. She licked her lips and tried again. 'Eggs and butter. And a cabbage.'

She made a little awkward gesture of proffering the basket, as though she thought he might want to inspect her purchases. Her eyes were fixed on him with a sort of horrified fascination, like a rabbit looking at a fox.

'You've been out into the streets?' he said silkily. 'Out into the shops to buy things? And you haven't been wearing gloves?'

'Oh — I — it —' She stammered, her eyes never leaving him, her hands massaging the handle of the basket helplessly.

Nicholas stood up. 'That was very naughty of you, my dear, wasn't it? You know I've told you you must always wear gloves when you go out, if you want to be a lady.' He turned away

415

and went to the cupboard in the corner. 'It seems you haven't learned that lesson yet. It seems to me that you need chastising again, to make you remember it properly. Am I right? You need a beating, don't you, on that portion of your anatomy so perfectly designed to receive it?'

She knew he liked her to say yes when he asked that question — it was part of the rules of his game — but the sound she made was hardly more than an exhaled breath.

He took from the cupboard the bound bundle of birch twigs, and turned back to her, feeling enormously good humoured now. A little joke occurred to him, and he decided, generously, to share it with her. 'It's a good job you bought the butter after all,' he chuckled. 'It will come in handy afterwards, to take the smart away.'

It was on the last day of the fair that James saw the horse. It could not have been there on the earlier days, for he knew he would have noticed it at once. It was the sort of horse one saw only once or twice in a lifetime. He stood a little way off, gazing at it in silence, knowing — as one knows quite certainly at such moments — that he had fallen in love.

The horse was a true black without a brown hair on him, standing sixteen hands, and quite the most beautiful animal James had ever been close to. His head was delicately sculpted, his neck powerful, his breast deep, his bone straight and clean. He was standing like a horse just waiting — longing — to be ridden away; not with one foot cocked, like most horses, but with his weight evenly distributed, his head up and alert — poised, one might almost say.

James let out a breath, and as if the horse had heard, he turned his head to look at James. There was a small, uneven white star on the broad black brow, the only marking of any sort. The fine ears pricked, the delicate nostrils flared as though to catch the scent of the man; the shining eyes regarded him with confidence, almost with benevolence. It was as if he was aware of his great and remarkable beauty. There is about some horses a something horsemen call *presence*. It is not beauty, though it often goes hand in hand with beauty; it is simply the quality of drawing all eyes, of seeming more real and vital than anything else in the vicinity. The black horse had presence: while James looked at him, he was unaware of anything else around him.

'— Papa?' Benedict's voice drifted into his consciousness as the world came back to him. 'He's a beauty, isn't he?'

The horse's attendant — owner? — came forward: a swarthy man with dark eyes and black hair in long lovelocks like a gypsy, though he was dressed neatly enough. 'You like my horse, sir?' he said. He did not precisely have a foreign accent; it was more that he spoke clearly and carefully as though English were not his native language.

'He's yours?' James said. He was not aware of the naked longing in his voice, but Benedict noticed it, and gave his father a troubled glance.

The dark man smiled a little. 'I sometimes think, sir, that it is a piece of impudence to talk of owning a horse like him. But insofar as any man has title to him, it is I.'

James had the accent now — it was the soft, careful diction of the far west of Scotland, or perhaps of Ireland.

'What do you call him?' he asked, drifting closer. The horse continued to look at him quietly; he felt as though the big, warm body were drawing him like a magnet.

'Lucifer,' said the man. 'On account of the star, which seems, just a little you see, to be falling.'

'Lucifer,' said James. He stepped to the side of the horse, and the horse turned to touch him lightly with his nose. 'Is he as good as he looks?'

'Just look at the bone, sir, and that lovely head. He's a sweet mover, a lovely ride. He has a mouth like a lady's glove, and goes like the beating of a man's own heart, to the lightest touch of hand or foot. He needs not whip nor spur. He moves straight and true, and jumps anything that you can see the sky over.'

James laid a hand on the glossy black shoulder, and a shudder of love went through him. The horse stood poised, seeming only lightly connected to the ground, though James's hands told him that he was put together with solid bone and powerful muscle, enough to carry him all day and still come home dancing. The legs were clean and cool; as James's fingers closed over the heel, the horse lifted its foot with perfect willingness — a small, round, neat foot, unshod and yet shewing no sign of raggedness: hard as flint, like an arab's hoof. Sound from the tips of his ears to the tips of his toes.

James's mouth was dry, his heart trotting like a dog. He would die if he didn't have this horse. He turned to Benedict. 'What do you think of him?' He asked it rhetorically, in the way a young man asks of his love, 'Isn't she beautiful?'

Benedict hesitated. 'He's certainly good-looking. But —'

'But?' James's eyes widened at the incomprehensible reservation. 'But what?'

'I don't know, Papa. There's something about his eye.'

'He has a beautiful eye!'

'Oh, yes, I know, but — well, he seems terribly full of himself, somehow. There's something — too composed about him. I can't quite explain.'

'I see that you can't,' James said with heavy irony.

'He is handsome,' Benedict said again, helplessly.

The dark man spoke again, politely, almost delicately. 'Were you thinking of him for yourself sir? Were you thinking perhaps of hunting him?'

'Hunting? Perhaps,' James said with belated caution.

'He would carry you all day and never miss a step. He's exactly what you want, sir. I know it here.' The man touched his breast. 'Once in a man's life, he needs a horse that isn't just a ride, but a companion. This is a *thinking* horse, sir.'

'How much,' James said helplessly.

'Five hundred.'

James heard Benedict gasp. 'Five hundred guineas?' he said, almost aghast himself.

The dark man smiled faintly. 'I'll make it pounds, sir, for the ready money. I must have it today. I go home tomorrow, and the horse with me, if he is not sold.'

'I'll get it.'

'Papa!'

'*I'll get it*! Don't sell him to anyone else. I'll get it now, and come straight back. Bendy, you wait here. Don't let anyone else have him!'

And James was gone, leaving Benedict staring after him, perplexed and worried.

CHAPTER TWENTY-ONE

Héloïse stood on the steps of the house and looked on doubtfully as the horse was led round the yard by Durban to James's directions.

'Well, what do you think?' he said at last, turning to her with eyes which were young with love in his no-longer-young face.

Héloïse felt helpless in the face of it. What was happening here? 'He seems very nice. But James, *five hundred pounds?*'

Durban spoke: 'Its not even as though he's an entire, sir. You can't breed from him.'

James's face hardened with resistance. 'He doesn't have to justify his existence in that way. Good God, can't you *see* —!' He appealed to Héloïse. 'Just once or twice in a lifetime, a horse comes along — it isn't a matter of a means of transport. You remember my old Nez Carré? He was more to me than almost any human being. And since he died —'

Héloïse met Durban's eyes across the yard. Between them the black horse stood poised and self-contained, as if aware of its beauty, expecting their homage. James's old horse Nez Carré had been a kindly, ugly, lop-eared bay gelding, as simple and transparent as most horses are. But the black was something quite different. He had an air of intelligence. He gave the impression that he was thinking all the time.

Well, why should that be a bad thing? Héloïse did her best for James. 'If you want him, my James, you don't need to ask my permission. It just seemed a great deal of money for a riding-horse.'

'For a gelding, sir,' Durban added quietly, 'with no name and no history.'

James was more confident now. 'All you need to know about him is what you see before you.'

'But James, the name— you must change it. You cannot call a horse after the Devil. It is not lucky.'

James grinned. 'You dear, superstitious thing! It's because of the star, you see — Lucifer, the falling star. Besides,' he forestalled her, 'he's not named after the Devil: Lucifer was his name while he was still an angel. It means bringer of light, which I should have thought was as lucky a name as you could want.'

'Has Father gone mad?' Nicholas asked, leaning against the doorway of the night nursery.

Benedict looked up, closing with an automatically defensive movement the book in which he had been writing. 'I don't think so. Why?'

'This new horse: the grooms are saying he bought it from a gypsy, and paid a fortune for it.'

Bendy looked away. 'You shouldn't listen to servants' talk.'

'Don't tell me what I should do! I shall do as I please! Is it true he paid five hundred guineas for it?'

'Pounds.'

Nicholas shrugged away the correction. 'Then he is mad! What's the point in selling all those reschooled horses, and then throwing away all the profit on some worthless hack?'

'You obviously haven't seen it. It's a very fine horse.'

'It can't be worth five hundred,' said Nicholas certainly. Benedict couldn't argue with that. 'He knows nothing about it, about its manners, its character — there must be something wrong with it, for a horse like that to be in the hands of a gypsy. When I think of all the hard work that went into those horses we sold —'

'It was mostly his work. I don't see why he shouldn't spend the profit as he wants.'

'Oh don't you, my lad? You pretty soon would if it was *your* inheritance he was squandering!'

For once Bendy almost lost his temper. 'Oh, don't go on

about your inheritance! You can't wait for our parents to die, can you, so that you can get your hands on it?'

Nicholas was startled. 'There's no need for that sort of —'

'Papa has been working all his life on this estate — and Uncle Ned before him — both of them working to keep it in good order, and asking nothing for themselves —'

'Papa's had a pretty good living out of it,' Nicholas sneered. 'He doesn't want for much, that I can see.'

'And you begrudge him that?'

'No — not precisely. All I say is —'

'Let him have the horse. He's earned it,' Benedict said shortly. And then, with a canny look, 'Besides, it isn't for you to say. Morland Place and everything in it belongs to our mother, not to you. And whatever you say and think,' he added as Nicky drew breath to reply, 'the estate isn't entailed. She can leave it to anyone she likes, so I wouldn't count my chickens if I were you.'

Nicholas reddened with anger. 'What do you mean by that? If you think she might give it to *you* —'

'I think nothing of the sort. All I'm saying is it would be a great deal pleasanter for everyone, and more dignified of you, if you could refrain from actually digging the grave until they're dead. Seeing you hanging around my parents carrying a spade over your shoulder is enough to put one off one's food.'

Nicholas breathed hard. 'Why, you insolent little urchin!' He stepped towards Bendy with hand raised, but Benedict didn't flinch. He faced his brother down, and Nicholas paused, and then lowered his hand. Slowly his glare was replaced with a secret smile. 'What a humorist you are, brother,' he said lightly, and turned away. He would let Bendy off this time, he decided — though he deserved a thrashing for his insolence! Just out of generosity, he would let him off.

The resignation of William Huskisson from the Cabinet — or his dismissal by Wellington, depending on your point of view — had unexpected repercussions. To replace him at the Board of Trade, Wellington chose Vesey Fitzgerald, the

Member for Clare, who had to stand for re-election in his constituency before he could join the Cabinet. Fitzgerald was one of the most popular of the Irish landlords, and had voted for Catholic Emancipation on several occasions; but in the by-election he was opposed by Daniel O'Connell, the leader of the Catholic Association, a quasi-military organisation of priests and peasants.

In spite of Vesey Fitzgerald's popularity, O'Connell won the by-election by a large majority, amid great excitement. This put the Government in an awkward position: O'Connell's election was legal, but as a Catholic, he could not sit in the House of Commons.

'Surely that solves the problem, then?' Lucy asked when Tom brought Jack Anstey to dine with her at the height of the crisis. 'They can just tell him to go away.'

Tom shook his head patiently. 'But he has been elected, and Fitzgerald has not. That's a *fait accompli*, Mama.'

'Not only that, ma'am' Anstey added, 'but come the next general election, O'Connell and his followers will repeat the tactic in other Irish constituencies. Can you imagine the fuss if Catholic after Catholic is elected and refused entry to the House?'

'Think of the fuss if they're allowed *into* the House,' Lucy countered. 'God knows, I've nothing against the Catholics, but *you* know how people feel, Danby.'

Lord Theakston nodded. 'Nevertheless, the Duke knows something must be done this time, m'dear. There's already unrest in Ireland. If O'Connell carries on his campaign, as Anstey suggests, we'll be facing civil war. That will do us all a great deal more harm than admitting a few Catholics into the Commons.'

'That's right, sir,' said Tom. 'The Emancipation's got to be pushed through, and as soon as possible.'

'The Duke will never get it past the King,' Lucy said.

But Danby shook his head. 'He's so ill these days, I don't think he has the mind to spare for caring about such things. He's half-stupefied with laudanum for most of the day, to counter the pain in his bladder. I don't think he'll give any resistance.'

423

So it proved. In January 1829, Wellington and Peel introduced the Catholic Emancipation Bill to the House, with
approval from the Duke of Clarence and indifference from His
Majesty. It passed into law in April, and all Irish offices of state
except viceroy and chancellor were opened to Catholics.

'It's a strange thing,' Lucy confided to Jack Anstey one day
when she met him walking across the Park, 'but your father
predicted this, you know, almost two years ago. When
Canning died — and Canning was *for* the Emancipation,
mind — your father said that his death would give a great
forward impetus to the liberal movement.'

'It's true, ma'am, that suppressing a thing sometimes
makes it stronger than leaving it alone.'

'Like pruning roses,' Lucy mused. 'All the same, it does
seem odd for it to be Wellington, of all people, who presented
the Bill and got it through. The victor of Waterloo, to be
leading a reform movement! Where will it all end?'

'It will be hard for him to resist further reforms now,' said
Anstey. 'He has alienated all the High Tories who might have
helped him to hold back the tide. Lord Eldon and his
supporters are furious with the Duke. They won't be satisfied
until they've brought him down.'

Lucy smiled. 'Let 'em try! I don't suppose the Beau cares
a snap about any of 'em.'

'He seems as contemptuous of them as of the Canningites,'
Anstey agreed. 'But there will be more and more pressure
now from the industrious and middle classes for reform —
especially Parliamentary Reform.'

'The Duke won't care for them either,' Lucy said. 'He's a
soldier, not a politician.'

Nicholas always felt a certain restlessness at the end of the
hunting season. He didn't care for fishing, and the shooting
was months away, and there seemed nothing to look forward
to. The sap was rising and the blood was restless, and young
men's fancies were expected lightly to turn to thoughts of
love; but to Nicholas love, as popularly constituted, could not
hold a candle to the excitement of the chase.

He had recently had his twenty-first birthday, and it had

passed not disagreeably. There had been a dinner and ball in his honour. His mother had given him a gold watch, his father had given him a smart tilbury of his own in which to rattle round the neighbourhood, and his allowance had been increased to a near-tolerable level. He had rather expected his life to change on reaching man's estate, but it seemed to go on in the same old way, and once the blessed thought-obliterating hunting was over, his spring restlessness came upon him worse than ever.

He could do anything he wanted, but there was nothing he wanted to do. He had mild amusement in setting himself to find out the details of Benedict's latest *amour*: the boy had fallen in thrall to a well-preserved widow who lived in a large house in Nunnery Lane. At the beginning of the affair Benedict had gone about in a state of blissful exhaustion which Nicholas found both amusing and irritating: the widow had a fine bosom and a knowing eye, and was no doubt teaching Benedict a great deal that he would later find useful. But there was nothing to be gained from the business from Nicky's point of view. He was hardly likely to be able to subvert a mature woman who knew her own mind; and he suspected that if he told his father about it, James was more likely to laugh and applaud than to take Bendy to task.

Nicky's own carnal interests were satisfied by the captive Annie, and his secret collection — now agreeably large — of curious books, which he liked to look at in complete seclusion, in his room with the door locked. As far as other entertainments went, he might have gone to London for the Season, but didn't see the point unless he were looking for a wife, which he was not. There were girls enough in York to flirt with and dance with when he had the inclination, and he had anyway sooner be a large fish in a small pond than vice versa.

So he passed his time in his club, drinking, talking, gambling a little; he spent evenings at the mess at Fulford Barracks at the invitation of some like-minded young officers and was often asked to dine there and play a hand or two of cards; and when he wanted a spree of a more violent sort, he attended illegal cock-fights at the cockpit just off Walmgate, and dog-fights in a warehouse by Layerthorpe Bridge. Soon, anyway, the invitations would begin to arrive to country house-parties, and the restless part of the year would be over. He had only to get through the intervening weeks somehow.

But it was during this period of restlessness that he decided to steal his father's horse. No-one but James had yet been allowed to ride Lucifer. Even his trusted man, Durban, had only been allowed to lead the black at exercise when James was not able to take him out; and that had happened very rarely. Like a man in love, James wanted to be constantly with his adored one. He rode Lucifer for preference all the time, and apart from the normal here-and-there journeys of daily necessity, he managed most days to take the big black out alone for a long ride purely for pleasure.

His love and admiration had not diminished with familiarity, and so far Lucifer had behaved himself so well in public that no-one any longer mentioned the extravagant price the master had paid for him. James had hunted Lucifer all through the winter, and the horse had proved his worth, carrying his rider surely and safely over all ground, and keeping him up with the first flight effortlessly. Only Héloïse remained uneasy about the horse, and that was purely because of his name, which she still thought unlucky. When James mentioned it in her presence, her hand showed a distinct desire all its own to make the sign of the cross.

So one day in a fit of irritable mischief, Nicholas decided take the horse and ride it, just to show them all — especially his father. It was a fine spring day, almost as warm as summer, and Lucifer, having been out with James in the morning, had been turned out for the afternoon in the high paddock up by Ten Thorn Gap. This paddock hadn't been grazed yet, and the new grass was lush and good. In fact Hastings had been saving it for the young mares when they had dropped their new foals and needed good feed to bring on their milk; but James was master, and if he said his horse was to be given the benefit, so be it.

No-one else would be likely to be up that way, and it would be easy enough for Nicholas to take the horse. Impossible, of course, to carry Lucifer's tack up there, even if he could have

426

got it out of the tack-room unseen. He would have to ride up to the paddock on Checkmate and swap over there, and hope Checkmate's saddle would fit the black.

Nicholas set off in good spirits, with the pleasant feeling of excitement that came from the anticipation of doing something he ought not. He reached the paddock without encountering anyone, and there saw Lucifer calmly cropping the grass, all alone in the paddock. He lifted his head as Nicholas appeared, and watched with interest as he rode up to the rails and dismounted. Checkmate whickered a greeting, but Lucifer only stood and looked, his ears pointing, his eye considering.

Catching him proved near impossible. Nicholas tied Checkmate up and started off towards the black across the paddock. Lucifer had gone back to grazing, and without appearing to watch Nicholas, simply kept moving away from him, head down, as though naturally eating his way in that direction. When Nicholas increased his pace, so did Lucifer. When Nicholas stopped, Lucifer apparently found a patch of grass to his liking and stopped too.

A bribe was evidently called for. Nicholas was horseman enough never to leave home without one, and so was able to produce from his pocket a rather wizened windfall apple, which he placed prominently on his palm as he walked towards Lucifer, making inviting chirruping noises. Lucifer lifted his head and watched, regarding the offering carefully. Nicholas stretched out his palm and took another step, his free hand ready to grab the black's headcollar. Lucifer stretched out his neck. Muzzle and apple, free hand and headcollar moved cautiously towards each other, closer and closer. An instant before the point of convergence Lucifer moved like lightning, snatched the apple and sprang away.

Nicholas cursed, lost his temper, and went running after the horse, who played him with the skill of a fisherman, cantering only just beguilingly out of reach until Nicholas was red-faced, sweating and exhausted, and had run himself to a standstill.

'Damn you, then, you black devil! Stay in your field until you rot! I don't care!' Nicky shouted almost tearfully, and turned away, stumping back towards the rails where Checkmate was tied. The game was not worth the candle. He'd like to see his father catch the beast when the time came! Checkmate whickered as he approached, and Nicholas thought the call was for him, and was almost touched. Only as he reached his hand out to the halter rope to untie it, a black muzzle slipped into his field of vision and blew on his fingers, and he realised that Lucifer must have been following him closely all across the field.

He reached out cautiously, expecting the black to jump away again, but having made a fool of him, Lucifer was willing to be caught, and stood still as Nicholas slipped his fingers through the headcollar. He showed no signs of wanting to escape. It was the work of a few moments to transfer the saddle and bridle, adjust them, and put Checkmate into the field. Then, almost holding his breath, Nicholas mounted and gathered the reins. At his command, Lucifer walked jauntily forward, his ears pricked. Nicholas rode up Ten Thorn Lane to the Knapton crossroads, and then turned off onto the open fields towards Harewood Whin, and put the horse into a canter.

It was a different experience. If what he had done before was riding, there had to be another word for this effortlessness, this sense of utter communion with a horse. Lucifer moved as though borne through the air, hardly touching the ground, his round hooves making a soft, damp sound as they struck the close, dense turf. He moved sweetly and in instant obedience to the slightest movement of hand or leg, turning this way or that almost as if in response to his rider's thoughts. The soft air parted round Nicholas's face, smelling of sun-warmed grass, and the moor fled away beneath them, while between the pricked, glossy ears the Whin grew nearer, a brown-grey mass beginning to be flushed with green.

'God,' said Nicholas, and it was the nearest he had come to prayer in many a year. An ear turned back to him enquiringly. Nicholas grinned with elation. What he had seen of Lucifer was as a candle to the sun compared with the experience of riding his father's horse. And perhaps, then, his father had not been so wrong after all. 'You beauty! You marvel,' he said aloud. 'God, what a horse!' And he closed his legs, asking confidently for more speed.

For the fraction of an instant nothing happened; then the black ears snapped down, flat against the skull. Suddenly, frighteningly, the mouth went dead at the other end of the reins: it was like a sound cut off, like a conversational voice going silent. The speed he had asked for was given him: Lucifer went forward as though shot from a gun, and Nicholas swayed out of balance for an instant with the surprise of it. Speed he had asked for, and it was his beyond all expectation; but now it was not his to command or control. Lucifer was galloping at full, furious speed towards the Whin, and Nicholas knew he could not stop him.

There was nothing to do but hold on. Nicholas crouched low, pulling on the dead reins automatically like a man shaking a corpse in the hope of reviving it. The ground went past in a blur; the Whin loomed up, a solid mass of close-packed branches — no path into it at this point. Nicholas had been bolted with before, more than once, in his twenty-one years, and he knew the rules. You stayed on and went with the horse. Sooner or later it would slow down — usually sooner — and its own instinct of self-preservation would keep it, and you, out of trouble. It was only at the last minute that he realised that Lucifer was not going to swing away and skirt the wood as any normal horse would. It was the ears which told him. For the fraction of a second they flicked forward, pointing, deciding, and then were clamped down again, and the horse, incredibly, increased its speed.

Instinct alone saved him. Nicholas knew with some primitive part of him which had nothing to do with reason that the horse meant to kill him, that it meant to gallop into the trees and smash him from its back against the low branches. All in the same movement he shook his feet free of the stirrups and flung himself desperately sideways out of the saddle. For a brief moment he soared painlessly through the open air, and then the turf came up and hit him sickeningly on the hip and shoulder. All the breath was knocked from him in one sob; but as he rolled over he saw the horse in a brief glimpse, all mixed up with sky and grass. He thought it would crash into

429

the wood in a mess of broken twigs, but it stopped, miraculously, with three bounces just at the edge of the trees.

It was a while before Nicholas could obey his horseman's instinct to get up and catch the loose horse. He lay as though flattened, gasping for breath, his body trembling with shock and the reverberation of the impact. He managed at last to roll over onto his knees, paused a moment with black flecks surging before his eyes, and then pushed himself unsteadily up. Lucifer was standing a little way off, his reins trailing; standing in that curious four-square way of his, his weight evenly balanced, looking at Nicholas. Nicky expected him to be difficult to catch, but he remained quite still and let him come up, only his ears moving, perhaps apprehensively, as though he wondered what the rider's reaction would be.

Nicholas took hold of the reins with a hand which still trembled, and stared at the horse consideringly. Lucifer, he thought, looked subdued — even, if it were not fanciful, a little depressed. Then he looked towards the trees where he had almost met his death. Yes, he thought, the place had been well chosen: the gap between two trees just wide enough to admit a horse, though the rider would probably have smashed both knees on the trunks; the thick branch under which a horse might duck, but low enough to whip the rider from the saddle, probably breaking his skull, or his neck, or both. Nicholas stared, still too physically shocked to feel nausea or even much surprise. It had not been complete madness, then. Lucifer had not bolted blindly, nor suicidally. He had chosen the spot carefully, with the intention of killing his rider.

'You devil horse,' he said softly. The ears moved questioningly, and the horse regarded him with that same air, both puzzled and depressed. 'I ought to beat you,' Nicholas said. 'I ought to flog you.' But — leaving aside the fact that he didn't yet have the strength, that his arms were still like strings of vermicelli — there was too much here to think about. He led the horse away from the trees, turned it to face the direction of home, and mounted cautiously. 'Walk on,' he said, giving the office.

Lucifer walked forward lightly and smoothly, as though nothing had happened; an obedient horse, well schooled and quite innocent. Nicholas, while not relaxing his guard, allowed his mind room to consider. So that was the secret, the reason that a horse so splendid had come to be sold in such a way, and by such a man. He was mad, of course, though it was a considering sort of madness. How many times had he killed, Nicholas wondered? And in how many different ways? For this was a thinking horse — no doubt he had other tricks stored up to play, just as the circumstances arose.

Most intriguing question of all, did his father know? Had Lucifer played his tricks on James yet, or had he so far revealed only the sweet and delightful face to his master. If James knew, he was keeping it to himself, and that was understandable: having paid so much so publicly, he would not want it known he had bought a pig in a poke. His pride would demand the secret be kept. Perhaps that was why he had not allowed anyone else to ride the horse, not even Durban.

But on the other hand, it might have been that Lucifer had been biding his time, and had not yet made any attempt on James. And if that were the case, the attempt was yet to come, and it could come at any time — to a rider utterly infatuated and utterly unprepared.

Unprepared. Nicholas's thoughts startled him so much that his hands checked the horse without his meaning to, and he had to send it on again. He must warn his father, of course, just in case he didn't know about Lucifer's other nature. Of course he must, otherwise there might be a horrible accident. James might be hurt, or even killed. He must be warned to be on his guard. Nicholas must own up to having ridden Lucifer without permission, even though his father would be angry, for the greater good.

Of course he must. And yet — it might all be his imagination, might it not? A horse wouldn't really plot to kill its rider. Horses weren't clever enough. Lucifer had just bolted — stung by a horse-fly perhaps, or merely startled by something unnoticed by Nicholas. In fact, if he hadn't thrown himself off, Lucifer would have stopped anyway, just as he did, before reaching the trees. The rest was just imagination, and there was no need to admit his crime. No

431

need at all. He would only get himself into trouble for nothing. No good would be done, because no-one would believe him anyway. And why should they? It was impossible, wasn't it? It was all his imagination.

In August Rosamund and Jes travelled down to Wolvercote to stay with Roland and Thalia. The Theakstons were also there, and Maurice Ballincrea came down for a few days in one of his migrations between the houses of his friends. Thalia was increasing again, pleased with the fact and very proud of young William, and was constantly urging her brother to marry and settle down.

'It's the tailless fox all over again,' Maurice said, shaking his head at her. 'Now Roland's managed to pen you up at last, you want to see me lose my freedom as well. Well, it won't do, Thally! I mean to have as much fun as I can, while I can.'

'But being married is fun,' Roland protested. 'Isn't it, Batchworth? Papa Danby, I appeal to you! You don't know what you're missing, Maurice, indeed you don't. I wouldn't be a miserable bachelor again for all the world.'

'Nor would I be a *miserable* one,' Maurice agreed. 'For those that don't like the state, the cure is to hand. Like my friend Ashley — no sooner decided that he ought to get married than he most conveniently fell in love.'

'You can hardly blame him,' Jes said. 'Minny Cowper is the most delightful girl — pretty, lively and sweet-tempered. I've heard her called the leading favourite of the Town.'

'By her mother, no doubt,' Lucy said somewhat sourly. Minny was Emily Cowper's daughter. Her given name was also Emily, so she was called Minny to distinguish her from her mother.

'No, by Princess Lieven, as a matter of fact,' said Jes. 'And whatever you think of Lady Cowper, you must admit that Minny is the prettiest girl of her season. Everyone's in love with her — young Talbot, Wortley, Russell —'

'I think you must be one of her suitors yourself,' Rosamund smiled at his enthusiasm.

He returned the look, but went on, 'I don't think your Ashley has much chance with her though, Ballincrea. What

432

has he? Three thousand a year at most. And from exactly the opposite interest as the Cowpers — they fervent Whigs, he stern Tory.'

'I don't know what the poor child has done to deserve to be sacrificed to the Shaftesbury family,' Lucy put in. 'With due respect to your friend, Maurice, he has an odious father and four beggarly brothers, all of whom are generally deemed to be mad; and Lady Shaftesbury must be the most unpleasant woman ever to wear shoes. And Ashley himself is such a stick, with his Evangelical enthusiasms, while she's quite a lively, merry little thing.'

Maurice was nettled into defence. 'Well, ma'am, the advantage is not universally considered all on his side. Not everyone likes the Lambs, or considers them sound.'

'Too clever and satirical — I know,' Lucy said. 'I've never liked Emily Cowper, and I suppose she epitomises them. And God knows who Minny's father is, for it isn't Lord Cowper, that's for sure.'

'Oh Mother,' Rosamund said reproachfully.

Lucy was unrepentant. 'I doubt whether Emily Cowper knows herself, though I suppose the favourite money is on Palmerston. How those Whigs like to nest together, to be sure! And Minny certainly seems to be an especial favourite with him. He writes her letters and sends her gifts, and brings her things back from Paris every year.'

'Men do sometimes take a fancy to other people's little girls,' Rosamund said innocently. 'Don't they, Jes?'

'Do they?' he responded. 'I'm sure I couldn't say.'

'I'm sure you could. Do you know, Mama, that he's struck up a perfect *liaison* with Sophie's little girl? He takes her out once a week driving in his carriage, and she writes a letter to him every Wednesday, full of secret jokes and shared allusions. I don't know whether to be jealous or despairing.'

'Now Ros, my dear —'

'I'm joking you, fool! But really, Mother, you should see Miss Fanny Hobsbawn when she's in full feather! There never was such a little temptress since Delilah took Sampson to the barber's shop.'

'She's very advanced for her age, that's all,' said Jes.

433

Thalia saw an opening. She hadn't heard her own child mentioned now for fully half an hour. 'William is too, isn't he, Roland? Do you know, he knows the name of ten different flowers; and he can recite the first five books of the Bible, and numbers up to twelve.'

'Remarkable!' said Lord Theakston kindly, seeing that no-one else was going to encourage her; and then, to divert the conversation away from William and his achievements, he asked, 'How is your railway coming along, Batchworth?'

'My railway? Would that it were!' Jes said. 'Though I must say I expect very material advantages from it, now that they intend to bridge the Irwell and bring the trains right in to Liverpool Road. From there it's only the shortest of hauls to my factories. I anticipate my transportation costs will more than halve once it's in operation.'

'Bridging the Irwell is it, now? What a feat of engineering the whole thing must be! Thirty miles long, isn't it? And solid rock to cut away above Liverpool, I understand.'

'Yes, sir — but the worst problem they've encountered is Chat Moss. There are many eminent engineers who have said that it will be impossible to take a railway carrying such a weight of goods across a bog like that. Francis Giles has said that if it can be done at all, it will cost more than a quarter of a million pounds —'

'Good God!'

'— but Stephenson says it can be done for much less, and I believe him. He has performed many a wonder already, which the experts dismissed as impossible.'

'I should like to see it,' Theakston said.

'When you next come to visit us,' Jes said, 'I hope you will both allow me to take you to see the Edgehill Tunnel.'

Lucy raised her eyebrows expressively. 'Take us to see a railway tunnel?'

Rosamund smiled. 'I've been to see it, Mama. It's quite one of the wonders of Liverpool. No-one visits anyone in Liverpool without being conducted through it.'

'What possible pleasure can there be in a tunnel?'

'Oh, it isn't dark or dangerous, I assure you,' Rosamund said. 'Its purpose is to pass goods down from Edgehill to the

434

Wapping docks by cable haulage, but it's such a wonder of engineering that they've made a promenade of it until the whole railway's finished. The walls are whitewashed and the floor levelled, and there are gas jets every fifty yards to light it, so it's perfectly pleasant. I've been twice already, and I've taken Sophie and Fanny too. There are plates fixed to the walls to tell you the names of the streets you're passing under. It's the most curious sensation to think of them being up above your head, with carriages rushing back and forth, and people walking to and fro.'

Lucy shook her head at the idea of such a sensation being sought for pleasure.

'Have you decided on the motive power yet?' Lord Theakston asked. 'I read in *The Times* that the Act of Parliament for the Newcastle and Carlisle railway expressly forbids steam locomotive engines.'

'There's a great deal of resistance to the idea from landowners up there,' Batchworth said. 'As far as the Liverpool and Manchester is concerned, there's still a division amongst members of the Board about the rival merits of locomotives and stationaries. Walker and Rastrick, the engineers, were commissioned to make a report on the question, and they came down in favour of fixed engines. But of course George Stephenson is very enthusiastic about locomotives, and since the report admitted that there were grounds for expecting improvements in the construction and performance of locomotives, the Board has come up with an ingenious solution. They are to hold locomotive trials, open to all, and with a prize of £500 to the winning engine, provided it can meet certain requirements of performance.'

'Five hundred pounds?' Roland said. 'That should certainly stimulate interest.'

'It already has,' Jes said with a grin. 'Henry Booth, the Treasurer, says that he began to receive letters within weeks of the announcement from all over the world, and from all sorts of people — not just engineers, but everyone who fancies himself an inventor. Engines were described which would tax the imagination of a madman, strong enough to pull a mountain out by its roots, and driven by every element

435

in nature. Hydrogen gas, high-pressure steam, columns of water, columns of mercury, pure vacuum! There was one ingenious machine described that managed without fire or steam, working in a circle to generate power at one end of the process and give it out at the other by the operation of frictionless wheels. Once set going, it would continue for ever by perpetual motion.'

'You see what tampering with nature does?' Rosamund said sternly. 'It simply encourages cracked pots to put themselves forward and air their mad ideas. They should stick to horses, and not tempt Fate to avenge itself on them.'

'I was just going to say much the same thing,' said Lucy.

'I know, Mama,' Rosamund said sweetly. 'That's why I said it.'

'Impudent child,' Lucy retorted, but a smile tugged at her lips. 'When is this trial to come about?'

'On the first of October, at Rainhill, where there's a level stretch of track,' Batchworth said. 'The locomotives will have to prove themselves capable of drawing a load of twenty tons weight at a speed of ten miles an hour, and of being able to continue to do so day after day.'

'Do you think they'll find one?' Roland asked. 'It sounds unlikely to me.'

Jes shrugged. 'Whether they do or not, it will be interesting to watch. The event looks likely to prove quite an attraction; and if the outcome is successful, it may change for ever the way we move goods about the country.'

'I don't see that,' Lucy objected. 'Ten miles an hour is not much faster than the canals; and if what little I understand about railways is true, they cannot even climb hills as canals can. They have to run on flat ground.'

'True. But they can go where canals can't, where there's no water. The construction is simpler. The speed is constant — no locks to hold things up — and after all, ten miles an hour is not an absolute. Once the principle is established and the mechanics understood, there seems no reason why the engines may not go twice as fast.'

Lord Theakston smiled genially at that. 'No reason at all,' he agreed; 'but equally no reason at all why anyone should want them to. Can it really matter whether your bales of cotton take three hours to come from Liverpool, or an hour and a half?'

'None that I can think of,' Jes said obligingly, 'except the fun of it. It is in the nature of mankind, sir: if a thing is possible to be done, sooner or later a man will do it.'

CHAPTER TWENTY-TWO

The Rainhill Trials finally began on Tuesday the sixth of
October 1829, on a fine morning, and amid great excitement.
Miss Fanny Hobsbawn, aged eight-and-a-half, told her
grandmother about it almost three months later at Christmas
at Morland Place, and still remembered every detail of what
she had seen, so impressive had been the experience.

'I'm glad it happened now,' her mother said, 'and not when
she was younger. It will be something she will keep the
memory of all her life. I know I shall!'

The trial ground was a stretch of level track almost two
miles long. The centre portion of one and a half miles was
marked with white posts, between which the performance of
the engines was to be measured. Beyond these the course
continued for a further eighth of a mile to terminal points
where fuel and water was available, along with a blacksmith's
shop for necessary repairs, and a weighbridge.

The ordeal decided upon was that each locomotive had to
haul a load three times it own weight and make twenty runs
to and fro over the one and a half miles of the course. An
interval was to be allowed after ten runs, which was the
equivalent of the journey from Liverpool to Manchester. The
course was to be 'taken flying', with the extension beyond the
posts used for getting up speed and braking. Timekeepers
were stationed at the posts with watches to note not only the
time taken for each run, but to record time lost at the
terminals in feverish repairs and adjustments.

At the middle of the course a large grandstand for
spectators had been erected beside the track, and was decked

with flags and bunting which fluttered cheerfully in the light breeze. To the rear of the stand a brass band was installed, playing pleasing and popular airs. A nearby tavern, lately and cunningly renamed the *Rail-Road*, was packed to overflowing with sightseers, who had crowded in from Liverpool, Manchester, St Helens and Warrington, and locomotive enthusiasts from even further afield. A number of ingenious gentlemen, whose usual habitat was the racecourses of old England, had set up their 'books' on the five locomotive engines to undergo the ordeal, and were already doing a brisk trade in relieving the ten thousand spectators of their spare cash.

There was also a large contingent of gentlemen of the press from all over the country, who had already identified the scientific and mechanical experts and obtained their opinion of the 'runners'. One of them, the *Cycloped*, entered by Mr Brandreth of Liverpool, was propelled by a horse on a kind of treadmill and was therefore disqualified by the judges as being outside the terms of the competition. However, as Mr Brandreth was a member of the Board they had to indulge him, and he was allowed to potter up and down the line with his machine in the intervals between the more serious trials. It provided entertainment during the sometimes considerable pauses caused by the mechanical complexities of its rivals. Indeed, the *Cycloped* attracted a great deal of praise from the more traditional thinkers among the spectators, who would always prefer what they could understand to the dangers of novelty.

Novelty was the name of another entrant, submitted by Mr Braithwaite and Mr Erickson of London. She arrived at the trial ground first, and was therefore able to show off her paces before the admiring spectators.

'She's based on the London steam-carriage,' Jes explained to his guests. 'You can see her origins in the four equal-sized wheels and the horizontal connecting-rods, which make her look like a road carriage rather than a railway engine.'

'They certainly make her appear very neat and workmanlike,' Jasper said. 'I like the way all the moving parts are hidden, too. She looks like a proper, finished carriage.'

439

'She looks to me more like a parlour tea-urn,' Jes said, a little less than graciously.

Fanny and Sophie, less demanding, thought the *Novelty* very pretty in her royal blue livery, with boiler and water tank clad in highly-polished copper which glinted like gold in the sun, and a pale blue flag with her name embroidered in gold fluttering from the rear. There was no dirt or toil or effort about her, and Fanny clasped her hands in rapture as the engine darted up and down the line, 'just like a dragonfly' as she later told her grandmama.

The *Novelty* also impressed the assembled scientific gentlemen, who told the eager representatives of the press that she was undoubtedly the best of the entrants and sure to win. She certainly seemed capable of amazing speeds, and the word soon filtered back through the crowds that on one run she had logged twenty-eight miles per hour!

'It seems that the other competitors need hardly have bothered to turn up,' said Sophie, watching with unabated fascination as the gleaming locomotive made another of her darting runs to enormous applause from the grandstand.

'This isn't the ordeal,' Jes reminded her. 'She isn't loaded; and anyway, it's sustained action that counts — the long grind of steady working. Though I must say that so far she looks very good.'

But almost as he spoke, there was an explosion from the vicinity of the engine, and then a fountain of sparks. The top-hatted figures of Braithwaite and Erickson could be seen running about in consternation as flame and smoke belched from the rear of the machine. Shortly afterwards the news filtered back through the crowds that the leather furnace bellows had burnt out, and the *Novelty* was put out of action for the time being.

A third contestant had failed to arrive — the *Perseverance* from Edinburgh had been badly damaged when the road waggon conveying it had overturned — so that left only two more. George Stephenson's entry was the *Rocket*, which had also been showing itself to the crowds, but without the acclaim of the dragonfly *Novelty*. Fanny apostrophised it as 'a black, ugly thing', and Sophie agreed that it looked clumsy and awkward compared with the other.

'You mustn't say so to Jes,' Rosamund smiled. '*Rocket* is his favourite.'

'Only because Stephenson and Booth have explained it to me,' Jes defended himself. 'Henry Booth — you know, the Treasurer of the Board — had the idea quite suddenly that to raise steam as quickly as possible the hot gases should be carried through the boiler not in one twelve-inch diameter tube — which to take the pressure has to be made of half-inch-thick iron — but in a multitude of little two- or three-inch tubes. They need only be one-sixteenth thick, so they can be made of copper, which transmits the heat much more readily. You see the point —'

'Yes,' said Jasper at once. 'You expose much more of the water in the boiler to a hot surface, so it will heat more quickly.'

'Exactly. It wasn't easy to do, but they have built *Rocket* with twenty-five little three-inch copper tubes. That ought to solve the problem of sustained steaming.'

'I still think it's ugly,' Sophie said placidly. 'And why did they choose yellow and black for its colours? It makes it look like a horrid great wasp.'

'Looks don't matter at this stage — it's performance that counts,' said Jes with dignity.

'But it doesn't go as fast as the blue one,' Fanny observed pointedly.

Jes turned to her. 'It will do, my love. Mr Stephenson isn't driving all out yet, because this isn't the real test. He's saving his best until the ordeal.'

'I wish they'd get on with it,' Rosamund said, glancing up at the skies. 'I'm sure those are rain clouds. In October, in Lancashire, a sunny day is as likely as not to turn off.'

'But the judges have agreed to try the engines in a certain order, and there's another to come before *Rocket* — the *Sans Pareil*,' said Batchworth, looking up the track. The light was growing silvery with the approaching rain. 'I don't see it anywhere. It was coming from Darlington by road. I hope it hasn't met with an accident.'

The news came back at last that the *Sans Pareil* had arrived

441

and was at one of the termini where a very disgruntled Mr Hackworth was struggling to mend a leak in the boiler and asked to be allowed more time to prepare his machine for the ordeal. Since it was now raining heavily, the judges announced that the *Rocket* would be tried the next morning, and declared the proceedings closed for the day.

By comparison with the trials and tribulations of the first day, the ordeal of the *Rocket* on the second day went off with almost tedious lack of incident. George Stephenson drove her himself. She was weighed in, hitched up to two waggons loaded with stone, the timekeepers took their positions, and it began. The engine chugged up the track at about fourteen miles per hour pulling the waggons behind her, and then down the track pushing them before her at the same speed. Nineteen times they passed the grandstand; on the twentieth and last trip, the engineer opened up the regulator, and the *Rocket* thundered past at full speed with a plume of white smoke streaming from her tall chimney.

'Twenty-nine miles per hour!' Jes cried triumphantly, looking at his own watch. 'That will show them all! I told you she could do it, didn't I my love?'

'You did,' Rosamund said, pleased that he was pleased.

'She still isn't as pretty as the blue one, though,' Sophie said.

'It doesn't matter what she looks like,' Jes pronounced. 'You saw for yourself how steady she was. She could do that all day long, week in and week out, which is what counts: strength and reliability. I don't think when it comes to it that *Novelty* has got what's needed.'

'I'll tell you what,' Jasper said, 'no matter how well or badly the other two engines perform, there'll be no more talk of horse-working or cable haulage after this. Your Stephensons have proved their point, Batchworth. Nothing could have been neater than that little engine tugging those waggons along. Nothing could have been more exactly the thing!'

'It will get better,' Jes said. 'The *Rocket* is only a first effort. Any little flaws or awkwardnesses will be ironed out as they go along.'

The other two contestants, tested on subsequent days,

442

proved unequal to the ordeal set them, and it was the *Rocket* which took the prize of £500. Perhaps more importantly for the Stephensons, the Liverpool and Manchester Railway bought the engine from them and ordered four more locomotives of the same type.

The Rainhill Trials and their result were widely reported in the newspapers. Discussion both about railways and locomotives was renewed in houses up and down the land, and nowhere more than at Morland Place. Benedict and Father Moineau were still great enthusiasts. They read every detail of every account of Rainhill that they could get hold of, endlessly discussed the advantages of eccentric rods and inclined cylinders, and debated the exact diameter of the ideal driving-wheel.

Nicholas and his mother were against the whole idea of locomotives, arguing variously that they were unnecessary as long as there were horses; that they were dangerous and unnatural; that they would never work in practice; and that they were inspired by the Devil and would bring ruin and destruction on the land.

The arguments were made more pointed by the fact that a Leeds and Selby Railway Company had been formed and was putting its Act through Parliament in the early months of 1830. Woollen goods from the manufactories in Leeds would soon be transported by railway to Selby to join up with the steam-boat service to Hull. The engineer, James Walker, had laid it out so that either horses or locomotive engines could be used, but after Rainhill few people doubted that it would be the latter which would hold sway.

And if there was to be a railway between Leeds and Selby, who could doubt that John Anstey's dream was not far behind, and that coals and milk and cloth and corn would one day soon be trundled into York itself behind one of those smoking monsters?

'If we don't make a stand against it, we'll have those infernal machines roaring through our own fields next,' Nicholas proclaimed, 'frightening our horses into fits and our cows out of milk, setting fire to our trees, and tearing up our peace for ever.'

'Never while I live,' Héloïse said fervently. 'Morland Place was left to me to protect and care for, and I shall never let such a thing happen to it. I begin to understand now why I was chosen to be its guardian,' she added in a low voice. 'My aunt would have died before she allowed the railway on her land, and so shall I.'

'But Mama,' Benedict said in half-amused protest, 'it isn't like you to make such extreme judgements, and especially when you haven't even seen a locomotive for yourself.'

'I don't need to,' Héloïse said firmly. 'I know it is wrong. God never meant such things to be. Besides, I have Sophie's account, if I needed confirmation. No good can come of them.'

Sophie had written to her mother to describe how she had had a closer encounter with one of Mr Stephenson's locomotives than she had ever expected to. After Rainhill the directors of the Liverpool and Manchester were eager to win over public opinion and spread the fame of their railway as far as possible, and to this end they laid on a number of private excursions. Select members of the public were invited to ride in special waggons drawn by one or other of the locomotives over a short section — four or five miles usually — of the track; with, if appropriate, a halt to view one of the engineering marvels of the route, a viaduct or bridge or cutting.

Sophie's account was thus:

'Lord Batchworth sent over the day before yesterday to say that the new locomotive engine, called *Dart*, had been delivered from Newcastle, and that if we should care to try her (locomotive engines are always called "her" and "she" you understand, like ships!) he would call for us in his carriage the next morning at eleven and take us to ride in her. Jasper was eager for it, and I must admit a certain curiosity myself, but I insisted that we should keep it from Fanny, for if she heard about it she would certainly want to go, and I was sure it must be too dangerous for her. Lord B was most upset as he had devised the treat with her in mind, since she had enjoyed seeing the ordeals at Rainhill so much. But Jasper agreed with me that we would not put our only child at such hazard, and so it was arranged.

444

'So yesterday the carriage came for us, and Lord Batchworth and Rosamund in it, and Rosamund in a lovely silk pelisse just a shade darker than my yellow gown I had at Christmas, Maman, with the ruched neck, do you recollect? She had a scarf tied about her hat, and warned me to put something similar over my bonnet, for she said the breeze would snatch it off when we were on the engine. So I sent in for a shawl, and then we were off.

'So we drove out to a place near Barton, and there was the *Dart* waiting for us, with a waggon fixed on behind with benches inside it to sit upon. Mr Stephenson — the father, not the son — was there, and looking very grand and Biblical, Maman, with his white hair and old-fashioned long coat. He was very proud of the new engine, and was eager to tell us that it had eighty-eight tubes (a prodigious number, you are to understand!) and also near-horizontal cylinders, which he assured us would make a smooth ride. I'm sure my brother can explain to you what these things mean. I cannot pretend to understand it all; but Mr Stephenson was so anxious to be agreeable and helpful that I smiled and nodded like anything just as if I did.

'Rosamund seemed much taken with the engine. She said, laughing, that it reminded her of a small, snorting horse which she felt much inclined to pat, and when Lord Batchworth encouraged her she did just that! I felt no such inclination. Close to, the engine seemed much bigger than I had expected, very black and fierce, full of smoke and smells and loud noises, and horribly alive. Do you remember, Maman, how I fainted when first I went to see the spinning machines in our factories? It was the same thing again with the *Dart*: the appearance of life in a thing one knows is not alive, is very horrible and frightening.

'However there was no escaping the excursion, so I took my place in the waggon with the others, who were in very high spirits. I was only glad I had carried my point about not bringing Fanny, for I was very nervous. I was to discover I had good cause! Mr Stephenson climbed onto the plate and pushed the lever, and so we started forward. It was the oddest feeling, Maman! To be travelling along so very smoothly, with no bumps as on a horse, more smoothly even than in a good carriage on a good road —and yet with no visible cause of progress, no horses, only the inanimate engine, is very strange. Just at first when we were moving slowly it was not unpleasant, but soon we began to go faster, and I began to be very afraid. We travelled to Kenyon, a trip of about five miles, in just a quarter of an hour, which means we went at twenty miles an hour. But Lord Batchworth told me that that was only the average speed. When Mr Stephenson was urged to "go it" we reached twenty-five miles an hour, and with just the same ease as the lower speeds.

'But Maman, this great speed is not to be borne! The pressure of the wind on my face made me feel that I could not breathe. To be flying through the air so fast, with no means of directing oneself, no power to stop, and dragged by an insensate machine that cannot even see where it is going, is *frightful*! I was filled with the conviction that the slightest movement or accident would cause instant death to all of us. The notion of being thrown out at such a speed, or colliding with anything, was so terrifying it made me feel sick.

'For the rest, the smoke was whisked away and was not troublesome, but there were a great many sparks, which seemed to me very dangerous indeed, and a great nuisance. One spark burned a hole in Rosamund's lovely pelisse, and another scorched Jasper's cheek quite painfully. I dread to think what would have happened if I had brought Fanny! Suppose one should have entered her eye? I should never have forgiven myself, and I have sworn privately she shall never go near one of these monsters. I am convinced no good can come of them. To be flying along at that speed is not natural: it has given me a headache which I have not yet got rid of. I think if I had had a weak heart, I should not have survived the experience; and though now that it is over I am glad to be able to say I have done it, I can say without hesitation that I never want to do it again.'

Rosamund's account of the excursion to her mother was naturally rather different in emphasis.

'I cannot convey to you the excitement of the sensation!

446

Imagine the best and fastest horse you have ever galloped upon, and then double that: Jes tells me the *Dart* can go at thirty-five miles an hour when she is let out! But then you must take away all sensation of effort, all friction, and substitute an absolute smoothness and a constancy of speed such as no horse can provide. One glides through the air like a bird, yet faster than any bird flies; and with nothing in front of one but the magical machine, with its flying white breath, rhythmical noises, and unvarying pace. We flew across Chat Moss in a moment! I looked down once at the ground just to the side of the carriage, and it was moving past me so fast I could not see it, only a kind of mist of brown and green. To be borne so fast and so smoothly is the strangest sensation, and yet I had a perfect sense of security. I was not the least bit afraid, though poor Sophie looked very pale when it was all over.'

The amusement and interest of Rosamund's letter was a brief respite from the other concerns which were preoccupying Lucy — and indeed all of London — that March of 1830. The health of the King was deteriorating rapidly. His condition was pitiable — his legs were so swollen he could hardly walk, he was blind in one eye, and had such palpitations and difficulty in breathing that he could not sleep lying down any more. There could be little doubt that he must die soon and the Duke of Clarence succeed. The Duke went frequently to visit his brother at Windsor, and it was reported that each time he left the presence, he cried for pity.

The Duchess of Clarence had not had a pregnancy for eight years, and it was now accepted that she would not produce an heir. This meant that the late Duke of Kent's daughter, the Princess Victoria, would succeed to the throne after the Duke of Clarence. With the failure of the King's health, there was renewed interest in the young princess, now ten years old, who had lived a very secluded life so far at Kensington Palace, hardly seeing anyone but her mother and her mother's adviser, a Captain John Conroy.

Conroy had been equerry to the Duke of Kent, and had somehow remained in the service after the Duke's death, having an unaccountable influence over the Duchess. He was popularly supposed to be her lover; certainly he had the authority of a father in the household, and was known to be both rapacious and ambitious.

'He means to be Regent,' Lucy said once, grimly, to her husband. 'If Clarence dies before the child is eighteen, it will be King John Conroy who rules.'

'Mrs Arbuthnot says the princess is a charming child,' Danby said. 'Pretty and high spirited, but perfectly civil and well bred.'

'What has that to do with it?' Lucy snapped.

'Only that if Conroy has the influence you suppose, he has brought the child up properly so far.'

'Ha!' said Lucy. 'Your Mrs Arbuthnot is doubtless impressed by being invited to Kensington Palace. I've heard the Duchess's entertainments there are quite regal these days.'

Danby shrugged that away. 'I shouldn't worry about Conroy, if I were you. He's an adventurer, but since everyone knows it, he's unlikely to be allowed to get away with it. You know the Duchess of Clarence wrote to warn the Duchess of Kent not to let him have too much influence over her. When she's queen, she'll keep an eye on the princess. She's very much attached to her.'

'But how long will she be queen?'

'Don't write off Clarence too soon,' Danby said. 'His health is good. He may reign for many years — long enough to avoid a regency, anyway.'

Other changes that were in the air were even more alarming. There was another slump in trading, and after three bad harvests the poverty of rural labourers in particular was so bad that there was talk of the possibility of riots. Unrest in France brought renewed fears that it might spread to England, and the radical elements in the country began to press again for Parliamentary Reform. It must be brought about, they said, to save society, or England would be convulsed with revolution in the 1789 style.

'I've heard all that before,' Lucy told Tom firmly when he repeated it to her. 'I didn't believe it then and I don't believe

448

it now. We'll never have revolution in England. The English are too sensible.'

'All the same, Mama,' Tom said, 'when the King dies there'll be a General Election, and that's bound to focus attention on Reform. There'll be talk — public debate —'

'That's all right,' Lucy said blithely. 'Let them talk all they like. Your seat won't be contested, and as long as Parliament is filled with people like you, the country won't come to any harm.'

March brought good news too: the Duke of Wellington finally brought the King to agree to give Mr Brummell a public position. He was to be consul in Caen at a salary of £400 per annum. The sum was not princely, but it was certainly enough to live on in a provincial French town, and the anxieties of his friends in England were at last relieved.

March also brought the birth of Roland and Thalia's second child — a girl, whom they named Lucilla.

'After you, Mama,' said the proud father.

'Hmph,' said Lucy. 'A plain English name was enough for my mother. Why do you have to rifle Latin for one?'

'Saint Lucy wasn't English,' Roland pointed out.

'You're becoming very argumentative as you get older,' Lucy replied, and eyed him curiously. 'Marriage has suited you, hasn't it?'

'Yes Mama. Very much.'

Lucy nodded. 'I chose well for you. But I wish Thomas would marry too. Can't you persuade him?'

'He says he can only love one woman at a time,' Roland smiled, 'and that's you.'

'Foolish nonsense,' Lucy said, trying not to look pleased. 'Well, you had better take me to see this little namesake of mine. When she's older, I'll teach her to ride, if you like.'

And that, as Roland knew, was the greatest sign of approval he could have hoped for.

At Morland Place, all these worries and concerns passed James by. He did not join in the railway argument because he had only the mildest and most passing interest in railways. The slump didn't worry him because the income from the

449

factories was only a small part of the estate. The rural poverty and unrest did not trouble the north of England, where work was plentiful and labourers generally healthy and prosperous. He didn't much care which of the sons of George III was on the throne, and had no doubt that the new talk of Parliamentary Reform would come to nothing as had all previous talk.

What did concern him was the challenge issued by Sir Arthur Fussell of Fussell Manor, Fulford. Fussell was a contemporary of his who had recently amused York society by taking a second wife in the form of one of Lady Grey's notoriously unmarriageable daughters. Miss Polyxena Grey was twenty-eight years old and had never had an offer until Sir Arthur — aged sixty-two and eight years widowed after a childless marriage to John Anstey's sister Lizzie — took a fancy to her.

Héloïse had been scandalised at the news of the marriage, not because of the discrepancy in age, but because Sir Arthur had been notoriously cruel to his first wife, and had lived a life of self-indulgence bordering on debauchery which had left him a very unappetising specimen of humanity. Miss Grey might be dull and plain, but she was 'a perfectly good girl', said Héloïse, 'and deserved better than to be forced into marriage with such a satyr'.

'How do you know she's been forced?' Nicholas asked idly. 'It might be her own choosing.'

Héloïse was indignant. 'She must know his reputation. No-one would choose such a man of her free will!'

'She might prefer it to staying at home with Lady Grey. Disappointment has made her temper savage, so they say.'

Héloïse would not believe it. But at all events the marriage went ahead, and the change in Sir Arthur was remarkable. He had Fussell Manor repaired and redecorated, ordered his new lady a smart barouche from York's leading coach-maker, bought himself new clothes, ceased to be seen wandering about the streets of York drunk at all hours, and generally seemed to be playing the part of an uxorious husband half his age.

It was when he came to order a pair of horses for his wife's barouche that he fell foul of James. He naturally wanted a pair of Morland bays for the rig —the smartest and best-looking pair Morland Place could provide, money no object — and approached James in his club to discuss the matter. James said he had just the pair — sweet goers, perfectly matched, and so gentle a lady could drive them. Sir Arthur arranged to go over the next day and look at them, and James ordered a fresh bottle of claret to celebrate the anticipated transaction.

It was half-way down this bottle that Sir Arthur brought up the subject of Lucifer.

'Whatever possessed a man of your experience to buy a horse from a gypsy? For you of all people to buy a pig in a poke —!'

James handled him gently to begin with. He was, after all, a potential customer. 'Ah well,' he said lightly, 'it's turned out well enough, in the event.'

'Well enough, has it? I wouldn't call parting with five hundred guineas for a commoner with no name *well enough*.'

'Lucifer is not a commoner,' James said, a little tersely. 'His breeding is stamped all over him.'

'It ain't stamped all over any papers, though, is it?' Fussell laughed. 'God, Morland, you was taken out for washing there, all right! Five hundred for a gypsy's horse! God bless my soul, what a joke!'

'He may not have it on paper, but he has it where it matters,' James said, growing riled. 'Handsome is as handsome does.'

'And what does this paragon do?' Fussell asked sneeringly. 'Pull a cart from the farmyard to the dung pit?'

'No such thing!' James snapped. 'He goes over any country, jumps anything he can see sky over, and has not his equal for courage and heart.'

'Fast as well, I suppose?' Fussell taunted him.

'He's the fastest horse in the Ridings.'

'Of course, you wouldn't care to back that up.'

'Over any country, in any going, against any company,' James said, his nostrils flaring.

Fussell leaned forward. 'I have a new horse I bought from Wixford over in Northallerton — a blood horse, with winners in his tree on both sides. He's by Thunderer out of Painted Lady, full brother to Vulcan, of whom you must have heard.'

He straightened up with a self-satisfied smile. 'Now I suppose you won't want to pit your gypsy nag against a real thorough-bred, will you?'

James put down his glass deliberately. He had a belated access of caution over the possible bad blood such a contest would inevitably breed — and Fussell was a customer after all. Two bay carriage horses in the hand, he told himself grimly.

'We're too old for this sort of foolishness, Arthur,' he said.

But Fussell scented victory, and pressed after it. 'Ha! I thought not. You know what the result would be. You know who would beat, if it were to come to it. Gypsy horse, ha!'

James's control snapped. 'With you in the saddle, your horse is beaten already. You always had the worst seat in the country, Fussell, and you've just proved you have the worst judgement too. It's hardly fair to take your money, but if you force it on me, I will.'

'Leave it to me to decide if it's fair. I'll pit my Jupiter against your dog-meat brute — yes, and my riding against yours! — for any amount you'd care to name. And if you refuse, I shall know you're a liar and a coward, and so will everyone else in York. Your reputation will be nothing.'

'Name the course,' James said, breathing hard. 'And say your prayers.'

'James, this is perfectly silly!' cried Héloïse, almost in tears. 'You must call it off. You must.'

'My love,' James said, looking uncomfortable, 'I can't do that. Not now I've accepted. Fussell will have spread it all over York by now.'

'What does it matter what people think?'

'It matters to me. And it matters to the business. I can't have it said that I wouldn't back one of my own horses to win over my own country.'

'Lucifer is not one of your own horses. He is not Morland-bred.'

'It doesn't matter. He will carry the reputation of Morland Place on his head just the same. And you needn't worry about the thousand guineas. Even if I were to lose it, I could cover

452

it all right — and I'm not going to lose it anyway. I shall have Fussell's thousand safe in my pocket by tomorrow night — and I shall buy you a diamond bracelet out of it.' He took up her hand to kiss it, smiling at her; but she didn't smile back.

'I don't care about the money — how can you think it? It is you I care about. James, you are not a young man any more —'

'Nor is Fussell,' James retorted, half amused, half hurt.

'Well, but I don't care about him,' Héloïse said hotly. 'He may break his neck if he wishes, and I shall not shed a tear. But you — you are my husband and my love, and you are *sixty-three years old*!'

'Not quite yet. Sixty-two if you don't mind — and I wish you wouldn't keep reminding me about it.'

'Don't joke,' she said tragically. 'Racing across country on a horse you don't know —'

'Oh for heaven's sake, Marmoset! I've been riding Lucifer for eighteen months now — and *don't cross yourself* when I mention his name! You've got a perfect obsession about him! I know that horse like the beat of my own heart. And for the matter of that, I know the country round here, every stick and stone of it. I've been riding and racing over it since I was three years old. I'm not going to get hurt, can't you get that into your head?'

She was crying, and he hated it.

'You won't mind me, I know that,' she said through her tears. 'You say you love me, but you will put me through this agony for your own stupid pride. I don't want you to ride in this race — that should be enough for you.'

'It's not fair of you to ask me like that. Making it a test of my love — it has nothing to do with it. Your fears are foolish —'

'Foolish?'

'Yes! I'm not going to get hurt. You're simply prejudiced against my poor Lucifer. And if it comes to pride, my love, I think you should examine your own conscience. You set out to have a battle of wills with me over this, and now you think you may lose you're attacking me with a woman's weapons.'

453

'Oh!' she cried, incensed. The tears dried up at their source.

James eyed her knowingly. 'Just examine your feelings at this very moment, and tell me that they aren't more anger than fear!'

Héloïse stared at him, her lips pressed tightly together, her eyes bright. After a moment she let out her breath quiveringly, and said in a quieter voice. 'Very well. But even if you were right about that, you are wrong about the race. It will not improve your reputation. People will not admire you for it. They are laughing at you — at both of you. Two foolish old men, that's what they are saying. Not a hero, James, but a clown.'

He was silent a moment, and she wished the words unsaid, knowing they had hurt him. Then he said quietly, 'Are they, indeed? Well, so be it. At least I will bring laughter to some people's lives.'

And with that he went away, leaving her with the ache of an unresolved quarrel in her heart.

Nicholas was James's best ally, which both surprised and touched him. He had always loved Nicky best in his heart, but had found it difficult to show it, and he had always feared Nicky didn't know it, and loved his mother better.

But now Nicky said, 'Oh, don't mind about Mama. She'll get over it. She'll be right as rain tomorrow. It's just woman's worrying, that's all. Which route are you going to ride?'

'It's point to point, from Rufforth to Providence,' James began to explain, and Nicholas interrupted.

'Yes, I know. I think you were very wise to make it so. You can choose your own line, and Fussell won't be able to compete with that. You can take Lucifer over ground he'd never dare to tackle.'

James looked at him with gratitude. 'You don't have any doubts about Lucifer, then?'

'I've seen you hunt him, and if Sir Arthur had, he would never have made this wager,' Nicholas said with a steady look. Then he got down to business. 'Now, obviously, the closer you can ride to a straight line the better, and there are

454

places where he's bound to take the easier route. That's where you can score over him.'

'Thank you, I hadn't thought of that,' James said ironically.

Nicky never noticed irony. 'The big thing is crossing the river. It seems to me that he's bound to go through Cattal so that he can cross by the Roman bridge; but you can go much more directly through Wilstrop Wood and past the old workings and then across the river where it narrows just below Wilstrop Cottage. You'll save the best part of a mile that way.'

'We fly across the river, I suppose?'

Nicholas widened his eyes. 'There's a weir at that point, with a causeway above it. You can simply walk across — the water's only fetlock deep.'

'And fast-running. If Lucifer slipped, we'd be whisked away over the weir in a trice.'

Nicholas shrugged. 'He won't slip. Why should he? You've often said he's as sure-footed as a cat.'

'True enough,' James said. 'I shouldn't like to try it with any other horse, though.' He frowned in thought. 'We'd better keep this conversation to ourselves, my boy. Don't mention the route to anyone else, or it might get back to your mother, and I shouldn't want her to worry. What with quarries and weirs, she'd be bound to think it was dangerous.'

'I won't mention it to anyone, sir,' Nicholas promised.

The morning of the race was mild and damp; a little breezy, with a touch of rain on the breeze, but the promise of a gleam or two of sunshine between the clouds.

Héloïse came out into the yard to see James off. His face was alight with enthusiasm, and she thought he looked younger than he had for years.

'Let me come to Rufforth to see the start,' she said again.

'Better not. Say goodbye to me here. It only prolongs the agony,' James grinned. 'I'll be back before you know it, anyway.'

'You're coming back by road?'

'Yes. Nicky and Durban have gone ahead to Providence. Durban will lead Lucifer home for me, and I'll ride back with Nicky in his tilbury. I'll be here in time for a nuncheon at noon — and a bottle of champagne for the famous winner! Now kiss me and wish me luck, my little Marmoset! Bendy will come back and tell you I got off all right.'

Lucifer was led out, looking fit and beautiful, and James mounted up. The horse took up the bit and mouthed it gently, standing four-square and poised, his ears moving back and forth, listening to his rider and assessing the other figures in the yard. Héloïse went forward with a titbit and offered it on her flat palm, and the big black horse looked at her thoughtfully for a moment before bending his neck to take it delicately, almost condescendingly.

'Good luck,' she said, looking up at James.

He smiled down at her. 'We won't need it. But thanks anyway. Come on, then, Bendy. I've got a thousand guineas to earn.'

CHAPTER TWENTY-THREE

For the first half hour, Sir Arthur Fussell was too eager to hear James declare him the winner to want to leave the finishing point, and he sat on his badly blown thoroughbred at the crossroads of the two Roman roads, looking first down one and then the other, expecting James at any moment to come crestfallenly into sight. Even when his horse began to shiver, he only removed himself to the inn just along the Cattal road, with an instruction to Durban to send his master along as soon as he arrived.

'I'll buy him a pint of best October by way of consolation, since I don't suppose they keep any wine. Send him down straight away, d'you hear? He's deuced late, ain't he? How a man can make so much of a short, easy point like that passes me! A mere eight miles over easy country! I could have walked it on my own feet by now.'

Only when he had gone did other members of the group gathered to see the finish begin to express their doubts. Sir Arthur's nephew, John Shawe, who was there as his official timekeeper, exchanged a glance with his friend Gussy Laxton and said, 'I wonder that he ain't here by now. All due respect to my uncle, but I'd have thought Mr Morland would get here first. You don't think he's met with an accident, do you?'

Nicholas looked worried. 'I'm beginning to wonder. He went off so fast that he should have been ahead of Sir Arthur all the way. But then,' with a look of relief, 'in that case, if he'd come a cropper Sir Arthur would have passed him, wouldn't he?'

'He must have struck out on a line of his own,' Durban

457

said. 'Did he mention anything of the sort to you, sir?'

Nicholas turned to look at him. 'No, he didn't. Of course in a point-to-point one rides one's own line, but he didn't mention any particular plan.'

'But he'd have to come through Cattal anyway, to cross the river,' said Jack Greaves, another friend of Shawe's. 'There ain't another bridge.'

'There's the Skip bridge,' said Laxton. 'We came that way; but it's a longer way round starting from Rufforth.'

'There's a footbridge at Mill Farm, sir,' said one of the grooms.

'No, that wouldn't take a horse's weight,' Nicholas said quickly. 'He couldn't have gone that way. Now let's think about it logically. Whichever way he was going, he'd start off heading straight for Marston Moor, and then he'd swing either left or right, depending on whether he was going for Cattal bridge or Skip bridge. Skip bridge is further, but he might have had a reason for going that way.'

'Well then,' said Shawe, 'suppose I drive back with Laxton down the Roman road across Skip bridge, and you drive back the other way through Cattal, Morland, and one of us is bound to come across him.'

'That won't do,' said Nicholas. 'I have to stay here in case he turns up. Besides, what if his horse went lame or something while he was still out on Marston Moor? It's a job for a horseman.'

'I'll go, sir,' said Durban quietly.

'No, better still,' said Nicholas, 'you give me your horse, and I'll go. You stay here with the tilbury, and if Papa turns up, you can drive him home and lead Lucifer behind. I'll go back through Cattal, which I think is the most likely way, and then ride over Marston Moor. I'll soon pick up the line. Someone's bound to have seen him.'

'And I'll do the same thing the other way,' said Greaves, who had come on horseback. 'Don't worry, Morland,' he added kindly. 'Ten to one the horse put his foot down a rabbit hole, and your pa's having to walk him home.'

'That's right,' said Bob Russell. 'Mr Morland's the best horseman in the Ridings. He won't have come to any harm.'

It wasn't until the middle of the afternoon that a message came in from Wilstrop Grange to say that Lucifer had been found wandering loose near the wood. He had a number of superficial cuts and grazes, and was slightly lame, so they had caught him and put him in the stables and would keep him until he was fetched.

'Wilstrop Grange?' Benedict said. 'What's he doing out there? He must have strayed a long way.'

'Cuts and grazes?' Héloïse said. 'That means he must have come down! Bendy, your father is lying somewhere hurt!'

'Not necessarily, Mama,' Benedict said quickly. 'The horse might have fallen after he got away from my father, however he came to do that.'

But Héloïse was not to be fooled. 'Come, my son, if he were not hurt, he would be back by now, or we would have heard from him.'

Benedict met her gaze reluctantly. 'If he were lying somewhere, the others would have found him by now. We must have thirty men searching every inch of the course. Nicky's been out all day.'

She had not been listening to him. 'You must go,' she said decidedly. 'Perhaps they have been looking in the wrong place. You were surprised the horse should be where he was.'

'Yes, but —'

'Go to where the horse was, and begin there. Do so, *mon fils*. Don't worry about me. I shall be all right on my own. Go and find your father, Bendy. Find him!'

On his wide wanderings on foot after foxes and badgers and other members of the animal kingdom, Benedict had visited most of the woods within a ten mile range of home. He knew Wilstrop Wood, a larger, wilder place than those nearer home; and he knew that beyond it, between the wood and Wilstrop Grange, there were shallow quarries, supposed to be the remains of Roman surface mines. The mental image of the horse, slightly lame and with a number of grazes, brought with it the unwelcome idea of a rolling fall down a shallow quarry side. It was not a pleasant picture, and he wished it

459

had not come to him, but now it had, he knew he must investigate. He could not at all account to himself for why his father might have been near the quarries in the first place, but if the horse had been up there, it must be looked into.

It was growing dark by the time he was crossing Marston Moor towards the wood. The short day was closing in, and the light rain, which had been blowing about all day on the breeze, grew steadier and colder as the wind dropped. His horse trotted unwillingly, ears laid back, seeing no sense in going away from home at this time of day. The turf of the moor looked strangely luminous in the dusk, and it passed hypnotically under his horse's softly thudding hooves. Bendy dared not push on into a canter, not in this light on uneven ground.

Near the middle of the moor was a close, and as Benedict came up to it, he saw that there were sheep in it, and the dark figure of a man just moving away. Moments later a low, swift shape rushed out of the gathering gloom and circled him before running back in response to a sharp whistle. Shepherd, with dogs, he thought. 'Hi, halloo!' he called. 'Don't go, I want to talk to you!'

The shepherd waited. As Bendy reached him he slid down from his horse's back, and said, 'Have you been out on the moor today?'

'Aye, sir,' said the shepherd, eyeing him with interest. Bendy didn't know him; but this was not Morland land. 'Browt the yows oop 'ere this morning. Had 'em over t'th' lane most of t'day.'

'You were out on the moor this morning with your sheep, then?'

'Aye. So Ah've said.'

'Then — then you must have seen a man riding a black horse across the moor — a big, black horse — going hell for leather?'

'Aye, oop t't wood,' the shepherd said, nodding in the direction of Wilstrop Wood. 'Straight as a die. Rode into't wood and Ah niver saw 'im again.'

'He rode into the wood?' Benedict said, frowning. Now what would he do that for? There'd be no reason to go through the wood to get to either of the bridges, and how else was he to cross the river? He surely hadn't meant to swim it?

The shepherd was watching him curiously. 'Aye, straight into't wood, goin' a lick. And so Ah told t'other young gentleman, when he axed me same question these four hours since.'

'What young gentleman would that be?' Bendy asked, his attention suddenly sharpened. 'Can you describe him?'

'Wan-faced young maister on a chestnut,' the shepherd said, watching his face cannily. 'Ah knowd '*im*, any road, though Ah didn't let on. Yoong Maister Morland o' Morland Place, that's who e was, no mistake. Ah've seen 'im in York, times Ah've tooken the ship in t'th'market. 'E's well known in York, young master.' He gave an unholy chuckle. 'Aye, well known in certain places!'

'What did the gentleman do when you told him about the black horse?' Benedict asked, a cold dread trying hard to gain foothold in his mind.

'Went off after 'im — i'th' same direction, any road,' said the shepherd. He cocked his head. 'Niver found 'im, see-min'ly.'

'Why do you say that?'

'Because *tha's* still lookin',' the man said simply. 'Who is it that's lost?'

'My father,' Bendy said absently. He felt in his pocket for a coin. 'Thank you for your help.'

'Nay, Ah don't want thy money. Go find thy father, lad.' He watched Benedict mount up, and then added, 'I 'ope for thy sake 'e warn't an enemy o' young Maister Morland o' Morland Place. That's a yoong man Ah wouldn't wish to get wuss-sides of.'

At the southern end, the wood tapered to a narrow belt of trees only about fifteen or twenty yards deep. Here Benedict found signs that a horse had gone through — snapped twigs and broken undergrowth — and on the farther side he found some hoof marks in the soft earth; but the light was fading too much to be able to follow them when they passed out onto the turf. In daylight, though, surely Nicky would have been able

461

to follow them? Why hadn't he found Papa?

But then, perhaps this was Nicky's trail he was following, not Papa's after all. Bendy rode northwards along the western edge of the wood, looking for another sign of exit, or more hoof marks, but found none until he came to the track which led to Wilstrop Grange, and then there were all too many of them. The track led through the wood and joined up on the eastern side with the track to Moor Monkton Grange and the Roman road. Bendy felt it was too far to the north to have been his father's line. He turned his horse and retraced his steps.

When he came to the broken place in the wood, he turned and rode straight forward, in as near as possible the direction in which he estimated the horse must have emerged. Wilstrop Grange, where Lucifer was waiting to be collected, was out of sight ahead and to the right of him. Straight ahead, much further on, was the river. Between here and the river were the old workings. He would look at them first, and if he found nothing, go to the Grange and ask for more help — men and lanterns, dogs perhaps.

He came to a place where rain gathering in a slight dip in the ground had created a puddle. It was obviously a more or less permanent puddle, for there was no turf there, only soft mud the ideal place for a footprint. He slipped from the saddle and went down on one knee, staring hard in the fluky twilight. There were a number of sheep-slots — he must be more or less following the line of a trod — and yes! two marks of shod hooves.

One was very deep and sharp, the toe of the shoe deeper than the heel: a horse going fast, probably cantering. The other was more even and shallow: a horse walking. One edge of it was superimposed on the deeper one.

Benedict stood up, staring about him in the darkness. If Lucifer had been running loose when he was found, there was no reason why he should not have crossed his own track, of course. But the second print looked larger than the first, and not so round, and Lucifer had notably small, round hooves. Benedict would have sworn the deep print was Lucifer's, and that the shallow print was not. But if the

462

second print was from Nicky's horse, what then? If Nicky had come up here this morning on the shepherd's information, why had he not said anything about it when he came home in the early afternoon to get more men for the search?

Well, perhaps the shepherd was mistaken, or lying. Or perhaps, having come up here and found nothing, Nicky had not felt it worth mentioning at home. Bendy started forward again, walking this time, leading his disconsolate horse behind him. The rain had eased off, and the clouds lifting a little revealed the last of a pink glow in the west. Behind him the sky was the more impenetrably black for it. Moonrise was a long way off, and it would only be a quarter moon anyway; but as long as there was a little starlight he felt he could find his way.

The first of the workings now. The chalk gashes showed up unearthly white in the failing light against the black of the turf. And here, at the lip of the shallow quarry on his right, was a place where the edge had been torn away recently, he would say from the raw, crumbled look of it. Benedict stopped, his heart like a cold stone in his chest. Something had gone over there, something large and heavy. He looked around him. There was nothing over which to hang the reins of his horse. He could only let it go, and hope it would stand still.

It was a short scramble, through loose stones, coarse grass and weeds, ragwort and young thistles, to the bottom, where the turf was rabbit-bitten, and there were hollows sheltering bramble bushes. His father was lying there, face down in the grass, one leg bent up, one arm flung out. His head was turned a little to one side, and his eye gleamed a little, dully, under his eyelid.

Bendy heard someone make a strange, hoarse sound, like a sob, and realised a second later it must have been him. He crouched down and laid his fingers against his father's cheek. He had had no doubt that he was dead — he was too still to be alive — but when the coldness of the cheek confirmed it he felt shock just the same, shock and fright and a childish desire to run and cry out for help. He wanted, like a very

463

young child, to run and find his mother, for her to make it all right again.

But one part of his brain was still functioning logically, and like a small, clear, faraway voice it was asking him why his father was dead. It was not such a very bad fall, after all, not sheer at any rate: more a sort of long slither. Like all horsemen, James had come off a thousand times in his life with no more than bruises. Steeling himself, Bendy laid his hands on the body and felt it over.

The leg that was bent up felt strange: the ankle was broken, he thought. That at least was understandable — falling with the leg turned under him, perhaps. But a broken ankle wasn't fatal. Bendy put his hands under the shoulders with the intention of trying to turn the body over, and as he lifted, he saw the head roll in a very unnatural way.

Shivering now, though not with cold, he let go the shoulders and took the head gently in his hands. The feeling was horrible, and though he had no medical expertise, it was unmistakable. The neck was broken. His father had died of a broken neck.

The horse was still there, dozing a little, its head a dark, cut-out shape against the last luminosity of the sky. It started as Bendy came up and almost jumped away, mistrusting the strange figure in the darkness. Bendy, his arms encumbered, called desperately to it, and it stopped, watching him suspiciously.

'Good boy, good old lad. Stand then, stand boy,' Bendy said soothingly. Oh thank God for good horses! He managed to get his arm through the rein, and then set about the difficult task of hoisting his burden over the saddle. Wilstrop Grange was the nearest, and they already had Lucifer. He would go there. They would help him. He didn't want to go amongst strangers just at the moment, but it was better than bringing his father home like this, flung across a saddle like prey.

Sophie was out of the carriage almost before the step had been let down, crossed the yard and flung herself into her mother's arms. 'Oh Maman!'

Héloïse held her close through her first paroxysm of

464

weeping, and when it eased a little, offered her handkerchief. Jasper had come up behind her, and the nurse holding Fanny's hand — Fanny looking bewildered, angelically fair in black. She looked at her grandmother hopefully — surely here would be normality? — and Héloïse tried to smile at her, but couldn't.

Sophie blew her nose, and then said, 'How can you be so calm? Oh Maman, how do you bear it?'

Héloïse shook her head. 'I don't know. I don't think I feel it properly yet. I keep thinking it was all a mistake, and that he'll come in and tell me so.'

Sophie looked at her, briefly and suddenly appreciating her mother's appalling loss. She had never loved anyone but Papa; and these two years past she had been dreading this very thing.

'I don't understand,' Sophie said, as tears surged upwards again. 'I don't understand anything.'

'It's God's will, my Sophie,' said Héloïse. 'That's what I have to keep telling myself. It is all God's will.'

'I don't know that I believe in God any more,' Sophie said in a small, defiant voice.

And now Héloïse managed to smile. 'That's all right,' she said. 'He believes in you.'

Lucy and Danby came. 'You look ill,' Lucy said bluntly to Héloïse. 'But on the whole, better than I expected.' She had thought that Héloïse would simply lie down and die without James, but though her face was marked with suffering, though she was plainly grievously wounded, she was still there, still on her feet and fighting. 'I admire you,' she said. 'But you always did have courage.'

Héloïse pressed her hand. 'Thank you for coming. Thank you both.'

'Well, there's only me now, isn't there?' Lucy said abruptly. 'And Harry in Cyprus. The ranks are growing thin.'

'Penalty of being the youngest,' her husband said gently. Lucy looked at him bleakly.

'Who will there be to come to my funeral?' she said.

*

465

Rosamund and Jes arrived; Rosamund with tears and embraces impartially for Héloïse, Sophie and Lucy.

'You're growing softer with age,' Lucy remarked.

'Oh Aunt, I know how you must be feeling,' Rosamund said quietly as she held Héloïse's thin body.

'Yes,' said Héloïse, 'I think you do. But your loss is worse than mine, *ma mie*.'

Rosamund couldn't speak about that. 'I don't understand how it could happen,' she said instead. 'Uncle was such a superb rider.'

'An awkward fall — an accident, that's all,' Héloïse said with a helpless shrug. 'It could happen to anyone.'

'And no-one was there to help him?'

Héloïse shook her head, her eyes distant with pain. 'He must have died instantly. There was nothing anyone could have done. I was afraid —'

'Yes?' Rosamund encouraged gently.

'I was worried that he did not die in a state of grace. But Father Sparrow says he loved riding so much that up to the last moment he must have been filled with a simple and innocent joy which is almost the same thing.'

Lucy bit her lip and turned her face away, and found, as always, that Danby's shoulder was there, and his large, clean, lavender-scented handkerchief at her service. She looked her gratitude at him, realising suddenly how lucky she was. *There is no-one at Héloïse's shoulder now*, she thought, *no-one's handkerchief at hand but her own*.

Thomas came up post, and Africa and her husband arrived by the mail, having left their boys with Polly. Polly sent her regrets: her fourth child was due almost any moment, and the pregnancy had been difficult. The doctor thought it unwise for her to travel. Thalia was still in child-bed, of course, and could not come, and Roland would not leave her, but Maurice came to represent her and his side of the family. John Skelwith and Mathilde came on the day of the funeral with their six children.

'And that's everyone accounted for,' Nicholas said.

Lucy, who despite having delivered Nicholas herself and

466

being his godmother had never liked him very much, thought he was much more upset about his father's death than she would have expected, and that it proved there was good in him after all. He was very pale, and had been suffering from fits of shivering and bouts of sickness. Héloïse, who doted on him, confided that he had hardly eaten since the news reached them of James's death.

'I wish you could speak to him,' she said, 'or recommend something to him. I worry about him so much. He isn't strong, you know. He must eat, or he will get ill.'

But any incipient sympathy she might have had for her nephew was nipped out when she said, 'And that's everyone accounted for.' Lucy managed not to turn and look, but out of the corner of her eye she saw Batchworth take hold of Rosamund's hand and press it. Of course everyone was not accounted for. There was still one of James's great-nieces lost in limbo, along with two of his cousins. Little Lady Charlotte Morland and her father and aunt were absent. The letter sent to inform them of James's death had received no reply.

James Morland, his mother's favourite son, was laid to rest in the family vault beside her. His bitch Fand had crept shivering to Benedict's knee the first night after his death, and so Bendy had taken over possession of her. The horse, Lucifer, had been shot — by Nicholas's order, and without consultation.

'But it wasn't the horse's fault,' Bendy had argued when he heard.

'Of course it was,' Nicky had said, staring past his shoulder. 'Papa was the best horseman in the Ridings. It must have been the horse.'

'But Papa wouldn't have wanted Lucifer punished. He loved that horse.'

'Well then,' Nicky had retorted, with what might have passed for a grin on a death's head, 'I've sent it to join him, haven't I?'

Bendy remembered that as he watched the coffin being lowered into the vault, and wondered, as he had wondered on and off for a week, exactly what had happened at the old

467

workings, both before and after. He hadn't taxed Nicky with the shepherd's story. That, and the hoofmarks in the mud, seemed now like a distant dream. Papa had broken his neck falling down the sloping side of the quarry — broken his neck in a riding accident. That was the only fact that mattered, or that had to be come to terms with. Bendy knew his father had always loved Nicky best, and that was only fair, since Nicky was the eldest. But Bendy had loved him just the same, and longed for his approval and affection; and now it was all over, and there would never be another chance to gain it. He wept for his loss and his mother's loss, and knelt and prayed along with Father Moineau for the peace of his father's soul; and added a private prayer of his own, that there would be horses in heaven for James Morland.

And afterwards, when everyone left the chapel and went upstairs to the long gallery for food and wine, Bendy called Fand to his heel and slipped out through the inner courtyard and the back door into the open air. It was a grey, blowy, damp day, the beginning of April; clumps of daffodils were bending wildly along the bank of the moat, and the gusts of wind brought the sound of sheep calling their lambs down from the fields. Fand ran here and there, burying her nose in the damp, good smells. Bendy began to cry, and turned to walk into the wind so that it would dry the tears on his face. It was in the nature of things that parents should die, and he knew and understood that. The hardest thing to bear was the thought that his father, loving life so much, must not have wanted to die. Bendy had the awful feeling that God had taken him before he was ready.

The grand ceremonial opening of the Liverpool and Manchester Railway took place on the fifteenth of September, 1830. The most elaborate preparations had been made, and interest in the railway had mounted to fever pitch.

'Which is all to the good,' Jes remarked to Rosamund. 'We want as much publicity as possible to get the thing off with a bang. Everything depends on it.'

'I should think so, indeed,' Rosamund said. 'It is a complete novelty, after all — a railway to carry passengers instead of freight! Are you sure it isn't a mistake?'

Jes grinned. 'No-one can be sure until it's put to the test. But there's been so much interest expressed since the Rainhill trials that the Directors are confident it's worth trying. We've certainly had more enquiries about passenger transport than the transport of goods. And after all, it doesn't matter a great deal to a bale of cotton whether it takes three hours or fifteen to get from Liverpool to Manchester, but it matters very much to a human being. Two hours each way on the railway means there and back in a day with time to conduct your business in between. Four and a half hours each way in a coach is a very different matter.'

Rosamund laughed. 'You don't need to convince me, my love. I am pining for another excursion on the railway, even if Sophie isn't. She called that dear little engine "the Devil's horse" and swore she would never let poor Fanny near one.'

'Poor Jasper too!' said Jes. 'He would dearly have liked a place on one of the ceremonial trains on opening day, but he's too loyal to Sophie to go without her. I hope you realise how lucky you and I are to be given tickets — and for the special train at that! People are offering the most absurd sums of money for a place on any of the trains, let alone the Duke's.'

'If William Huskisson can arrange for the Duke of Wellington to be present at the opening, acquiring tickets for his friend Batchworth must be simplicity itself.'

In spite of all the excitement, and careful planning, and guest-lists studded with eminent names, the atmosphere about the opening of the railway was not as blithe as it had been hoped a year ago after Rainhill. The slump was biting hard, and there was widespread unemployment, hunger and unrest in the country, especially amongst rural labourers. It was expressing itself down in the south-east in an outbreak of rick-burning and machine-smashing, which everyone feared might spread and escalate.

There had been another revolution in France in July, and the Bourbon Charles X had been ousted by the Orleanist Louis Philippe with his tainted egalitarian blood. Fear that this might encourage a revolution in England was widespread. The Whig adherents were agitating for Parliamentary

Reform to stave it off; the Tory adherents feared Reform almost as much as revolution.

The King had died at Windsor in June, and his brother Clarence was now King William IV. He was proving a kindly, sensible, hard-working monarch, with an unexpectedly good grasp of business; but the general election occasioned by his succession had laid open an ants' nest of discontent. Only a quarter of the seats were actually contested, but public opinion had expressed itself very firmly in favour of reform and against the old privileges. In the face of this, the Duke of Wellington, known to be rigidly against reform of any sort, had never been more unpopular — particularly in the north, where Peterloo was still remembered with bitterness.

Rosamund had very naturally asked her husband why the Duke had been invited as guest of honour, since the Company was anxious to secure popular success and approval for their revolutionary venture.

'It's largely Huskisson's idea,' said Jes. 'He hopes that the occasion might bring about a reconciliation between him and the Duke, and I must say there are many of us who agree with him. We need men like Huskisson in the government; and something must be done to soften the Duke's attitude, or there really will be trouble. If he can't be brought to yield to a measure of reform, we may well find ourselves facing revolution.'

Rosamund remembered the talk of revolution at the time of her first marriage, and begged leave to doubt that it would ever come to that; but trouble which fell short of revolution was still to be feared and avoided at all costs. She remembered Peterloo, and Jes being brought in to Hobsbawn House unconscious, with blood pouring from his face. She never wanted to witness anything like that again; so she hoped along with her husband that the idea would work and the guest of honour would have his heart softened by the occasion. The Company was certainly taking great pains to secure his safety, though perhaps that only went to prove his unpopularity: the line was to be heavily guarded along its whole length, and there were to be soldiers at the Manchester terminus, in case the huge crowds which were expected to

470

turn out to see the engines arrive should turn nasty. Not only that, but to guard against sabotage every point and crossing between Liverpool and Manchester was to be removed, except those at the termini, and one crossover at Huyton.

Jes and Rosamund stayed the night of the fourteenth of September at the Royal George in Liverpool, and set off early the following morning to be at the Company's yard at Crown Street in time for the arrival of the Duke.

'It's a pity we're all still in Court mourning,' Rosamund said as they went out to their carriage. 'It would have been nice to see other colours than black amongst the guests — especially since gowns have so much cloth to them these days.'

Sleeves were very wide and full this year, not just puffed at the shoulder but bellying out at elbow-level before narrowing again to the cuff; and skirts were wider too, with gathers at the waist making them almost bell-shaped. Rosamund had been used all her girlhood to the slender 'Greek' fashions, and had yet to become used to having so much material hanging about her.

'You look very lovely all the same,' Jes said. Her gown was of plain black taffeta, her mantle of black cashmere edged with fox, her wide silk bonnet, set well back from the face, a sober affair, except that the bows of black ribbon which decorated it were piped with crimson. 'Black suits you, though I suppose one ought not to say it. But it shows off your white skin and glorious hair.'

Rosamund turned to smile at him. 'Not so glorious as it was, my love! I found three grey hairs there yesterday. Poor Moss was so shocked she pulled them out and begged me not to tell you. She's afraid you won't love me when I grow old and ugly.'

'You will always be young and beautiful to me,' Jes said. 'If Moss doesn't know that by now, she's a fool.'

The Crown Street yard was crowded already with the eminent guests who were to travel on the Duke's train, while fascinated spectators lined the road and packed about the gate to watch the arrivals and catch a glimpse of the trains. The Duke's train — carrying eighty of the most distinguished

471

guests including members of Parliament, the directors of the Company, civic dignitaries from the two towns, and of course the Earl and Countess of Batchworth — was to be drawn by the *Northumbrian*, and driven by George Stephenson himself.

There were seven other trains, and six hundred guests had been given tickets in different colours according to which engine was to draw them: the *Dart* purple; the *Arrow* pink; the *Meteor* brown; the *Comet* red; the *Phoenix* green; the *North Star* yellow; and old *Rocket* herself light blue. It had been decided that the Duke's train should travel alone on the southern line, and lead the way, while the others followed at close intervals but on the northern line. Seventeen miles out from Liverpool, at Parkside, all the engines would stop to take on water, and when that was done the Duke's train would remain stationary while the other seven trains passed it, so that all the passengers could catch a glimpse of the guest of honour.

At last an open barouche swept into the yard, drawn by four white horses, and from it descended the Duke himself, all in black, of course, and enveloped in a long cloak, grim and unsmiling as he always was in public. He was accompanied by the Home Secretary and the Marquess of Salisbury, and when they had been greeted by the Directors of the Company and shown to their seats, a single cannon boomed out as the signal to start, and the *Northumbrian* chugged slowly forward through the Mount Olive cutting.

'It's incredible to think that this was solid rock only a short while ago,' Rosamund said. 'Look, there's already moss growing on it, and ferns and little plants.'

'We're down in the bowels of the earth, really,' Jes agreed, looking out at the tall cliffs of grey granite to either side. 'And look at all the people who've turned out to see us! They've forgotten their grievances for the time being at least.'

Along the top of the cliff, lining the bridges which arched over the cutting, at every vantage point was a mass of cheering, applauding spectators. As they passed Rosamund saw face after face, mouths wide with approval, eyes wide with wonder. When they passed over the Sankey Viaduct, the canal below was packed with barges and the barges and the meadows to either side packed with people, a sea of pink faces turned upwards, a reed-bed of waving arms and fluttering handkerchiefs.

'This is a momentous day,' Jes said. It's a great beginning, you know. This is something quite new in the experience of mankind.'

Rosamund gave him an amused smile. 'Yes, my love! Of course it is.'

'No, don't laugh,' he said seriously. 'I'm not merely being enthusiastic. Just think of this: in all of history, since the world began, man has been able to travel over the earth only as fast as a horse can run, and no faster. The Egyptians, the Romans, the Greeks — every civilisation has been limited in the same way, until ours — until this moment.'

Rosamund reached across and took his hand, and nodded. It was a great thought — a sobering thought.

'There's no knowing where we may go from here,' he went on. 'We have broken free, Ros. I believe there is nothing the machine can't do. We only have to work out how.' He pressed the hand he held, and smiled at her. 'I'm glad I have lived in this age. And think of the wonders our children may witness!'

He meant it metaphorically, of course, and her face showed nothing; but her heart grieved all the same that there would be no children of her body and Jesmond's to see those wonders and marvel at them. In a week from today she would be thirty-three years old, and since Charlotte was born she had never once conceived. It was her punishment, she understood that; but she wished it need not be his, too.

They reached Parkside in four minutes less than an hour. 'A steady seventeen miles an hour,' Jes said with satisfaction. 'Hullo! Everyone seems to be getting down.'

'Not everyone,' Rosamund said. 'Just some of the gentlemen. I suppose they want to stretch their legs.'

'It will make room for you ladies to move around. You'll want to sit over on this side so as to see the other engines come past, won't you?'

Rosamund divined his intentions. 'Go on, if you want to,'

473

she said. 'I don't mind if you leave me alone.'

'Oh no,' he began to protest, and then, as a group went past the window, 'Ah, there's Huskisson, taking a walk between the lines! Poor man, he gets very stiff sitting still. Ever since the King's funeral, he's had dreadful rheumatism in one leg and hip. Kneeling down hour after hour in St George's Chapel did it for him. I wonder whether the Duke will acknowledge him when he passes the state coach?'

'I can see you are dying to find out,' Rosamund smiled, 'so why don't you get down and promenade with them? I shall be quite happy watching everything from the window.'

'You don't mind? Thank you, my love. Let me see you comfortable first. If you take this seat, you will be able to see right up the track if you just lean out a little. You might even see the Duke's glove waving to the passing crowds.'

'Thank you. Of course, that's the nearest I can ever hope to come to such an eminent personage,' Rosamund said drily. 'Go on with you!'

Jes opened the door and jumped down onto the space between the southern and northern tracks. It had been laid and sanded especially for the occasion, and made a pleasant place to walk, and many of the gentleman were enjoying the opportunity to light a cigar and talk to their friends. Jes greeted various acquaintances as he hurried to catch up with Huskisson, who was a little ahead of him, in a group with some other friends, Holmes and Birch, Calcraft, and Prince Esterhazy, the Austrian ambassador. The Duke had moved to a corner seat of the state coach in order to watch the other engines pass and to be seen by the guests, and as Jes caught up with the tail of Huskisson's group, he saw that the Duke had seen the Member for Liverpool. There seemed to be a breathless pause: would he notice him? The grim, beak-nosed face did not soften; but the Duke nodded slightly, and made a small gesture of acknowledgement with his right hand.

The world which had held its breath now let it out again, and Huskisson and his group hurried forward to make the most of the opportunity. Jes joined the rear of the group. He wanted to hear what was said; and he felt he should pay his respects to the Beau, under whom he had served in France, even if he was not precisely his most fervent political ally.

The Duke opened the door of his carriage and Huskisson stepped up to it. The Duke held out his hand, and Huskisson shook it, and the two men began talking with at least an appearance of cordiality. Jes strained his ears to try to catch what was being said, but there was too much noise. Indeed, there was a steadily increasing din which, after a moment's perplexity, he realised was the sound of an approaching engine. He jerked his head round, and saw that it was the *Rocket* bearing down on them on the northern line, pulling the third train — *Phoenix* and *North Star* having already gone past them.

'I say look out!' Jes shouted. 'Clear the line there!'

Someone else took up the cry. 'Get into the carriages. Get in! Get in!'

The space between the lines, Jes thought, was quite wide enough if a man stood close to the stationary train. He stepped back and flattened himself against the Duke's carriage, and saw several others doing the same. There was no real danger — but of course there were those who had not had his experience of engines, who had never been so close to one of these moving, snorting, steaming monsters before. There were cries of alarm, and every evidence of panic on the part of previously self-contained men.

The cry was taken up 'Get in! Get in!' and other doors were flung open by people still on board. *Rocket* came thundering on, fast as a cantering horse, but black and insensate, five tons of fire-breathing iron. Calcraft was scrambling up into a compartment now, and a small forest of hands reached out and grabbed Prince Esterhazy and dragged him up bodily. Huskisson made an attempt to climb up into the Duke's carriage, but with his stiff leg and solid weight he could not do it. He stepped back down and looked round, dithering with anxiety. The door of the Duke's carriage, standing open, blocked the space between the lines. As Jes watched, Huskisson, apparently to get round it, stepped out onto the northern line, into the path of the oncoming engine.

Several people shouted a warning. Jes filled his own lungs to tell his friend to look out, as, limping clumsily on his game

475

leg he clambered round the open door, stumbled, and fell.

Even at the last minute, Jes somehow expected the engine to stop. This was a new age, and man had freed himself at last from the horse; but Jes and everyone else present had been brought up in the world of horse transport, and probably all of them, except perhaps the engineers, instinctively expected the *Rocket* to behave like a horse, to stop herself at the last moment, or veer away. But *Rocket* was not a living thing, for all her feminine pronouns. Jes saw William Huskisson lying with his game leg doubled over the line, blinking in a dazed sort of way at the approaching engine; and the next instant he had disappeared.

It all happened in the fraction of a second. The breath Jes had drawn in to shout a warning was let out in a terrified noise, half bellow, half scream, as the Rocket thundered on, unstoppable, over the fallen man, over the human flesh, the leg of a living person, his friend Huskisson. There were too many screams at that moment for anyone to know if Huskisson cried out. People were running, shouting, half mad with horror — for the horror of it was far greater than if it had been a horse-drawn cart which had knocked the man down. It was the fact that he had fallen, and yet still the engine had come on, which was so sickening and shocking.

The engineer must have been trying to stop, for the train halted before more than the first few carriages had passed over the body. Jes had no idea he was moving until he found himself, one of half a dozen, beside Huskisson, frantically lifting him clear of the line. His leg and thigh were hideously crushed, seeming to bear no resemblance to human flesh any more. Huskisson was still alive, and still conscious, though his face was yellow-white as wax. He met Jes's eyes, though Jes had no idea if he knew him.

'I have met my death,' Huskisson whispered.

They laid him down beside the track, and Jes became aware of the babble of sound, human voices crying, speculating, supplicating, and in the background the hissing, sighing voices of the engines — devil voices, inhuman, mocking.

No-one seemed to know what to do. It was George Stephenson who cut through the fog of indecision, took command, gave precise orders, which everyone obeyed instantly, glad of leadership at such a moment. The *Northumbrian* was uncoupled from all but her leading carriage, into which Huskisson was tenderly placed, though he was barely conscious by now, and plainly close to death. Then Stephenson climbed up onto the footplate, opened the regulator, and set off in a cloud of steam at full speed for Eccles.

As the engine dwindled on the distant track to a flying mote, Jes recollected his wife, and hurried back to the carriage to see that she was all right. She was plainly very shocked, but bearing up with her usual courage.

'I've seen wounded men before,' she said. 'I'm all right.'

'Not like this,' he said, chafing her cold hands. 'And not for a long time.'

'It must be far worse for you. You were so close to it, you saw it all. My dear,' she added with a horrified glance, 'there's blood on your coat.'

Jes glanced too, and sat down rather abruptly beside her. 'Oh my God,' he said. 'I can hardly take it in. Poor Huskisson! Poor wretched man! And after all his enthusiasm, after everything he's done to bring this day about! Without him, without his help, there never would have been a railway. You remember it was he who persuaded the Marquess to come in?'

'Yes, I remember. And now he's the first victim. It's ironic.'

'The first? The only one, I hope and pray,' Jes said quickly. 'God, it was a terrible thing! Even though I knew it was an engine, in my deepest heart I expected it to stop of its own accord, as a horse would.'

'Our children won't make that mistake,' Rosamund said grimly. 'It's natural that we should. What will happen now?' she went on, to divert his mind from the horror. 'Will we go on, or back?'

'I suppose we ought to cancel everything and go back, out of respect,' Jes said. 'But on the other hand, there will be huge crowds waiting at Manchester for the spectacle. If it doesn't come, there may be trouble.'

477

'How so? Won't they just go away if they're told what happened?'

'You know what mobs are like. They'll probably think the Duke doesn't dare face them. Or else some exaggerated story of disaster will start circulating, and they'll panic.'

'I suppose so,' Rosamund said, frowning in thought. 'But, just a minute — how are *we* to go anywhere, forward or back? Mr Stephenson has gone away with our engine.'

'So he has, by Jove! Well, they can cross one of the other engines over and —' He stopped as he remembered the security arrangements which had been made. 'They can't even do that. All the crossings have been removed. We're stranded!'

Rosamund gave him a grim sort of smile. 'So much for your new age, my love! These locomotives have yet to prove themselves superior to horses, I think. I wonder if, after today, people will be so eager to trust themselves to them.'

The Duke having given his decree for going on to Manchester, it was left to the engineers to devise a means of making it possible. After much debate, the *Phoenix* and the *North Star* and their trains were all coupled together, and a chain was stretched from the rear and attached to the remaining three carriages of the Duke's train, and in this extraordinary way they were able to steam slowly up to Eccles.

Here they found the *Northumbrian* waiting, with the news that Huskisson had been transferred to the vicarage and was even now being attended by a doctor. The engine was coupled up again, and the trains continued on their way. The drama was not yet over, however, for as they approached Manchester, they found not only the banks of the long cutting lined with spectators, but the lines themselves blocked with a dense mass of people. The engines had to slow to a crawl to prevent any further bloodshed, and it soon became obvious that these were not enthusiasts come to cheer, but a mob which had somehow escaped the military guard and had come to protest.

At snail's pace the trains crawled through the mob, hearing

478

beyond the windows the sullen roar of its anger, seeing the contorted faces surging up to the glass and away again, the banners and the crudely-painted placards swaying above the massed heads — *Remember Peterloo!* and *Bread and Reform* — hearing the ominous thud and tinkle of stones and brickbats thrown at the passing carriages, catching the briny odour of fear and hatred in the air. The passengers rode in tense silence, keeping their countenances rigidly, showing no fear, meeting no other eye. Rosamund and Jes held hands tightly below the line of the windows, staring fixedly ahead, each privately vowing that if the worst came to the worst they would sell their lives dear defending the other. Suddenly the noise of the wheels changed, the crowd seemed to have melted away, and they were rumbling over the iron bridge at Water Street, with the brownish-grey waters of the Irwell below them and Manchester station ahead.

Jes said, 'Thank God, we're there. We're safe.'

'We still have the return journey to do,' Rosamund said, turning to look at him.

He shuddered. 'No! Enough is enough, for one day. We get down here, and go straight to Sophie's house for the night. We can send for our things tomorrow. I want four walls around me and a view from a window that doesn't move. And a large brandy.'

'What about the ceremonial luncheon?' Rosamund said. 'Don't you think we ought to stay for that? I know it's after half past three, but —'

'I don't think anyone will be worrying about that,' Jes interrupted her grimly. The train was steaming into the station, but the station had already been invaded by the crowds, and were being held back only with difficulty by the soldiers. It was time for quick thinking. Already those who had lined the cutting would be running back to join the mob here. In a few minutes it would be impossible to get out of the train at all.

'Come, love, we must leave now, and quickly,' he said. 'Take my hand, and don't let go for anything. When I lift you down, run for that warehouse over there.'

Rosamund nodded, her face pale but calm. Thank God, he

thought, for a sensible woman! He kissed her lips quickly, opened the door and jumped down. The noise from the crowd was louder out here, and even as he turned to jump Rosamund down, he saw the first of them breach the thin red wall of the soldiery and come running across the open space between them.

'Run,' he said simply. Rosamund's hand was tight in his; her other hand snatched up her skirts, and she ran like a young girl, straight across the line of the mob and into the doorway of the new goods warehouse, where the festive luncheon had already been laid out. There were flowers and flags and bunting here, and anxious servants gathered to wait on the guests, and a welcoming committee looking pale and terrified. What an end to the day! As Jes and Rosamund halted, panting, inside the door, someone stepped forward, hardly knowing whether to welcome or commiserate.

'Sir — my lord — are you —? Is his grace —? Is it true that —?'

Jes cut firmly through the stammering.

'My good man, anything you may have heard, however unlikely it sounds, is probably true. And if you would be so very kind as to direct us to the most private door to this place, we will make our escape before anything even more bizarre happens to us.'

Late that night, Jasper and Sophie retired to their bed-chamber, having said good-night to their unexpected guests, whom they had provided with dinner, accommodation, a change of clothing, and sympathetic ears.

'Poor Mr Huskisson,' Sophie said, unclasping her necklace in front of the dressing-table. She had sent her maid to bed as they were so late. Jasper could unhook her — a process which he always seemed to find inexplicably pleasurable. 'What a dreadful thing!'

'A great loss to the country,' Jasper said, removing his neckcloth. 'He had work to do for the good of England which may now be a long time doing.'

'But such a dreadful way to die,' Sophie said, sticking to her own point. 'It seems that Maman was right about

480

railways. When she hears about this, she'll be more determined than ever not to allow a railway to cross her land. Poor
Bendy will have to keep his passions to himself.'

'It won't hurt him to do that,' said Jasper. 'All the same, my
love, however many there are who think the same way as your
mother — and there will be plenty — it isn't going to change
anything.'

'Isn't it? But surely people won't want to ride on these
locomotives now they know how dangerous they are?'

'Huskisson's death was a tragic accident, but it was nothing
to do with riding on locomotives — any more than being run
down by a gig makes it dangerous to ride in carriages.' He saw
her frowning reflection in the glass, and walked over to stand
behind her, placing his hands on her shoulders. 'Batchworth
is right about railways, just as he was right about power looms
and factory machines. They *are* the future, and it's no use our
fighting against them. We will only hurt ourselves. You can't
change the course of history.'

'I suppose not,' Sophie said, though more out of the habit
of agreeing with him than because she accepted what he said.

'It is God's will,' he said, knowing from long experience
what she was thinking. 'God gave us the curiosity to ask
questions and the wits to answer them, didn't he?' He undid
the first hook of her gown and bent his head to kiss the nape
of her neck. 'Your mother said that to me once, and you know
your mother's always right.'

Sophie regarded herself in the glass, and her eyes shone,
dark and bright, reflecting the candlelight.

'There's something else that Maman was right about,' she
said.

'What's that, my love?' Jasper asked, undoing the second
hook.

'When I was very little I asked her once why people had to
die, and she said it was to make room on earth for new
people.'

'Did she, my darling?' Another hook, another moth-wing
kiss.

'Yes, she did. I thought of that when Papa died, you know,
because Bendy said to me that he thought Papa hadn't

481

wanted to go yet, and I reminded him of what Maman said, and said perhaps it wouldn't be so very bad if he was making room for someone who very much wanted to be born.'

Jasper stopped with his hand on the fourth hook, and met her eyes with a quizzical look, in which hope hardly dared to dawn. But the expression on her face was not to be mistaken.

'Have you — have you any notion that anyone in particular wants to be born, Sophie mine?' he asked carefully.

She smiled at him in a way that made him feel breathless and exalted and lit up inside, as though he had eaten half the stars of the midnight sky in one gulp.

'Oh yes,' she said softly. 'I have a very good notion who it might be.'

sphere

To buy any of our books and to find out
more about Sphere and Little, Brown Book Group,
our authors and titles, as well as events and
book clubs, visit our website

www.littlebrown.co.uk

and follow us on Twitter

@LittleBrownUK
@LittleBookCafe
@TheCrimeVault

To order any Sphere titles p & p free in the UK,
please contact our mail order supplier on:

+ 44 (0)1832 737525

Customers not based in the UK should contact
the same number for appropriate postage
and packing costs.